UNFORGETTABLE

A Legal Thriller

Deborah Hawkins

This is a work of fiction. The names, characters, places, and incidents are products of the author's imagination and have been used fictitiously. Any resemblance to actual persons, living, or dead, events, or locales is entirely coincidental.

Published by Deborah Hawkins
ISBN:978-0-9992180-6-8 (print)
ISBN:978-0-9992180-5-1 (ebook)

For he would be thinking of love
Till the stars had run away
And the shadows eaten the moon.

W.B. Yeats

CONTENTS

PROLOGUE

Early Morning Hours, February 14, 2019, Rancho Sante Fe, California

She balanced on one foot at the top of the mahogany staircase to prove to herself that she wasn't drunk. The highly polished steps spiraled invitingly to the black-and-white marble floor below in the mansion's front hall. So much unrelenting criticism about her drinking from her husband and his harpy daughter. But lately her agent and Michael Bernstein had joined them. They were nothing but a chorus of broken records. *Nora, you're drinking too much. Nora, you shouldn't drink alone. Nora, you'll fall down those stairs to your death one night if yous keep on drinking.*

Of course, they were all wrong. She'd been a dancer before she'd made it as an actress. She had perfect balance. She could stand here all night on the ball of one exquisite foot. In fact, she'd do that. She'd show them. They'd find her here in the morning, poised and serene, at the top of the grand staircase, like a goddess waiting to welcome her worshipers. And she was a goddess. She was Venus, the goddess of love, and this was the dawn of her festival day.

The clock in the hall chimed, and the sound startled her.

Suddenly, she began to sway. She felt her weight shift forward. She reached out and grabbed the bannister. But only for a moment. She steadied herself on both feet and let go of the handrail. In a moment, she'd resume her one-footed stance.

But not yet. She swayed again and tipped toward the stairs. Fear pierced her like a knife. She reached out and grabbed the mahogany balustrade once more. It was smooth and cool under her palm, like one of her polished crystals, and it soothed her sudden terror.

That was it. Crystals. A session with her crystal therapist would drain away all the stress that had sent her to the wine bottle that night. And a massage. She'd tell her personal assistant to book the appointments in the morning.

She swayed again, and this time she gripped the banister and didn't let go. Okay, maybe she'd drunk too much. But only just this once. It had been a terrible day. All of the most important people in her life, and a few of the unimportant ones, had come by, one after another, to tell her that she, the most talented actress of her generation, was washed up.

But of course it wasn't true. She was only forty-six. God, Meryl Streep was past seventy and still working. Everyone remembered Nora Carson as Angelique in *Unforgettable.* The movie was a classic like *Casablanca.* She would always be a major draw at the box office. The doomsayers were wrong. Her career was far from over. She was still gorgeous. Granted, her colorist had to mix the perfect shade each month to hide the gray strands in her shoulder-length chestnut hair. And her wide hazel eyes, framed by perfectly arched brows, had become nearsighted. But contact lenses fixed all that. And regular injections from her

Beverly Hills plastic surgeon took care of any tiny lines or sags that had appeared in her exquisite heart-shaped face. One day, she'd have to have a full facelift, but not yet.

For now, all she had to do was lose the twenty pounds that tarnished her five-foot-eight frame and find the right script. Of course, that was the problem. So few scripts came her way these days. She had asked Lachlan to front the money for her own production company without success. But she was still one of the most beautiful and desirable women in the world. She could get what she wanted from her husband.

Everything was beginning to spin. No, that was just her imagination. As long as she hung on to the handrail, she was fine. She was going to resume her one-footed goddess pose in a moment. The world would arrive to worship her in the morning. A massage, some crystal therapy, and a low-carb diet would prove that Nora Carson was far from finished.

She threw back her head and laughed out loud at the thought of vanquishing her enemies. She shook with joy from head to toe as she contemplated Lachlan, begging her to take him back. Then suddenly her hand wasn't on the reassuring railing anymore, and her feet weren't under her, and she was falling, down and down into darkness.

* * *

February 14, 2019, San Diego Channel 10 Breaking News, 11:30 a.m.

Early this morning, the body of acclaimed actress, Nora Carson, was found at the foot of the main staircase in the Rancho Santa Fe mansion that she shared with her husband, famed Irish poet,

Lachlan Adair. According to a spokesman for Mr. Adair, he was in Boston at the time of his wife's death and is devastated by the news. Deputy Coroner Dr. Gus Tavoularis of the San Diego County Coroner's Office has issued a statement saying Ms. Carson's death appears to be an accident.

BEGUILED

CHAPTER ONE

Thursday, February 14, 2019, Offices of Goldstein, Miller, and Mahoney, Emerald Shapery Center

At five p.m., forty-five-year-old Cameron Rhodes was sitting in his twenty-ninth floor corner office at Goldstein, Miller, studying the view of San Diego Bay and wondering how soon he'd be able to leave. He'd closed a huge corporate merger just an hour ago, worth millions in attorney's fees to the firm, and he desperately needed some downtime after three weeks of round-the-clock preparations for the deal. He would have already been gone except for a meeting that Hugh Mahoney had scheduled for five thirty. Cam's personal cell phone rang, and he picked it up, hoping Hugh was calling to cancel the meeting. But it was his wife, Jessica.

"Hi, darling."

"Hi, Jess."

"Are you on your way home?"

"Not yet. Hugh's got something he needs to talk to me about."

"But the girls and I have barely seen you for the last three weeks because of that merger. Didn't it close today?"

"It closed."

"Then tell him he'll have to wait until tomorrow. Or get someone else."

Cam studied the little waves in the bay, twinkling in the late afternoon sunlight like a handful of diamonds scattered across the water. Jess had been a rising star in the litigation section until she'd walked away from certain partnership when their second child was six months old. Her father had been a name partner in an old-line Baltimore firm, and therefore she understood the nuances of big-firm politics in a way that outsiders did not. She knew that Cam was one of the few young partners who could refuse one of Hugh's requests because his grandfather was Tyler Marshall Miller, the Miller in Goldstein, Miller. It had been a foregone conclusion that Cam would join the firm after law school and a foregone conclusion that the nepotism cloud that had hung over his father Blaine's head throughout his legal career would hang over Cam's, too. He hated the fact that people thought his professional success was based upon his family connections rather than on his own hard work as a Yale undergrad, his position as a law review editor, and his legal abilities which had attracted a formidable list of Fortune 500 clients.

"I'll be out of here the minute the meeting is over."

"Well, make it a quick meeting. Your mother's moved the start time of the party from seven thirty to six thirty because McKenna is coming."

"But she's in London."

"Not tonight. She's in LA on a shoot, and she's coming down with Nash on the train. But they've got to leave by nine thirty to get the last train back to LA."

"Isn't Nash afraid he'll be mobbed by fans? Doesn't he want to burn up the road with his Ferrari?"

"He's usually safe in his ball cap and glasses. Besides, the traffic down and back is always terrible."

"True." His younger brother had refused to follow in the family's legal footsteps and had become a very successful actor. "Look, Jess. You know I'd rather be on my way home."

"I know. If you aren't back by six, the girls and I will go on without you. Addison's coming then so that the cousins can entertain each other while we help Jackie."

"That's thoughtful."

"Try to be there as close to time as you can. You know how much these family parties mean to your mother."

They're her whole life. "I promise to be there by six thirty."

CHAPTER TWO

Thursday, February 14, 2019, Offices of Goldstein, Miller, and Mahoney, Emerald Shapery Center

"Thanks for staying around this afternoon," Hugh Mahoney said as he folded his six-foot frame into the inadequate chair in front of Cam's desk at precisely five thirty.

Cam had purposely put him in the client chair to avoid the longer meeting that would have ensued had he made him comfortable on the sofa that faced the expanse of San Diego Bay. He was never entirely comfortable around Hugh even though he was a close friend of his parents. So close, in fact, that he was a regular at his mother's endless family parties.

"Coffee?" Cam poured himself a cup from the pot his secretary had brought in minutes before Hugh's arrival.

"Sure, thanks."

Cam felt Hugh's striking dark eyes, framed by thick-lensed glasses, studying him as he served the coffee. Hugh had undergone a transformation in the last five years, but he still looked rumpled in his clothes, no matter how expensively he was dressed. His life had changed forever when he'd taken on the wrongful death case of a young widow, Kathryn Andrews, and in the course of that litigation, Hugh had gone from being the most powerful plaintiff's attorney in America to the head of an Innocence Project that he ran with his daughter, Erin. Cam had turned most of the work of running the firm over to Mark Kelly, the managing partner. But he still stepped in when something involved one of his many close friends. And despite what Cam's wife thought, saying no to Hugh when one of his cronies needed help was nearly impossible. Hugh would pressure you until you gave in. Cam sipped his coffee and braced himself.

"I know you've just finished a major deal and—"

"And my family has almost forgotten what I look like."

Hugh smiled, unfazed. "How is Jess? Litigation misses her. How old are Callie and Stephanie now?"

"Eight and six."

"In school, then. They'll be out of the house before you know it. Tell Jess to come back to work. We need her."

You don't understand that I couldn't work these hours if she wasn't at home with the girls. But he decided to humor him to end their meeting quickly. "Sure, Hugh. Is that why you wanted to see me?"

If this were all he wanted I'd be ecstatic, but I know better.

"Well, no. But I do want Jess back. She's dynamite in front of a jury. I needed to talk to you before you left today because a client's daughter needs some help that I think only you can provide."

"What kind of help?"

"What do you know about Lachlan Adair?"

"Nothing. Never heard of him."

"He's a well-known Irish poet and author."

"I wasn't an English major at Yale."

"Right. I remember. I thought maybe you'd heard of him because of the movie they made from one of his novels. It was called *Unforgettable.*"

"Jess and I don't have much time for movies. Two kids, demanding job. You know what I mean."

"Look, I know you don't want to be here this afternoon."

"If I stay much longer, I'm going to be in trouble with Jess and my mother. She's having her annual Valentine's blowout tonight, and it starts at six thirty."

Hugh frowned. Cam could see that he didn't like crossing Tyler Miller's daughter, but something was pushing him to do it anyway. "Couldn't you be a little late?"

"Why?" *I'm ready to remind him that I'm Tyler Miller's grandson and tell him to leave and come back on Monday.*

"Lachlan's wife was found dead this morning, and his daughter called and asked if I could find someone in the firm to help the family in case there are any complications from her death."

"What kind of complications?"

"So far the San Diego County Sheriff's Department and the coroner are saying it was an accident, but Raven is worried that they might change their minds."

"Who's Raven?"

"Lachlan's daughter."

"She's afraid her father might be a suspect?"

"He was in Boston when Nora died."

"Then why is she worried?"

"She'll have to tell you. She's just arrived from Dublin, and I came to ask if you'd meet with her right away."

"Right away as in how right away?"

"She's staying at Lachlan's condo in the Pacific Gate building on E Street. I told her you'd come over after we talked."

"You want me to meet with her at five forty-five on a Friday afternoon after I just spent three weeks pulling off a huge merger that I closed an hour ago?"

"I know it's asking a lot, but Raven's worried about her father."

"How can she be worried about him if he was in Boston when his wife died?"

"We didn't discuss the details."

Cam shook his head and didn't bother to control the exasperation in his voice.

"The answer is categorically no, Hugh. I don't do criminal defense as you well know."

"But you've worked on business deals that involve author's rights and author's affairs. You're the only one in the firm with that kind of experience. Raven said this could involve his literary rights to the novel that became the famous movie."

"I can't see how that could be true."

"It's not clear to me either, but she was very concerned."

"Then I'll talk to her about it on Monday."

"But she needs advice before Monday. The sheriff's office has contacted her and has asked to speak with Lachlan."

"I thought he was in Boston."

"He's coming to make the arrangements for Nora. He'll be here tomorrow."

"Nora?"

"Nora Carson. His wife."

"The actress?"

"Right. Do you know her?"

"No. Maybe Nash does. I'd have to ask him. Nash, by the way, is another reason why my mother is going to be furious if I don't show up tonight. He and McKenna are coming down from LA for the party. McKenna's in from London, one night only."

"Look, this won't take long. Raven is just three minutes away over on E Street. Just go see her for fifteen minutes, and then tell her she'll have to come in on Monday if that's not enough. You'll still make your mother's party close to time."

"But I don't do criminal law, Hugh."

"You did early in your career."

Oh, God, I've been checkmated. "My grandfather insisted that I spend two years in the public defender's office to get trial experience before I joined the firm. It's been sixteen years since I did any criminal work."

"Look, Lachlan isn't likely to be a suspect. And if he becomes one, I'll put an attorney from our white-collar crime section on the file. At this moment, you're the perfect person to help the Adairs because of your unique background. Please, Cam. I know your grandfather and your father, too, would want you to help the firm out."

Clever. Hugh always gets what he wants. He knows I try to live up to Blaine's expectations.

"Okay. I'll run over to E Street, but only for a few minutes."

"Thanks, Cam. I'll call her and tell her you're on your way."

CHAPTER THREE

Thursday, February 14, 2019, Offices of Goldstein, Miller, and Mahoney, Emerald Shapery Center

Cam put his cell phone, a legal pad, and his laptop into his briefcase, slipped on his black overcoat, and grabbed his car keys. He considered calling Jess or his mother to say he might be late, but he should be there close enough to time that it wouldn't matter. It was five minutes to six now, and the Pacific Gate was only three minutes away. He could almost walk faster than he could drive, but he wanted to have his car with him so he could head straight for Coronado when his meeting was over.

He'd reached his parking space when his cell phone rang. *Damn! He didn't have time for calls at that moment.*

"Where are you?" Hugh demanded.

"I'm in the garage. I'm about to unlock my car."

"Glad I caught you then. I just talked to Raven. She's not at the condo. She decided to stay at the guesthouse at Lachlan's estate in Rancho Sante Fe. The address is 2530 Via Del Charro."

"That's a thirty-minute drive, Hugh. Over an hour round trip and it's nearly six o'clock. If I spend any time at all with her, I'll be late for Mother's party, and Jess will be furious. And she's already furious because of the last three weeks."

"Jess is a pro," Hugh insisted "Besides, you'll be at the guesthouse no later than six thirty. You can spend a half hour with Raven and make it to your parents' place by seven thirty. You'll only be an hour late."

"Look, this can wait until Monday. Call her and tell her I'll see her in the office at nine on Monday morning."

"But she's afraid the sheriff will want to talk to her father as soon as he arrives, and he's in flight at this moment. She needs to talk to you tonight. A half hour tops."

"Okay, okay."

Cam sighed and got back into his black Mercedes S-Class and headed out. At least it was Friday afternoon, and traffic was light as he made his way to the I-5 North. He'd have to find a way to get rid of this as soon as possible, and that should be easy enough to do if it became a criminal case.

* * *

Thursday, February 14, 2019, 2530 Via Del Charro, Rancho Santa Fe

It was dark by the time he reached Rancho Santa Fe. Via Del Charro was a narrow two-lane road lined with dim yellow streetlights and spindly eucalyptus trees.

He drove slowly because it was difficult to make out house numbers in the dark. Eventually he came to 2350 and turned into the driveway. But he had to stop at the massive wrought iron gate that confronted him. It showed no sign of opening in response to his car positioned directly in front of it. Hugh hadn't given him a phone number for the mysterious woman somewhere on the other side of this intimidating barrier. He eyed his phone and considered what to do. Of course he should call Hugh. But if he did, he'd lose his excuse to leave. He glanced at his watch. Five minutes to six. If he backed his car out and headed for the I-5, he had a chance of making his mother's party on time and seeing Nash and McKenna.

He hesitated for one more minute and then began to ease the big car backward. But just as he did, the gate started to swing open slowly.

Damn! He'd lost his chance of escape.

He stopped backing up and waited for it to open fully. Then he eased the Mercedes forward. In his rearview mirror, he saw the gate begin to close the moment his taillight cleared the opening. He stopped and watched in equal parts fascination and horror as the heavy bars slowly swung into place.

I'm trapped. No, that's ridiculous. But then, why do I feel that way?

His heart was hammering as if he'd been on a long run. He looked ahead to see if he could see Lachlan's mansion, but it wasn't visible. The driveway was narrow like the main road and was also lined with tall, thin eucalyptus trees.

He drove slowly and cautiously down the winding road. He saw no signs of a house, but surely there was one in this direction. He glanced over at the clock in the dashboard and saw that it was six thirty-five. His lateness for the party had now been firmly established. Well, there was nothing he could do about it except drive on in the dark and hope that he'd find the guesthouse quickly.

Cam followed the pavement as it curved to the left. Suddenly an enormous white villa appeared on the right. He found himself headed toward a gigantic two-story wedding cake that had an impressive portico with a pair of ornately carved front doors in the center, framed by impressive columns.

He stopped in front of the house, but it looked so dark and lonely that, instead of turning the engine off and getting out, he remained in the driver's seat, studying the windows staring back at him. Tiny lights scattered in the flower beds provided the only illumination. The blank windows looked like rows of blind eyes. Cam shivered involuntarily even though he was wearing his heavy overcoat. Someone had died there less than twenty-four hours ago. It could possibly be a crime scene.

Pull yourself together. You don't have much time to waste on this case right now. Find this woman, listen to her story, and get out of here.

It was a good guess that the guesthouse was behind the mansion. He put the Mercedes in gear and headed down the drive again. It continued to meander for another fifty yards before it branched off to the right. Relieved that he had made some progress toward finding the mystery woman, he turned and found himself still in the dark, traveling parallel to the mansion's lawn on his right. A thicket of eucalyptus trees on his left blocked his view of what lay beyond.

He continued down the drive that paralleled the immaculate lawn. In the distance he could see the large square of the pool behind the mansion and a tiny outbuilding that must be the pool house. The water looked dark and cold in the February night, and it made Cam shiver again. If the mansion had a guesthouse, it wasn't here. Hugh had sent him on a fool's errand. Cam's anger flared like a torch in the darkness. He was upset with Hugh and with himself for giving in to his demands.

He was relieved to see that following his current route past the pool would bring him to another right turn that surely would take him back to the main drive. As soon as he hit that, he was going to head left and out of this deserted and seemingly haunted place. He prayed that whatever invisible force had opened the gate to let him in would open it to let him out.

He was still traveling about twenty miles an hour because the road was so narrow and winding and because it was so dark. But as he neared the end, he began to increase his speed. He was going about thirty miles an hour and was continuing to accelerate when a woman in white appeared in the middle of the road only a few feet in front of his car.

I'm going to hit her! Is she a ghost? Where did she come from?

Panicked thoughts whirled through his head as he stomped on the brakes as hard as he could and hoped that the tons of metal headed toward the white figure would stop before it was too late.

He closed his eyes and prayed as he braked. He didn't want to see the impact when he hit her. Maybe she was a ghost, and somehow this was all a bad dream. *But I'm strictly a rationalist. I don't believe in ghosts.*

The Mercedes jolted to a stop with a horrible screech. Cam kept his eyes closed for one more minute, preparing himself to deal with a seriously injured woman.

In the silence, he heard a tiny scratching sound at the driver's side window. It seemed much louder than it doubtless was because the night was now so still around him. The noise came again, this time accompanied by knocking on the window.

Cam opened his eyes. The woman was standing next to his car. She was wearing a white wool coat and a fluffy white hat that hid her hair completely. When she backed away slightly to allow him to open the door, he could see that she was wearing a pair of brown leather boots. She had riveting light-blue eyes that, in the illumination from his headlights, he could see were the color of the sky.

"I'm Raven," she said when he managed to get out of the car and hold on to the driver's door for support. "You must be Cameron. Hugh said you were coming."

Even though Cam's heart was beating so hard that he couldn't get his breath to speak, the soft musical lilt in her voice immediately charmed and soothed him.

After a few seconds he was able to say, "What were you doing in the middle of the road?"

"Looking for you." She seemed to have nerves of steel. Almost being hit by a Mercedes the size of a small tank hadn't appeared to frighten her in the least. "I knew you wouldn't find the guesthouse unless I came out to flag you down. I saw you miss the turn after I opened the gate."

"But why stand in the middle of the road?"

"It was the only way to get your attention."

She was so tiny. She seemed like one of the fairies from his daughters' bedtime stories who suddenly appeared to cast spells on unsuspecting travelers. Her husky, melodious way of speaking felt like an enchantment wafting over him even on a raw February night.

Don't be ridiculous. You're in shock because you thought you'd hit her.

In his stern cross-examination tone, he said, "You scared me to death."

"Sorry." She gave him an impish smile that belied any trace of apology. He was annoyed that his accusation hadn't impressed her.

"Look, I don't have a lot of time tonight. This is just a preliminary consultation. I've got some family matters to attend to. I came up here as a favor to Hugh. Could you show me the way to the place you're staying, so we can get this over with?"

"Of course!" She smiled again, and without another word walked around the front of the car, opened the passenger door, and got in.

Cam hadn't expected that. He continued to stand by the driver's door, trying to steady himself.

She leaned across the car and patted the driver's seat invitingly and said, "Well, stop scowling and get in. You said you were in a hurry."

She had taken control of the situation and that only made him angrier.

Get a grip and get this over with.

"You'll have to back up just a little," she said after he got in and restarted the car.

"You've gone just past the turn."

Going backward seemed to be a metaphor for this case, he decided as he put the car in reverse. Even though he didn't believe in spirits, he still had his personal collection of professional prejudices about his work. A rough start to a case was an omen.

When he had reversed far enough, Raven pointed to the turnoff to the guesthouse. It was even narrower than the main drive, and it was also lined with eucalyptus trees. If you didn't know it was there, you'd never find it.

The one-car roadway wound through the trees. No sign of a house. Cam began to wonder if this was a bad dream. If it was, he was ready to wake up. But as suddenly as Raven had appeared in front of his car, the little white replica of the main house appeared straight ahead. He was relieved that it was fully lit, inside and out.

* * *

She took his coat and hung it next to hers on a coat-tree in the front hall. When she pulled off her hat, her dark hair fell to her shoulders in rich, thick waves. Cam felt a jolt of completely inappropriate desire. He imagined running his fingers through it. Her eyes met his as if she knew, and he quickly looked away.

I need to get out of here. I've been happily married for fifteen years. Tight jeans and furry white sweaters mean nothing. What's come over me?

"The sitting room's in the back. I've only just arrived, but I managed to get the gas fire going before I came to find you."

He followed her down a short hallway lined with images of Lachlan's book covers. Raven paused in front of the only photograph. In it she was standing next to a tall, fit, handsome older man who had an impressive head of very dark hair and her light-blue eyes.

"That's me da," she said. "He's the reason I needed to see you right away."

Her use of the Irish expression for father made her seem childlike and vulnerable. Cam wondered how old she was. He guessed mid-thirties.

"Hugh said you were worried that your stepmother's death might have repercussions for him."

"That's right. Come sit in front of the fire, and we'll talk. I'll put the kettle on for tea. Or would you like some Jameson? Or coffee? You're American. I bet you'd rather have coffee. Or Jameson in your coffee?"

"Honestly, I don't have time for tea. Hugh said you were concerned about your father being interviewed by law enforcement. I need to answer your questions and get going."

"Everyone has time for tea," she said. "Sit down in front of the fire and relax for a moment while I brew a cup."

He took a seat on the couch and took out his legal pad. The warmth of the fire was soothing and somehow reassuring after being lost in the cold dark outside. He began to relax, despite knowing that he didn't have much time to spend here.

The kitchen and the sitting room were divided only by a breakfast bar, so Cam could see her as she turned on the kettle and put the teapot and two cups and saucers on a tray.

She looked up at him and smiled mischievously "Making tea fascinates you?"

"No, I—" He was irritated because she obviously enjoyed catching him off guard. He looked around the room and noticed the walls were lined with original paintings of traditional buildings and cottages and landscapes that clearly were not in Southern California.

"Did your father paint these? I assume they're all scenes in Ireland."

"Right. But they're mine. His gift is words. Mine is images. I do abstract ones, too. They're in the main house."

"So you're an artist?"

"Among other things."

"Such as?"

"I'm a solicitor."

"You're an attorney? You don't look old enough." *Oh, God, why did I have to say that?*

But she didn't seem offended. She gave him another impish smile as she poured hot water into the teapot. "Is it impossible to be an artist and an attorney at thirty-six?"

She didn't pronounce the *H* so that it sounded like "tirty." He realized that her Irish accent was part of her allure.

"I—well—no. But since Hugh said you needed to talk to an attorney urgently, I didn't expect you to be one yourself." *Stay rational and focused. Jess and your mother are waiting.*

"Well, I am. After I finished my undergraduate degree in art history at Oxford, I went back to Dublin and studied law at Trinity College because I could see that my father needed someone to handle his affairs. He's a great poet and a visionary, but not much with practical affairs. It was a natural fit for me to become his solicitor. But I don't have any experience with criminal law or the American police, so that's why I called Hugh before I left Dublin and asked him for help. I'm starving. I'm going to make a few sandwiches. Would you like some, too?"

"Actually, no."

"In too big a hurry. I get it. What am I making you late for?" She gave him another playful look and a smile that said she knew he found her attractive.

He needed to do something to break the spell that was slowly drawing him away from everything except her hypnotic voice and her sky-blue eyes that seemed to look right through him. He thought of Jess's darker blue eyes as an antidote to the enchantment she was weaving.

Jess! God! He should have called her before he left the office. But originally, he'd thought he was only going as far as E Street. He looked at his watch. Five minutes past seven. He needed to wrap this up fast.

"A family party. I—I need to give my wife a call." He hated the way he stammered when he felt that she'd read his mind.

She raised her eyebrows slightly at the word "wife," and then she said, "You can go into my studio if you need privacy. Back down the hall, first door on the left."

Cam felt that she was challenging him to leave her. "Fine. Thanks."

He got up and headed down the hall. Her studio was lit by a dim lamp with a green glass shade sitting on a small wooden desk under a window. An armchair slipcovered in a tiny flower print was tucked into the corner by the desk. Unlike the pristine white sofa and chair in the sitting room, the slightly saggy little chair made her studio feel homey. Two easels holding two unfinished landscapes occupied the center of the room. Paintbrushes and tubes of paint were arranged neatly in front of each. He assumed that the large light-blond antique cabinet that covered the back wall housed the rest of her art supplies.

He dialed Jess's cell, praying she'd answer. But no luck. He left a voicemail explaining Hugh's last-minute demands and promising to be there before the party was over.

In a final attempt to reach a live person, he dialed his mother's phone, too. But Jackie's bright, brisk voice invited him to leave his number and promised to call him back. Defeated, Cam repeated the same explanation, hoping one of them would check their messages, so they would know why he was going to be so unexpectedly late.

Raven was sitting on the sofa, staring at the fire, when he came back to the sitting room. She'd put the tea tray on the table in front of the couch. She was so absorbed that she didn't turn when he came in. Cam felt awkward because he didn't want to startle her.

But she knew he was there. "Come sit," she said without taking her eyes off the fire. She patted the seat next to her.

He would have preferred the chair at the end of the sofa, but he obeyed.

Her eyes left the fire and fixed on his. He felt that awkward jolt of intimacy again.

"Have a sandwich," she suggested, offering him the plate. "I made them while you were making your call. And I've poured your tea."

He picked up the flowered mug and took a long sip. It was dark and rich, and he could have sworn she'd laced it with Jameson after all. The tiny triangle of brown bread, smoked salmon, and cream cheese that she'd offered him disappeared in two bites. He helped himself to another.

"Did you reach your wife?"

"Her voicemail." *Which means I need to get out of here fast.*

"Her birthday?"

"No, Valentine's Day. My mother gives these family parties to celebrate every holiday she can come up with no matter how obscure, and everyone has to be there. She loves having us all together."

"You must have a big family."

"I have two sisters and a brother."

"And you are the oldest."

"How did you know?"

"Lucky guess. Are you the only lawyer?"

"No. My mother's father was one of the founding partners of Goldstein, Miller, and my father is the assistant head of the litigation section."

"So you followed in their footsteps?"

"Something like that."

"What about your mother who gives these parties?"

"No, she's not an attorney. My wife is—was—an attorney."

"What does she do now?"

"She looks after our daughters. Callie is eight and Steph is six."

"Are you the only one with children?"

"No, my sister Addison has two girls, the same ages as mine. Her husband is an attorney."

"I'm not surprised. What about your other brother and sister?"

"Nash is five years behind me. He's an actor. He lives in Los Angeles. My sister McKenna, who's two years younger than Nash, lives in London. She's an assistant fashion editor for *Vogue.* They're coming down from Los Angeles tonight for my mother's party."

The firelight was warm, and Cam was now pretty sure she'd loaded his tea with whiskey. That had to be why her lilting voice and fascinating eyes had made him answer so many personal questions. His attempt to break her spell by calling Jess had only deepened it.

"So you're Nash Rhodes' brother?"

"Do you know Nash?"

"Nora did. I hope you don't mind my questions about your family."

How did she always seem to read his mind?

"It's not part of a standard client interview."

She laughed as she poured more tea for both of them. "I know. It's just that I was also hoping we'd turn out to be friends."

Her eyes locked on to his in another one of those looks that felt inappropriately intimate. *She's flirting with me. I should mind, but I don't.*

He glanced at his watch as he spoke. Seven forty-five. *Where had the time gone? It doesn't feel as if we've been talking very long at all.*

"I'm keeping you from your party." He saw an unmistakable trace of disappointment in her eyes that he willed himself to ignore.

"Why don't you tell me why you wanted to see me? Hugh said something about literary rights to a novel that became a famous movie. He said you were afraid something about the rights situation would make the police change their minds about Nora's death being an accident."

"It's a long story, and you don't have time for a long story right now."

"How about on Monday then?"

"I'm afraid that the sheriff might call my father in for an interview before Monday."

"Then give me the short version of the long story."

"I'll try. My father wrote a novel called *Unforgettable* in 2004 that was a huge hit. In 2007, it was made into a movie with Nora Carson in the title role as Angelique. She married my father that year, the beginning of a truly miserable situation for everyone involved.

"Recently, the producer of *Unforgettable* contacted my father about making a sequel. The contract granting the right to make the original movie provided that my father would have approval over any sequel and that he would be the screenwriter. My father agreed to write the script, but he didn't want Nora in the movie."

"What about the producer? Did he want her?"

"No, he didn't. But Nora's contract to play Angelique said that she had the right to play that role again in any sequel."

"So your father was going to write the screenplay without her character in it?"

"Exactly. Angelique would be dead when the new movie opened."

"But I doubt that would make the sheriff change his mind about Nora Carson's death."

"It would if he knew that my father and Nora had had bitter words about the sequel, and Nora had threatened to go to court to enforce the Angelique clause in her contract."

"So your fear is that the sheriff will somehow find out about all this and decide that your father killed Nora so she couldn't interfere with the new movie?"

"Exactly."

"But I don't see why you are worried if he was in Boston when Nora died."

"I'm worried because he is both Irish and a poet. We Irish

like to tell stories, so he likes to tell stories. But, above all, he likes to tell his own story."

"Why is that a problem?"

"Because I don't want the authorities to hear about his miserable marriage to Nora and their fight over the sequel. I read that in slip-and-fall cases, it can be hard for the authorities to tell a murder from an accident, and sometimes innocent people get convicted based on rubbish testimony from so-called accident experts."

"I'm not in a position to say," Cam told her. "I don't do criminal defense work. Hugh sent me because I've had some experience with literary rights."

"But he said you used to do criminal law."

"A long, long, time ago. So long ago that it doesn't count. I'm sorry, but it's nearly eight."

Her eyes were full of disappointment again. They plainly said that she was attracted to him and didn't want him to leave. And he felt something, and it was something that he didn't want to feel and didn't want to name. She seemed so tiny and delicate and vulnerable. And beautiful.

I need to get out of here. "Look, regardless of phony accident reconstructionists, you've got nothing to worry about if your father was in Boston last night–"

"He definitely was. He was sleeping with one of his students. He teaches Irish Literature at Harvard. He's known for his way with words and his way with women."

"Well, then stop worrying."

She gave him the look that said she wanted him to stay.

"I'm sorry, but I've got to get going."

CHAPTER FOUR

Thursday, February 14, 2019, 2530 Via Del Charo, Rancho Santa Fe

Cam stood up to take his leave when suddenly a sound like someone trying to break through a door startled him. His eyes went automatically to the back door that led into the kitchen. Thankfully, it didn't have a window, but it was vibrating with the efforts of someone on the other side who was trying to force it open. At that moment, all the lights in the house went out. Apparently, there was more than one would-be intruder, and number two had just cut the power.

Cam considered trying to escape through the front door, but it was too risky. There was no way to know how many of them were out there or where they might be positioned. He felt Raven grab his arm and pull him down the hall a few steps and into the closet, opposite the front door. His heart was pounding so hard that he couldn't speak. He could feel Raven trembling beside him in the darkness and without thinking, he put his arm around her and pulled her close. The pounding on the door grew louder. Cam realized that whoever it was knew that the house was occupied because all the lights had been on and his car was out front. Maybe Nora's death hadn't been an accident, and maybe this was her killer on the other side of the door. If he broke it down, he'd find their hiding place for sure. Cam wouldn't let himself think about the rest of it.

The pounding and rattling seemed to go on forever.

"Do you have your phone on you?" Raven whispered.

"No. It's in my briefcase on the coffee table. Any idea who's trying to get in?"

"None." He felt her burrow closer to him, and he hugged her a little tighter.

Suddenly, after what felt like an eternity, but which was actually probably only a few more seconds, the pounding stopped.

Cam listened to the blessed silence for a few minutes and then whispered, "I'm assuming we're going to hear a window smash soon. I think we've just got to take our shot at running for my car. It's right outside the front door."

"The house has security glass. The back door is high-security, too. That's probably why they didn't get through."

Cam remained still, listening intently. After a period of silence, he said, "I'll venture out and see what's going on. Stay here."

He opened the door and stood in the hall for a moment to orient himself. A faint thread from a distant landscape light close to the house lightened the darkness. He moved carefully down the hall toward the kitchen. On this side, there was no evidence of damage to the back door. He moved back to the front hall and peered out cautiously between the blinds. His car was right where he left it. The front yard was deserted.

He went back to the closet, but Raven had already opened

the door and stepped into the hall. She slipped into her overcoat which had been hanging on the coat-tree and handed him his.

He took it but didn't put it on. "We need to call the sheriff and stay here until he comes," he told her.

But she shook her head. "It'll make them think Nora's death was suspicious. You can drive me down to the condo. I'll come back for my bag tomorrow with my father. Put your coat on. Let's go."

She began to undo the lock on the front door, but Cam reached out and grabbed her hand. "We can't do that! I'm sure whoever is out there is just waiting for us to make a rush to the car."

"We'll be fine. Come on."

He could see that her mind was made up. He pulled on his coat and followed her outside. They paused only long enough for her to lock up the guesthouse. He still did not see anyone around, but he gunned his car down the drive and took the twisty road to the security gate faster than he should have. He held his breath when Raven got out to punch in the gate code manually, but still there was no sign of whoever had tried to break into the guesthouse. Cam drew a long breath of relief as the gate closed behind them, and he sped off toward the I-5.

CHAPTER FIVE

Thursday, February 14, 2019, the Pacific Gate Condos, Downtown San Diego

Cam had expected more conversation from Raven on the trip downtown. But she was quiet as the Mercedes slid almost silently through the cold night. The clock on the dashboard said nine fifteen when he parked in one of the visitor spaces in the underground parking garage on E Street.

"If you hurry, you could still see your sister."

"McKenna and Nash are already gone. They had to catch the last train to LA. And all the kids have been sent home to bed. Tomorrow is a school day. I should walk you to your door just to make sure you're safe."

"Thanks."

"I still think we should have called the sheriff."

"I don't." She opened the car door and got out, apparently to prevent further conversation.

He followed her through the lobby, past the massive security desk, which was reassuring, and to the elevator. She punched a button and the car began to move slowly at first but then more rapidly as they rose higher and higher until they reached the top floor of the building. The doors opened, and she got out.

The penthouse. The poetry business must be better than I thought.

She crossed the hall to a pair of impressively carved double doors and unlocked the one on the right. He followed her inside but paused after he crossed the threshold as he waited for her to turn on the lights. The condo was a huge square of glass, surrounded by the night sky and lit only by starlight and moonlight. He felt as if he'd stepped into a magical land from the fairy tales that Callie and Steph loved. He looked around, trying to anchor himself in reality. From where he stood, he could see straight through the living room into the kitchen and the dining area beyond. A hall on his left appeared to lead to some bedrooms.

But Raven didn't reach for the light switch. Instead, she closed the door and walked across the living room and paused in front of the glass wall to gaze at the view. The almost full moon seemed to be peering in at them.

She turned to Cam and whispered, "Come, look."

But he remained by the door. The closet episode had been pure fear and panic. This was different. He was married. He had always been faithful to Jess.

"Just a quick peek," she urged, motioning for him to cross the room to her. "We're on the forty-first floor. You don't get to see a view like this every day. It's magnificent. It'll calm your nerves."

Cam sighed and obeyed. As he stood beside her, he looked down at the specks of emerald, sapphire, ruby, and diamond twinkling below. Suddenly, he felt as if he were standing on a cloud, hovering over a dark, airy world of colored lights. She was right. It was soothing to stand beside her in the dark. He'd fallen under her spell again. If she offered him a nightcap, he'd be unable to refuse.

"I should go." He summoned all of his will to resist her apparent magic.

"Would you consider staying for a drink? Something stronger than tea. I'm still feeling the effects of the break-in. I'm not quite ready to be alone yet. Since you've missed your party, would you mind terribly?"

I'm hopelessly lost at this moment because I don't mind. "Of course not."

When she came back with two glasses, she motioned for him to sit beside her on the sofa.

He took a sip. The whiskey was smooth and mellow, and he surrendered to his fascination with her.

"Better?" She gave him that look that said more than it should have.

"Better." He nodded. "Why didn't you want me to call the sheriff?"

"Because they'd associate this with Nora's death, and it's not related."

"How do you know?"

"Because whoever was trying to get in was after things in the guesthouse."

"Such as?"

"My paintings. You saw my work. I've shown internationally. And some rare first editions of my father's books. Most of them are in the main house, but he kept a few in the guesthouse. And he has guns."

"Guns?"

"He's something of a collector. There's a gun safe in the room he uses as his study."

"Who knows about the weapons and the art?"

"Anyone who knows my father and me would know. If I had to guess, I'd say the intruders were likely employees on my stepmother's staff, either currently or in the past. Nora employed a housekeeper and three or four maids and five gardeners to look after the grounds."

"Sounds expensive. Your father footed the bill?"

"Yes. Nora claimed that she paid for everything, but her income had dried up to almost nothing."

"How do you know?"

"I told you. I'm my father's solicitor. I'm responsible for all of his affairs. I see his financial statements every month."

"So why not report the burglary to law enforcement?"

"Because they always suspect the family when someone dies, don't they?"

"Not if you father was in Boston, and you were in Dublin."

But her intense blue eyes were troubled. She took a long sip of whiskey and then said, "I just don't want the details of my father's marriages smeared all over the press."

"How many times has he been married?"

"Three. Have you heard of Sinead O'Mara?"

"No. Another actress?"

"A famous Irish poet. She and my father were married in 1973. They were both twenty-three, and she was heavily pregnant. My half brother James was born in December, just before Christmas. That lasted for eleven years."

"What ended it?"

"I would say my father's career, but in truth, it was his infidelity. Sinead and my father were equally famous when they married. But Trinity College offered him, not her, the professorship in Irish Literature. That made him very famous in literary and academic circles. In 1981, Harvard offered him a professorship, and he took it. Sinead didn't really want to leave Ireland, but she loved my father and she went. She's since written a lot of poetry about being torn between love of a man and love of a country."

"How did they wind up separating?"

"Lachlan met my mother, whose name is Victoria Duncan and who is also Irish, when he'd only been at Harvard for a year." Raven paused to gauge the effect of her story on him. Then she continued. "Victoria had been a student at Trinity College in Dublin when my father was still teaching there, and she pursued him to Harvard by participating in a one-year study abroad program. As I said, Lachlan was never one to be faithful, but Sinead loved him enough to always look the other way."

"So how did your mother manage to break up your father's marriage?'

"She's a tricky one. And determined. Deep down, she's always known she's not a great literary talent. And she's incredibly jealous of Sinead to this day because she's the real deal when it comes to being a poet. My mother set her sights on my father because, as his wife, she could command the respect she craved in literary and academic circles, the kind of respect she would never receive on her own.

"Sinead wanted to stay with my father and ignore the affair, and he wanted to stay with her. Not only was she the great love of his life, but she was his equal as a literary talent, and he loved her and respected her for that."

"So why did he leave her?"

"My mother got herself pregnant. She lied about using contraception, and then she blamed him for the pregnancy and threatened to destroy his career at Harvard unless he married her."

"How old was your half brother?"

"Only ten. It's a testament to Sinead's character that, to this day, she has never failed to be kind to me and to make me welcome whenever I'm in Ireland. And she's still wonderful to my father, too."

"So how long were your parents married?"

"From 1984 until 2007."

"What ended their marriage?"

"Not what, who. Lachlan continued to have affairs. That drove my mother crazy but not as crazy as the poetry he published about his continued love for Sinead. Literary critics always say that my father kept retelling his story with her to ease the grief of losing her."

"Any truth to that?"

"Probably. All the Irish poets are deeply romantic pessimists. Do you know anything about William Butler Yeats and his hopeless love for Maude Gonne?" Raven gave him that intimate look that was hard to resist with that much whiskey in him.

"Afraid not. I majored in economics in college."

She shrugged at his admission of ignorance and went on. "She was an English-born Irish revolutionary who was the most beautiful woman of her day. She broke Yeats' heart when she married Sean McBride, a fellow Irish republican. At any rate, after a lot of years of poetry celebrating his love for Sinead, my father published *Unforgettable*. The novel is about the sadness of a man who is forced to give up the woman he truly loves for a pregnant mistress. My mother wanted to leave him the moment the book was published, but she had too much to lose if she did. She had a minor position teaching writing at Harvard but only because she was Mrs. Lachlan Adair. If she left my father, her marriage and her career would have been over."

"What about your father? Did he want a divorce?"

"No. He didn't see the point of divorcing my mother and ruining the little bit of fame she had among academics as his wife. He isn't capable of being faithful, but he's not heartless. He didn't love her the way he loved Sinead, but she'd tolerated his affairs and even accepted the fact that he didn't live with her so that he could be free to sleep around."

"Who did you live with?"

"My mother until I was seven. Then she sent me to boarding school in Dublin."

"When you were only seven?"

Raven nodded. "She didn't want to be bothered with me. She was focused on promoting her career as an academic."

"So if your mother's career depended on her connection to your father, why did he eventually divorce her and marry Nora?"

"In a word: publicity. *Unforgettable* was number one on the New York Times bestseller list for over a year. Michael Bernstein, the producer, won the bidding war for the movie rights, and every actress in Hollywood wanted to play Angelique because Da made her the epitome of the woman no man can forget: beautiful, talented, desirable, and endlessly forgiving. Once a man has been with her, he will never want to be with anyone else. Nora won the role and set about convincing everyone that she, too, was unforgettable."

"And that meant destroying your parents' marriage?"

"Yes. Nora did the same thing to my mother that she had done to Sinead: she went after my father relentlessly. She knew the movie was going to be a hit, but she also knew that it would be a bigger hit if she had an affair with the creator of Angelique. And the movie would be the biggest hit of all if their fling ended in marriage. Not only would she have played Angelique, she would *be* Angelique in the eyes of the world."

"And how did your mother feel about that?"

"She fought it tooth and nail."

"And lost?"

"Lost might be too harsh a word. My father felt guilty about divorcing her to marry Nora, and her divorce settlement was more than generous. But my mother didn't see it that way. She was, and still is, eaten up with bitterness. There's no one in the world who hates Nora Carson as much as my mother does."

* * *

Raven's spell had dissolved Cam's sense of time. The upstairs windows were dark when Cam pulled into his driveway at midnight. Of course, the girls were long ago in bed, but since the master suite was on the back of the house, he didn't know about Jess. He studied the white clapboard, green-shuttered, three-story colonial for a few more seconds. It was an East-Coast style house surrounded by lush California palms and blooming hibiscus. Jess felt at home in a house that reminded her of the houses in her old neighborhood in Baltimore. She filled it with traditional antiques and colorful but slightly worn Persian rugs. The atmosphere was warm, inviting, and cozy.

Inside, Cam took off his overcoat and hung it in the hall closet. He took off his shoes and went upstairs first to Callie's room and then to Steph's. Both girls were sleeping soundly in their frilly pink-and-white canopy beds.

He turned and went back down the hall to the master suite. The light under the door said that Jess was awake and waiting for him. She was sitting in one of the wing chairs by the window, wearing dark-blue pajamas and reading a book. He could see an empty wineglass on the table. She looked up as soon as he came in.

"Oh, thank God, Cam. I was worried."

"Sorry. Obviously, things didn't go as planned."

"Hugh's client had a long story to tell?"

"Something like that." He went into the walk-in closet to change into his pajamas. Suddenly, he wondered if he smelled of Raven's perfume. He hoped he didn't because he was too tired to take a shower.

"How was the party?" he asked as he buttoned his pajama shirt.

"That's why I waited up."

"I'm sorry that I missed McKenna and Nash."

"Oh, they were fine. They understood. We all know that Hugh makes last-minute demands that are hard to get out of. It's Jackie I'm worried about. You should go see her tomorrow, if you can."

"I will. I refuse to go back to work until Monday after having to work tonight."

"Was the meeting with the client that bad?"

"I didn't meet him. His daughter, who is also his solicitor, was the one who wanted to talk to me. She was at the Adair guesthouse in Rancho Santa Fe, and someone tried to break in while we were there. I didn't make the party because I had to drive her to their condo downtown." It was close enough to the truth to get past his conscience.

"You witnessed an attempted burglary? Did you call the police?"

"It's the sheriff's jurisdiction out there. And yes, we witnessed the attempt, but no, Raven Adair didn't want to call law enforcement. It's a complicated story. Why are you worried about my mother?"

"She thinks your father is having an affair. And she's got the evidence to prove it."

CHAPTER SIX

Friday, February 15, 2019, Caminito Bella Luna, Coronado, California

Cam didn't set an alarm the next morning. He woke at eight and immediately called the office to say that he wouldn't be in. Then he showered and pulled on sweatpants, a T-shirt and hoodie, and a pair of Nike running shoes.

He went down to the kitchen to make himself breakfast. He was unusually hungry because he'd missed supper last night. Jess had pinned a note on the fridge saying that she was meeting a friend for coffee after dropping the girls at school. Cam cooked himself a large plate of scrambled eggs and slathered his toast with the strawberry jam his mother made from the berries in her extensive garden. He didn't look forward to an interview about his father's perceived infidelity for many reasons. First, his reaction to Raven made him uncomfortable. He knew that he would never act on those feelings, but he didn't like having them in the first place. He didn't want to believe that his father not only had been attracted to another woman but had crossed the line.

But more importantly, as his mother told the story, his parents' marriage was based upon a genuine and deep love and not upon the fact that she was Tyler Miller's daughter. If Blaine Rhodes had married Jacqueline Miller to ensure his success at the firm, Jacqueline Rhodes refused to even consider the possibility.

According to his mother, she and Blaine, who had been a summer intern during his second year of law school, had fallen in love at first sight during a fancy formal firm party to welcome the law students. It was not at all incredible because in those days, Jacqueline had been a tall, slim blonde with fascinating wide-set brown eyes. She had majored in art history at Wellesley where she had discovered that she hated living on the East Coast and, after graduation, had come straight home to the mansion in La Jolla where she had grown up as an only child. Cam's daughter Callie was a mini version of her grandmother and destined to be as sought after one day.

For the most part, Cam himself had inherited his father's striking good looks. Like Blaine, he was six feet tall with a trim, muscular build. He had his father's very dark hair and both parents' brown eyes. But unlike Blaine, who had a stern expression, Cam had Jackie's round, open face which gave him a likeable, approachable look even when he wasn't smiling.

Although Blaine was sixty-nine, he was still attractive, so his mother's fears were not entirely unreasonable, Cam reflected as he finished his eggs. Still, deep down he didn't believe that Blaine would betray her. Although he resented having his success attributed to nepotism rather than to his legal training at Yale just as much as Cam did, Blaine had seemed to delight in having the money to give Jacqueline Miller all the things that her heart desired: the nine-bedroom house in Coronado with the backyard pool, the four children, and the nannies to take care of them so that she had all the time she wanted to pursue her passion for gardening.

He rinsed his dishes and put them in the dishwasher and headed out, fortified by the food but still not looking forward to hearing his mother's suspicions. As he slid into his Mercedes, the sight of Raven in the middle of the path last night popped into his head along with a string of anxious thoughts. Should he call her? Had she been all right after he left her at the condo? He had barely stopped the car in time to avoid hitting her. She might have been hurt. *I shouldn't be thinking about her now. But I am.*

The memory irritated him so much that he put his Mercedes into reverse and gunned it a little too aggressively out of the driveway. He took deep breaths during the three-minute drive to his parents' house to get his temper back in order and to banish any more thoughts of Raven. Likely her father wouldn't be charged with Nora's murder because he had an alibi, making it equally likely that Cam would never see her again.

He parked in the gravel circle behind his parents' three-story, pink stucco, Italian-style villa and headed for the back door. The sound of raised voices made him pause on the steps. A minute later, his father, dressed in a suit and wearing his black cashmere overcoat, ran into him as he burst through the door, obviously in a tremendous hurry.

"Excuse me, Cam. I'm late for the office." Blaine pushed past him, and a few seconds later, Cam saw his father's black BMW leave the driveway. The knot in his stomach tightened as he entered the kitchen.

Jackie turned from unloading the dishwasher and gave him a hug. She felt thinner, Cam thought. And her face, although mostly unlined, looked drawn and her eyes had the sad expression that she wore when someone disappointed her.

"Sorry about last night, Mom."

"We all know you wanted to be here. Have you had anything to eat?"

"I have."

"Oh, that's too bad. I have a sausage and egg casserole left from your father's breakfast. Anyway, what about a cup of tea and some cake from last night?"

"Tea, is fine, but no cake." He'd just had coffee with his own breakfast, but she would be hurt if he refused everything.

He watched her start the electric kettle and lay a tray covered with a blue-and-white mat with a blue teapot, two mugs, a sugar bowl, and a small pitcher of milk. Tea was one of her many rituals like her family parties and her work in her garden and the monthly book club that she had started when she was first married.

Watching her perform the familiar steps and being in the kitchen with her was comforting. It was a warm, inviting space that she'd updated three years ago with dark-blue tile and warm-yellow walls giving it a Mediterranean feel that harmonized with the villa style of the house. He noticed that she had tiny pictures of her four granddaughters propped amid the orchids, basil, and oregano plants in the greenhouse window.

When the tea was ready, she picked up the tray and said, "Let's go to the den."

In some ways, he would rather have stayed in the kitchen

where he could make a quick exit through the back door if and when her anxiety became too much for him to handle. But he obediently followed her through the dining room where garlands of tiny red and pink hearts were strung along the pale-green walls. A massive arrangement of hearts and flowers in the center of the mahogany table that seated eight seemed to reproach him for missing the party. She led him into the cherry-paneled den, which was furnished with a comfortable overstuffed red sofa and matching chairs accompanied by various side tables. She had filled the wall of shelves opposite the floor-length windows that overlooked her garden and the pool with books and many photos of family memories, including Cam and Jess on their wedding day. It wasn't hard to tell what was most important to Jacqueline Rhodes.

She sat down on the sofa and began to pour the tea.

"Dad seemed stressed this morning."

"He didn't want breakfast. He said it would make him late for work. I insisted. You'd never think that he's been retired from the firm for eighteen months."

Cam accepted the mug that she handed him and took a sip. He felt awkward asking about the state of his parents' relationship, so he put it off by asking, "When will McKenna be back?"

"Probably Thanksgiving. And, of course, Christmas."

Cam smiled when he thought of Christmas. Her celebrations rivaled anything Hollywood could dream up. All nine bedrooms were always full, and there was a Christmas tree in every room along with a twelve-foot Douglas Fir in the hall. Steph and Callie always lay awake all night on Christmas Eve, trying to get a glimpse of Santa landing on the roof outside their room. He didn't want the conflict between his parents to end these happy memories. He considered not bringing it up at all, but he knew he'd be letting his mother down if he didn't listen to her fears. As the eldest, she'd always confided in him first. She called him her rock.

So he took a deep breath and said, "Jess told me you needed to talk to me."

"Your father is having an affair." She tried to keep the emotion out of her voice, but she didn't succeed.

"No, Mom." Cam put his tea down and gave her a comforting hug. He had never seen that kind of pain on her face. "He wouldn't do that to you—to us—our family."

"Oh, but he would. And he has been doing it for a number of years now."

Cam's heart skipped a beat. The tone of her voice didn't leave any room for doubt. "How did you find out? Did you ask him? Did he tell you?"

"No. For years, I've handled the household bills including your father's personal credit card. His secretary takes care of his business card. Some years ago, I kept finding charges that looked like out-of-town trips for work. When I asked him why he put work trips on his personal card, he always said that he'd used the wrong one by mistake. But it kept happening. Finally, after a few years, he opened a new personal account and started taking care of everything himself."

"So he just mixed up his credit cards. I've done that."

"That's not the whole story. Two years ago, he started leaving receipts around the house from the new personal card."

"And?"

"And they were for some of the same restaurants and hotels that he'd said were work trips charged to the personal card by so-called mistake."

"Where were the charges from?"

"In the beginning, they were from New York, Boston, and Washington, DC."

"But he had clients there."

"Yes, but he didn't stay in B & B's and boutique hotels when he went to see them. The firm has deals with the hotels that it books repeatedly for firm travel, and they are always big five-star hotels close to the office."

"That's true."

"Do you think he had a different mistress in every city?"

"No. I think she was meeting him in places where he had work. He'd stay on a few days to see her, and I wouldn't question him because he told me he was on business."

"But he's not still doing that since he retired. He's in the office a few days a week and here the rest of the time."

"That's true," Jackie agreed. "But I think he's still seeing her."

"Is he ever gone overnight?"

"Once or twice in the eighteen months since he's retired. He always said he was traveling for one of the clients he kept."

"That could be true."

"It could be, but I don't think so. And he missed the party last night."

"He missed the Valentine's Day party? That's one he's always tried to make."

Jackie nodded.

"What was his excuse?"

"Work."

Cam sipped his tea thoughtfully, trying as hard as he could to find some hole in her logic. "Well, it's possible. I'm on a different floor, so I couldn't say. Have you asked him about it?"

"I did years ago when I found those receipts before he changed his card. But I had the feeling that he wanted me to find all that stuff. He wanted me to know that he was seeing someone else."

"But why would he do that?"

"Because he wanted a divorce, and he didn't want to ask for one while my father was still alive. Then when your grandfather died two years ago, he started leaving the receipts around again, thinking I'd file for divorce."

Cam shook his head. "This doesn't sound right to me. You and Dad have always been so happy together."

"That's the story we've told, but there has been a woman here and there over the years. You father is a very attractive man, but I suppose you know that because you are, too."

Cam felt another twinge of guilt about last night and Raven. *But this is different. I'm never going to see her again.* "Did you ever ask Dad about those occasional women?"

"No, I looked the other way for all our sakes. Fortunately, they never lasted long. But this one is different. It's lasted." Jackie's eyes filled with tears. "Because he really loves her."

Cam reached out and hugged her again. She felt thin and frail. A wave of anger suddenly took hold of him. He let her go and said, "I'm going to talk to Dad and get to the bottom of this."

"No! No!" Jackie was suddenly in a panic. "You have to promise me, Cam, that you won't say a word to him."

"But why not?"

"Because it will be the end of all this." She used both hands to gesture to the magnificent house and the photographs on the shelves across from them. "Don't you see, if he tells the truth, he'll also say he wants a divorce, and I will lose the family that I've work so hard to create. I don't want to lose *us*." She was crying hard as she spoke, so Cam put his arm around her again and held her quietly for a few minutes, stroking her hair and telling her everything was going to be all right.

CHAPTER SEVEN

Wednesday, February 20, 2019, 4212 Ocean Way, Coronado, California

By Wednesday, Cam had convinced himself that all had returned to normal. He was relieved that he had heard no more from Raven, and he was also relieved that his mother wanted to bury her head in the sand and pretend that her marriage was built on an unshakable love. And he was happy that he and Jess had managed to find enough time and privacy for themselves to make love twice over the weekend.

All was well, he told himself as he prepared to turn out the light at eleven o'clock on Wednesday night. Whatever fantasies or actual acts of infidelity had threatened the stability of his world last week, they were all in the rearview mirror.

And then his cell phone rang. Cam switched the light back on and looked to see who was calling. Hugh. Oh, God. What could he want at this hour?

Beside him, Jess asked, "Who is it?"

"Hugh."

"That's ridiculous. Turn it off and make him wait until business hours."

Cam hesitated for a split second and terminated the call. *After all, I'm Tyler Miller's grandson. He can't fire me.* "You're right. He can talk to me at the office tomorrow."

But just as Cam reached up to turn off the light, the text alert went off. Cam sighed.

"Is that Hugh again?" Jess asked.

"It is. He says that Lachlan Adair has just been arrested at the airport for the murder of his wife. The daughter wants me to pick her up at the E Street condo and go down to the jail with her."

"But you don't do this kind of work anymore."

"And that's what I told him when he dragged me into this on Valentine's Day. But I suppose I have to go because I'm the one who's met with the client's daughter. Hugh promised he'd put a criminal defense attorney on the case if Lachlan was arrested, so after tonight, I won't be involved."

He leaned over and gave her a long kiss. "I'll try not to wake you when I get back."

* * *

She was standing in the brightly lit lobby of the high-rise when he parked near the front door. She was wearing the white wool coat and the fluffy white hat. She ran to him when he entered the building and threw her arms around him.

"Thank God, you're here! They handcuffed Dad as he was getting on the red-eye back to Boston. He called me from the jail."

She smelled of jasmine and musk, and even under the heavy coat, Cam could feel her lithe, supple body through the soft knit of his sweatpants and hoodie. He told himself that his involuntary response to her meant nothing.

He released her and stepped back. "There's not much we can do tonight."

"But I have to see him! I have to know that he's all right, and I have to take his medications to him in case he can't come home in the morning."

It took them less than five minutes to reach the San Diego Central Jail. By some stroke of luck, Axel Saldana, the number two in the district attorney's office was still there, overseeing the paperwork related to Lachlan's arrest.

"What are you doing here?" He said when he saw Cam. "I thought you gave up working on the criminal side ten years ago!"

Axel had just been starting his career as a deputy district attorney when Cam's grandfather had forced him to do the two-year stint in the public defender's office. They'd done trials together. Axel had always looked the part of a prosecutor. He was six feet tall, with intense dark eyes and hair so closely cut that his head appeared to be shaved.

"Sixteen years ago," Cam told him. "The firm sent me because I've done some business work for the Adairs. Hugh is appointing someone from the criminal defense team in the morning."

"Well, here's the discovery packet of what we have so far. Police reports, CSI findings, and the coroner's report. You can pass it on to whoever takes over the file."

"This is Ms. Adair, Lachlan's daughter. She'd like to see her father, and she has brought his prescriptions."

"We can't let those into the jail," Axel said, "but give them to Deputy Blake over there. He'll write them down for our medical to prescribe and give them back to you when you leave. Mr. Adair isn't supposed to have visitors tonight, but I'll make an exception for you, Cam, since we know each other. Fifteen minutes only in the Attorney Interview Room."

"Thanks."

Axel himself led them down the steel-gray hall to the interview room which was small and sparsely furnished with a gray metal table and four chairs. The window in the door was covered in bars. A moment after Cam took a seat next to Raven at the table, the door stirred and Lachlan entered in the custody of a deputy.

"Fifteen minutes," Axel admonished the deputy as he left the room. "Leave the cuffs on and wait outside."

"Yes, sir."

When the door closed behind them, Raven started to get up to give her father a hug. Even in orange jail scrubs, he had an air of professorial dignity. Cam could see why he had a reputation as a ladies' man. He was taller than Cam, around six feet two, and his height made him an imposing figure. He was even more good-looking in person than he had been in the photograph that Cam had seen in the guesthouse. Raven had inherited his dark hair and light-blue eyes. But unlike hers, which could be flirty and mischievous, Lachlan's were calm and kind.

"Don't," Cam cautioned. "They're watching, and they'll think you're passing him some sort of contraband."

She glanced in the direction of the door and sat down.

"It's all right, daughter," Lachlan said. "It's a far cry from the Maze."

"I know, Da. But still, you shouldn't be here." There were tears in her eyes as she spoke.

"I'm Cameron Rhodes, from Goldstein, Miller."

"Thanks for coming," he said. Like Raven's, his accent also made the word sound like "tanks."

"Did they give you any idea of why they changed their minds about your wife's death?" Cam asked.

"No. They didn't say anything except 'you're under arrest' when they handcuffed me."

"How long have you been in San Diego?"

"Since last Friday. Nora didn't have any other family, so it was up to Raven and me to arrange her memorial service. We held it this morning, and then her solicitor read her will in the afternoon."

"How did she dispose of her property?"

"She was virtually penniless. She was living on her income from me."

"And that was expensive for you?"

Lachlan shrugged. "As Raven will tell you, nothing has been too expensive for me since *Unforgettable.* The book and then the movie changed our lives. I could afford Nora, and I can afford your firm's fees, too."

Cam smiled. "Well, that's good to know. I'm not going to be your attorney after tonight. I don't do this kind of work anymore."

Lachlan looked disappointed. "But Raven said you were going to be my attorney if they arrested me. She said that you understood the literary rights problem about the sequel to the movie."

"I do, but you need an attorney whose expertise is criminal defense. I'm very rusty on criminal law," Cam said. "All of our attorneys in the criminal defense section are excellent lawyers. Hugh will find someone whom you feel just as comfortable with."

CHAPTER EIGHT

Wednesday, February 20, 2019, Pacific Gate Condos, Downtown, San Diego

Raven was silent on the short drive to E Street, but when Cam pulled up in front of the lobby to drop her off, she put her hand on his arm and said, "Please come up with me."

"Not now. It's twelve thirty."

"And your wife is waiting for you?"

"No. I'm sure Jess is asleep. She has to be up at six to get the girls ready for school."

"Callie, age eight, and Stephanie, age six. See, I remembered. Please come up for a drink. I—I don't want to be alone right now. I'm frightened, and I need to talk to you."

Cam looked down at her dainty hand on the sleeve of his jacket and remembered how she'd stood bravely in the middle of the road on that first night. But she did look worried now. The confidence and even defiance that had attracted him initially had vanished. But somehow, she was even more appealing this way.

I shouldn't do this. But I'm not going to have anything to do with this case after tonight. One more time won't hurt.

* * *

Stepping into the unlit condo felt exactly the same as it had last Thursday night—like stepping into a dark, enchanted land. As before, Raven summoned him to the glass wall overlooking the city where the lights glowed like a vast net of diamonds, emeralds, and sapphires stretching toward the ocean. He stood next to her, bathed in starlight and moonlight, unable to resist the magnetic pull of her beautiful eyes that seemed to see through the defenses to his feelings that he was trying to muster.

She let them stand together gazing at the magical city spread out before them for several minutes before she turned on the soft overhead lighting.

"Have a seat on the couch, and I'll fetch a drink."

Cam sank into the luxurious down sofa and reminded himself sternly not to let this go too far. It was already twelve forty-five. He should down this drink quickly and be on his way.

"Here." She handed him a crystal whiskey glass with a generous pour. He took a sip, entirely unprepared for the rich vanilla, caramel, and spice notes that lingered on his palate. He had never tasted anything like this before. He glanced over at the bottle on the table and read Midleton Very Rare Irish Whiskey. The most expensive whiskey in the world.

She saw him glance at the label and said, "It's amazing, isn't it? I thought something special might persuade you not to give up on Dad."

Her eyes said that she found him special, and he reminded himself again that he mustn't let this go too far. He cursed his body for responding to her. The hat and coat, of course, were gone. She was wearing simple black wool pants and an equally simple long-sleeved black sweater that complimented her hair and made her eyes seem even more striking. A large, creamy oval pearl dangled from each ear, and her perfume intoxicated him.

Okay, I've fallen under her spell again. But I've got to resist. "What is the Maze?" he asked.

"The Maze is the jail in Northern Ireland where the British imprisoned those who were fighting to expel the Crown and create a united Irish State. My father was held there as prisoner in the mid-seventies when he was in his early twenties. The British refused to treat him as a political prisoner, but that's what he was."

"Because of his poetry?"

"Oh, no. My father was involved in the resistance to the Crown's presence in Northern Ireland. He's famous in our country not only as a poet but as a great Irish patriot."

"Do you mean that he was a member of the IRA?"

"Even to this day, the Irish Republican Army is loath to give up the names of its members." Raven studied him carefully for a long moment. Then she asked, "You've led a perfect life, haven't you?"

The question startled him. "I—Well, no. No one has."

"But you have," she insisted. "You've got a big, close family. Your parents are rich. You went to private school and to the best universities. Your wife has the same background. You have two perfect daughters. I bet you live in a big, perfect house. You've never deviated from fulfilling your family's expectations."

"I suppose that's true." Once more her eyes held his, and he felt suspended in her enchanted world that drew him in and made him want to remain there forever.

But magic was a dangerous proposition, and he was a realist who didn't believe in magic. He forced himself to let go of the feeling that he was drifting along on a gossamer cloud. He said, "I wouldn't call my life perfect. Uneventful, perhaps, but not perfect."

"I think I chose the wrong word. 'Perfect' really doesn't apply to life, does it?"

"No, it doesn't."

"But by 'perfect,' I just meant that you seem like someone who's always moved in a world of people just like yourself—wealthy, privileged, and intelligent. You've never had any moments of rebellion or asking yourself what you really wanted."

"I never gave that much thought. But it's true. I've never considered wanting a life different from this one."

"Tell me about Jess. You must be very happy with her."

I'm letting her do it again. I'm letting her lure me into telling her all about myself. It's the whiskey. No, not just that. The soft light and her perfume and everything about her.

"We met at Yale. Her father was a big-name partner in a large law firm in Baltimore before he passed away. Jess would have gone to work there if she hadn't married me and come out here."

"What does she look like?"

"Blond, blue eyes. Almost as tall as I am. Thin. She runs."

Raven gave a little shiver and laughed. "Goodness! I hate running. Your parents were happy when you married her, weren't they, because you all belong to the same tribe?"

"Same tribe," he said thoughtfully. "I never thought of it that way. Yes, that's true. But isn't that true for you, too? You're the daughter of a wealthy, famous poet who, like your mother, is respected in academic circles. You belong to that tribe."

"I don't. I didn't choose an academic life. My father's name would have been an entré into those circles, but I didn't want to hang on the edges of his fame the way my mother does.

"I'm not like you. I wasn't born rich. My father was living on a professor's salary and wasn't even particularly famous when I entered the world. And then, when I was three years old, he moved out so that he could pursue other women even though he didn't divorce my mother. He didn't become wealthy until 2004 when I turned twenty-one. My life hasn't been like yours."

"Okay, I agree. But what does this have to do with your father's time in a Northern Ireland prison?"

"Because I don't want you to stop being Dad's attorney, and I'm afraid that you've led such a conventional life that if I tell you the truth about what he did during the Troubles, I won't be able to talk you out of dropping him as a client."

"But I've already told you that I'm leaving. The new lawyer will contact you in the morning."

"But Dad doesn't want a new lawyer, and I don't want a new one for him."

"Raven, I haven't tried a criminal case for sixteen years." *But you make me feel as if I'm willing to try this one.*

"But will there really be a trial? Won't they let Dad go when they find out he was in Boston that night?"

"It depends on how convincing his alibi witness is."

"Her name is Leslie Ryan. I'll email her contact information to you."

"And have you talked to her?"

"Once."

"Don't. If Axel finds out, he could accuse you of witness tampering."

"Does this mean you'll stay on?"

"I'll think about it. But if I do, I'll be asking Hugh to associate a criminal defense specialist. That's going to double your father's legal fees."

"He can easily afford it."

"You were going to tell me something about your father that you thought would shock a man who has led a 'perfect' life."

"Actually, it would shock anyone."

"What is it, then?"

"Lachlan is a trained killer."

SPELLBOUND

CHAPTER NINE

Thursday, February 21, 2019, Offices of Goldstein, Miller, and Mahoney, Emerald Shapery Center

"How was the arraignment?" Hugh asked at eleven thirty the next morning.

"Uneventful. I'm surprised I remembered how to do it after so many years."

"Not guilty plea and bail setting. Not complicated. It's like riding a bicycle."

"Not exactly."

"Did the court grant bail?"

"Yes, although Axel argued strongly against it. Irish national. Flight risk, all that."

"Did Lachlan surrender his passport?"

"Without a whimper. And coughed up five million for the bond."

"The Adairs are adamant that they want you to stay."

"I know. I heard all about it from Raven last night. I didn't get home until two in the morning."

"Ouch!"

"I told her I'd stay, but you've got to associate someone from the criminal defense team. I'm too rusty to go it alone."

"Exactly what I was thinking. And I've got the perfect attorney: Meg Courtney. She's a senior associate who's just transferred from our New York office. Former federal prosecutor. She'll be an asset for sure."

"Thanks, Hugh. I'll go see her this afternoon."

* * *

Meg Courtney's office was on the same floor as Cam's, on the same side of the elevator but farther down the hall. At two o'clock he headed that way carrying a copy of the police report and hoping to find her free.

She was not yet a partner, but she had a spacious office. Cam knocked on her open door before he realized that no one was sitting behind her desk. He turned to leave, disappointed that she wasn't in.

But a voice called out, "I'm over here."

An attractive forty-something blonde with striking green eyes was just getting to her feet as he reentered her office. She was dressed informally in a dark-green sweater and jeans and brown leather boots. She'd been sitting at a child-sized table in one corner with the little boy who rose to his feet along with her. He was eyeing Cam quizzically with an identical pair of expressive green eyes. But that was where the resemblance ended. The child's face was rectangular and solemn, and he had a thatch of very dark hair and a dusting of freckles across his nose.

"I'm Meg," she said, offering her hand. "Hugh said you wanted to talk today. I was going to come down to your office after my babysitter picked up Finn. I couldn't send him to preschool this morning because he's coming down with a cold, and I don't have a regular babysitter until three every day."

"Don't apologize. My wife and I have two girls, and we had our share of children-in-the office days until it got so complicated that Jess decided to stay home after the second one."

"I'm afraid that's not an option for me. I told Hugh I may not be the right attorney to help you. Finn's father only sees him occasionally, so I'm a full-time parent."

"I take it he's still in New York."

"So Hugh told you that Finn and I have just moved to San Diego?"

"Yes. He said you'd only been here a few months."

"I like it here." Finn suddenly spoke up. "I'm four," he added solemnly. "We have a whole house, and I have my own room, and we can go to the beach on weekends."

Meg smiled at Cam as she opened a box of Legos. "In New York, he had to share a room with me." To Finn, she said, "Here's your astronaut set. Why don't you make one while Mr. Rhodes and I talk?"

"Okay." The little boy returned her smile. Then, in a serious tone, he said, "I'm going to be an astronaut some day because I like to count the stars at night."

"He's very grown-up for four," Cam observed as they walked over and sat down in the client chairs in front of Meg's desk.

"Yes, he is," she agreed as she reached for the police report in the middle of her desk. "He's a great kid, and I like it being just the two of us, but I'm going to have to get a nanny soon if I expect to make partner."

"Are you up this year?"

"I told Hugh I'd rather wait until next year. I'm an eighth-year associate, but with the move and everything, it's too much right now."

"Hugh said you were a federal prosecutor before you joined the firm."

"That's right. I joined Goldstein, Miller in 2014, and they gave me credit for my time in the U.S. Attorney's Office. Listen, I just want to be sure that you understand that I tried to talk Hugh out of assigning me to this case because of Finn."

Cam smiled. "And I tried to talk Hugh out of assigning it to me because it's been sixteen years since I did my brief stint as a PD. If it's any consolation to you, I don't think this is going to last very long."

"Why not?"

"Lachlan has an alibi for February 14. He was in Boston, sleeping with a student named Leslie Ryan."

"And he told you that?"

"His daughter, Raven, who is also his solicitor, told me about the student."

"When is the preliminary hearing?"

"Next Wednesday."

"Would he be willing to waive the ten-day rule to give us more time to prepare?"

"No, I asked him at the arraignment this morning. He and his daughter are sure that the charges will be dismissed based on the alibi evidence."

"Since neither of us wants this case, we should both hope

that Ms. Ryan turns out to be as convincing as the client thinks she is. When can we talk to her?"

"She'll be here on Monday."

* * *

"You were late last night," Jess said as Cam climbed into bed beside her and prepared to turn out the light.

"Two a.m."

"You were at the jail that long?"

"No, the daughter wanted to talk to me afterward."

"Until two in the morning?"

"She insisted that I stay on as her father's attorney."

"But I thought you were quitting after the arraignment this morning."

"I did, too. But Raven talked to Hugh, and Hugh, of course, wants to give the Adairs what they want."

"Are you the only attorney on the file?"

"No, thank God. Hugh's assigned a very senior associate, Meg Courtney, to work with me. You'd like her. She's a single parent with a precocious four-year-old named Finn. She's ideal for this case because she's a former prosecutor."

Jess turned and rolled away from him and frowned at the ceiling. Then she said, "I don't want you involved in anything that's going to take you too far away from us right now. The girls need you, and I need you. And I think your mother is going to need you quite a bit in the next few months."

"I know. I'll be here for all of you. But I think the thing with Dad is going to blow over."

"Then you're in denial just as much as Jackie is. This is an affair that has lasted for years."

"But they've been married for far longer than that affair, if it even exists. And besides, Dad is retired now, and he doesn't really have time to see someone else on a regular basis."

"But that's the danger," Jess insisted. "Apparently, he's really in love with this woman, and now that your grandfather is gone and your father's career at the firm is all but over, nothing is making him stay with Jackie anymore. He's free to ask for a divorce or just initiate proceedings himself."

"He wouldn't do that!"

"And I think he would."

Cam stared at her, too horrified to reach over and turn out the light.

Jess gently took his hand and said, "If I'm right, that's why all of us will need you a lot more than the Adairs in the next few months."

He smiled and leaned over and kissed her on the cheek. "Don't worry. The Adairs will be out of my life by next Wednesday. He has an alibi."

CHAPTER TEN

Monday, February 25, 2019, Offices of Goldstein, Miller, and Mahoney, Emerald Shapery Center

"Do I have to testify?"

Cam felt sorry for the thin young woman sitting in the middle at the mahogany table in the firm's small conference room on the twenty-ninth floor. She ran her shiny red fingernails through her long blond hair and fixed her large brown eyes on Lachlan beseechingly as she spoke. After she settled her hair, she began to twirl the star charm on her bracelet in an obvious effort to soothe her nerves. If they used her as a witness, they'd have to find something for her to wear besides jeans and a denim jacket.

"Why don't you tell us about the night of February 13, and then we'll decide," Meg suggested.

Leslie shrugged. "There's nothing to tell. Lachlan—I mean Professor Adair—and I had dinner, and then I stayed over. He gave me breakfast, and I went back to my apartment in the morning."

"Where did you have dinner?"

"At Tony's. It's a little Italian place near his house in Beacon Hill."

"Do you have the receipts?" Meg asked Lachlan who was sitting at the end of the table with Raven. The horrible image of his mother clutching her box of credit card receipts popped into Cam's head.

"Actually, we ate in that night," Leslie said quickly before he could answer. "Lachlan cooked for us."

"Are you sure? Which was it?"

"Actually, now that I think about it, we ate in, but we ordered from Tony's," Leslie said.

"Any receipts?" Meg looked at Lachlan.

He shook his head. "Who keeps pizza receipts?"

"Did you use a credit card? That would be on your statement."

But he shook his head again. "Tony's is cash only for delivery."

Cam felt a knot forming in his stomach. So far, Leslie Ryan wasn't impressive as a witness.

"How do you know Professor Adair?" he asked. "Are you an undergraduate or a graduate student?"

She seemed offended by his question. "I'm twenty-nine and a Ph.D. candidate."

"I apologize. You look very young."

Leslie stopped twirling her star and frowned. "Look, I really, really don't want to go to court. I thought I could just sign a statement or something like that."

"I'm afraid it doesn't work that way," Cam told her. "How long have you and Professor Adair been together?"

"Oh, a few months. Since just before Christmas."

"And you knew about his wife?" As he spoke, the image of his mother tortured by those tiny scraps of paper returned.

"Of course. Everyone knows that he's married to Nora Carson."

"But that didn't matter?" Cam continued, still haunted by the thought of his mother's anguished face.

"Look, this wasn't meant to be anything long term." She sounded exasperated. "Lachlan sleeps around. Everyone knows that. Can I go now? I've told you everything I know about that night."

"You can't leave San Diego before Wednesday," Raven said. "You will have to testify for Lachlan."

Cam frowned. "Meg and I are going to make that decision, Raven. And we haven't made it yet."

"Of course. I'm sorry. I just meant that she should stay until the two of you decide."

"Here." Meg pushed her legal pad across the table to Leslie. "Write down your contact information for us, and Cam and I will let you know by this afternoon if you need to stay until Wednesday. Are you at a hotel?"

"No, at my aunt's house in Mission Hills."

Leslie wrote her information on the legal pad and pushed it back to Meg, who read it carefully. Then she said to Cam, "Do you have any more questions for Ms. Ryan?"

He shook his head.

"Okay, I'll walk her to the elevator," Meg said, "and I'll explain what we have to decide before Wednesday on the way."

* * *

"Why wouldn't you use her?" Raven asked when Meg came back.

"Because she's risky."

"Why don't you find her convincing?" Lachlan asked.

"She's nervous, she doesn't want to testify, and her memory wasn't very good."

"You mean the dinner mix-up?" Raven frowned.

"Just everything about her," Cam replied. "You have to remember that this is a preliminary hearing and the district attorney has the burden of showing probable cause to hold Lachlan on the murder charge. The police report is very thin on evidence. In a nutshell it says that Nora died sometime between midnight and two a.m. Lachlan's DNA has been found in the house, but that's meaningless because it was his house, and he had lived there. They have surveillance footage of a black Range Rover entering the security gates at the foot of the drive at eleven forty p.m., but there's no license plate visible and the house's surveillance camera does not show the car arriving at the house. I think we have a good shot at getting the charge set aside without Ms. Ryan."

"And I agree," Meg said.

CHAPTER ELEVEN

Monday, February 25, 2019, Pacific Gate Condos, Downtown, San Diego

At seven thirty p.m., Cam felt suspended in the night sky once again as he sipped a glass of Chateau Margaux and studied the waning moon that stared back at him through the glass walls of the Adair condo. He could hear Raven moving about the kitchen as he inhaled the smell of the chicken that she was roasting in the oven.

Of course, he hadn't planned to be here. But he'd gotten home at six forty-five only to find Jess and the girls on their way out the door to Jackie's monthly book club meeting. As he'd stood in the window, watching the Cayenne pull out of the driveway and feeling grateful to Jess for supporting Jackie, Raven had rung him.

"Can you come over tonight? I need to talk to you. Please. It's important. I can give you dinner if you haven't eaten."

Although he knew he should have said that he couldn't talk about the case without Meg present, Cam guessed that Raven had more to say about Leslie Ryan, and it would be advantageous to put a stop to the idea of her as a witness once and for all. Besides, despite his best intentions not to let himself be flattered by Raven's attention, he found her fascinating. Now, as he stood sipping her superb wine, the tiny traces of guilt that had gripped him as he left a note for Jess evaporated. Once more the spell that Raven wove pulled him out of his world and into hers.

"Where's Lachlan?" Cam asked as he sat down at the table in the dining room set for two.

"He's found a pub close by. He's carousing and reading his poetry to anyone who's as drunk as he is."

"He's on bail, Raven. He's not supposed to be out drinking."

She shrugged. "Then he'll find out the hard way, won't he?"

"If his bond is revoked, that will be used against him at the hearing on Wednesday."

"That's what I wanted to talk to you about. The hearing. But first, food."

The roast chicken was perfectly cooked. The tiny peas swimming in butter sauce were an exquisite accompaniment along with colcannon, a comforting mix of potatoes, cabbage, butter, and cream. Her hand brushed his lightly as she handed him each dish in turn. He told himself it was an accident, but it didn't feel like one.

He said the first thing that came into his head to stifle the feelings that her touch had aroused. "You're an excellent cook." *Stupid, banal remark. Get a grip.*

She smiled. "Thanks. I've always made good use of my holidays in France to hone my cooking skills. I'm lucky you could come tonight. Your wife didn't object?"

"My mother has a book club every month at her house. Jess

takes Callie and Steph to play with my sister Addison's girls."

Her light-blue eyes studied San Diego's night skyline through the glass wall behind Cam for a minute before she said, "What lucky little girls to be part of such a big family. I always wanted that."

"You said you had a half brother."

"James, yes. He's ten years older than I am. And I have a half sister, who's just twenty-one this year. Her name is Skye. Her mother was another one of Dad's students."

"Do you see much of her?"

"No, not really. Skye's mother got married when she was four, and her stepfather adopted her. Dad hadn't had much contact with her until she came to Harvard as an undergrad. She graduated this year and took a job in New York. They got pretty close when she was in college, but I barely know her."

"And that's it for you? A half brother and half sister?"

She nodded. "At least, that's all that Dad and I know about it. Given his wandering ways, others could always turn up."

Cam ate in silence for a few minutes, considering the smoldering anger that he felt toward Blaine for his infidelity to Jackie.

"You're thinking about something awfully hard."

"No, not really." He knew he was on dangerous ground because she had a way of worming things out of him that he never intended to tell her. "I'm guessing that you want to persuade me to use Leslie Ryan at the hearing on Wednesday."

"Dad needs the world to know that he wasn't in San Diego the night Nora died. Leslie is the only person who can say that."

"But you realize that she didn't say that very convincingly in our meeting this afternoon."

"Look, anyone with any common sense would be upset at the prospect of having to testify in court."

"Why is her testimony so important to you and Lachlan?"

"Because it proves he didn't kill Nora. I realize you think the DA hasn't enough evidence to hold Dad on the murder charge, but I'm not as optimistic as you are because, as I told you when we met, I know that there are innocent people who've been convicted of homicide because some expert was able to exaggerate an accident into a deliberate killing. Dad is sixty-nine years old, so any sentence of any kind would be a life sentence for him. Leslie knows he wasn't in San Diego that night even if she isn't very artful at telling the story."

"But you realize there's no guarantee that a judge is going to believe her?"

"Of course. But it's a risk I want you to take for me and for my father."

* * *

Jess met him at the door in her pajamas and robe when he came home at midnight. She was holding a cup of hot chocolate. It was a specialty of hers, made from real chocolate instead of a powder that came in a can.

"You're late again." Her tone was factual, not accusatory.

"I had to meet with Raven Adair about an alibi witness whom she wants us to call at her father's preliminary hearing."

"Wow, this is like going back to your early public defender days. I haven't heard the words 'alibi witness' out of your mouth for a long time."

"I'm wishing I hadn't heard them tonight, either. Hugh owes me for this."

"Want some?" She held up the cup of hot chocolate invitingly.

Cam's stomach rolled at the thought of pouring liquid chocolate into the sea of Jameson in his belly. "No, thanks. I'm learning that the Irish tolerance for whiskey exceeds mine. To be honest, I've got to go upstairs and sleep this off." She was his wife, and she knew when he was drunk, and there was no point in trying to lie about it. "But before I do that, how was Mom tonight?"

"She was fine. Her head is firmly in the sand, and she's determined to keep it there. Did you resolve the alibi witness problem?"

"Kind of, sort of." He finished hanging his overcoat in the hall closet and closed the door. "It looks like the Adairs are going to insist on having us call the student Lachlan was sleeping with on February 13 in Boston. She wasn't impressive when we met with her, and Meg and I don't think we need her because the DA doesn't have enough evidence to point to Lachlan, but Raven's terrified of what will happen without her."

"So you're going to do it?"

"We'll keep her on standby and maybe by the end of the hearing on Wednesday, the Adairs will see that we don't need her. Come on, let's go to bed. We both have to be up at six."

CHAPTER TWELVE

Wednesday, February 27, 2019, San Diego County Central Courthouse, Downtown San Diego

"She's a no-show," Meg whispered to Cam as they sat at the defendant's table with Lachlan at eight thirty on Wednesday morning, waiting for Judge Bennet Walker to enter the courtroom and call the preliminary hearing to order. "She met with me yesterday in my office, and we went over her testimony, and I know she understood that she had to be here first thing this morning."

"Where is she?" Cam asked.

"Her aunt said she left for Boston on the red-eye last night."

"Well, then that settles that." He smiled at Meg. "We don't have to worry about her performance as a witness because she isn't going to be one."

* * *

But Leslie Ryan's flight, Cam reflected that evening, as he described the day to Jess while they sat in the den sipping hot chocolate after the girls had gone to bed, was just the beginning of the surprises.

Axel Saldana's first witness was the deputy coroner, Maria

Sanchez. After she testified to the preliminary facts of height, weight, and date of the autopsy, Axel homed in on the most important part of her findings.

"Did you find evidence of drugs in her system?"

"Alcohol, but no narcotics. Her blood alcohol level was 0.02. That would be mild impairment of speech and vision and coordination. Alcohol did not contribute to her death."

"What was her cause of death?"

"Broken neck, caused by the fall."

"What about bruising on her body?"

"Her torso was heavily bruised. She had a large bruise on her left arm and leg. That was the side she impacted on."

"Were you able to determine a time of death?"

"I think she died around midnight."

"And what did you conclude about the manner of death?"

"Her death was a homicide."

"Why did you rule out accidental death?"

"She wasn't drunk enough to lose her balance on the stairs. She was pushed."

"And what brought you to that conclusion?"

"The heavy bruising on her back. She fell on her side. I believe that someone applied strong force from behind."

"Thank you, Dr. Sanchez."

As Axel returned to the prosecution's table, Judge Walker looked at Cam and asked, "Any questions, Mr. Rhodes?"

"A few, Your Honor."

Cam took Axel's place at the podium and asked, "Dr. Sanchez, what were the DNA results from the fingernail scrapings taken from Ms. Carson?"

"Only her DNA was present."

"So there was no evidence that she fought off an attacker?"

"True, but I don't believe she ever saw the person who pushed her."

"Thank you, Dr. Sanchez." Cam sat down.

"Call your next witness," Judge Walker said to Axel.

"Your Honor, we call Michael Bernstein."

Cam heard Lachlan, who was sitting between himself and Meg, draw in a sharp breath. He hoped that the judge had not noticed his client's reaction.

A trim, dark-haired man who looked to be in his early fifties took the stand with a calm, confident air. He was wearing a well-fitting dark-gray suit that added to his aura of authority and professionalism.

After Axel had taken him through the preliminary facts of identity and relevance, he asked, "And did you see Nora Carson on the evening of February 13, just a few hours before her death, Mr. Bernstein?"

"I did. I had invited myself to dinner that night."

"And what time did you arrive at Ms. Carson's home?"

"Around seven thirty."

"And why did you invite yourself?"

"To discuss the sequel to *Unforgettable.*"

"Did Ms. Carson have a role in the sequel?"

"No, and that was the problem I wanted to solve with her. She believed that her contract for the original movie gave her the right to play the lead role in any sequel. Her husband thought his contract gave him the right to keep her out of the movie. My attorneys had advised me that her claim was stronger than his, and she could stop production if we tried to go forward. So I went to see her that night to work out a solution."

"Did you personally want her in the new movie?"

"No, I didn't. I thought she was too old."

"How old was she?"

"Forty-six. But it wasn't just her age. She hadn't had a good part in a hit movie in quite some time. Both of these facts made me agree with Lachlan that she wouldn't be a draw at the box office."

"Did you tell her that?"

"Yes. She wasn't happy to hear that news. I offered her fifteen percent of the movie's gross if she'd give up her contract rights to a part."

"And did she agree?"

"No. She vehemently refused."

"What were her exact words to you?"

"You'll make that sequel over my dead body."

"Thank you, Mr. Bernstein."

"Mr. Rhodes?" Judge Walker looked at Cam.

"Thank you, Your Honor." Cam took the podium, inwardly fuming. The Adairs hadn't told him about any talks between Bernstein and Nora Carson. He was about to do the unforgivable: ask a question that he had no idea what the answer would be.

"Mr. Bernstein, did you ever discuss your offer to Ms. Carson with my client?"

"Yes. He agreed to it, although he wanted to offer her a lesser percentage based on the net proceeds."

"And did he know on the night of February 13 that she had rejected your more generous offer?"

"I assume he did. I sent him a text message after the meeting."

"And what time did you leave Ms. Carson's house that night?"

"Around eleven thirty. I texted Lachlan as I was leaving."

This isn't going well, and I have a feeling it's about to get worse. The knot in Cam's stomach tightened as he took his seat, and Axel replaced him at the podium. Meg looked over and gave him a tight smile. *She knows we're in trouble.*

"Just a few additional questions for you, Mr. Bernstein. What kind of car were you driving that night?"

"My red Tesla."

"And could you identify the car in this picture for us?"

"That's my car exiting the security gates at the end of the Nora's driveway."

"And what is the time stamp on that photo?"

"It says 11:33 p.m., February 13, 2019."

"This is a printout of your text messages from that night. Could you read the time of the message that you sent Lachlan Adair?"

"11:31 p.m. I sent it from my car before I headed down the drive."

"And one last question. Do you own a black Range Rover?"

"No, I do not."

"Thank you, Mr. Bernstein."

"We'll take a fifteen-minute recess," Judge Walker said.

Out of the corner of his eye, Cam saw Axel and his assistant leave the courtroom. Since they were out of earshot, it was safe to talk here. Raven had gotten up from her seat behind the bar and had come to huddle with them.

"Clearly, these are facts Meg and I didn't know about," Cam began.

"But they don't matter," Raven insisted, "because Dad was in Boston. That's why I told you we needed Leslie Ryan. Where is she?" Cam thought he heard a note of desperation in her voice.

"When she didn't show up this morning, I called her aunt," Meg said. "She flew back to Boston last night."

"She panicked," Raven said. "I was afraid of that. Well, as you said, their case isn't very strong. We didn't need her."

So far we don't, but I have a feeling that's about to change.

Axel's next witness identified herself as Alicia Cortez, Nora's housekeeper. Cam guessed she was in her midthirties. She had long dark hair that she nervously tossed over her shoulder from time to time as she answered questions. She kept her large dark eyes fixed intently on Axel as if to make sure that she understood everything correctly. She was slightly overweight but very pretty, and her light flowery dress added to her air of youth and truthfulness.

"And how long had you worked for Ms. Carson?" Axel asked.

"Going on five years."

"And did you work for the defendant, as well?"

"I was Ms. Carson's employee. Mr. Adair only visited occasionally. He lived in Boston."

"So Mr. Adair and his wife did not live together based on your observations?"

"That is correct."

"Did Mr. Adair visit his wife on February 13, 2019?"

Oh, God. Here it comes. Cam glanced at Meg who nodded imperceptibly. *I'm glad I'm not alone on this file.*

"Yes," Alicia Cortez said. "He called around ten o'clock that morning and said that he wanted to come over between eleven and eleven thirty. Ms. Carson was very excited about his visit."

"Why?"

"Because she thought he was coming to tell her that he would agree to write a part for her in the movie that she wanted to be in."

"Was that the sequel to *Unforgettable*?"

"Yes. She talked about it all the time. She thought it would restart her career."

"Were you present for the conversation between Professor Adair and his wife?"

"No. I was working in the living room across the hall. They were in Ms. Carson's study."

"So you couldn't hear what they were saying?"

"No. I didn't hear anything until the shouting started."

"How long before that happened?"

"I would guess they talked for about a half hour. I was nearly finished with tidying the living room when I heard Ms. Carson yelling, 'You'll never make that movie without me!' Then I heard china breaking, and the door to her study burst open and Professor Adair came out with blood running down his forehead. I could see that Ms. Carson had thrown one of her antique vases at him. She had come to the door, and he was in the hall, holding his head. He was furious. He yelled, 'I'll kill you before I'll give you a part in this movie.'"

"Are you sure that's what he said?"

"Absolutely. And then he threw open the front door and ran outside to his car."

"Did you see the car he was driving?"

"Yes. He left the front door wide open, and when I went to close it, I saw him leave in a black Range Rover."

"Thank you, Ms. Cortez."

"Any questions, Mr. Rhodes?"

"No, Your Honor."

* * *

"That's horrible," Jess said. "More hot chocolate?"

"No. I'd consider a scotch right now, but I won't sleep well if I do."

"Well, at least that was the worst of it."

"No, the lowest point came after that. Axel showed the surveillance footage of a black Range Rover driving through the security gates at eleven forty p.m. Fortunately, the camera didn't capture a license plate number. But then he showed records from the Fairmont in Del Mar that showed Lachlan checked in on the afternoon of February 13 and did an express checkout the next morning. He listed the car he was driving as a black Range Rover."

"Which means, he had motive and opportunity to kill his wife," Jess said.

"And poor little Leslie Ryan fled to avoid perjuring herself."

CHAPTER THIRTEEN

Thursday, February 28, 2019, Offices of Goldstein, Miller, and Mahoney, Emerald Shapery Center

"This is all my fault," Raven said at ten thirty the next morning. She was sitting at the far end of the conference table with her back to the window. She was wearing a pale-blue dress and a simple string of pearls. The sunlight behind her accentuated the contrast between her dark hair and her clear eyes. She was a breathtakingly beautiful woman, Cam thought, even when her expression revealed that she was deeply worried.

"Please don't be too hard on her," Lachlan said. "It wasn't her idea, originally."

In a starched white shirt worn without a tie and an Irish tweed sport coat, he looked every inch the distinguished academic.

"Was it yours, then?" Cam asked with a frown.

"Neither of ours originally," Raven said. "Leslie came to us and asked if she could help Lachlan."

"And you suggested a false alibi?"

"No, she did," Lachlan said. "At the time, she didn't know that I was in San Diego on February 13 and 14. She thought I was in Boston, so it wouldn't be a very big lie to say that she was with me."

"I gather she has feelings for you," Meg said.

Lachlan shrugged slightly. "All of the female students do. And I have feelings for them. I love beautiful, intelligent women. I can't help myself."

He ended with a charming smile that made Cam wonder if he was coming on to Meg, too. If he was, she was ignoring him.

"My inability to love and be faithful at the same time was my undoing," Lachlan continued. "I suppose Raven told you about Sinead, the great love of my life. I lost her because I was sleeping with Raven's mother."

"She did tell me that story," Cam agreed. "But why weren't you honest with Meg and me about your whereabouts when Nora died?"

"Because Leslie offered to say that she was with me that night, and we all thought her statement would make everything blow over quickly. Obviously, we were wrong."

"So tell us about everything you did on February 13," Cam said.

"I arrived from Boston around eight thirty that morning. I went straight to Michael's house in La Jolla to talk about his idea of giving Nora a percentage of the profits from the sequel if she would agree not to pursue a role in the movie. As he said, I thought his offer was too generous. He gave me breakfast, and I decided to talk to her myself to see if she'd take less. That didn't go well, as you know."

"And then?" Cam prompted.

"I was upset when I left Nora's. I checked into the Fairmont in Del Mar, and I called Michael to tell him that I'd quarreled with her."

"What did he say?"

"That he'd try to persuade her to accept a deal that night."

"And after that?"

"I sat by the pool and worked on my new novel until it was time for Seamus to meet me for dinner. We ate at the Michelin-starred restaurant in the hotel and afterward we drank in the bar until it closed."

"Seamus?"

"Seamus O'Malley. He's been my friend since our university days."

"So there should be surveillance footage from the hotel of the two of you in the bar?" Meg asked.

"I would think so."

"When did you go back to Boston?"

"The next morning. I caught an early flight. The news about Nora was waiting for me when I got home."

"Raven described you as a 'trained killer,'" Cam said. "Is that true?"

Lachlan frowned and looked away toward the window and San Diego Bay. He said dreamily, "The light on the water looks like a thousand gold coins this time of day, doesn't it? It's as if all the souls lost in the Troubles are shining up at us, telling us they aren't really gone."

"The Troubles?" Cam asked.

"The fight for Irish independence and to unite Ireland that began when I was a boy in the sixties. One day, when I was twenty, the British came to our farm in County Sligo which is not far from the border with Northern Ireland. They accused my parents of hiding an Irish Republican Army gunman who had killed a British soldier in Belfast.

"It wasn't true, but the soldiers wouldn't listen. They dragged my bedridden mother downstairs and beat her on the front lawn. They shot all of our sheep and cattle, and then they shot my father in the legs and left him a cripple for life. Finally, as they left, they burned our house. They found the gunman a few hours later, at another farm close by, and executed him. No trial, nothing. Just shot him on the spot. So I decided to take his place."

CHAPTER FOURTEEN

Friday, March 1, 2019, 4212 Ocean Way, Coronado, California

"I don't think anyone's heart was in it tonight," Cam said to Jess as he changed for bed. "Mom shouldn't have insisted that all of us come for dinner."

"You're right," she agreed as she finished brushing her teeth in the en suite bath.

Cam watched her shake the water out of her toothbrush before putting it in the holder. It was something she did every night before she came into their bedroom to turn down the bed. Suddenly, the intimacy of her familiar routine made him feel guilty for having Raven on his mind all evening. She had texted him this morning.

> *"I hope you can understand why I wanted you to use Leslie. I hope you can forgive me. Can you get away for a drink this weekend?"*

Of course I couldn't. But I wanted to, and I was upset with myself for wanting to. But still, I wanted to. Was this how my father felt about the other woman? Torn between what he knew was right and what he wanted?

Cam couldn't get the image of her in the light-blue dress,

sitting in the sunlight, with her lovely, sky-blue eyes clouded with worry out of his mind. If it had been anyone else, he would have terminated the firm's representation. But the thought of never seeing her again was devastating. And besides, how could he blame her for trying to save her father?

"I'm glad Nash came down," Jess said as she climbed into bed and pulled up the covers. "But it wasn't the best night to get all of us together."

Cam thought of the strained conversation at the dinner table, everyone trying his or her best not to open the wound that his parents' marriage had become. Even Callie and Steph and Addison's girls, sitting in their own corner at the children's table, had been subdued.

"He's staying over tonight. Maybe he'll be able to talk to them."

"To Blaine and Jackie?" Jess frowned. "What could he say to them?"

"Suggest counseling?"

"Jackie thinks Blaine would leave before he'd do that. And I agree with her."

Cam got into bed on his side and adjusted his share of the covers as he considered his blunt, no-nonsense father who rarely showed emotion of any kind.

"I have to say, I think the two of you are right," he said. "But this game we're all playing that they are still happily married isn't working, either."

"You and Nash can talk about it in the morning at T-ball. I told him you'd be bringing the girls."

Cam did not relish the thought of the cold, windy bleachers

in Tidelands Park at eight thirty, filled with bored, upscale professional parents nursing Starbucks adult sippy cups while their offspring took turns trying to hit a ball atop a post.

"The girls don't really like T-ball," he pointed out.

"All their friends play. They want to be with their friends."

Cam reached over and turned out the light and settled himself on his side of the bed. He doubted that every eight- and six-year-old really liked hacking away at a big plastic ball on windy Saturday mornings, and he suspected that the whole exercise had more to do with parental ambition to imbue their offspring at an early age with the necessity of "building a resume" to ensure they would one day lead lives identical to those of their parents.

Sleep eluded him. He kept thinking about Raven despite his best efforts not to. She'd been right about his life. It wasn't perfect, but it was boring and predictable, and he was raising Callie and Steph to follow in those footsteps.

The bedside clock said one a.m. when he finally slipped out of bed and quietly went downstairs to the living room where he contemplated the liquor cabinet and wondered if alcohol would quiet his mind or send it racing into a higher gear. But before he could decide, he heard the sound of a vehicle stopping in front of his house. *Oh, God. It's Nash. Something's happened at my parents' and he's come to get me.*

Cam put down the bottle of scotch and peered through the blinds, expecting to see his brother's red Ferrari. But instead, a small gray sedan was parked across his driveway. His heart began to beat faster. Who could be watching his house? And why?

He considered going outside to confront the occupant of the

car, but then it occurred to him that there could be more than one. The only safe answer was to call the police, but his cell phone was upstairs, and they no longer had a landline.

He'd moved the blinds only slightly in order to look outside, so he was pretty sure that whoever was in the car did not realize he was watching it. He gently released the blind to its normal position and tiptoed upstairs. He was able to find his phone on his nightstand and go back downstairs to make his call without waking Jess. He prayed that she and the girls would sleep through this.

But just as he reached the living room again, he heard the sound of an engine springing to life. He peered through the blinds and saw the little gray car disappearing into the night.

CHAPTER FIFTEEN

Saturday, March 2, 2019, 4212 Ocean Way, Coronado, California

The next morning, Cam couldn't get the vision of the car lurking at the end of his driveway out of his mind as he sat on the bleachers in Tidelands Park, sipping coffee and watching Callie and Stephanie waiting for their turns to practice whacking at the ball perched on the tee. The weather was chilly and blustery, and the wind that whipped around him was damp and smelled of the sea. He was cold and bored, and he could see that Callie and Stephanie were, too. Given their own wishes, they would have been home playing with the princess dolls that McKenna had brought them from London.

The sight of his brother Nash running toward him momentarily lightened his mood. Nash was wearing a puffy black jacket, jeans, and Air Jordans. The wind played with the lock of hair that fell over his forehead as he jogged toward him. Cam's younger brother had Blaine's height and his dark hair and Jackie's gentle brown eyes. And although he had Blaine's rugged good looks, he had Jackie's expression of openness and kindness even in repose. Cam knew that Nash was talented as an actor, but his looks had played a role, too, in his success.

Cam left the bleachers and came down to intercept his brother in a bear hug. "I'm freezing and Callie and Steph are miserable," he said. "Let's go to Café 1134 and talk."

"Fantastic idea."

* * *

They settled in the tiny loft at the coffee shop where there were only two tables and it was less likely that they'd be interrupted by Nash's fans, although he was a regular in town because of his family visits, so most of the residents respected his privacy. The walls of the little shop were painted light yellow and lined with the work of local artists. The warmth and color were a welcome change from the blustery wind, gray sky, and cold bleachers at Tidelands Park.

Cam put Callie and Steph at one table where they happily dug into carrot cake and hot chocolate. He and Nash took the other and sipped their lattes in silence for a few moments.

Finally, Cam asked, "How were things with Mom and Dad after we all left?"

"Polite, very civilized. He helped her with the dishes. They're still sleeping in the same room."

"That's something at least. I keep hoping Mom is wrong."

"We all are, but I think there's evidence to back up her suspicions."

"You mean that little box of receipts?"

"Not just those. I've run into Dad a few times in LA or New York with various women on what looked like dates."

"Are you sure? I mean, all of us go to dinner with colleagues when we're on travel."

"Concerts? Theater? The opera?"

"It wouldn't be outside the bounds of reason. If he was traveling with another partner in the firm who shared his interests."

"That's true. He's always introduced me to whoever he was with. He didn't mention a professional connection, but I always assumed there was one."

"Could have also been a client," Cam suggested.

"True." Nash agreed.

"I wanted to talk to him, but Jess says I shouldn't because Mom doesn't want anyone to confront him."

"I have to agree with that," Nash said. "Mom's whole life is this family and being Blaine Rhodes' wife. I don't see how she'd survive without that identity."

Cam sipped his coffee and considered his brother's point.

"You're very quiet," Nash observed.

"I was thinking about Jess. I don't think her identity is tied up in being Mrs. Cameron Rhodes."

"But it's different for her. She had her own career, and she chose to walk away. Mom never aspired to anything other than being Dad's wife. If she loses that, she loses everything."

"She still has us."

"But it wouldn't be the same for her," Nash said. "Surely you know that."

"I do."

"In some ways, I wonder how they got together in the first place," Nash said. "Hasn't it ever occurred to you that our parents are opposites?"

"Opposites? She's the daughter of a successful attorney. Dad's a very successful attorney."

"They come from the same tribe, but they are opposites as people."

The word "tribe" made him remember Raven's assessment of his marriage to Jess.

"Dad's world is entirely rational," Nash went on, "full of hard edges and requirements. On the other hand, Mom's all about dreams and individuality. Her world consists of soft, blurred lines and beautiful things like fresh flowers and tiny, exquisite celebrations. You and Addison live in Dad's hard-edged, meet-expectations world. You became a lawyer; she became a lawyer's wife. McKenna and I chose the magical realm."

"Why didn't you want to practice law after you graduated from Stanford and passed the bar?"

"Because I wanted to be an actor, not a trial lawyer. And I didn't want to turn into Dad."

Cam was quiet again. Then he said, "Maybe you're right about Dad's world being full of expectations, but Mom has expectations, too."

"Such as her husband would be faithful because his marriage to her meant that his career rested on pleasing our grandfather?"

"Yes."

"And now Tyler's dead, and our father has established his place at the firm based on his own merit, so he could leave Mom if he wanted to."

Cam frowned. "What you're saying is true, but the thought of Dad breaking Mom's heart like that is too horrible to even contemplate."

"Agreed."

Callie and Steph interrupted them with demands for one

more piece of cake, and their childless uncle was happy to fetch it for them.

"Jess isn't going to be happy about that," Cam said when Nash rejoined him after putting the cake and two clean forks into each delighted little girl's hand.

"Jess isn't going to know unless you tell her. Dad said that unUncle Hugh has made you Lachlan Adair's defense attorney."

Cam smiled at the family name his siblings had always used for their grandfather's law partner. "He has. He's dragged me back to the world of criminal defense, kicking and screaming. At least, I've got a co-counsel who knows what she's doing."

"Who's your second chair?"

"No, co-lead. Meg Courtney. She's a senior associate who's transferred in from New York. Divorced, single mom with a really sweet little four-year-old boy, Finn. The dad's still in New York. She's a former federal prosecutor. Raven Adair told me that you knew Nora."

"Ah, so you've met the gorgeous and fascinating Raven."

Cam felt a twinge of guilt, but then reminded himself that he'd done nothing wrong. "And her father, of course. Tell me about Nora."

"She was her own worst enemy," Nash said thoughtfully. "She started as a dancer, but she hurt her back, so she moved into acting. She did a brilliant job of the Angelique role, and after that, she had her pick of romantic leads. But she liked to drink and party, and I think she was always in a certain amount of pain because of her back. She put on weight that she didn't take off, and she refused to transition into the kinds of supporting roles that she'd have been really good at."

"Did you ever work with her?"

"For a short time a couple of years ago. It was a rom-com. We started shooting, but the producers pulled the plug three months along. They said that Nora and I had no chemistry, and she looked too old for the part. I was relieved because I had seen the dailies, and I agreed with them. Nora, however, was desperate for the exposure and devastated by the producers' decision. She begged me to go on with it if Lachlan would fund a production company for her. Thankfully, he refused."

"Did you know anything about a sequel to *Unforgettable*?"

"Yes. Michael Bernstein approached me about playing a supporting role, and I was interested because the original movie was so popular. But I turned him down after he told me about the fight for control between Lachlan and Nora. I didn't want to wait around while the two of them duked it out. One of the worst things about that three-month stint with her on the movie that got abandoned was listening to her go at Lachlan. He'd come from Boston to visit her on set, and she'd spent hours in her trailer telling him off."

"Did he raise his voice to her?"

"Not really. My trailer was close by, and I could hear the sound of their voices. He always sounded calm and rational. When he'd had enough of her hysterics, he'd just leave."

"Do you think he'd be frustrated enough with her to kill her?"

"I'm not sure my opinion matters much because I only knew them for a short time. The thing is, that sequel was going to bring in a lot of money. *Unforgettable* was one of the highest grossing movies of all time, and it had a very sad ending.

Bernstein was right to think that all the fans would come back to see if things turned out better the second time around. I could see Lachlan just getting fed up with Nora and deciding to put an end to her opposition. Everyone in Hollywood knew she drank too much and took pills for her back, so a fall down the stairs would be quite plausible."

"Did you ever see what kind of car Lachlan was driving on these visits?"

"He always traveled in a black Range Rover owned by Lachlan's buddy, Seamus O'Malley. Seamus was among the first to figure out how to track buying behavior on the internet. He runs a company called Celtic Analytics that has an office in San Diego. Nora told me that he keeps a fleet of Range Rovers for his friends and executives to use."

"Would Seamus have a motive to kill her?"

"The little bit that I know about Seamus came from Nora. He was Lachlan's friend, not hers, but she never indicated he had any ill will toward her."

"Do you know anyone who drives a small gray sedan?"

"Why?"

"There was one parked in front of my driveway last night at one a.m."

"What model was it?"

"I don't know. It wasn't directly under the streetlight. All I could make out was the color and four doors. Maybe some sort of Toyota or Nissan. I heard the sound of a car stopping, and I thought that you'd come to tell me that there was a problem at Mom and Dad's."

"Could it be someone associated with the Adairs?"

"So far, everyone we know about, including the unidentified person who killed Nora, drives a black Range Rover."

"It was probably just some tourist who liked the look of your house. Did you call the police?"

"I was about to, but it left before I found my phone."

"I wouldn't worry about it unless it comes back."

CHAPTER SIXTEEN

Sunday, March 3, 2019, Offices of Goldstein, Miller, and Mahoney, Emerald Shapery Center

On Sunday afternoon, Cam went to the office at three o'clock because the house was empty. Jackie had suddenly invited Addison and Jess and her granddaughters to tea at the Hotel Del.

"It's last minute, but I think we should go," Jess told him after Jackie's call.

"Refusing her would hurt her feelings."

"True. I'll go to the office. Sunday afternoons are a good time to catch up."

"You might want to pick up something to eat on the way home. You know we'll be full after all those sandwiches and scones."

* * *

Even an international law office is quiet on Sunday afternoons. Almost all of the associates who worked nights and weekends had gone home to show their spouses and significant others that they were still alive.

Cam was happy to have some time to focus on clients other

than the Adairs, and he had a very productive afternoon. Around four thirty, he saw Meg and Finn pass his open door, heading in the direction of her office. A few minutes later, they came back. Meg was holding Finn's hand and carrying a thick folder. She knocked on his open door, and he looked up and smiled.

"Great minds think alike?" he suggested.

"Something like that. I was going to go over my notes from our meeting with Lachlan tonight. Want to talk about what to do next tomorrow?"

"That would be great," Cam agreed.

"I got to have breakfast with my Dad this morning!" Finn suddenly volunteered.

"Hush!" Meg looked uncomfortable. To Cam, she said, "Sorry. Too much personal information."

"No, not at all. I'm glad he comes to town to see Finn. It must be nice for you to have a little break."

But Cam sensed that he'd strayed into sensitive territory because she gave him an uneasy smile as she turned to leave. *What had happened in New York? She doesn't like to talk about it. But her personal life isn't my business. Still, I feel for her. It's tough to be a single parent and make partner in this firm.*

* * *

He found enough loose ends to occupy himself for another hour. He doubted that Jess and Steph and Callie were back yet from Jackie's. He hadn't asked about Blaine's whereabouts, but he gathered that the sudden invitation to tea had been the result of his father's leaving Jackie alone that afternoon.

He was suddenly seized with the impulse to go up to his father's office on the floor above to see if he was there. Cam strongly suspected that Blaine was at work, and he hoped the news would help allay his mother's fears and persuade her that her concern about an affair was groundless.

As soon as he got off the elevator, he could see that the door to his father's office was closed. That likely meant he was there. Cam hurried down the hall, tapped briefly on the door, and opened it. Blaine was sitting at his desk, reading something.

He looked up, startled. "What's going on, son?"

"Nothing. I was catching up while Mom has tea with Jess and Addison and the girls, and I thought I'd say hi if you were here."

Blaine leaned back in his chair and smiled. "I hope tea means that your mother will be in a better mood by the time I get home. She was angry with me for coming in today, but I needed to go over these depositions before I see the client tomorrow."

Cam suddenly felt guilty for buying into Jackie's suspicions. "I think she thought you'd have more time to spend with her when you retired," he offered.

Blaine shrugged. "Probably. But I told her that there were some cases that I couldn't and didn't want to walk away from. It was only meant to be a partial retirement. Are you headed home now?"

"In a few minutes. I'm going to order some food for pickup. Jess warned me that they'd all be full of sandwiches and scones from the Del. Are you leaving soon? We could go somewhere for dinner."

"Going to have to rain check that. I still have two more depos to take a look at."

"I'll leave you to it then."

Cam smiled happily as he headed back to his own office. Here was confirmation that Jackie was imagining things. He decided not to order food but to stop at his parents' house on the way home. His mother always had something in the fridge to feed stray children who stopped by, and he could deliver the good news to her and Jess and Addison at the same time since it was highly likely everyone was still there.

But just as he was gathering his things to leave, his cell phone rang. Raven. *I should make her wait until tomorrow.*

"Hello?"

"Cam, I'm at the USCD Hospital in Hillcrest. I think Dad may have had a heart attack. I'm here alone. Could you come?"

CHAPTER SEVENTEEN

Sunday, March 3, 2019, UCSD Medical Center, Hillcrest

He found her in the waiting room on the cardiac care floor. The waiting room was tiny, and they were the only occupants. She was sitting on one of the red plastic chairs that faced a television, which, thankfully was turned off. She looked lost and small in a long black coat that seemed to swallow up her tiny figure. Her face was pale and drawn, but he could see relief in her eyes when he walked in the door.

He took the red plastic chair next to hers and said, "How's Lachlan?"

"I don't know. They took him up to radiology for tests about an hour ago. I hope you don't mind that I called. I was going crazy sitting here alone."

"No, I'm glad that you did." *And honestly, I am glad, but I wish that I wasn't.* "What happened?"

"He's sixty-nine, and he has angina, but he thinks he's indestructible. He went out carousing last night with Seamus. I told him he couldn't go, but he wouldn't listen which is typical of him where Seamus is concerned. He's a horrible influence on my father."

"Is that the Seamus O'Malley of Celtic Analytics?

"Yes. How did you know about Celtic Analytics?"

"I spent some time with Nash yesterday. He told me about working on a movie with Nora that was abandoned after a few months."

"*Summer Love*," Raven said. "Nora was lucky that they pulled the plug on that one. Anyway, Dad and Seamus found some pub downtown and drank themselves silly until the wee hours. When Dad got up this morning, he complained of chest pains. His medication usually takes them away, but they got worse all afternoon until he finally agreed to let me bring him here. I hope your wife didn't mind that I called."

"I was at the office. Jess and the girls have been with my mother all afternoon, and I was supposed to get dinner on my own tonight, anyway."

"Are you hungry? I'll be okay here alone if you want to go to the cafeteria and get something."

"You don't look all right. You look exhausted and scared."

Suddenly, there were tears in her eyes that he could tell she was fighting to suppress. "I'm sorry," she said.

"Don't be. I understand."

"It's just that he's all that I—" But she couldn't finish her sentence. The tears took over, and she covered her face with her hands to try to hide them.

"It's okay to cry," Cam said as he took a handful of tissues from the box on the table next to his chair and laid them in her lap.

"Thank you." She picked them up and dabbed ineffectively at her eyes.

On impulse, Cam reached over and put his arms around her. She laid her head against his shoulder and continued to cry softly.

At that moment, the door opened, and a tall man with gray hair, wearing light-green scrubs entered and hurried over to them.

"I'm Dr. Benjamin," he said. "Is this your husband, Ms. Adair?"

White-hot embarrassment shot through Cam that he did his best to hide. He let go of her and willed himself not to remain intoxicated by her perfume.

"No, this is Cameron Rhodes, my father's attorney. How is he?"

"We don't see evidence of a heart attack. It looks like an acute bout of angina. We are going to observe him overnight, just in case. He's sedated, but he's asking for you."

"I'll wait here while you go," Cam said, anxious to reestablish the professional boundary that he had just crossed.

"No, come, too," she insisted.

He walked beside her as they followed the doctor to Lachlan's room.

The sight of Lachlan tied to tubes and monitors dealt Cam an emotional punch that he wasn't prepared for. It was like seeing a majestic tree after being felled by an ax. Raven hurried over to his bedside and put her arms around him as best she could.

"Da," she said softly and kissed him on the cheek.

He seemed to struggle to open his eyes. He smiled at her and then closed them again. He mumbled, "Love you."

"And I love you, too." She put her arms around him and hugged him as much as the various monitors attached to his body would allow. "I want you to be okay."

The desperation in her voice produced an unexpected and unprofessional jolt of sympathy for her in Cam. Lachlan opened his eyes and gave her one more brief smile, then closed them once more.

Raven was crying again. She accepted the tissue that Cam handed her as she sat down on the edge of her father's bed. "I want to stay," she said.

"He's all right. He's just groggy from the sedative. There's no need for you to be here all night because he's going to sleep," Dr. Benjamin said. "It would be better for everyone if you went home and got some rest, too."

Raven's anxious eyes went from her father to the doctor, and then to Cam.

She's alone and even more afraid than that night in the closet at the guesthouse. I can't just dump her at the condo and walk away. And I don't want to, either.

"The doctor's right, Raven. The hospital will call if anything changes, but it doesn't look as if it will. There's a great French restaurant close by. I'll take you to dinner."

CHAPTER EIGHTEEN

Sunday, March 3, 2019, Bleu Bohème, Adams Avenue, San Diego, California

Cam felt a twinge of guilt as he sat across from Raven in the candlelight, drinking Bordeaux. The exposed stone walls and wooden tables created a rustic bistro atmosphere that complimented the French menu. This was one of Jess's favorite restaurants, and he'd never been here without her. *But surely she'd understand why I had to invite Raven to dinner. Hugh was right. Jess is a pro. Then why do I feel uneasy? Because I'm sitting across from a beautiful woman, and I'm falling under her spell again.*

"Thanks for coming tonight," Raven said.

"It's—"

"Don't say 'my job.'"

Before Cam could speak again, the salads arrived, intricate concoctions of greens, pears, grapes, and goat cheese.

"I shouldn't have said that," she observed after a few bites.

"It's all right."

"No, it isn't really. I just can't help feeling that we're—"

Is this how it started with Blaine? A professional relationship that felt as if it should be more? But wait! Tonight I established that he isn't having an affair. And neither am I.

"We're friends and colleagues," Cam interrupted her before she could move into more dangerous territory. He could sense that she knew what he was actually feeling, and he didn't want to give her the opportunity to speak the truth. "You, me, and Meg. We're in this together for Lachlan. Do you mind if I ask you why you said he was all you had? What about your mother?"

"Victoria?" Raven raised one perfect eyebrow and considered his question. "I told you before, I've never been more than a means to an end for her. With me da, it's different. He was the one who flew me back to Boston to spend the holidays with him and whatever girlfriend was current at the time. When I grew up, I could see how much he needed me because none of his girlfriends was ever permanent. Lachlan values me because I take care of him, but to Victoria, I'm just a ticket to academic fame that got punched and thrown away years ago."

The sadness in her voice tugged at Cam's heart. "I'm—"

"Don't say 'sorry'!"

"How did you know that I was going to?"

She shrugged. "I don't know. I'm Irish. I've got a touch of second sight."

I hope that doesn't mean you know how much I want to hold you again and tell you everything is going to be all right.

Their entrées arrived, Coquilles St. Jacques with lobster risotto for her, Beef Bourguignon for him.

"This is lovely," she said after a few bites. "It's like being in Paris."

"Jess loves this place." As soon as the words were out of his mouth, he regretted them.

Her expression said that she was disappointed by the reference to his wife, but she smiled and smoothed things over. "Well, then she and I have another thing in common besides being attorneys and liking you."

As usual, she'd deftly managed to cross the line from professional to personal. And, as usual, Cam didn't entirely regret it. But he knew that he had to turn things around.

"But don't you resent the way Lachlan treats women?"

"Asked the father of two daughters. Sorry, I couldn't help teasing you just a little."

I think you mean "flirting with me." So much for moving the conversation away from the personal realm.

"But, seriously, doesn't it bother you?"

"You mean, how could I have sympathy for a womanizer?"

"It sounds so blunt when you say it, but yes, how could you?"

Raven smiled dreamily. "It's not sympathy that I feel for me da. It's love. He loves beautiful women. He can't help himself. Love of beauty drives him. He's Irish and a poet and a romantic. I can't fault him for that."

"Tell me about your father and Seamus O'Malley."

"They go back to university as Dad told you. They've always been drinking buddies. Seamus is Dad's wingman. He isn't as attractive to women, but he profits from Dad's charm."

"You mean he picks up the leftovers?"

"That's a bit harsh. He's never married, and when you ask him why, he always says he's never managed to fall in love. Although, I sometimes think cynically that he's stayed single to prevent the risk of having to split his fortune in a divorce."

"Was he a member of the IRA, too?"

"Be careful. I haven't said that Da was a member. No one knows for sure who is in and who isn't."

"Wouldn't killing for them back in the day mean he was in?"

"Not necessarily. But to return to the topic of Seamus. He got a job with Microsoft when it was just getting started. From there, he founded his own company in Dublin."

"Isn't he headquartered here now?"

"No. He picked San Diego instead of San Francisco for his West Coast office, but home base is still Dublin. He shuttles back and forth on the company jet."

"Nash said Seamus keeps a fleet of black Range Rovers that he always allowed your father to use when he was in town."

"Your brother knew about the cars?"

"He saw your father come and go from that movie set in them."

"I see. It's true. Seamus has always put his vehicles at Dad's disposal."

"How did Seamus feel about Nora?"

"I don't think he had much contact with her."

"Nash said that Nora wanted to start that movie back up, and she asked Lachlan to fund a production company for her."

"And he probably told you that Lachlan said no."

"That's right."

"But Lachlan didn't say no. I did. *Summer Love* was a silly, trivial mess, and Nora was too old to play the lead, but my father would have given her the money if I hadn't put a stop to it."

"Why did you do that?"

"My father is very wealthy, but that doesn't mean he should throw away money on a cringeworthy movie."

"Shall I clear the plates?" The waiter appeared out of nowhere.

"Please." Raven smiled. "And bring dessert. We'll have the chocolate mousse with two spoons."

"Coffee?"

"No, Jameson on the rocks."

I should speak up and say 'coffee and no dessert for me.' This is supposed to be a business dinner. Or is it?

After his drink arrived, Cam sipped his whiskey slowly and watched her savor the creamy dark chocolate. Her eyes sparkled in the warm candle glow. She apparently had put her anxiety over Lachlan aside temporarily.

"Hey, that's not fair. You're supposed to help me with this."

"Okay." And he picked up his spoon and dug in. The smooth sweetness on his tongue immediately reminded him of Jess's signature hot chocolate. Guilt stabbed him as he thought of sitting side by side on the sofa, sipping it in cozy domestic contentment.

But I don't need to feel guilty. She'd take a client to dinner under these circumstances.

"A penny for your thoughts," Raven said.

"Just glad to see that you're cheering up. Lachlan is going to be okay."

She seemed to sense that he wasn't being truthful about where his mind had been wandering. "Will your wife mind that you had dinner with me?"

"No." *Although, actually, she would probably mind this.*

The waiter appeared again, and Cam asked for the check. He could see the disappointment that he felt at the end of their evening in Raven's eyes.

* * *

Cam both dreaded and anticipated the moment when he'd step into the magic of the darkened Adair condo with Raven. As before, she summoned him to the window to take in the city gleaming like thousands of jewels below. He felt as if she had spread the entire world at his feet.

"I never get tired of this," she whispered.

"It's lovely." *I didn't say you're lovely, too, but I wanted to.*

"Can you stay for another drink?"

"No." *But that's not true. I could. The message I left with Jess said I was at the hospital with the Adairs. I could still be there. But something might happen if I stay, and I think Raven knows that, too.*

She sighed deeply and said, "Please? Just one more. I don't really want to be alone right now."

But he shook his head. He was having to fight too hard against the impulse to grant her wish and that meant that he was on very dangerous ground. "I really can't. I've got to be in the office early tomorrow."

She smiled and leaned over and kissed him softly on the cheek. It was such a natural gesture that it seemed appropriate even though it wasn't. "Good night, then."

"Good night." He stopped himself from returning the kiss and headed for the door, still in the dark . He was acutely aware of her walking beside him. Now he profoundly regretted turning down her invitation for another drink.

When they reached the door, she put one hand on the knob and one on his sleeve. "Wait!"

"What is it?"

"If anything happens to Dad tonight, may I call you?"

"Of course." She looked so small and vulnerable in the dark, and Cam wished he didn't have to leave her. When she opened the door, he could see tears gleaming in her eyes. On impulse, he leaned over and kissed her on the cheek. And then he turned and headed for the elevator, realizing that he was powerless against her magic.

TRAPPED

CHAPTER NINETEEN

Monday, March 4, 2019, 4212 Ocean Way, Coronado, California

Cam woke late on Monday morning, but it didn't matter. He'd been in the office yesterday, and he was caught up. He was entitled to take his time getting in today.

He glanced over at the clock. Eight a.m. He could hear his children's voices downstairs accompanied by the sound of doors opening and closing. A few minutes later, he heard Jess's Cayenne pull out of the drive. The school run. Suddenly, he pictured himself with Raven last night and guilt overwhelmed him.

By the time he had showered and dressed, Jess was back. He had just begun to brew himself a cup of coffee when she entered the kitchen through the back door. She quickly shed her light-blue jacket and hung it on the coatrack. Then she hurried over and gave him a quick kiss on the cheek.

"It must be cold outside."

She laughed. "Was that a cold kiss?"

"It was."

She laughed again. "You were late last night. How's your client? Did you have to eat awful hospital food?"

She doesn't suspect a thing. Thank God. "He had a bad bout of angina. The doctor said he'd send him home this morning. How was tea?"

"Honestly, a bit depressing. Jackie was sure that Blaine was out with the other woman. She put the girls at a separate table and talked about it endlessly to me and Addie."

Cam poured his newly brewed coffee and took a sip. Then he said, "Dad was at the office."

"What? Are you sure?"

"I went upstairs to satisfy my curiosity, and there he was at his desk, reading depositions."

"Thank God! You have to tell her, Cam. Right away."

"I will. I was planning to stop by before going to work."

* * *

He found Jackie in her garden. She was in the back, pruning the climbing roses. The sun had begun to warm the air by nine o'clock, but she was still wearing the red windbreaker that had been her defense against the chilly air that had produced Jess's cold morning kiss.

"Hi, Mom!"

Her face lit up when she turned and saw him coming toward her. "Cam!" She opened her arms and gave him a hug. "What brings you by this morning?"

"I've got some news that I think you'll be glad to hear."

"Come inside, and I'll make us a cup of tea."

In the kitchen, Cam watched her go through the familiar ritual of covering a tray with a flowery mat and then adding mugs and condiments while she waited for the water to boil in the electric kettle. She carefully measured the loose tea and added the hot water. It was something he'd seen her do a thousand times as a prelude to soothing a hurt or offering advice or, sometimes, giving a reprimand.

"Let's go sit in the den," she said as she picked up the tray.

They settled side by side on the sofa, and Cam accepted his mug from her and took a sip.

"I really enjoyed being with Jess and the girls yesterday," she began as she drank her own tea.

"I'm glad." But Cam remembered Jess's comment that the afternoon had been depressing because Jackie had talked about Blaine the entire time.

"Jess said you were at the office."

Cam felt a twinge of guilt. But she couldn't know, of course, about Raven and dinner and being with her at the condo last night. *And besides, nothing happened, and I'm not going to let it happen.*

"I was, and that's what I wanted to talk to you about."

"Your father said that's where he was going when he left yesterday morning, but I knew he was lying."

"No, he wasn't." Cam shook his head. "He was sitting in his office reading depositions at five o'clock. I was curious, so I went to see if he was there, and he was. He'd been there all day reading depos, and he told me he was sending out for food because he hadn't finished yet. He was preparing for a meeting with a client today in one of the cases that he didn't give up when he retired. Mom, you need to get over this paranoia. That little box of receipts that you've been hanging on to is meaningless."

Suddenly, there were tears in her eyes. Cam set down his

mug and put his arms around her. She began to cry softly into his shoulder. Holding and comforting her brought back holding and comforting Raven last night. *But nothing happened, and nothing is going to.*

His mother leaned away from him and picked up a napkin from the tea tray to wipe her eyes. She gave him a warm smile. "Thank you for this, Cam. Thank you so much."

* * *

By the time Cam reached his office, it was ten thirty, and the sunlight was brightly streaming through the windows. He felt as if he had passed through a trial by fire and had reached a safe haven because just as he was about to start his car to leave his parents' house, he'd received a call from Raven, followed by a text because he hadn't answered his phone.

> *"Can you go with me to pick up Dad at the hospital? He'll be ready to leave in twenty minutes."*

Cam had been horrified by how much he had wanted to say yes. The need to see her had seemed to well up from some empty place inside him that he'd never realized was there. But he was fresh from wiping away his mother's happy tears at finding out that her marriage was whole and sound. No matter what he wanted, he knew what he had to do to keep his own safe.

> *"Can't this morning. Glad he's well enough to come home."*

He hated himself for hesitating for a full minute after he'd finished typing the text before pressing send and starting the car.

But now he was in his own world where he was safe, and he was determined not to be tempted to stray outside these bounds again. He couldn't let himself think about how small and vulnerable Raven had felt in his arms last night or how her scent had enchanted him in the darkness in the condo. Instead, he willed himself to see Jess's tall, athletic figure as she'd entered the kitchen that morning and to remember how the cold morning air had chilled her lips.

* * *

"Would it be okay to meet in my office? Finn's with me today. His after-school babysitter had a doctor's appointment." Meg appeared at his door at two o'clock, the time they'd set to talk about the Adair case. She was wearing a dark skirt and a white blouse tied with a soft bow at the throat. She looked professional and pleasant but also tired, and her face seemed drawn as if she was worried about something.

"Of course. I've got quite a bit to tell you about happenings over the weekend."

He picked up his file and a yellow pad and followed her down the hall. When they reached her office, he saw that Finn was seated at his little table, deeply absorbed in building a Lego robot. He followed Meg to the grown-up-sized table on the other side of her office and sat down. She took the chair opposite him where her file was already open.

Suddenly Finn looked up from his robot and said, "I got to spend yesterday with my dad, but then he had to go home. I wanted to go with him, but he said I couldn't."

Meg winced and said sharply, "We're going to talk about work now, Finn. Please play quietly until we're finished."

The little boy's face fell, and Cam felt sorry for him and for her. He said gently, "I'm sure he'll be back very soon to see you again."

The words seemed to comfort Finn. He smiled and went back to his Lego project.

"Sorry," Meg said.

"Don't be. It's got to be hard for both of you. At least his father comes in from New York once in a while to see him."

Meg gave him a tight smile and opened her file and said, "What happened over the weekend that you wanted to tell me about?"

"Lachlan had an acute bout of angina, and Raven asked me to come to the hospital. After we knew he was out of danger, I took her to dinner."

"Did you learn anything interesting?"

"She told me that Seamus O'Malley and Lachlan go back a long way. Seamus shuttles back and forth on his private jet between his main headquarters in Dublin and his West Coast office here. He's made his fleet of Range Rovers available to Lachlan for years."

"I did some research on Seamus," Meg said. "He and Lachlan have done fundraising for various Irish politicians and causes. Lachlan is deeply revered in Ireland for fighting the British."

"So Raven has said."

"You might want to take a look at the Irish papers. They're full of indignation because he's going to be put on trial for murder in the States. Did Raven say anything else interesting?"

"Actually, this bit came from my brother, the Hollywood actor. Nash was in a movie with Nora that was never finished. He said that Nora often raised her voice to Lachlan whenever he visited her on set, but Lachlan remained calm, and when he'd had enough of her, he'd just leave."

"That might help us a little with establishing Lachlan's nonviolent character," Meg observed, "but I doubt we could convince a jury that Lachlan would just walk away from making this sequel."

"Nash said that, too."

"Is your brother Nash Rhodes?" Finn suddenly exclaimed from his corner. "He plays Sam in my favorite movie!"

"I'm afraid your brother has a fan," Meg smiled apologetically. "Finn is in love with the one about the dog who objects to all his owner's girlfriends until the dog finds the one he likes. I've lost count of how many times we've watched it. Close to a hundred, I think. It's silly. That's why Finn loves it."

"I gather Nash plays Sam, not Tucker." Cam smiled.

"That's right."

"I have a poster of Sam and Tucker in my room," Finn announced.

"I'll see if Nash will autograph one for him," Cam offered. "And I'm sure he'd like to meet you, Finn. He comes down often for my mother's family events."

"Yeah!" The usually solemn little boy stood up and did a short, joyful dance beside his table.

But Meg was not pleased. "Sit down, Finn, and be quiet, please. We're still working here."

"Sorry."

Cam could see that the reprimand had hurt him deeply. He spoke softly so only Meg would hear. "It's okay for him to have something to look forward to. I know Nash would enjoy meeting the two of you."

But Meg shook her head and said a bit sharply, "No, really. It's kind of you, but it would be an imposition. Finn's confused enough about the male figure in his life as it is."

Cam suddenly remembered her face when Finn had said he'd wanted to stay with his father. "I'm sorry. I shouldn't have said anything. You're right of course."

She looked relieved. "Thanks for understanding. I know you meant well. Did you learn anything else interesting from Raven last night?"

"Nora asked Lachlan for the money to start her own production company to revive the movie that she was making with Nash. He refused on Raven's advice."

"So her decision to stop production of Lachlan's sequel could be payback for not funding her movie?"

"The thought crossed my mind. But I think the production company was less important to Nora than having a role in the sequel."

Meg sighed. "We don't seem to be finding anything that helps us put together a defense."

"Not so far."

"I think we should hire a slip-and-fall expert," she said.

"You mean someone to give an opinion that it was an accident? But it wasn't. Someone pushed her."

"Expert opinion is usually for sale. And I'm sure you've defended guilty people before using experts."

"All the time in my public defender days. You're right. We should go shopping for an expert."

"I'll take care of it."

"Thanks. What about talking to Michael Bernstein?"

"You read my mind. It would be nice to know if Michael Bernstein was the only one at Nora's dinner on February 13. And Nora had a longtime agent, Sonia Siebert. I feel certain that Lachlan wasn't the only person Nora was at odds with. Sonia could probably tell us the names of at least some of her other enemies."

"I like that idea."

"Bernstein has a house in La Jolla, but it's just a vacation place. I checked this morning, and he's available in his Los Angeles office next Monday. And Sonia said she'd see us then, too."

"We can take the train up. The traffic is always terrible. But we probably won't be back until around six thirty. Can you leave Finn that long?"

"He can sleep over at a friend's house. He'll love having a slumber party on a school night."

CHAPTER TWENTY

Friday, March 8, 2019, the Pacific Gate Condos, Downtown San Diego

For the rest of the week, Cam fought his thoughts about Raven. She hadn't texted him again after he'd refused her request on Monday to accompany her to bring Lachlan home. The harder he tried not to think of her, the more thoughts of her overwhelmed him. He found his mind wandering during important client meetings. At home, he thought of her nonstop as he went about his usual evening routine: dinner, homework, bed with Jess. At any given moment, his grip on reality could be overcome by a memory of her eyes, her scent, and most of all, how she had felt in his arms.

Had unforgettable memories like these overwhelmed Blaine? No, Cam had established that his father, at least currently, wasn't having an affair. But there was that little box of receipts that supported his mother's suspicions more than he wanted to admit. Had an almost uncontrollable urge like this one pushed his father over the edge at some time in the past?

He assured himself that his willpower was stronger than his father's. He had, after all, led the ordinary life that Raven had commented upon. And as she'd also observed, he'd never strayed outside of his own tribe when it came to finding friends and a mate. Nash had been right: Cam had chosen to live up to the hard edges of Blaine's expectations instead of following his heart into Jackie's softer world of dreams.

Although Cam spent the week assuring himself that he could withstand any temptation that his memories of Raven presented, at the same time, his intuition told him that temptation was out to get him. And he knew beyond any doubt that he was right when he saw Raven's name on his caller ID at noon on Friday.

"I need to see you right away," she said when he answered.

"How's Lachlan?"

"Back to being himself."

"I hope he's not out carousing again."

"I can't control him. That will never change. But I really must see you. It's important."

"Can't it wait until Monday?" But he knew the answer even before he asked the question.

"No. Maybe a quick drink here after work? I won't keep you long."

But you can keep me as long as you want because I'm free.

"Don't forget you're on your own tonight," Jess had reminded him that morning.

"Right. I remember. You're chaperoning the Girl Scout sleepover at the Blanchards'."

Girl Scouts was another activity that Jess forced Callie and Steph to do because all their classmates participated. Cam had no doubt that they would have preferred to spend Friday night in their own beds.

"What about T-ball tomorrow?"

"I'll take them. You're off the hook this weekend."

* * *

One moment before he rang the bell at six, he told himself that he still had the power to walk away. He could go back to his car and call her and say that something had come up and he would see her in the office on Monday. But he knew he didn't want to leave, and he was relieved when she opened the door even before he touched the bell. She was dressed all in black in a turtleneck and soft, billowy pants. Her hair was loose around her shoulders, and she pushed it back with her graceful hands to reveal large pear-shaped diamonds dangling from her ears.

"Thanks for coming," she said. "I promise not to take up too much of your time."

"It's all right. Jess is chaperoning the girls at a Girl Scout sleepover that had to be moved from the park to someone's house because they couldn't pitch tents in the rain."

"So you've got time for dinner, then?" she asked as he handed her his raincoat to hang in the closet.

"I suppose I have. But isn't this rather short notice?"

"Not at all. I can throw together a fettuccine Alfredo in the blink of an eye. I've had lots of practice when Dad comes in roaring drunk at two a.m. Come into the living room, and I'll pour a whiskey for us. Unless you'd rather have something else."

"No, that's fine." He followed her into the glass-walled living room where the lights of the San Diego skyline sparked in the dark. He could feel himself falling slowly under her spell and the enchanting night sky. He took off his suit jacket before he sat down and loosened his tie.

"Here's your drink. Why don't you just take off that tie and be comfortable?"

He handed her his coat and tie and sat down and sipped the whiskey. It slid down with that pleasant burning tingle that, a second later, made him feel warm and relaxed all over.

When she returned from disposing of his clothes, she poured a drink for herself and sat down close to him on the sofa. She took a sip and said, "I was a Girl Scout at school. In Ireland, we call them Girl Guides."

"What was it like to be sent away from home so young?" he asked. "I can't imagine sending Callie and Stephanie away from home right now."

Raven smiled. "For me, it was the best thing in the world. I was very important at school because of my father. I got lots more attention there than I did at home."

"But your parents were in Boston."

"And very preoccupied with their own lives. If for some reason my father couldn't fly me back to the States for a holiday, Sinead would have me. She and James and Tom, her husband, lived on a sheep farm in Galway. I actually preferred to spend the summer with them. She is the most remarkable person. Even when I was little, I could see why she is the love of my father's life."

"What is she like?"

"Very tall and thin. Long dark hair and large dark eyes. Oval face, perfectly balanced, lovely complexion. She has always worn beautiful tweeds and shawls and sweaters that she knits from the sheep's wool that she dyes herself. She sings and plays the Irish harp and writes beautiful poetry and prose. She's very famous now, although she wasn't as famous when I was going to Galway on my holidays. I've always wished that I had been her daughter instead of Victoria's."

The deep longing in her voice touched him. "Did you get on with your half brother?"

"Very well. He always took care of me back then."

"Where is he now?"

"All over. The Middle East, mostly. He's a journalist for Reuters. You must be hungry. Come into the kitchen and keep me company while I make the pasta."

He picked up his drink and followed her into the spotless white and chrome kitchen and watched as she tied on a dark-blue apron, filled a pot with water, and took greens out of the refrigerator for a salad.

"You know there's a portrait of Sinead in my father's study that I painted several years ago. It's just down the hall if you want to see it. Second door on the left."

His curiosity aroused, Cam left the kitchen to take a look. The first room he passed was her art studio. The next room he came to was Lachlan's study. Books lined the walls, and a large cherry wood desk occupied most of the space. The portrait was hung opposite the desk so that Lachlan had a constant reminder of his loss whenever he was working there. She was, just as Raven had said, strikingly beautiful. The likeness was so authentic that Cam almost expected her to speak.

He left the study and started back toward the kitchen. But he paused at the doorway of Raven's art studio. He remembered the pictures that he'd seen that night at the guesthouse and her assertion that she had exhibited in international shows. Curious, he went in to have a look.

The work in progress on her easel gave him a shock. He stopped and stared at a half-finished portrait of himself.

"Do you like it?"

He looked up and saw her standing in the doorway. "I—"

She entered the room and came to stand beside him. She studied her work and mused, "The eyes aren't right. They're flat, and your eyes are warm and kind. I'll keep trying."

"I'm flattered." It was all he could think of to say.

"How did you like Sinead's portrait?"

"She's beautiful."

"I hope you don't mind that I decided to paint you. It's because I haven't been able to stop thinking about you."

* * *

Because of the rain, Cam guiltily expected Jess and the girls to have abandoned their tents at the Blanchards' when he rolled into the driveway at two a.m. He was relieved that the drive was empty of Jess's SUV, so his transparently false story wasn't going to be needed.

When he went inside, he found the house as deserted as he'd left it. He'd had so much to drink that he'd taken a huge risk in driving home. But his car had to be in its usual spot when Jess returned in the morning so that everything would look normal.

But things weren't normal. As much as he assured himself that they were as he changed into his pajamas, he knew better. He wasn't quite sure how he'd managed to turn down Raven's invitation to stay the night, purportedly in the guest bedroom, because he'd wanted to stay so much.

After dinner, they had settled on the sofa again with a second bottle of wine.

"I'm glad that you didn't mind my painting your portrait," she said as she sat down very close to him. "I thought it could be a thank-you gift at the end of everything."

He smiled. "I'm actually very flattered. But so far, it doesn't look as if we're winning this case, so I'm not sure you're going to have anything to thank me for. When you called, you said you needed to talk to me about something. What is it?"

"Dad and I want this case to go to trial right away. How soon can we get it over with?"

"Well, technically, the trial must happen no later than April 22, but Meg and I have just begun our investigation. We don't have a defense for Lachlan yet."

"Dad didn't kill Nora."

"I know you want to believe that," he said, "but he had motive and opportunity. And, as you've told me, he has killed before, more than once—professionally."

"That was a war. He killed as a soldier."

"If you want to put it that way."

"I do want to put it that way. Look, being charged with murder is taking too great a toll on Dad. That's why his angina flared up. I want you to get a date for trial and get this over with before it kills him."

Her haste made Cam uneasy. "I'll have to talk to Meg about it. I don't think she'll be happy about being rushed to go to trial."

"But I'm not rushing you. I know who killed Nora, and it wasn't my father."

"I'm listening."

"It was my mother. There's your defense."

"Victoria? But she lives in Boston."

"Not now. After my parents' divorce in 2007, she got a job as an assistant English professor at the University of California at San Diego in La Jolla. She lives in La Jolla, not far from the university and a short drive from my father's house in Rancho Santa Fe. And as I've told you, she hated Nora more than anyone else in the world because she lost a lot of prestige in academic circles when she was no longer Mrs. Lachlan Adair."

"But why would she decide to kill Nora twelve years after the divorce?"

"Because she was going to hold up the sequel to *Unforgettable*."

"But that affected your father's pocketbook."

"No, it affected my mother's, too. My father felt guilty about the divorce, and he wanted to remain on friendly terms because of me and because both of them knew the same people in the academic world, so he gave my mother a very generous divorce settlement. As part of that, she received a percentage of the profits from *Unforgettable*, both the book and the movie. And she received a percentage from any sequel that might be made later."

"So if Nora held up the movie, Victoria would lose money?"

"A lot of money," Raven said. "And then, too, as part of that same settlement, my father made Victoria his literary executor. After his death, she'll be paid a percentage of what his works continue to earn. She has an incentive to want the exposure that a sequel to *Unforgettable* would bring because it will make all his work more valuable for her later on."

"But what evidence do you have that your mother went to Nora's that night?"

"She was driving one of Seamus's black Range Rovers."

"How do you know?"

"I asked Seamus to send me a list of all the people who had a vehicle in his fleet on February 13 and 14. My father, of course. But Victoria had one, too."

"But how would she have known that Nora turned down Michael Bernstein's offer for a percentage of the receipts?"

"Whether Nora took the offer or not didn't matter to my mother. She just wanted her gone. First, she'd lost my father to her. Now, she was going to lose a lot of money no matter what Nora did. If Nora took a percentage of the profits, that would reduce my mother's share from the movie. If Nora turned down the offer, she'd lose even more because she'd block the sequel."

Cam was quiet as he thought over what she'd said.

She studied his expression anxiously. He was only too aware of how close her face was to his.

"You're very quiet," she said. "You don't believe me, do you? I know that asking you to use Leslie as an alibi made me look like a liar, so I asked Seamus to email you a copy of the Celtic Analytic's vehicle roster so that you could see that I'm telling the truth. Isn't it obvious? My mother knew that Lachlan was driving one of those SUVs that day."

"But how did she know?"

"Because my father had told her that he was coming to town, and Seamus always provided transport. My mother knew that as much as my father hated Nora, he wouldn't hurt her. So if she wanted Nora gone, she'd have to do it herself. And since my father was in town, everyone would assume that he was responsible."

"But wouldn't it hurt your mother's financial interests even more if Lachlan went to prison?"

"Not at all." She shook her head as she poured herself some more wine and topped up his glass. "If Dad goes to prison, Victoria will take over running his literary business."

"So even before his death, she'd be in charge?"

"Right. Don't you see the beauty of her scheme? She could get rid of Nora and get her revenge on my father by sending him to prison. This is my father's defense. We have to go to trial right away, so that he can be acquitted and go on with his life."

She studied him earnestly, and Cam could see that she was hoping for his agreement. But at that moment, he was focused on her clear blue eyes and little else. He'd had too much to drink, and he almost didn't care.

The silence stretched on long enough for her to guess what was actually on his mind. She moved almost imperceptibly closer to him and asked softly, "Don't you agree that Victoria has come up with the perfect payback for Dad and Nora?"

He was still lost in her hypnotic eyes, but he managed to say, "It would take more than Seamus's vehicle roster to convince a jury."

She leaned closer and whispered, "You've had too much to drink."

"I know."

"You should stay the night."

"I know."

"Come on, then." She put her glass on the sofa table and stood up and took him by the hand.

Every part of him responded to her so strongly that the jolt brought him back from the brink of getting up and following her. "You know that I can't."

"But you can have the guest room."

"But you know that I can't."

Cam turned over and laid his hand on Jess's smooth pillow as if it were a talisman to protect him from Raven's spell. He'd played with fire tonight and come frighteningly close to burning down his very ordinary life. He vowed not to do it again.

CHAPTER TWENTY-ONE

Monday, March 11, 2019, Santa Fe Depot, Downtown San Diego

The sight of Meg, looking crisp and professional in her navy suit as she waited for him in the train station on Monday morning, cheered Cam. She looked calm and relaxed, and he wondered if the prospect of a day without being torn in two by parent and attorney responsibilities might be the reason. He, on the other hand, remained unsettled and agitated as he nursed his guilty conscience and tried to reassure himself that his wife suspected nothing. His worst moment had come at noon on Saturday when Jess and the girls had found him still asleep.

"Cam! Cam! Are you all right?"

He had no choice except to admit that he had a hangover and a pounding headache.

But Jess had only chuckled at the news. "That'll teach you to drink alone in an empty house."

He'd given her a weak smile and collapsed again on his pillow, desperately trying to think of a way to stifle the pain in his head and to smother his conscience.

But a little later, his guilt had stabbed him sharply once more when she came in with a tray of scrambled eggs and toast.

"Food will help," she decreed. And, indeed, it had.

But now it was Monday, and he was boarding the business class car with Meg, fully focused on his work and determined to stay that way.

"The coffee isn't bad, but I can't recommend the cellophane-wrapped muffins," he told her as they seated themselves and arranged their briefcases.

"I've had enough coffee for now. I stopped at Starbucks after I dropped Finn at school."

"Is he going to be okay today?"

"Fine. He barely slept last night because he was so excited about his sleepover."

The train pulled out of the station, and Cam watched the city roll by as they headed north. He debated for almost an hour before he decided that he had to tell Meg Raven's theory about her mother. Mercifully, she did not question the impression that he created that he learned all this new information in a phone call late on Friday afternoon while he was still at the office.

"It's plausible and attractive," Meg said. "But you're right. Seamus's roster isn't enough to prove it."

"Maybe we'll get lucky, and Michael Bernstein and Sonia Siebert will have better information for us."

"Maybe." The trouble is Raven is now in a huge hurry to go to trial. She thinks the stress of being a defendant caused Lachlan's angina attack."

"But we need time to build some sort of defense." Meg said. "If we have to go now, Lachlan will be convicted for sure."

* * *

Michael Bernstein's suite, with an expansive view of Beverly Hills and the Pacific Ocean, occupied the entire forty-fourth floor of one of the two Century Plaza Towers, one of the two tallest buildings in California. Meg and Cam did not have to wait long before his receptionist ushered them out of the sterile chrome and glass waiting area into Bernstein's equally sterile office.

He was on his cell phone when they walked in. He gestured for them to take the chairs in front of his desk, made from a single slab of glass with chrome accents. He looked exactly the same as he had at Lachlan's preliminary hearing: trim and fit, with salt-and-pepper hair and kind brown eyes, although today he was wearing a pair of round horn-rimmed glasses that gave him both a boyish and a scholarly air. His dark-gray suit and white shirt, worn without a tie, was the quintessential California business look.

"I've got to go," he told the person on the other end of his call. "Some people are here who want to talk to me." He turned to Cam and Meg and said, "I'm sorry. We're still trying to figure out if we can make that sequel. You're here about Nora, aren't you? You're Lachlan's attorneys."

"We are. I'm Cameron Rhodes."

"Meg Courtney."

They all stood to shake hands and then resumed their places. Michael Bernstein gave Cam a long appraising look before he said, "You're related to Nash Rhodes, aren't you? I see the family resemblance."

"He's my younger brother."

"Very talented actor. I hope you'll give him my best and tell him to have his agent call me. I've got a project in the works that would be perfect for him."

"I'll pass on your message," Cam said, slightly annoyed that Bernstein was treating him like an errand boy.

"But that's not why you're here, of course." He seemed to sense Cam's reaction. "You want to know about Nora."

"That's right," Cam agreed. "My brother said that she had her pick of leading roles in romantic movies after *Unforgettable* but then got too old for those parts and refused to move on to mature roles."

"Nash pretty well summed it up," Michael Bernstein said. "She was incredibly talented, and she could have been working all the time if she'd just been willing to be realistic about aging."

"You testified at the preliminary hearing that you didn't want her in *Unforgettable* because you thought forty-six was too old and because she hadn't had a hit movie in a long time. Were there any other reasons that you didn't want her?" Meg asked.

"Well, those two alone would have been enough to discourage investors. But in addition to that, she and Lachlan couldn't get along, so the movie would be plagued by feuds between the screenwriter and the female lead and that would inevitably cause delays and run up production costs. And then, too, Lachlan wanted a younger woman for the part, and since his contract locked him into writing the script, it was more important for me to make him happy and that was easy to do because we both agreed that Nora shouldn't be in this movie."

"And you told her that on the night of February 13?" Meg asked.

"Well, I had told her that before February 13, but I did tell her again that night when I offered her a share of the profits."

"Why wouldn't she take you up on the offer? Didn't she need money?"

"Yes and no. She wasn't bringing in anything in her own right at that point other than a few hundred dollars here and there from residual rights from various performances. But she had all the money she wanted from Lachlan."

"Even though they didn't get along?" Meg frowned slightly.

Michael Bernstein nodded. "I never asked him why, but I've always assumed he did it to buy peace. Nora never knew how to back off. She'd keep coming and coming at you until you'd given her what she wanted."

"So she was determined to be in the sequel?" Meg asked.

"And that's why she wouldn't agree to a share of the profits. She fully intended to go to court to stop the movie if I didn't give her the role of Angelique again."

"Who was going to play Angelique?" Cam asked.

"No one. Lachlan intended to kill her off at the beginning of the movie using a body double for Nora. He wanted the female lead to be a twenty-something who reminds the male lead of Angelique, and he had someone in mind for the part."

"Who?"

"Nora's personal assistant, Kiara Blake. Lachlan was sleeping with Kiara, and that fact, along with Lachlan's determination to give her the lead, infuriated Nora."

"Were you willing to give Kiara the part?" Cam asked.

"I thought it was a bad idea. She's only twenty-five, and she doesn't have much acting experience. She took the job with Nora because she thought she'd be able to get close to the big names in the industry."

"Looks like she succeeded," Cam observed.

"That's true. She was at Nora's on the night of February 13 because she wanted to see me."

"Did she have dinner with the two of you?"

"Oh, no. I was there to persuade Nora to do something that she didn't want to do. If any of my attention had been on Kiara, I'd have had no chance with Nora. Kiara knew that I didn't want to deal with her that night, but she forced the situation by going for a swim in Nora's pool, and she made sure that I saw her in her bikini as I left."

"Did you speak to her?"

"No. I didn't want to encourage her. I was going to try to talk Lachlan out of using her in the film because I didn't think her name would help us attract investors. We needed someone like Emma Stone or Jennifer Lawrence."

"So she was still at Nora's when you left?" Meg asked.

"I saw her go into the house as I was driving away."

"Did she live with Nora?"

"No."

"So she was in the house close to the time of Nora's death?"

"I can't say when she left."

"Did she drive a black Range Rover?"

"No. She had a white Honda Civic."

"Would you say that she was capable of killing Nora?"

"Yes, definitely. When I heard that she was dead, I immediately thought of Kiara because she wanted that part so badly, and Nora was going to shut down the entire film to keep her from getting it."

"And you said that Lachlan was sleeping with Kiara?" Meg asked.

"Yes, he was. But you have to put that in perspective. Lachlan sleeps with any attractive woman who will give him the opportunity. Kiara wasn't particularly special in that regard. He liked her, and she was available for the movie, so he pressed me to use her. I'm pretty sure I could have talked him out of giving her the part if I'd pointed out the monetary consequences of giving an unknown the leading role."

"What about Victoria Adair?" Cam asked. "Raven says she had a financial stake in the movie, and she hated Nora."

"All of that is true. She was very disruptive when we were shooting *Unforgettable* because she suspected Nora was making a play for Lachlan, and, of course, she was right."

"Did you see her at Nora's that night?"

"No. Victoria is the last person Nora would have invited to her home for any reason. The hatred was mutual. In addition to all her other motives, Nora wanted to hurt Victoria's financial interest in the movie."

"Raven thinks Victoria was driving the black Range Rover that went through the security gates at eleven forty. Did you happen to see a black Range Rover that night headed toward Nora's as you left?" Cam asked.

"No. Nine minutes passed between the time I left and when that black car entered. I was gone before it got to the security gate. I do know that Victoria has a silver BMW."

"Raven thinks her mother wasn't driving her own car that night," Cam said.

"I couldn't say. But there is one more thing I think you should know before you leave."

"And that is?" Cam prompted.

"You'll hear a rumor at some point that Nora blackmailed me for the part of Angelique. That's not true. We were a couple for less than a year before I met my wife. That was more than twenty years ago. Nora was brilliant as Angelique. She won that part fairly, and it had nothing to do with any personal relationship."

CHAPTER TWENTY-TWO

Monday, March 11, 2019, 9601 Wilshire Boulevard, William, Morris, Endeavor, Beverly Hills

"You're Nash's brother," Sonia Siebert said as she greeted them in a conference room in the William, Morris, Endeavor Agency in Beverly Hills. Although she was barely five feet tall, and so thin that a strong wind would sweep her off her feet, her body-hugging red dress accented with a simple gold necklace and earrings and her perfectly coifed chin-length blond hair conveyed an air of power and authority. Cam noticed the telltale signs of a facelift in a mouth stretched a little too far to be entirely normal and a wide-eyed look that seemed out of character in her otherwise entirely professional demeanor. He guessed she was in her fifties, trying to look ten years younger.

"I'd love to have him as a client if he ever decides to change his representation," she said.

"I'll let him know." Cam felt the same irritation that he'd felt earlier in Michael Bernstein's office, but like Bernstein, Sonia moved on quickly.

"You're here about Nora. My assistant said that you represent Lachlan."

"That's right," Cam said.

"Dreadful marriage. I felt sorry for them both."

"Were you Nora's agent at the time she married him?"

"Oh, yes. She and I went way back to her earliest breaks as an actor after her dancing career ended. The marriage was more of a publicity stunt for *Unforgettable*."

"So we've been told," Cam said.

"Nora should have let him go," Sonia went on. "What little there was between them was long over. I told her that many times."

"So she confided in you?"

"Absolutely. An agent is part business advisor, part therapist, and part confessor."

"What did she tell you?" Meg spoke up for the first time.

"Lachlan wanted a divorce, but she didn't. She thought he was still in love with her and would come back even though he had never been faithful to her from the earliest days of their marriage. Of course, I knew that was a delusion, just like her delusion that she could still play romantic leads."

"When was the last time you spoke with her?" Meg asked.

"We had lunch at her house on the thirteenth."

"What time did you arrive and how long did you stay?"

"I believe I got there around one o'clock, and I left around four. I stayed longer than I'd intended to because I was trying to calm Nora down. Lachlan had been there earlier, and they'd had a fight, and Nora was still upset about it."

"Because he'd threatened to kill her if she interfered with the sequel?"

"No, that's not why she was overwrought. She never took

any of Lachlan's threats seriously. As I said before, she was delusional about Lachlan's feelings. He hated her, and he wasn't coming back, but she believed in every fiber of her being that he would return because she considered herself irresistible to men. During their quarrel that morning, she had thrown a vase at him and cut his forehead. Nora rarely acknowledged wrongdoing, but she was suddenly afraid that their marriage was really over because she'd hurt him. I tried to tell her that their marriage had been over almost from the beginning, but that only upset her even more."

"Why did you pick that day for lunch with her?" Meg continued.

"Because I knew that Michael was coming to dinner that night, and I knew that he was going to offer her a very favorable financial deal to give up her right to be in the sequel. I wanted to talk her into taking the deal."

"But shouldn't you have been trying to get her into the movie instead of out of it?" Meg asked.

Sonia bristled at the suggestion. "Of course not! My job is to act in my client's best interest. I knew that Lachlan was going to write the screenplay, and I knew how much he hated her. There was no way she'd have had a sympathetic character to play if she'd insisted on being in that movie."

"You mean this time around, no one would have liked Angelique?" Meg suggested.

"Right."

"Did you make any headway with her?" Cam asked.

"None. And it was too bad because Michael was willing to offer her a part in another movie in addition to a share of the profits from the sequel if she'd agree to play an age-appropriate role. He had a movie in the works called *The Matchmaker*, and he was going to offer Nora the lead."

"Why didn't she want that part?" Cam asked.

"Because it was for a forty-something woman, which is exactly what Nora was, who sets up a matchmaking business after being divorced and who can find the right man for all her clients but never for herself. Nora insisted that she only wanted to play twenty- or thirty-somethings. When I made her see that was unrealistic, she accused me of telling her that her career was over. But I hadn't told her that at all. And Michael liked Nora. They had history. He was willing to help her get back on her feet if only she'd accept a role that she could actually shine in."

"My brother told me that after the shutdown of the movie he and Nora were in, she wanted to start her own production company. Do you know anything about that?"

"I know all about it. Even the title of that project was ridiculous. *Summer Love.* I saw the dailies. I guess Nash told you that he and Nora had zero chemistry. It was painful to watch. At first, she wanted to start a production company to revive it, but I persuaded her that it wasn't salvageable and pointed out that a production company would give her an opportunity to find really good parts for herself since her offers were dwindling. And, too, for all her faults, Nora was generous with young actresses trying to get a start. That's why she took on Kiara as her assistant. She didn't expect her to stab her in the back by going after Lachlan and the lead role in the sequel.

"Anyway, Lachlan was willing to fund a production company for her. He was always willing to give Nora money because that would buy peace between them. And then, too, he realized that she could actually make a go of it. Nora had better commercial instincts than anyone gave her credit for. She had a plan to make movies that would have been financially successful. Despite her myopia about wanting ingenue roles for herself, she knew there was a huge audience of women over forty who were just waiting for movies that would speak to them. Those were the movies she wanted to make. In some ways, Michael and Lachlan are wrong about the sequel to *Unforgettable.* The original audience is considerably older now and would love to see Angelique, in midlife, reconcile with her former husband, who regrets his infidelity and who has been pining for her for so many years. But Raven, the oracle, put a stop to it. She predicted that Nora wouldn't succeed."

"I take it you aren't fond of Ms. Adair." Did he sound too protective of Raven? Cam's gut tightened as he wondered if he'd given himself away.

"She's an astute businesswoman who guards her father like a dragon, but she hated Nora passionately and that clouded her judgment. I think Lachlan would have received a good return on his investment if he'd backed Nora's production company."

"Was anyone else at Nora's that afternoon while the two of you were having lunch?" Cam asked to get away from Sonia's opinion of Raven.

"Her staff. She had three housemaids and a housekeeper and several gardeners, but they were working outside, of course."

"What about her personal assistant?"

"She had the afternoon off. Nora didn't want her to overhear us talk about the sequel."

"Would it surprise you to know that Kiara came back that

night while Michael Bernstein was there?" Cam asked.

"I wasn't surprised when Michael told me about it. And the bikini."

"Did you stay in San Diego that night?"

"No. I went back to LA."

"Was Kiara capable of killing Nora for the role in the movie?" Meg asked.

"I don't know. I've wondered, of course. Michael said that he saw her go into the house as he was leaving."

"What about Raven's mother, Victoria?" Meg continued.

"She'd be perfectly capable. She's as cold as an iceberg, like Raven."

Cam felt the impulse to contradict her but managed to hold his tongue.

"What about Raven?" Meg asked.

"She says she was in Dublin that night," Sonia replied. "But who knows for sure? Her reputation for the truth is not sterling."

CHAPTER TWENTY-THREE

Monday, March 11, 2019, Aboard the Pacific Surfliner, Southbound to San Diego

Cam listened to the steady clack of the train's wheels on the tracks as they picked up speed leaving Union Station in downtown LA. He tried to hypnotize himself with the sound so that he couldn't think or feel. He'd never considered Raven as a suspect, yet there it was in plain sight: she had as much interest in Nora's death as her father and her mother and access to Seamus's cars, and she'd been instrumental in setting up that false alibi for her father that had fallen through.

Had what felt like unmistakable attraction been an act to throw him off her actual trail? Sonia was right that they had no proof, other than Raven's word, that she'd been in Dublin when Nora died. After all, he'd been lied to about Lachlan's whereabouts until the evidence from the preliminary hearing had forced a confession.

Cam downed the little bottle of red wine that the steward had handed him with the business class box of chips and crackers and waved him down for another.

"Are you all right?" Meg asked. She had set the snack box

aside and was sedately sipping the house coffee and studying her notes, a model of professional decorum.

"Fine. Just thirsty."

"You know, that's one step up from what we all drank in high school."

His laugh sounded uneasy and nervous even to himself as he unscrewed the cap on bottle two and poured it into the transparent plastic cup. "I can't picture you sneaking around with a bottle of wine as a teenager."

He was surprised when she looked hurt. "You think I've always been a thirty-eight-year-old, slightly frazzled single mother, with her career hanging by a thread?"

"I—I don't think that." But she could tell he was lying. That was the only way that he had ever pictured Meg Courtney.

"Yes, you do. It's all right. But I once had a life of spontaneity and wasn't serious about everything. It's just that now it's all too much for one person, but I have no choice."

Cam realized that if he'd been entirely sober, her opening up to him would have made him uncomfortable. But now he was lulled by two six-ounce bottles of middling-to-fair wine and listening to her took his mind off the distinct possibility that Raven had been playing him. But would she have painted his portrait if he hadn't meant anything to her at all? *Stop thinking about that! You're married. It makes no difference whether Raven was sincere or not.* But, of course, no matter what he told himself, it did matter.

His phone buzzed, and he looked down to see a text from Jess.

"You're on your own for supper tonight. We're eating

early with Jackie and Blaine."

Well, at least his mother and father were sitting down to dinner together. That was a good sign. But Cam wasn't pleased to be cut loose because now he could act on his impulse to find a way to see Raven and ask her for the truth.

For the rest of the trip to San Diego, Cam fought with himself about what he would do when they arrived. As the Surfliner wound down the coast, he vacillated between planning to go straight home and planning to go straight to the Adair condo.

When the train came to a complete stop at Santa Fe Station at seven thirty, he and Meg gathered up their briefcases and got off. Meg glanced at him curiously as they walked along the sidewalk toward the station, but she didn't say anything until they reached the front door.

"Are you sure you're all right?" she asked. "You still seem a little edgy."

"Maybe I am," he agreed. "We got a lot of new information today. It's difficult to assimilate it all right now." *New information that I don't want to be true.*

"Well, go home and rest," she suggested. "I'm parked in the back of the lot. You don't have to walk all that way with me."

His first impulse was to take his leave and hurry off to his own car, which was in the other direction. He could text Raven and arrange to be at the condo in under ten minutes. He imagined another impromptu supper with her.

But the lights in the parking lot were just thin trickles through the darkness, and the thought of letting Meg go alone down the long line of parked cars in the dim light didn't sit well with him even in his state of guilty infatuation. They'd had a long day of work and travel, and suddenly it occurred to him that she would be going home to an empty house because she'd given Finn permission for a sleepover. There was a way to make up for hurting her feelings earlier, and at the same time, he could remove temptation from his path.

"Let's have dinner," he said.

"But aren't you having dinner with your family?"

"My wife sent me a text. They didn't wait for me. Finn's got plans for the night, so you're alone, and I'm alone, too. We can talk over the case and what we learned today about potential suspects other than our client. We'll pick a place close to your house. Where do you live?"

"In La Jolla Shores. Finn wanted to be close to the beach."

"That's perfect. There's a fantastic little farm-to-table place close by called The Yellow Door. Have you ever been there?"

Meg shook her head. "Finn won't eat anywhere that doesn't serve pizza or chicken nuggets."

"Then all the more reason to take advantage of tonight. It's a tiny place, but some of the best comfort food I've ever tasted."

"Really, Cam. Thanks, but I'm tired."

"I am, too, but we both have to eat. Tell you what. I'll drive us there in your car and afterward, I'll take an Uber back here to pick up mine."

That way, I can't drive straight from your place to the Adair condo after dinner.

"I— Really, Cam. That's sweet, and it's a tempting offer. I don't get many nights away from Finn and a chance to eat in a grown-up restaurant, that's true. But I should go on home tonight."

"No, you shouldn't."

"Well—"

"Not 'well.' Yes."

CHAPTER TWENTY-FOUR

Monday, March 11, 2019, The Yellow Door, La Jolla, California

At eight p.m. on a school night, they had The Yellow Door to themselves. The living room and dining room of the tiny cottage in the Bird Rock section of La Jolla had been combined to form one cozy space accented with warm red walls and furnished with ten small tables topped with yellow-checked tablecloths and tiny rainbow-hued Tiffany lamps. The fire in the fireplace added to the homey, welcoming feel of the room on the cold March night. It was a family-run business, and Cam had been here with Jess often, but tonight Madame Le Clare took their orders for French onion soup and cassoulet without betraying any curiosity about his companion.

"It's been a long day," he observed as he sipped a glass of cabernet.

"It has."

"You look a little worried. Was everything all right with Finn when you called from the car?"

"He's fine. It's just—well—odd to be without him for a night."

"Doesn't he spend time with his father in the summer when school's out?"

"I—we—"

Her face and her tone said he'd hit a very sensitive nerve. *I've got to remember to stay away from the subject of her marriage.* Fortunately, the soup arrived at that moment.

They ate in silence for a few minutes, and Cam sensed that her discomfort was growing, not diminishing. Work was a safe subject, so he said, "I wasn't expecting to find so many potential suspects."

"Neither was I." She looked relieved by the shift in topic. "Nora's house was a veritable hive of activity on February 13."

"I bet there's a lot more surveillance video than the prosecutor has given us. That house and the grounds had to be full of cameras. It's impossible to believe that there's only one picture of a Range Rover coming through the gates that still exists, especially since so many people went to see her that day."

"I can lean on Axel," Cam offered.

"That's okay. I'll talk to him. I'm an ex-prosecutor, and I'll be able to persuade him to give us everything."

"Okay, thanks." Cam nodded in agreement, but the suggestion made him uneasy. *What if they found out that Raven had been at Nora's that night?*

"You're right about the food," Meg said as Monsieur Le Clare removed their empty soup bowls and replaced them with steaming plates of cassoulet. He could tell that she was beginning to relax at last. Her eyes sparkled in the candlelight, and she smiled as she sipped her wine. "I must think of some way to bribe Finn so that I can come back here."

"I expect the Le Clares would do some version of chicken nuggets if you told them that your return depended on it."

Meg laughed. "Good idea. I might give it a try."

He suddenly realized that she rarely laughed, and he wanted to ask her if she had any life other than Finn and work. But he remembered how she'd reacted when he'd asked if Finn spent summers with his father, so instead, he asked, "So what else did you do in high school besides drink middling-to-fair wine?"

"I didn't drink much of that. I didn't like alcohol in those days. I was working pretty hard to get a scholarship to Brown. My parents were high school teachers, and they couldn't afford it, but I had my heart set on going there."

"And did you?"

"I did. I got the scholarship."

"Brothers? Sisters?"

"None."

"I bet your parents enjoy Finn. Are they close enough to see him often?"

"No. They passed away before he was born."

"So you and Finn are really on your own, except when his father comes to see him?" The minute the reference to her ex was out of his mouth, he kicked himself mentally.

"Finn and I are a good team."

"Of course, I can see that."

"I'm not sure we're going to stay in San Diego." She spoke thoughtfully.

"But why? Finn seems so happy here. He has his own room and he loves the beach."

"So you remembered that?"

"Sure. He's a memorable kid. Special."

She studied his face for a moment in the candlelight as if

making up her mind about something. Then she said, "You're a very thoughtful person."

He laughed. "My mother says that, too. Don't give up on California yet. If you go back to New York, you'll be in another tiny apartment, and the Goldstein, Miller hours aren't any better there than here. You'll probably need a nanny even more."

"We wouldn't go back to the city. I grew up in Rochester, and I'd look for a job in a small firm where the hours are better or maybe set up shop on my own."

"If I were Finn, I'd rather be at the beach in January than in Rochester in the snow. You just need more time to make friends here. Besides Nash, I have two sisters. One is in London, but the other is here. I think you'd like Addison. Her two girls are older than Finn, but they love little kids. And you'd like my wife, Jess, and our two girls also love younger children. My mother gives lots of family parties, but she invites friends to some of them. You should let me put your name on her list."

"No, really. That's kind of you. But Finn and I are fine. He has lots of friends from school, and I don't really have time to socialize."

So that was the answer. She had no life outside of Finn.

"Well, the offer is open if you change your mind."

"Thanks."

* * *

Cam called the Uber before they left the restaurant, so it was waiting for him when they arrived at her house, a small blue cottage two blocks from the beach.

"You don't have to walk me to the door," she said as she

parked in the drive and turned the engine off.

But Cam remembered the mysterious car at the end of his own driveway over a week ago. "You're going into a dark house alone. The driver will wait two minutes, I'm sure."

He followed her up the walk and waited while she unlocked the front door and turned on the lights. He caught a glimpse of her living room as she stepped inside, lots of reds and blues and greens. Jess would call it Boho and artsy. Cam would have expected her house to be as controlled and conventional as her work clothes and her office furnishings. There was a side of Meg that he hadn't expected to find, and he liked her more for her individuality.

But she wasn't going to invite him in. He had the distinct feeling that she was ready to be alone, and he couldn't blame a single parent for enjoying a rare evening of solitude.

Cam said good night and got into the Uber for the ride back to the train station. As soon as they pulled away from Meg's, he began to think about Raven again. Ten thirty. It would be nearly eleven by the time he reached his car. Too late to call to see if he could stop by the condo.

It was better this way, he told himself. He needed to stop thinking about her. Sonia was right. She could be a suspect. In fact, she and her father could have conspired Nora's death. They both had a financial interest in the sequel, and Lachlan would save thousands by not having to support Nora anymore.

But as he paid the Uber driver and got into his own car and headed home, he couldn't stop himself from thinking about that portrait she'd been painting and how it had felt to be alone with her. By the time he turned onto his own street, he had convinced himself that Sonia was wrong. Raven hadn't been involved in Nora's death. But his musings ended abruptly as his house came into view. All the lights were out except the one in the living room, which meant that Jess was still up, probably waiting for him. And there, at the end of his driveway, was the small gray sedan, lights and engine off.

Cam's outrage at someone watching his house where his wife and children were alone overcame any fear that he felt. He jammed on his brakes and jumped out of his car, leaving it in the middle of the street. But the minute he started toward the sedan, determined to find out who was inside, its engine came to life. It sped away with its lights off. Cam strained to make out a license plate number, but it was too dark.

He got back into his own car and realized that he was shaking from head to toe, whether with anger or fear or a combination of both he could not say. He pulled into his driveway and sat for a while, breathing deeply to calm down, and waiting to see if the car came back. When he was sure it wasn't going to return, he went inside to find Jess sitting in a chair in the living room, reading a book. She looked up and smiled.

"How was your trip?"

"Fine. How was dinner with my parents?"

"Tense. We can talk about it tomorrow."

CHAPTER TWENTY-FIVE

Tuesday, March 12, 2019, 4212 Ocean Way, Coronado, California

In the morning, Cam went with Jess on the school run and insisted on breakfast at Clayton's Coffee afterward. He told himself that he didn't feel guilty about his almost constant fantasies about Raven since Friday night, but at a deeper level, he knew that guilt was driving him, and at the same time, he felt protective because of the mysterious car.

"You said it was tense last night with my parents," he prompted after they'd ordered hash browns and scrambled eggs.

"It didn't start out that way, but during dinner Jackie came up with one of her grand plans, and Blaine wasn't at all pleased."

"What was Mother up to?"

"A mandatory Rhodes family affair on Sunday."

"This coming Sunday? Isn't this rather sudden, even for her?"

"Yes, it is. And that was Blaine's problem with it."

"So what are we all supposed to show up for?"

"A Children's Pops Concert downtown at Symphony Hall at two, followed by drinks and tapas at their house afterward."

"Bit of a long day, even for the Rhodes family," Cam observed as their food arrived.

"Right," Jess agreed as she dug into her eggs. "Blaine said so, and that set Jackie off. It was as if she was deliberately challenging him to tell her that she was asking too much."

"So how do we talk her out of it?"

"I'm afraid she's already bought the tickets and hired a caterer for the evening cocktail party."

"So we can't talk her out of it?"

Jess shook her head. "This is some sort of test that we all have to pass, but Blaine especially. You know, Cam, maybe you're right that Blaine isn't having an affair, but something's going on with him. He's different from the way he used to be."

Cam shrugged. "I can't say that I've noticed any differences. He's always been preoccupied with work and a little resentful of being known as Tyler Miller's son-in-law. I think he's having trouble adjusting to retirement. He hasn't learned how to stay out of the office yet."

"Maybe." But she didn't sound convinced. "Sorry the girls and I stood you up last night. Did you meet Nash for dinner in LA before you came home?"

A surge of guilt washed over him, but Cam told himself he had nothing to feel guilty about. He hadn't been with Raven.

"No. I was with my co-counsel, Meg Courtney."

"Oh, the one with the little four-year-old boy who you said was so cute and precocious?"

Is it my imagination or does she look relieved? It's my imagination.

"That's right. Finn was sleeping over at a friend's house because Meg was getting back late from LA. And I could see she really has no life outside of Finn. So I suggested we grab dinner at The Yellow Door and talk over the case."

"Oh, The Yellow Door. What a great idea! You're so thoughtful, Cam!" And she leaned across the table and gave his hand a squeeze. "Did she like it?"

"She did." Cam thought of the longing on Meg's face when she'd said she wanted to come back, but Finn would be hard to convince. "She's talking about leaving San Diego and going back to New York. She hasn't been here long, and Finn likes it here. I tried to talk her out of it."

"She needs friends."

"That's what I told her. I said she'd like you and Addison."

"Well, then, invite her to Jackie's for the cocktail party Sunday night. Finn could play with the girls. They'd spoil him."

"I know." Cam's heart surged with love for her kindness and generosity at the same time that he shivered inwardly at the thought of how close he had come to crossing the line with Raven on Friday night. "I'll give it a try. Finn loves one of Nash's movies. I'm sure he would be over the moon to meet him."

"The one about the dog?"

"That one."

Jess laughed. "The girls loved *Sam and Tucker*, too. We could arrange a showing in Jackie's den and have Nash pop in as a surprise."

Cam's heart surged once more as he asked himself what he'd done to deserve such an amazing, thoughtful wife.

She picked up the check and leaned across the booth and gave him a kiss on the cheek. "My treat. Yours next time. I've got to get going. I promised Jackie I'd help her shop for favor bags for the kids on Sunday."

"Wow. She's going all out."

"Right. I told you, this is some sort of loyalty test."

"We'd better not fail it then."

"Absolutely." She gave him another quick kiss and got up. "Don't rush. Finish your coffee. I'll see you tonight. Pork chops for dinner. Your favorite."

"Can't wait." And he sipped his coffee for another ten minutes, meditating upon the myriad details of his life that he shared with Jess and no one else.

CHAPTER TWENTY-SIX

Tuesday, March 12, 2019, Offices of Goldstein, Miller, and Mahoney, Emerald Shapery Center

Cam had turned his phone off during breakfast and decided to leave it off until he reached his office. But when he sat down at his desk and turned it on, he saw that Raven had been texting him frantically for the past two hours.

"*Sonia said you were at her office yesterday. I have to see you!*"

He stared at the list of messages from her that all said the same thing for a long time, wondering what to do. He was still full of the domestic glow of being with Jess, and somehow it didn't feel right to allow himself to fall under Raven's spell so soon after leaving his wife. But how did she know about his meeting with Sonia?

He told himself he would make it quick as he dialed her number.

"Oh, thank God! I've been texting you all morning."

"I turned my phone off. Jess and I were at breakfast."

"I—I see." Her disappointment was palpable. "I need to see you."

"Your message said something about Sonia."

"Yes. She said she met with you and the other attorney on Dad's case."

"When did she say that?"

"This morning. She called to talk to Dad but wound up talking to me instead. She wanted to know how the sequel was coming."

"How is she involved in that now that Nora's dead?"

"She's representing Kiara. If Nora had lived and taken Michael's deal, Sonia would have received fifteen percent of Nora's profits from the movie. With Nora gone, Sonia needs another way to get in on the action. Look, I don't like doing this over the phone. I need to see you."

And I need to see you and that is exactly the reason why I shouldn't. "I've got a meeting here in an hour, and my afternoon is full."

"What about now? It won't take long. I'm three minutes from your office."

He was filled with a mixture of hatred for himself and joyous anticipation as he took the elevator down to the parking garage to get his car. As he exited the garage and headed down Broadway, he promised himself to treat this like the business meeting that it was meant to be.

But that promise was immediately in jeopardy when she answered the door. She was wearing her black trousers and turtleneck and a painting smock. She looked overjoyed to see him.

"I've got something to show you," she announced, taking him by the hand and leading him toward the hallway to the bedrooms. He followed her, telling himself that he wasn't tingling all over because she was holding his hand.

She pulled him into her studio and pointed triumphantly to

the portrait of him. Fresh paint and used brushes in front of it told him that his arrival had interrupted her work on it.

"I've got the eyes right at last," she said. And, in truth, they had lost the wooden look that Cam had noticed before. They were kind and gentle. Loving even. Was that true to life? At that moment he didn't care. He was overwhelmed by a feeling he didn't want to name.

"I don't know what to say."

"Say you like it."

"I do. Very much."

"Good! Then let's go to the living room. I've made coffee for us."

He followed her back down the hall and took a seat on the couch. A minute or two later, she appeared with a tray and handed him a cup. The coffee was deep and rich. Suddenly, he thought of sitting on the couch with Jess at home, sipping her hot chocolate.

I shouldn't be here. I should have made her come to the office.

"I don't have a lot of time," he began.

"Just like the night we met." She smiled. "Only that night it was a family party that you had to get to."

"Well, today it's an important client, so what did you want to tell me?"

"That I really was in Dublin the night Nora was killed. Sonia said that you were doubting me."

"It was actually Sonia who suggested that you might not be telling the truth."

"Sonia doesn't like me."

"Why?"

"Because I nixed Nora's production company."

"But how did that affect Sonia, personally?"

"Because she was counting on getting a lot of roles for her clients in the movies Nora wanted to make. Sonia hates me because I forced Dad to say no. Sonia knows that I was in Dublin on the night of February 13-14."

"How does she know?"

"Because we had a phone conversation that day. She was trying to persuade me to influence my father to write some sort of role for Nora in the sequel. A bit part that would make her happy enough not to interfere with making the movie."

"But how would that prove you were in Dublin?"

"Because there's an eight-hour time difference. She called from LA around five p.m. and woke me up at one o'clock in the morning. My phone records have the time of her incoming call." She thrust several sheets of paper toward him.

Cam took them from her and studied them briefly. The black print seemed to blur as he felt her studying him intensely. She seemed to sense the effect she was having on him. After a few seconds, she said, "You have to believe me."

He looked up from the phone bills and met her intense gaze with his own. "Why do I have to?"

"Because I'm telling the truth. And because—" Her voice trailed away as if he knew the end of her sentence without having to hear it. Her eyes still held his.

But he wasn't satisfied with the unspoken. "And because why?"

"Because you know the way I feel about you."

* * *

He found Finn at his little table in Meg's office that afternoon at three thirty.

"She's not here," he announced when Cam entered. He looked up and gave him a big, confident smile that warmed Cam's heart. "She said to tell you that she'd be back in a minute."

"Okay." Cam put his file folder and legal pad on Meg's grown-up-sized table and walked over to look at Finn's Lego project.

"It's a spaceship," he announced. "Like the ones at the Air and Space Museum."

"So you've been there with your mom?"

"Yes." Finn smiled.

"And you like it here in San Diego?"

Finn nodded his head vigorously. "My mom keeps talking about moving back to New York. I don't want to go." He looked sad.

"I don't blame you. Maybe she needs to make some friends here, and then she'll want to stay."

Finn brightened. "Yes! She needs some friends, so we can stay. I don't want to leave my friends here."

"Am I being talked about?" Meg smiled from the doorway. She was carrying a bag of CDs. "Sorry to be late. These just came over from the prosecutor's office, and I wanted to make sure I took possession of them right away. They're from the cameras at Nora's house. I called over there this morning, asked what else they had, and they sent these."

"Finn and I think you'd like San Diego better if you had friends here. My mother is having one of her parties on Sunday, and my wife and I are inviting you and Finn. Jess thought our girls and Finn would enjoy watching his favorite movie. Callie and Steph love it, too."

Although Finn looked hopeful, Meg shook her head. "It's not good for either of us to be out late on Sunday night with a whole work and school week ahead."

Finn gave Cam a sad look and went back to building his rocket ship. Meg motioned for Cam to take a seat at the big table.

"I think we should divide these up to review," she said.

"I agree." Cam paused for a minute to consider what to say about Raven. Certainly, he wasn't going to say he'd gone to the condo. "Sonia told Raven about our meeting with her yesterday. Raven called this morning to say she was in Dublin the night Nora died and Sonia knew that."

"So they don't like each other. I'm not surprised."

"What's more interesting is that Sonia now represents Kiara who Lachlan wants for the female lead in the sequel."

"So should we put Sonia on our list of suspects?"

"I think we should. Sonia stood to make a lot of money if Nora took Michael Bernstein's deal. But she didn't take it. It's possible that Sonia got rid of Nora in order to represent Kiara and get her cut that way. Sonia says she left San Diego that night, but I'm not sure I believe her. Thanks for taking the lead on getting these videos out of Axel. I'll get to work on my share right away."

"And I will, too. Want to touch base on Friday to see where we are?"

"Good idea." Cam gathered up his share of the CDs and waved goodbye to Finn who smiled and waved back.

Meg followed him into the hall and closed her office door so that she could speak without Finn overhearing her. "I don't mean to be ungrateful for the invitation. I'm guessing that you'd planned to introduce Finn to your brother as part of the showing of *Sam and Tucker*."

"My wife suggested it," Cam said.

"And it's a very sweet idea. I'm touched and deeply grateful. But as I told you before, Finn's confused enough about his father. It wouldn't help if he met 'Sam' who is not a real person anyway. It's best if we don't do that to him."

"I'm sorry. Of course you're right."

CHAPTER TWENTY-SEVEN

Sunday, March 17, 2019, Copley Symphony Hall, Downtown San Diego

Cam parked the Cayenne in the lot across from Symphony Hall, turned off the ignition, and sat for a moment, bracing himself to face the afternoon. He'd dropped Jess and the girls at the front door to meet Jackie who had texted that she was waiting in the lobby while Blaine parked their car. He could see Nash's ostentatious red Ferrari a couple of rows away, so he was already inside too.

Cam took one more deep breath, got out, and headed across the street. The lobby was crowded with parents and children, but it was easy to spot the Rhodes clan. Steph and Callie were huddled with Addison's girls, comparing notes about the dolls they'd brought to hear the concert. Jackie was laughing at something Jess or Addison had said, and Nash was deep in conversation with their brother-in-law, Kurt.

Everyone was connected to Tyler Miller, the patriarch, in some way. As Cam headed toward them, he thought of Raven's observation: they all belonged to the same tribe. Maybe that was the reason for his fascination with her—she wasn't part of this tribe. He'd wanted to see her all week, but at the same time, he'd held his breath whenever he'd reviewed his share of the surveillance tapes from Nora's house, hoping she wasn't there. So far so good, but there were more to go.

During the week, he'd had a hard time turning down her multiple invitations to meet for a drink after work, but he'd made himself do it. Still, not seeing her had fueled his desire to see her even more. *When would his sanity return? What if it didn't?*

"Cam! Over here!" His mother waved as he approached. "Your father should be here any minute. He must be having trouble finding a space."

Cam's heart turned over. There were plenty of empty spaces in the parking lot across the street.

"It's ten minutes until the concert starts," he said. "Why don't we go in and take our seats? Dad will find us."

But Jackie shook her head. "I have all the tickets. He'll be here soon."

So they remained in the lobby as the rest of the patrons moved into the concert hall. Cam could see the anxiety rising on everyone's faces as the minutes ticked by.

Finally, at three minutes to two, Nash took Jackie gently by the arm and said, "Come on, Mom. We don't want the girls to miss the concert."

"But your father—"

"I'm sure he's all right," Cam said. "Go on in. I'll try to call him."

And, of course, when he tried, there was no answer.

* * *

That night, Cam got into his pajamas quickly and went down the hall to check on Steph and Callie. The drinks and hors d'oeuvres portion of the evening had been very tense, and he wanted to see how much of the grown-ups' discomfort had rubbed off on his daughters. Thankfully, each one seemed oblivious to the family-wide anxiety and heartbreak.

Jess had just stepped out of the shower when he returned to their bedroom. She was standing in front of the foggy mirror, wrapped in a towel, using another towel to dry her curly blond locks.

"Are the girls okay?" she asked as Cam entered.

"Fine. They are absorbed in their dolls and the concert. They loved the music."

"That's a relief!" Jess dropped her towels and quickly pulled on an ankle-length white nightgown. "I'm surprised they didn't ask you why Grandpa wasn't there."

"They never mentioned it." Cam got into bed and set the alarm on his phone for seven. Then he turned out the light on his side to discourage further conversation. The last thing he wanted was a rehash of the day's events. He himself had been in turmoil all afternoon, not only because of his father's absence, but because Raven had messaged him that morning with an invitation to dinner, and he'd been surprised at the depth of his regret that he couldn't accept it. All evening at the tapas party, his dutiful side had struggled against his rebellious wish to walk out the way Blaine had. Now, he was exhausted by hours of inner conflict that he was ashamed of and that he dared not reveal to anyone.

Jess turned off the bathroom light and went around to her

side of the bed. Before getting in, she picked up her phone and set the alarm. "I'll be up at six," she said.

"Ugh! Couldn't you make it seven?"

"No, sorry. I want an hour to myself before I have to get the girls fed and off to school. I'll try not to wake you."

But Cam knew that she would.

"We should have made Jackie come back with us," she said as she put her phone on its charger and turned out the light on her side of the bed. "It didn't feel right to leave her in that house alone all night."

Cam didn't answer, hoping silence would end the conversation. He didn't want to relive the heartbreaking moment when he'd received a curt text from Blaine saying that he wouldn't be home. Cam wished he could forget the look on his mother's face when he'd delivered that news.

"Don't you think we should have insisted?"

"We did insist, and she refused." Despite his best efforts, he couldn't keep the edge out of his voice. He felt his anger rising no matter how hard he tried to push it away. A day of his own conflicting and guilty emotions had left him almost fully drained of the willpower he needed to keep them in check. "Don't make too much of this, Jess. She'll work it out with Dad. She always does."

"No, she won't. He's walked out on her. I told you when we had breakfast at Clayton's that she dreamed up this sudden family event to test his loyalty after you told her that he wasn't having an affair. And he very obviously failed that test by humiliating her today in front of all of us. He's made it clear that he doesn't want to work it out with her."

"That doesn't mean he's having an affair," Cam insisted even though he knew his father's behavior proved exactly that.

"Of course it does."

"Not necessarily. It just means that he's tired of being required to show up whenever she decides to string up some paper hearts and serve cookies on matching napkins."

"Cam!" Jess sat up and turned on the light on her side of the bed, her own anger rising to meet his. "How could you possibly say such a thing? Jackie's family events are her whole life. You know that!"

"Is a preoccupation with table settings, party menus, and treats for favor bags, a 'whole life'?" *If she hadn't put us all on call today, I could have made an excuse to see Raven. Oh, God, this is why I'm spouting Rhodes family heresy. But I don't care.*

"Have you taken leave of your senses? Jackie's so-called trivia is the glue that binds this family together."

"Well, reasonable minds can differ on that!"

"I think you should sleep in the guest room."

"I agree."

* * *

He stalked down the hall to the room that Jackie had refused. He was vibrating with anger and regret that he hadn't been able to get away to see Raven. Part of him acknowledged that he'd been rude and unkind to Jess. She was right that Blaine had behaved badly, but at that moment, Cam felt some sympathy for his father's need for freedom from family responsibilities.

He turned down the bed and started to get in, but something drew him to the window. The guest bedroom was on the front of the house, overlooking the drive and the end of Ocean Way.

Cam peeked through the blinds and there it was. A little gray Fiat 500 was parked under the streetlight at the end of his driveway. His anger, which had been dimming, now flared. He opened the door and hurried down the hall and down the stairs. He grabbed his Burberry from the closet and threw it on over his pajamas and ran out into the night to confront the occupants of the car.

As he drew closer, he expected to hear the engine start and to see it disappear as it had before. But this time, it didn't. He slowed as he drew nearer, suddenly aware that he might be approaching someone who was armed. But it was too late to run back to the house, and he was an easy target as he stood under the streetlight, so he continued toward the gray sedan, his heart hammering so hard in his chest that his breath came in gasps.

He stopped about two feet from the driver's door. The windows were tinted so he couldn't see inside. He stood transfixed under the weak light from the streetlight, wondering if he was about to be shot. His heart rate sped up as the window began to roll down slowly. He expected to see the barrel of a gun pointed at him at any minute.

The window continued to wind down. But just at the moment when he thought he was going to see the weapon, a woman's face appeared. Raven. His heart seemed to stand still.

"You?" Cam could feel his lips moving, but only slightly. It was barely a word, more like a breath. He was as surprised and enchanted as he'd been that first night when she'd popped up in front of his car at the Rancho Santa Fe mansion.

"I—"

"No, never mind. Not here. Move over. I'll drive. I know where to go."

She slid over into the passenger seat. Cam got behind the wheel, oblivious to the fact that he was wearing his pajamas under his trench coat and his house slippers. The engine came to life when he turned the key. He made a half circle around his cul-de-sac and turned right onto the cross street, Ocean Terrace. From there, he moved onto Ocean Boulevard.

He drove until he found a parking spot that suited him next to the sidewalk on the ocean side of the street. He was drunk on her perfume by the time he turned off the engine and said softly, "Come on."

They walked along the sidewalk until they came to a bench facing the water. He pulled her down beside him and put his arm around her. Her tiny form was wrapped in a long black sweater that felt like Jess's cashmere shawl. She looked up at him in the dim light of a distant streetlight, with eyes so full of love and longing that his heart turned over. He leaned down and cradled her chin in his hands and kissed her, tentatively at first, but then long and deeply.

Eventually he let her go. She leaned back and studied his face before she asked, "You're not angry that I came to find you?'

"No."

"It's just that I couldn't stop thinking about you."

He kissed her again, then said, "It's the same with me. I've been miserable all week because I couldn't get away to see you."

She snuggled into the curve of his arm again and laid her head on his shoulder. They sat like that for a long time, watching the black waves tumble into little curves of lacy foam on the wide white beach. Cam closed his eyes and savored the breeze that caressed his cheeks and ruffled his hair. His body responded to the warmth of Raven's cuddled against him.

"Are you sleeping?" Her soft lilt seemed like music meant only for him.

"No." He opened his eyes and smiled at her. "Just savoring the peace of being with you at last."

"Look, there's a seagull. They don't always fly at night. He looks lonely."

Cam observed the lone white bird, soaring over the black waves. "Hunting for food while all the others are sleeping."

"Probably. But he still looks lonely."

"Are you ever lonely?" The question just popped out before Cam had time to think.

"Sometimes." She turned from the sea to study his face again. "Da's busy with his life; my mother is useless as a companion."

"But surely there's someone—"

She reached up and put her finger over his lips. "No, there isn't. At least, not until now."

He kissed her again. Just for now, he wasn't going to think about how impossible this was. He threw off the weight of the day-long effort to please his mother and to play out the happy-family script that she had written and decided to have what *he* wanted, if only for a short time and regardless of the consequences.

"What is your wife going to think about this?" Raven asked when he let her go.

"She isn't going to know. We had a fight at bedtime, and officially I'm sleeping in the guest room. I was turning down the bed when I saw your car."

"Didn't she hear you leave the house?"

"It doesn't matter if she did. She'd assume that I went to my parents' house. Their marriage is in trouble." And now that the restraints were lifted, he began to pour out the story of his mother's suspicions, his own belief that they were unfounded, and Jess's anger over his being able to see Blaine's point of view.

"Family show-ups would get wearisome," Raven agreed. "You were in such a hurry that first night because of your mother's party." She leaned up and gave him a long kiss. "And I didn't want you to go. Even that first night, I wanted us to be together."

He sat quietly studying the little waves running toward the sand on tiny white foam feet. He tightened his embrace a little because he was dreading the moment when he would have to let her go.

"What are we going to do?" she asked.

"I don't know," Cam said to the infinite ocean, stretching toward the black horizon. "But we'll find a way."

Had it been like this for Blaine? Had he experienced a moment when love became so intoxicating that there was no room in his heart for anything else?

BLACK MAGIC

CHAPTER TWENTY-EIGHT

Monday, March 18, 2019, 4212 Ocean Way, Coronado, California

Time ceased to exist for Cam as he sat on the bench, holding Raven in his arms. Eventually, she dozed against his shoulder, and he, too, dropped off. He woke with a start just as the sky began to lighten. He suddenly felt as if they were being watched. He looked around but saw no one. Still, he was uneasy.

"What's wrong?" she asked.

"I didn't realize you were awake."

"Something startled you, and when you jumped, it woke me. Is something wrong?"

"No. I was having a bit of a bad dream." Since he couldn't see anyone watching them, he decided not to tell her about his hunch.

She snuggled into his shoulder once more and said, "Well, let's get comfortable again. And this time, you'll have a good dream."

"You know I can't, Raven. The sun's coming up, and I have to go home."

She opened her fascinating eyes and studied him carefully for a few moments. Then she said, "Tonight then. Dad's going to be out with Seamus. Come to the condo?"

"Okay."

Cam drove her Fiat to within two blocks of his house. Before he got out, he gave her a long kiss and said, "Until tonight." Then he made his way home on foot, hoping that his neighbors would not see him walking around the neighborhood with his Burberry thrown over his pajamas.

He was thankful that the front door was still unlocked. That meant that Jess hadn't been up since he went outside to identify the car watching their house. He tiptoed up the stairs and crawled into bed in the guest bedroom. The clock on the bedside table said four fifteen. He lay still and watched the dawn begin to creep through the blinds. He was on fire with feelings he had never experienced before.

He was in love. He let himself say the words out loud once as if to convince himself that it was true. He felt giddy and light-headed, and he wondered how he could manage to wait until tonight to see Raven again.

It had never been this way with Jess. She was the suitable match that Blaine and Jackie would accept. And by the same token, he was the rising young lawyer that her parents expected her to marry. In Raven's words, they were from the same tribe. But this—this was unlike anything Cam had ever experienced. It was as if all the colors of the rainbow had suddenly announced that they were his personal property.

Eventually, he dozed off. The sound of the front door closing behind Jess and the girls leaving for school woke him at seven thirty. He decided to get up and shower and, with any luck, be on his way to the office before she returned. Last night's glow had turned into this morning's overwhelming guilt. He hoped she didn't know that he'd been out most of the night.

But luck was not on his side. She came in through the back door at eight thirty just as he was filling his travel mug from the pot on the kitchen counter. She paused, coat still on, to watch him add cream and screw on the lid.

"I'm sorry that I told you to sleep in the guest room."

"It's okay."

"I heard you go outside at some point."

"I needed a walk to calm down."

"You have a point about Jackie's preoccupations."

"But you're right that they hold the family together, trivial though they may seem."

"She shouldn't have made us all show up yesterday with things that tense between herself and your father. It was wrong."

"Were Callie and Steph still okay about everything this morning?"

"Fine. They only said that they liked the music and wanted to go to another concert."

The thought of his daughters deepened Cam's sense of guilt, yet at the same time, he longed to be with Raven again.

"I'm relieved to hear that."

"And they liked the tapas. I'll go check on Jackie this morning. If she has leftovers, I'll bring them home for the girls. And maybe Blaine came back after all."

"Maybe."

"You don't sound optimistic."

"I'm not. I'm going to stop on my way to the office and see how she's doing. And I'll tell her you'll be by a little later."

"Okay." Jess smiled. A few seconds later, she stopped him on his way to the door and gave him a long, lingering kiss on the mouth. When she let him go, she said, "No more guest room."

* * *

Cam reached his parents' house in less than five minutes. His mother's white BMW was the only car in the driveway. Obviously, Blaine hadn't come back last night.

He entered through the kitchen door. The house was very still. Even the little decorative lights that Jackie left on all the time had been turned off.

He headed into the dining room next. It, too, was cold and lifeless. All the crepe paper streamers and paper roses were gone. The long dining table was empty. All traces of last night's party had vanished.

The next room was the family room, and the next was the large living room. As with the dining room, all signs of last night's party had disappeared.

She must be upstairs asleep. She exhausted herself cleaning all of this up last night. That's why she didn't hear me come in.

But as he walked into the front hall, he saw her. She was lying in the middle of the floor, surrounded by bits of paper scattered like snowflakes across the polished oak floor. She was wearing her nightgown and her head was turned toward the massive front door as if she was expecting someone to come through it. The little box that had held the evidence of Blaine's infidelity was upside down, several inches from her right hand.

Even as Cam rushed over to her, he knew it was too late. She wasn't breathing, and he couldn't find a pulse as he knelt beside her. She was cold, and her body had begun to stiffen. She'd been dead for some time. His hands were shaking as he took his phone out of his coat pocket and dialed 911. Then he called Jess.

"They're sending an ambulance," he told her, "but it's too late. Will you call Addie and Nash?"

"Of course, and then I'll be right over."

We shouldn't have left her alone. We shouldn't have left her alone. The mantra spun in his head as Cam sat by her, crying uncontrollably.

CHAPTER TWENTY-NINE

Monday, March 18, 2019, US Grant Hotel, San Diego

The Rhodes gathered a few at a time at Cam's house throughout the day.

First, Cam, Nash, and Blaine arrived at two that afternoon after the police documented Jackie's suicide and released her body for burial. Without Jackie, the Bella Luna house had lost its cozy charm. Shortly after that, Addison and Jess made the school run and brought back Jackie's four granddaughters who had been given a child's version of the news. McKenna would not arrive from London until the next morning at nine.

Overwhelmed by grief and guilt, Cam had little to say all afternoon. Instead, he listened as his siblings decided that the memorial service would be on Friday in Jackie's garden. When the pizza and soda arrived for late afternoon lunch/early dinner, he patiently arranged them on the dining room table, all the while thinking about Raven. And he continued to think about her as he helped Jess make up the guest room with clean sheets for Nash. He knew he would have to get her out of his mind, of course. But for now, he could not.

At nine thirty, Blaine announced his intention to return to

the Grant Hotel where he had spent the previous evening. Everyone except Cam had had too much to drink, so he offered to drive Blaine downtown. When they reached the hotel, Blaine invited him up for a scotch.

"I know all of you blame me," his father said as he settled into one of the velvet club chairs in the living room of his suite. "But it's not my fault."

"We blame ourselves," Cam said, sipping his club soda because he still had to drive home. "She made us leave last night, when we all knew that we should have stayed."

"Why did you listen to her?"

"She was so sure that you'd come home, and she wanted to be alone with you."

"I thought about going home, but I needed more time. That concert command performance made me angry."

"So you came here and got a room and drank away the afternoon?"

"That's a bit harsh, son. I went to the office for a while, and then I decided I didn't want to go to her party that night, either."

"Why didn't you just tell her you didn't want any part of her plans?" Nash asked.

"I tried. She wouldn't listen. I thought I could make myself do it, but finally, it all seemed too much."

"But why?"

"I don't know. Maybe just too many years of pretending to avoid conflict with her finally boiled over. Maybe it was too many years of being unhappy and trying not to be."

"She always said your marriage was a great love story," Cam reminded him.

"That was her version."

"What was yours?"

"I don't believe in great love stories. Do you?"

Cam's guilt cut through him like a knife, but he hoped that it didn't show. Keeping his face as neutral as possible, he said, "No, of course not."

"Your mother had become paranoid and unreasonable," Blaine said. "It became harder and harder to deal with that."

"You mean her belief that you were having an affair?"

"Exactly. No matter how many times I denied it, she refused to believe me. And she hung on to that ridiculous box of meaningless receipts."

Cam's eyes suddenly teared as he thought of the bits of paper surrounding his mother's body that morning and her face turned expectantly toward the front door, waiting for Blaine to come home. "I did see some of them," he said to Blaine.

"And?"

"And she had a point. Boutique hotels, B & Bs. Not the places the firm always puts us up."

"Do you really think that means I was having an affair?" Blaine sounded more exasperated than angry. "I've been on firm travel for more than thirty years. Wouldn't it make sense that I'd get tired of the same accommodations, year after year?"

"I see your point. I told her she was wrong."

"And she was. Look, Cam. Your mother and I led mostly separate lives for our entire marriage. It had nothing to do with affairs. You know that. We just had different responsibilities."

"Then I retired, but not the way she wanted me to. She wanted me to be a much bigger part of her life than I had ever been. But parties and entertaining and gardening have never been interesting to me. I didn't retire in order to become an extension of your mother's life. In fact, I never intended to give up law entirely. But rather than face that truth, Jackie made up fantasies that perfectly normal charges for business entertaining somehow proved I was being unfaithful. She could have accepted that our lives in retirement were going to go on pretty much the way they always had. Instead, she made herself miserable telling herself stories about infidelities that never took place."

* * *

By ten fifteen, Cam could see that the alcohol had made Blaine drowsy enough to sleep. He wished his father good night and headed for his car in the parking garage.

He had volunteered to drive Blaine to the hotel to have a few private moments with him to resolve his mother's suspicions once and for all. But he had driven his father downtown for an additional reason: to give himself the chance to see Raven. He hadn't been alone long enough to call her during the day, and so he had to deliver the news of his mother's death through a text message. He had intended to make the five-minute drive to the Adair condo when he left his father's room, but by the time he reached his car, he was in turmoil over whether or not he should let himself see her.

It wasn't an affair, he told himself. *Yet*. But he told the accusatory voice in his head to be quiet because he was certain that he wasn't going to let it become one. Still, the voice of temptation reminded him that Jess would never know about a short visit to Pacific Gate. Yet the voice of responsibility told him that anything other than going straight home would be disrespectful to his mother's memory. He resolved the conflict by exiting the parking garage and turning away from E Street, toward home. In a few blocks, he reached the entrance to the Coronado Bay Bridge and glanced in his rearview mirror. A black Range Rover was following him.

CHAPTER THIRTY

Tuesday, March 19, 2019, 4212 Ocean Way, Coronado, California

Cam woke with a start at two a.m. He looked over to see if he'd awakened Jess, but she was still sleeping deeply. He shifted from his side to his back and contemplated the ceiling for a moment. Then he closed his eyes and willed himself to go back to sleep so that he didn't have to think about seeing Jackie crumpled at the foot of the stairs. But he couldn't get it out of his mind.

He got up carefully and tiptoed down the hall, past his children's room and past the guest room where Nash was sleeping. He wondered if a double whiskey would numb him enough to let him go back to sleep, but a drink didn't sound good at two in the morning. Jackie would have made tea. It was warm and soothing, not harsh like alcohol. He decided on a cup of tea.

He tiptoed downstairs, found the kettle, and made himself a cup of apple-spice, one of Jess's favorites. He went into the living room and sat in one of the wing chairs to sip his comforting brew without bothering to turn on a light. As he sat in the dark, he turned over the events of the day, one by one, ending with the mystery of the Range Rover.

It had followed him until he turned onto his cul-de-sac. The sight of the big black car behind him had unnerved him, and he'd been relieved when it sped away. He'd hurried to park his Mercedes and head inside to bed, his anxiety suddenly cancelled by grief and exhaustion.

But now, in the wee hours, he wondered if it had driven away to throw him off and then returned. What if it had been sitting outside, watching his house for hours while they all slept?

He maneuvered the blinds carefully so that he could look out without being noticed. His heart began to beat faster but not because the Range Rover was there. Raven's little gray Fiat was sitting under the streetlight, exactly where it had been the previous night. He backed away from the window and picked up his mug of tea. He sipped it slowly and tried to imagine that his mother was in the room. He knew what she'd say: finish your tea and go back to bed. Somehow, when Cam had believed in Blaine's infidelity, his own flirtation with Raven had not seemed a real betrayal. He had been able to tell himself that, after all, Blaine had once been gripped by an overwhelming passion. But now that his father had explained convincingly that his affair had been the product of Jackie's loneliness and her imagination, Cam's feelings for Raven aroused a higher degree of guilt than previously.

He sipped his tea and tried not to remember being with her last night. But the memory was too strong: the warmth of her tiny body against his, the sensual smell of her musky perfume, her lilting voice, and her deep, passionate kiss.

He left his half-empty mug on the table under the window and walked into the hall. He took his Burberry out of the closet and put it on over his pajamas. Then he opened the front door and slipped outside without a sound.

She moved to the passenger seat when she saw him coming. He opened the driver's door and got in. They drove to the spot on Ocean Boulevard where they'd been the night before. Neither felt the need for words. He took her hand, and they made their way to the same bench facing the ocean where they sat down, entwined in each other's arms. He leaned down and gave her a long passionate kiss.

Afterward, as he had the previous night, Cam held Raven and listened to the waves as they rolled on shore. There was more breeze tonight and the smell of brine was stronger. He was still aching over the loss of his mother, but holding her comforted him in a way that nothing else had and in a way that he could not explain.

The silence stretched on comfortably until she said, "I didn't expect to see you tonight. I just felt close to you sitting there in the car. I thought all of you were asleep and no one would know."

"I woke up and couldn't go back to sleep. I kept seeing my mother lying at the foot of the stairs."

"You were the one who found her? How horrible for you."

"Yes. If only it had really been an accident. The tragedy of it all is that she thought my father was having an affair. And he wasn't."

"Why did you look outside? Were you looking for me?"

"I didn't think you'd be there. A black Range Rover followed me home after I took my father to his hotel. I thought it might have come back to watch my house. Why would Seamus have me followed?"

"You don't know for sure it was one of his cars."

"True. But how likely is it that someone else who owns a black Range Rover followed one of Lachlan's attorneys home tonight?"

"Not very likely. Did you get a license plate number?"

"No."

"If it comes back, maybe you can get one."

"I hope it doesn't return. It might be Nora's killer. I don't like the idea of that person watching my house where my wife and children are sleeping."

Raven laid her head on his shoulder and whispered, "I want you to be safe."

Suddenly, something seemed to fly past them out of nowhere. A split second later, Cam heard *tick, thud* and then again, *tick, thud. Oh my God. The sound of a silencer.* The only cover was the concrete bench. It wasn't much, but still holding Raven, he rolled under it, huddling as far back as he could, his body shielding hers.

Tick, thud. Tick, thud. The bullets were landing all around them. The shooter must be walking toward them. Cam held Raven as tightly as he could and prayed.

Tick, thud. Tick, thud. And then, miraculously, silence. A second later, Cam heard cars driving by on Ocean Boulevard, followed by the sound of tires screeching as another car made a fast getaway.

"I think he's gone," he whispered to Raven. "But let me go first to make sure."

He let go of her, rolled away from the bench, and stood up cautiously. No sign of the gunman, but there were expended casings scattered across the sidewalk.

A second later, she was standing beside him, holding her wrist.

"What's wrong?" he asked.

"Nothing."

"It doesn't look like nothing. Right now, we need to go back to the car as fast as we can because the shooter is likely to come back to recover those casings. We don't want to be here when he returns."

Cam put his arm around her, and they hurried down the sidewalk and across the few yards to her Fiat. He opened the passenger door for her, and as he did, he saw blood dripping from her arm. As soon as she was settled, he hurried to the driver's side and got in. He pulled away from the curb abruptly.

"Hey, take it easy," Raven said. "Where are we going?"

"To the hospital. You're bleeding. And from there, we'll call the police."

"No!"

Her denial was so sharp that it startled him. "But we have to call them."

"No, we don't. Do you want your wife to know about this?"

"I—"

"Of course you don't."

"Okay, no police. But you need medical attention."

"No, I don't. I'm fine, and I can drive myself back to the condo. In his paramilitary life, Dad treated a lot of wounds. He can take care of this. We have to get you home now before your wife wakes up."

"You're sure you can drive?"

"Positive."

Cam suddenly remembered the way she'd stood fearlessly in the path of his monstrous Mercedes that first night. She was much tougher than she looked. "Okay. I'll park a block from my house and walk the rest of the way. But you promise to call me the minute you get back to the condo?"

"Absolutely."

CHAPTER THIRTY-ONE

Tuesday, March 19, 2019, 4212 Ocean Way, Coronado, California

At eight o'clock, Cam woke to sunshine, birds singing, and the realization that his world would never be the same. His mother was dead, he was falling deeply in love with a woman who was not his wife, and he'd been shot at only a few hours ago.

He headed for the shower, only to realize that the left sleeve of his pajama top was covered in blood. He found a trash bag under the sink and stuffed his pj's into it.

Since it was eight o'clock, Jess was on the school run. He slipped on his robe and went downstairs to dispose of his bloody garments in the bottom of the trash can under a pile of bagged garbage before she could return and see them.

As he showered, he examined himself for any signs that he'd been hit by the gunfire. Thankfully, he was unscathed. He put on a pair of gray slacks and a blue-checked shirt that Jess had given him for Christmas and went down to the kitchen to make himself some breakfast. He was sitting at the kitchen table eating his scrambled eggs and toast and sipping black coffee when Jess came back.

"The girls decided that they wanted to go to school today,"

she said as she took off her coat and hung it on a peg by the back door. She walked over to the coffee pot and poured herself a cup and then sat down at the kitchen table opposite Cam.

"Did you think they were over Jackie enough to go?" he asked.

"'Over' isn't the right word. We're all going to have a hard time adjusting to the fact that she's gone. But they would rather be with their friends than moping here."

Cam nodded. "Makes sense."

"How are you doing?" Jess reached out and squeezed his hand gently. "You were out again last night. Couldn't sleep?"

"That's right."

"You were gone for quite a while."

"Sorry. I didn't mean to wake you up."

"I had trouble sleeping, too. I started to get up and come find you so we could walk together. Nash was here with Callie and Steph."

Cam felt a sharp stab of guilt. "Is Nash up?" he asked to change the subject.

"Up and out. He went to the Grant to have breakfast with Blaine. He was going to wake you to go with him, but I told him you'd been out late, so it would be better to let you get your sleep."

More guilt. Oh, God, what am I mixed up in?

"What did Blaine have to say for himself when you took him back to his suite?"

"That Mother just imagined an affair. That she'd expected too much closeness after he retired. He pointed out that they'd always led very separate lives, and he hadn't retired in order to be a part of her gardening and entertaining interests."

"Sounds a bit harsh," Jess said.

"No more harsh than my father's usual."

"I suppose so."

Jess was silent for what felt like a very long time to Cam. He could tell that she was thinking over a question that she wanted to ask. His stomach tightened as he dreaded what was coming. Finally, she looked him in the eye and asked, "Have we—I mean do we—lead separate lives?"

"I—I'm not sure I know what you mean."

"Yes, you do." It sounded like an accusation. *Does she know about Raven?* "My life is centered on the girls, their school, their activities. Yours is all about your work, especially this criminal case that Hugh made you take on."

Does she know about Raven? There's no way that she could.

"The Adair case is not a forever thing, Jess. You know that. And we are both involved in our daughters' lives."

"But it just seems to me that more and more it's me, Callie, and Steph. The school run. Girl Scouts. Book club." Her eyes suddenly filled with tears.

"I don't think there'll be any more book club," Cam said softly. "That is, unless you or Addison keep it going."

Jess wiped her eyes. "Jackie would have wanted us to. But right now, it would make all of us too sad."

Cam got up and went around the table and bent down and put his arms around her. She stood up and snuggled into his embrace. *She doesn't know about Raven. Thank God!*

After a few seconds she pulled away, wiped her eyes again, and asked, "I see you're business casual today. Are you going to the office or going to join Blaine and Nash at the hotel? Addison and McKenna are meeting them there at ten to plan Jackie's memorial. Addie called and asked both of us to come, but I was thinking this is more of a Rhodes sibling job."

"No, you should come. Mom thought of you as her daughter, too."

CHAPTER THIRTY-TWO

Tuesday, March 19, 2019, the Pacific Gate Condos, Downtown San Diego

Cam left the family meeting at eleven o'clock. There was mostly agreement about the service on Friday, but a major controversy erupted over Blaine's plans to sell the house immediately. The thought of losing it heightened everyone's grief, and Nash insisted that he would step in and buy it if his father refused to change his mind. But Blaine declined his offer and continued to insist that the house had to go.

"Your mother died there. I don't want to live in it anymore."

Although the sight of Jackie at the foot of the stairs would haunt Cam for the rest of his life, he didn't agree with his father He hoped that Nash would prevail. But he didn't want to listen to the family argument that was brewing. Raven was on his mind, and he wanted to make sure that she was all right. And he wanted to know if Lachlan could shed any light on who had targeted them last night. So after telling Jess that he needed to head to the office and arranging for Nash to take her home, he texted Raven his news. She replied, "*Come as soon as you can.*"

* * *

Lachlan, wearing his usual distinguished-professor tweeds, answered the bell and invited Cam in. He looked him over from head to toe as he stood in the front hall, and then he said, "So glad you're all right. Me girl is resting. Come this way."

Cam's heart beat a little faster as they walked toward the living room where he could see that Raven was curled up on the couch, swathed in a fuzzy white blanket. She didn't get up, and it seemed natural to cross the room and lean over and give her a kiss on the cheek. She put her arms around him and returned the kiss on his cheek.

"Are you all right?" Her eyes were a bit sunken, her face pale, and a thick bandage was wrapped around her left wrist.

"I'm fine. Just tired. I decided to take it easy today. Shouldn't you be doing that, too?"

"No, I need work to take my mind off everything. The family just met to decide on the service for my mother."

"I'm very sorry to hear that," Lachlan said.

"It's hard," Cam told him.

"Sit here." Raven sat up and drew her blanket around her and patted the seat beside her and Cam obeyed. If Lachlan hadn't been in the room, he would have kissed her again. He was being drawn to her once more, but this time, instead of resisting, he liked the feeling.

As he took the chair opposite, Lachlan said, "She had a bullet fragment in her wrist."

Cam looked over at Raven. "I told you that you needed to go to the hospital last night."

"I took care of it here," Lachlan said. "Not very deep. Lots of practice on gunshot wounds in the old days."

"It was better this way," Raven said.

And, indeed, it was. If Cam had taken her to the ER in Coronado, the world, including Jess, would have known that they had been under gunfire together in the small hours of the morning.

"Does this have anything to do with the black Range Rover that followed me home after I took my father back to the Grant? I assumed it was one of Seamus's vehicles."

"The car didn't belong to Seamus. It was likely the gunman who shot at you and Raven."

"But why shoot at us?"

"Because I have secrets, and I have enemies, and one or more of those enemies is afraid that I might have shared some of those secrets with my defense team."

"But why would you do that? Is there something from your past that would help us prove you didn't kill Nora?"

"No, of course not. My work during the Troubles was long over by the time I met her. But I know details about crimes that Scotland Yard has tried for years to solve. Someone is afraid that the Yard might pressure the locals to offer me a way to stay out of prison in exchange for information they've been trying to get for decades."

"Information about who?"

"I have too many enemies to try to guess which one or ones the Yard is interested in. Probably all of them."

"Would you take a deal?"

"Not if it meant prison time. I'd be a snitch and, therefore,

I'd be a dead man as soon as I walked through the door."

"So whoever these enemies are, they now know where I live with my wife and daughters?"

"I'm afraid that's true. Seamus has agreed to keep some of his people on you and your family and on me and Raven."

"Seamus?"

"He has a past, too."

"And, therefore, his own security people?"

"Exactly."

Oh, God. I never bargained for this. Should I tell Jess? What about Meg and Finn?

"Is my co-counsel in danger?"

"She could be."

"She has a four-year-old boy."

"I'll tell Seamus. Give me her address."

CHAPTER THIRTY-THREE

Tuesday, March 19, 2019, Offices of Goldstein, Miller, and Mahoney, Emerald Shapery Center

He went straight to Meg's office as soon as he reached the firm and was relieved to find her there. She was sitting behind her desk, studying something on her laptop with a troubled expression. He knocked on the open door to announce his presence. When she looked up, he could see a faint puffiness around her eyes as if she'd been crying. He immediately thought of the difficulty that she seemed to have with her ex and how much she hated to talk about it. He didn't want anything to get in the way of the news that he had to share with her, so he decided not to ask what was wrong.

"I wasn't expecting you to be back at work so soon," she said. "I'm sorry about—"

"Don't say it. I know." Suddenly, he realized that he wasn't ready to be here, and if she offered him sympathy, he'd begin to cry again.

She nodded as if she understood. "Okay. If you're here, there must be an important reason. Come in and sit down."

He crossed the room and took the chair in front of her desk. "Where's Finn?"

"At school."

"Who's picking him up this afternoon?"

"My babysitter. Why?"

"You should go yourself. For the next few days, at least."

She looked troubled, just as Cam had expected her to. She got up and came around her desk to take the chair next to his as if she needed greater proximity to process the news of this threat. Now that she was closer, he could definitely see traces of tears around her eyes.

"Does this have something to do with Lachlan Adair?" she asked.

"Absolutely."

"Tell me."

"Lachlan has old enemies from his IRA days. Someone came to town to make sure that he doesn't tell any secrets if, for example, the FBI and Scotland Yard should lean on Axel to offer him some kind of plea deal in exchange for giving evidence to the Feds against his old comrades."

"How do you know there's a gunman after Lachlan?"

"Raven was wounded in the wrist last night. She couldn't sleep and went for a walk near the condo."

The lie sounded plausible enough.

"Were the police involved?"

"No. Lachlan fixed her up at home. He says everyone connected to him is at risk."

Meg looked grave. "Do Lachlan's enemies know where we live?"

"They've found me. Someone followed me last night after I dropped my father at the Grant. He's staying there because he doesn't want to go back home right now." Another version of the truth, but close enough.

"So someone could have followed me home, too?"

"And to Finn's school, and to any parks you've taken him to, and, of course, here to your office."

Cam watched as Meg considered this news in silence. She was obviously frightened, so he wanted to comfort her. "Look, don't worry. Lachlan has arranged for some of Seamus's people to provide protection. Seamus has a past, too."

"No bodyguards, please." Meg held up one had as if to ward off a blow. "That will terrify Finn. He won't agree to leave the house, even for school."

"I'll tell Lachlan that they need to stay out of sight."

"No, I'll handle this. I'll be sure to pick Finn up from school myself and keep him here with me until I'm ready to go home."

"But that's not practical," Cam said. "You can't take him to every meeting you have for an indefinite period of time."

"Well, I'll bring him and the sitter here, then. She can watch him in my office when I'm in meetings. What about you? What are you going to do?"

"I'm going to ask Jess to take Callie and Steph to visit her mother in Baltimore. Maybe Finn could go stay with his father for a little while in New York."

"No!"

"But he'd be safe there."

"That's not an option," Meg said curtly.

"He could go with Jess to Baltimore. Callie and Steph would spoil him."

"That's a generous offer," she said, warming slightly, "but he doesn't know your wife or your daughters. He'd be afraid to be with strangers."

"I won't push you," Cam said. "But he seems like a very grown-up little boy who likes new adventures to me. I think he'd be fine with it."

"No." The chill returned. She turned her head toward the glass walls of her office and stared at the view of the city below for several seconds. Then she began to shake her head slowly, and a tear rolled down her cheek.

Cam reached out and put his hand lightly on her arm. "Meg, just think it over. You've got too much on your plate as it is. When I talk to Jess about all of this, I'll talk to her about Finn, too. That way, if you change your mind—"

She wiped away her tear and steadied herself and met Cam's gaze. "I won't change my mind, but thanks. I'm sad because this will delay my plan to move. If I leave for upstate New York now, whoever thinks I know secrets will come after me and Finn. So I have to stay here until the threat is gone. That probably means until Lachlan's case is over. I'm sorry, Cam. It's not you. I like working with you. But I don't want to stay here."

"But Finn wants to stay."

"Finn's too little to make that decision."

CHAPTER THIRTY-FOUR

Tuesday, March 19, 2019, 4212 Ocean Way, Coronado, California

Cam waited until bedtime to talk to Jess. It was hard to pretend that everything was normal through dinner and bedtime with the girls. But it helped that the only conversation was about Jackie and the memorial service on Friday.

"There's something we need to talk about," Cam said at nine o'clock after Stephanie had finally been persuaded to go to bed and stay there.

Jess smiled. "I'll make hot chocolate."

"Good idea."

Cam leaned against the kitchen counter with arms folded and watched her go through the familiar ritual of heating milk and melting chocolate and then combining them into her smooth, signature beverage. When she handed him his cup of the rich, dark liquid, she smiled and said, "Penny for your thoughts. No, wait. I can guess them. You're thinking about watching your mother make tea."

"I am."

She laid her hand on his arm sympathetically. "I was thinking about that, too. Let's go sit in the den."

They settled side by side on the couch. When she cuddled against his shoulder the way she always did when they had talks like this, Cam felt a measure of relief and guilt.

She doesn't suspect anything about my relationship with Raven. Oh, God. Has it become a relationship?

"What's on your mind?" she asked as she sipped her chocolate.

"Lachlan Adair has warned me that his life is in danger along with the lives of everyone connected to his case."

"What?" Jess sat back and stared at him. "Because he killed his wife, he and his entire defense team are in danger? Surely he's exaggerating."

"He isn't. His old IRA comrades are afraid the Feds will lean on the state to offer him a deal if he agrees to name names from his past."

"But surely those crimes are so old that the statute of limitations has run on them."

"Not the murders."

"But I thought those people would never inform on each other."

"That's what his daughter says. But at Lachlan's age, any sentence is a life sentence. If the state offered to let him plead to something like involuntary manslaughter that would justify putting him on probation, it's hard to see how he wouldn't be tempted to take it and spill what he knows to save himself."

Jess was silent for a few seconds, apparently considering the magnitude of the risk. Then she asked, "What does 'in danger' mean exactly?"

"It means someone sent a shooter to town who happened to

find Raven walking alone near the condo last night. She was wounded, fortunately not seriously, in the wrist."

The more often I repeat this, the more it begins to feel true.

"It sends shivers down my spine to think that you've been out wandering in our neighborhood two nights in a row."

"Point taken."

"At least Lachlan's enemies don't know where we live."

"But they do."

Jess was suddenly in full alarm mode. "How do you know?"

"Someone followed me home after I took Dad back to the Grant last night."

"Did you tell the police?"

"I stopped at the station on the way home tonight. They said they'd run extra patrols. And Lachlan's friend Seamus has security people that he's sending to watch us here. But I don't think that's going to be enough."

"You're right. I think I should take the girls to my mother's for a while."

"That's exactly what I was going to suggest."

"We'll leave on Friday after Jackie's service. That will give me time to get lessons from their teachers. Actually, it will be good for them to spend some time with their other grandmother. Losing Jackie is hard for them."

"It is," Cam said.

"I hope Blaine doesn't sell the house. It holds so many memories for everyone in the family. I can't bear to think that Sunday is the last time we'll ever be there. Don't let him do it, Cam."

"I'll try my best. Nash can probably save it if Dad actually puts it on the market."

"But Blaine said he wouldn't sell it to Nash."

"We'll think of something."

"What about your colleague, Meg? Isn't she in danger, too? And her little boy?"

"She is. I tried to talk her into letting Finn come with you and the girls. He's very grown-up. He wouldn't be a problem."

"Callie and Steph would love to have him along. Mom has plenty of room. I wouldn't mind, either. I always wanted three." She looked sad, and Cam squeezed her hand gently. She'd miscarried two years after Stephanie was born, and the doctor had said more children weren't likely.

"Well, if Meg changes her mind, I'll tell her that Finn's welcome in Baltimore. But she was adamant that he should stay here with her."

"How long do you think we'll have to be away?"

"I don't know. I would guess until Lachlan's trial is over. Everyone involved wants to fast-track it. Raven has wanted a quick trial from the beginning, and that would suit Meg, too. She's in a hurry to get this case over and move to upstate New York."

"So she hasn't changed her mind about San Diego?"

"She hasn't even though Finn wants to stay."

Jess leaned over and gave him a long kiss on the mouth. Then she said, "You know how much the girls and I will miss you."

"And how much I'll miss all of you."

"What are your chances of getting an acquittal?"

"Slim to none."

BEWITCHED

CHAPTER THIRTY-FIVE

Monday, March 25, 2019, Offices of Goldstein, Miller, and Mahoney, Emerald Shapery Center

At nine o'clock on Monday morning, Cam contemplated his view of San Diego Bay as he waited for Meg. They had agreed to meet that morning to talk about the Adair case.

He had spent his weekend in his empty house, going through the case file, trying to find some fact that they could develop into a defense. He'd dropped Jess and the girls at the airport on Friday afternoon after Jackie's service that morning. Jackie had had a lot of friends, and the little garden had been overflowing with people who had come to remember her. After eulogies and speeches, the guests had been offered refreshments on the lawn because Blaine had refused to open the house. As the nonfamily members ate tiny sandwiches and drank champagne to celebrate Jackie, the family had gathered petals from her roses and then walked the few blocks to the ocean to scatter them with her ashes in the calm sea under the bright morning sun.

Now, reliving those moments and studying the light waves dancing on the blue bay as he waited, Cam thought of the unexpected sense of relief he'd felt as the last of Jackie's ashes mixed with deep-red rose petals had gradually disappeared into the clear green Pacific waves. He couldn't explain the feeling. His grief over her loss was as deep as ever. He told himself it came from knowing that all the tension over the arrangements for the service was now over, but he also wondered if some of his relief was attributable to his decision that he would be strictly faithful to Jess from now on.

But he'd still had the impulse to drive straight to the condo as soon as he'd left her and the girls at the airport. He hadn't seen Raven since Tuesday. She'd sent him pictures of her painting in her studio, the only evidence of her injury a gauze wrap on her left wrist. He'd thought about her constantly on Wednesday, but as the day of Jackie's memorial approached, he'd felt more and more guilt when his thoughts strayed. His father had not been unfaithful; therefore, he told himself he had lost his justification for his own fantasies about being with Raven.

His resolve had wavered several times over the weekend when she'd either called or texted. But he'd messaged back that he was working on Lachlan's case, and that had been enough to keep her from urging him to come to the condo. He'd looked out at the streetlight every night before going to bed alone, hoping to see the little gray Fiat. But, of course, that would have been far too dangerous under the present circumstances.

"Sorry to keep you waiting."

Cam looked up to see Meg hurrying into his office. She was still wearing a light coat and carrying a large bag that he could see contained the Adair file. She'd come straight to his office without going to her own first.

She took off her coat and draped it over one of the chairs in front of Cam's desk. She sat down in the other and pulled a yellow pad out of the large bag. She looked up at him and smiled. "How was your weekend?"

"Quiet. Everyone left on Friday afternoon. Lots of time to read the file. How about you?"

"A little tense. Finn was cross because I didn't want to go to the playground or walk on the beach. How's our client's daughter?"

"I haven't heard anything else," Cam lied. "I assume she's recovering. Shouldn't you and Finn go to a hotel?"

"It would be too upsetting for him. Any ideas about how we're going to defend Lachlan and get this over with?"

"I came up with two possibilities over the weekend."

"Probably the same ones I thought of: a third party culpability defense. We'll claim the killer is either Kiara or Victoria. So that means that we have to come up with some credible evidence that we can get admitted at trial that points to one of them."

"You read my mind."

"I was thinking we should start with Kiara. She had a strong motive, and she was definitely at Nora's that night. We should talk to her. Maybe we can do it today. She lives in Del Mar. I'll call her and see if we can set something up."

"What about Finn?"

"What about him?"

"He can't go with us to interview a witness. Who's picking him up from school?"

"I was going to meet the babysitter there and bring the two

of them back to the office. I want to have my eye on him whenever he's not in school."

"Then if Kiara agrees to a meeting, I'll go."

* * *

Monday, March 25, 2019, The Condos at Del Mar Highlands

Kiara Blake lived in a small condo development perched on a bluff overlooking the Pacific in Del Mar. There were three small buildings of nine units each. Cam easily found hers in Building Three on the third floor at four o'clock that afternoon.

She opened the door and invited him into the living room with the ocean view and motioned for him to take a seat on the sofa.

"I'm making coffee. Want some?"

Cam said yes to be polite and proceeded to divide his waiting time between watching the waves wear away the beach below and studying Kiara's six-one, curvy frame through the pass-through to the kitchen as she measured coffee and added water to the pot. She was wearing khaki shorts and a simple white T-shirt and brown leather sandals. Her long blond hair was wound into a messy bun at the nape of her neck. She wasn't wearing any makeup, but she didn't need any. She was a strikingly gorgeous woman. Cam could easily picture her rising from Nora's pool like Venus rising from the sea to entice Michael Bernstein into giving her the lead in the new movie.

"Here you go." She handed him a mug and sat down on the opposite end of the couch. She sipped her own coffee thoughtfully for a moment before she said, "Poor Nora."

"Were the two of you friends?"

"Maybe in the beginning when I first went to work for her.

She was generous in helping new talent when it suited her, and it suited her with me."

"But that changed?" Cam sipped his coffee which was surprisingly good.

"It did. You've talked to Sonia and to Michael. You know the whole story about me and Lachlan and the sequel."

"Didn't that seem disloyal to you? Going behind Nora's back to take something she wanted after she'd helped you?" *Who am I to talk about loyalty when my wife is on the other side of the country, and I'm obsessed with another woman?*

"Some people would call it disloyal. I didn't."

"Why? Because it benefitted you?"

"Yes, but it benefitted Nora, too."

"Your sleeping with her husband and taking her role in the film benefitted her?"

"Look, she and Lachlan were long over. She was the only one who didn't know it. And he had never been faithful to her or to any woman. I'm sure his daughter has told you that."

"She has." The reference to Raven made him uncomfortable as it always did. Cam concentrated on keeping his face neutral. "But you still haven't told me why you think your relationship with my client benefitted Nora."

"Because I was the right person for the lead. I would make the project successful. Nora would have had more than enough money to start that production company she wanted so badly if only she'd been smart enough to take the share of the profits Michael offered her instead of trying to block everything."

"Sonia and Michael had doubts about your ability to carry the movie."

"I know." She polished off her coffee and set her mug on the table decisively. "But I didn't have any doubts. In fact, I don't presently have any doubts. Michael is going forward with the project, and Lachlan has promised me the lead."

"Is that why Sonia is representing you now?"

"So you know about that?"

Cam nodded. "What happened that night at Nora's? You were there. Michael saw you get out of the pool and go into the house as he was leaving."

Kiara gave him a sly smile. "That was the plan."

"You do realize that you're a suspect in Nora's death? You were seen going into the house at eleven thirty. The coroner thinks she died around midnight."

She waved her hands dismissively. "Of course, I know all about that. But I'm not a suspect. The DA's investigator has already been here and cleared me."

"How did he do that?"

"She. The investigator was a she. She cleared me because I didn't kill Nora. I went into the house that night to talk to her. Sonia was there, too."

"Sonia? She said she went back to LA after they had lunch."

"Well, then she lied. She had already figured out that Lachlan was never going to let Nora be in the movie, and she realized that he could force Michael to use me."

"So she decided to represent you?"

"Yes. It made sense, don't you see? She had influence with Nora, and she thought she could talk her into taking the deal, which, as I said, would have let Nora make her own movies."

"Didn't Nora understand that?"

"She did, but she was stubborn. She thought playing Angelique again would restore her career and bring Lachlan back to her. And she thought the money she'd earn from the role would let her make her own films. In other words, she thought she could have it all without having to give up being in the sequel."

"So you went in the house that night. Did Sonia come with you? Was she driving the black Range Rover that passed the security gates at eleven forty?"

"No. I couldn't see who was in the Range Rover. It drove past the main house and later when Sonia and I left, we saw it parked by the guesthouse. We assumed that whoever was inside was waiting for us to leave."

"Why didn't Sonia's car show up on the security camera?"

"She came in the back way."

"The back way?"

"Don't you know about that?"

"No. Lachlan's never mentioned one." *Or Raven.*

"The drive to the guesthouse forms a V. The right side of the V connects with Del Charro."

"Why didn't Sonia come in from the front?"

"Because she didn't want Michael to see her as he was leaving. The swim in the pool was her idea, but she didn't want him to know that."

"Why was Sonia there to pick you up?"

"She was disappointed that she hadn't been able to budge Nora that afternoon at lunch. She thought the two of us together might make her see reason."

"As in pushing her down the stairs?"

"Absolutely not. As hard as it is for you to believe, Sonia and I both cared for Nora a lot. And there was a future for everyone if Nora could get the money to make her own projects. I'd get good roles; Sonia would make tons of money; Nora would restore her career. Nora was very much alive when we left."

"Do you have any proof of that?"

"Absolutely. Here, let me get my phone. Do you want any more coffee?"

"No, thanks."

She gathered up both mugs and went into the tiny kitchen. A minute later, she came back with an iPhone in a glittery case. She scrolled through it for several seconds and then sat down on the couch close to Cam and handed him the phone.

"Here. Nora sent this message to both of us at 12:03 after we were in Sonia's car."

Cam read, *"Not washed up, you bitches!!!!!"*

"Scroll down," Kiara commanded, "and you'll read my reply at 12:06."

> *"Think about all the movies you could make!!! We love you, Kiara and Sonia."*

He handed the phone back to her. "So the DA knows that she didn't die at midnight?"

"His investigator knows. She asked me to agree to let her have my phone records, and of course I said yes."

"What about the Range Rover?"

"Like I said, it was parked by the guesthouse as we left. There was a person on the driver's side, but neither Sonia nor I could see who."

"Could you tell if it was a man or a woman?"

"No."

"Where did the two of you go after you left Nora's?"

"Sonia was staying at the Fairmont, so we went to the hotel's bar and had a nightcap. And then I took an Uber home."

"Since Sonia lied to us about staying in San Diego, how could we verify that you and Sonia were actually together that night?"

"You could talk to the bartenders at the Fairmont. One of them was an actor, and Sonia thought he had potential. His name was Michael something. Blond, tall. Surfer look. Sonia gave him her card and took one from him. She could give you his full name."

"Lachlan says that he and Seamus were at the Fairmont bar, too, until it closed. Did you and Sonia join them?"

Kiara shook her head. "They weren't there."

Cam felt a sinking feeling in his stomach. "Are you sure? Lachlan explicitly said he was at the hotel bar with Seamus O'Malley."

"He told me he was going to be with Seamus that night, but he didn't say they'd be at the hotel. And they weren't. You look upset."

"Do I? Annoyed, perhaps. Not upset. Thanks for talking to me about all this."

"Anytime. You're Nash Rhodes' brother, aren't you?"

"I am."

"Would you put in a good word for me? Tell him I'd love to work with him."

CHAPTER THIRTY-SIX

Monday, March 25, 2019, the Pacific Gate Condos, Downtown San Diego

Cam was seething as he drove south on the I-5. Suddenly this case was mired up in lies. Axel knew that the coroner's testimony at the preliminary hearing was false, yet he'd done nothing to correct the error with him and Meg.

And here was yet another lie from Lachlan! He shouldn't let himself be upset. His gut had always told him that Lachlan hadn't closed down the bar with Seamus at the Fairmont on February 13. And Cam had had a hunch ever since the debacle of the prelim that Lachlan was completely and utterly guilty. Of course he'd been the shadowy figure in the Range Rover waiting for Kiara and Sonia to leave. True, Cam had learned in his public defender days that clients rarely admitted guilt even under cover of the attorney-client privilege. But there was something about the way that Lachlan had played him that made him more resentful than he probably had a right to be.

It all had to do with Raven, he reflected as he sat in bumper-to-bumper traffic, something that did nothing to improve his mood. Was she playing him, too? Or did she genuinely care about him? He realized that although he was angry with Lachlan, he was far more angry about the prospect of finding out that Raven had been in on her father's lie. How could he find out the truth? But did he want to?

The traffic began to flow again, and Cam gunned his car into the fast lane and mashed the accelerator hard. As he did, he suddenly remembered Raven standing fearlessly in front of his monstrous machine on the drive in front of the guesthouse on that cold February night. When he'd jumped out of the car, his heart pounding because he thought he had hit her, he'd felt as if his life had changed forever when she'd smiled at him. But no, he told himself, that couldn't be true. He shouldn't let his imagination run away with him because he didn't believe in love at first sight.

Yet somehow, wondering whether Raven's feelings for him were real amped up his anger with Lachlan's lie about his whereabouts on the night of Nora's death. Kiara described seeing someone in the black Range Rover waiting by the guesthouse. It could be Lachlan just as much as Victoria.

Cam suddenly felt a burst of the freedom that comes from knowing no one is watching the clock at home, waiting for his return. The whole evening was his to do as he wanted. And he wanted to drive to the condo and confront Lachlan.

* * *

At five thirty there was no one at the security desk in the lobby, so no one asked any questions as Cam headed for the elevator to the penthouse. One part of his mind registered the security breach, but he didn't give it much thought.

He rang the doorbell at the penthouse and identified himself over the intercom.

"Oh, I'm so glad you've come!" Raven said as soon as she opened the door. She put her arms around him and hugged him while he was still standing in the hall. But her face changed when he stepped inside. "You're upset. What's wrong?"

"Is Lachlan here?" Despite his anger, Cam reacted to her embrace. She was wearing a dark-blue sweater that highlighted her eyes, and her hair was loose around her shoulders. He felt the hard jolt of attraction that being in her presence always aroused in him. For a brief moment, he wanted to forget his anger and take her in his arms.

"He's in his study."

"I have to talk to him."

"What's happened?" She looked concerned.

"He lied about where he was on the night Nora died."

"You'd better talk to him then. This way."

He followed her across the foyer and down the hall to Lachlan's study. As they passed her studio, he looked in, suddenly curious about what she'd been doing when he interrupted her. He saw a half-finished landscape on her easel and a crumpled smock draped across a chair as if she'd taken it off quickly when she'd come to answer the door. And he saw the portrait she'd painted of him prominently displayed on a small chest of drawers that stood against the wall.

She noticed his curiosity about her studio and said, "I was painting this afternoon. It takes my mind off unpleasant things. I think I've finished your portrait, but I'm studying it to make sure."

She stopped in front of the closed door to Lachlan's study and knocked.

"Da, Cam's here to see you."

A moment later, Lachlan opened the door. His dark turtleneck and tweed slacks made him look very professorial as usual.

"Is something wrong?" Cam saw surprise and apprehension in his eyes.

"Yes. I have to talk to you."

"Come in, then. We can talk here. Should Raven fetch you a whiskey?"

"No." Cam knew that his anger was obvious, but he didn't care. He sat down on the little sofa across from Lachlan's desk. Lachlan sat down on a chair opposite.

"Should I go?" Raven asked.

"No, stay." Lachlan pointed to the vacant end of the sofa.

"I think this should be a confidential interview," Cam said.

"I don't have any secrets from my daughter." Now Lachlan sounded angry. "Why have you come bursting into our house this afternoon?"

"Because you've lied to me and Meg. Again."

Cam had expected Lachlan to look uncomfortable when he confronted him, but his face remained neutral. He noticed that his eyes shifted briefly to Raven and then back to Cam's before he answered.

"I've already told you that I have secrets and that it's best that you don't know them. Which 'lie' are you here to talk about?"

"I talked to Kiara Blake this afternoon."

"I know that she and Sonia were at Nora's that night," Lachlan said. "We all wanted Michael to use Kiara instead of Nora in the sequel. They were there for some indirect persuasion."

"And then they went to the bar at the Fairmont where Sonia was staying. And neither you nor Seamus was there. You told Meg and me that you spent the evening at the hotel bar after dinner."

"This is another subject that it's best you know nothing about."

"I can't lie to the court and the jury and tell them you were at the Fairmont when I know you weren't."

"All right. I admit that I wasn't at the hotel. But I was with Seamus."

"And where were you and Seamus?"

"At his office."

"But you don't work for Seamus," Cam objected.

"That's true. I don't. But our business that night had nothing to do with Celtic Analytics."

"So what took you to Seamus's office?"

"Leftover business from the old days."

"IRA business?"

Lachlan shook his head. "None of us admits to membership. Hasn't Raven told you that?"

"She has, but I think you've as good as admitted it when you talk about your 'work during the Troubles' and the fact that it caused you to have enemies who shot at me and Raven on Saturday."

Lachlan shrugged. "Maybe. Maybe not. I'm not admitting that I am or ever was a member of the IRA."

"What was your meeting about?"

"It was a discipline matter. That's as much as I can tell you."

"Discipline? What kind?"

"It's best that we not talk about it."

"I'll decide what's best. You've told me that my life is presently in danger, yet I really have no idea why. I want an answer to my question: what kind of discipline?"

"You'll wish I hadn't told you."

"I'll take my chances."

"An execution."

"For what?"

"Being an informant."

"But I thought the IRA was no longer active in Ireland."

"That's as maybe, but when we find a snitch, even if the snitching took place long ago, we still exact the price that every snitch must pay."

"So you ordered a killing?"

"Not me personally."

"But the group did, didn't it? And you were part of that group?"

"Two members of the disciplinary counsel make the decision, and none of us ever know who the two are on any given occasion. I can say that I wasn't one of them this time. But I didn't dissent from what had to be done."

"Was what happened to me and Raven on Saturday payback for that execution?"

"No. As I told you before, I have a lot of enemies who want me dead. In my time, I killed a fair number of people. The Irish have long memories, so there are many who've put a price on my head."

"Why did you lie about being at the Fairmont?"

"Because the less you know about me, the safer you and your family are. And you couldn't have used the truth anyway because a secret meeting isn't much of an alibi."

"What else have you lied about?"

"Don't keep pushing this, Cam. You'll regret it."

"I'll be the judge of that. What else have you lied about?"

"Truthfully, I've lost track at this point. Sometimes, I think my whole life has been a lie since the day the British shot up my family and I decided to take the place of the lad they executed. But I haven't lied about Nora. I didn't kill her."

"Kiara and Sonia saw a black Range Rover parked at the guesthouse that night. The person inside was waiting for them to leave. Was that you?"

"Of course not."

"But you hated Nora, didn't you?"

"Sometimes. Mostly at the beginning of our marriage. At the end, money would buy peace, so hating her really wasn't necessary. Raven says you've sent your family away."

"After your warning, I thought it best."

"It was. Don't tell me where they are, but are they far from here?"

"Yes."

"I'm relieved to hear that. And what about your colleague's child?"

"My wife would have taken him, too, but Meg wouldn't agree."

"She should have. We're all in a great deal of danger right now, and that won't change until my trial is over. I want a trial right away."

"But Meg and I aren't ready."

"Then the two of you must get ready. I am directing you to set a trial date without delay."

"Please say you don't mean that."

"I never meant anything more in my life."

CHAPTER THIRTY-SEVEN

Monday, March 25, 2019, 4212 Ocean Way, Coronado, California

It was strange to come home to an empty house. Normally, at seven the lights would be on, Callie and Steph would be finishing their homework, and Jess would greet him with a kiss and a plate of food that she'd been keeping in the oven because he'd missed dinner at six. But tonight, the kitchen was cold and dark when he stepped inside, and the stillness made him feel unbearably alone.

A shower, a beer, and a frozen pizza were only minimally comforting. Lachlan's demand for an immediate trial kept replaying in his head. He told himself not to panic. Some sort of defense would turn up to keep him from being convicted.

He tried to call Jess, but her phone was off. It was eleven o'clock in Baltimore, and he was sure they were all in bed.

Next he tried Nash, but he texted back that he was out to dinner. Cam wondered if it was a business meeting or a date. But he knew he shouldn't ask.

Meg was third on his list.

"Am I interfering with Finn's bedtime?" he asked when she answered.

"I just turned out his light."

"Is everything all right with you two?"

"No one lurking around as far as I can tell. We're locked up for the night. What about you?"

"Same. Uneventful. The house is too quiet without Jess and the girls. I wanted to give you a brief rundown of my meeting with Kiara and let you know that Lachlan is demanding an immediate trial."

"Did you see him, too?"

"Yes. After I talked to Kiara, I went to the condo and confronted him because he keeps lying to us. He wasn't at the Fairmont that night."

Cam began to feel less lonely as he narrated the events of his afternoon.

"So Kiara and Sonia aren't suspects, and we have a new time of death," Meg observed when he concluded.

"Yes. And Axel hasn't turned over the reports of his interview with Kiara nor has he turned over those text messages that put Nora's time of death later."

"Then it's good you went to see Kiara. I wonder if he's withholding anything else. I'm still reviewing the surveillance videos from Nora's house. Nothing interesting yet."

"It's got to be Lachlan," Cam said.

"So you're not impressed with his story of an IRA secret execution counsel at Seamus's place?"

"Are you?"

"No."

"Can we talk him out of an immediate trial?"

"I don't think so."

"Then I'll see when we can get into court to set a date when I get to the office in the morning. He's going to regret demanding this."

"I know."

* * *

Somehow, he'd sensed that she would call that night, so Cam wasn't surprised when Raven's number appeared on his phone just as he ended his call with Meg.

"I need to see you." The tension in her voice was too real to be an act. "My father's gone out with Seamus, and I need to talk to you. Could you come back for a few minutes?"

Nine o'clock. Too early for bed, but late enough that he should tell her to come to the office in the morning. But he'd wanted to see her all evening, and he'd had to restrain his impulse to call her instead of Jess and Nash and Meg.

So he said, "Sure."

* * *

He sat beside her on the sofa in the half-dark of the condo's living room. She'd already poured a whiskey for them both, and it was waiting on the coffee table. He'd known from the minute that he'd heard her voice on the phone that he wasn't going to treat this as a business meeting. He should, but he couldn't.

He took a sip of his drink and studied her for a few seconds. She looked troubled and upset, and he sensed that her emotions were genuine.

"What's wrong?" he asked.

"When you were here earlier, I could see that you think my father is guilty. He isn't."

Cam studied her again for a few seconds in the low light.

Before he could say anything else, she went on, "I'm terrified of losing him. For too many years to count, it's been hard for me to feel anything except terror at the thought of losing Lachlan." She paused and then added quickly, "And, more recently, terror at the thought of losing you."

Stunned by her honesty, Cam continued to study her for a few moments, vacillating between what he wanted to say and what he should say.

She read his dilemma, she added, "I'm sorry. I overstepped. I didn't mean to make you uncomfortable. The thought of never seeing you again does terrify me, but I shouldn't have said it. You must miss your family."

"Of course." He took another sip of whiskey. He knew he meant what he'd said about missing Jess and the girls, but at the same time, when he was with Raven, everyone else seemed to disappear. He was relieved when she changed the subject.

"You've got to believe me when I tell you my mother killed Nora. She had the most to gain: control of Dad's literary rights and revenge on the woman who had stolen her husband. Don't you see? She was driving one of Seamus's Range Rovers that night."

"But so was Lachlan."

"But he was with Seamus at Celtic Analytics."

Cam frowned. "Honestly, I want to believe that. But his story keeps changing."

"But he can't help that." She sounded desperate, and there were tears in her eyes. He reached out and wiped away the one that had overflowed onto her cheek. She took his hand and held it for a few seconds before he gently took it back.

"Why does he have to lie?"

"You and I both know that you can't put his IRA past in front of a jury."

"That's true. But since we can't do that, Lachlan doesn't have an alibi for that night."

"And that's why we have to prove it was my mother."

"But we don't actually have any evidence that it was Victoria. All we have is the image of a black Range Rover going through the security gates shortly before Nora died. Kiara saw the car parked by the guesthouse as she and Sonia were leaving. Whoever was inside was waiting for Nora to be alone."

"That's something my mother would do."

"It's something anyone would do who wanted Nora out of the way of the sequel."

"You have my testimony that my mother hated Nora."

"But there's the housekeeper's testimony that your father threatened to kill her that morning during their argument."

"He's Irish. He exaggerates. And Nora never took Dad's threats seriously. She refused to believe that he didn't love her."

"Sonia told us that."

"Well, it's true."

"Unfortunately, a jury isn't likely to believe that Nora didn't feel threatened."

"But I know Dad didn't mean it seriously, and I'm sure he didn't kill her. Can't you find a way to get a jury to believe that?"

"Not without more time. Can you talk your father out of an immediate trial?"

"No." She looked deeply disappointed. "Once his mind is set, he never goes back."

"Then that doesn't leave much for Meg and me to work with."

Raven looked away toward the night sky and the twinkling lights of the city. Cam saw a few more tears slide down her cheeks. He reached over and wiped them away.

They sat in silence for a few minutes, and then she laid her head on his shoulder. He could feel her body shake as she cried quietly. He put his arms around her and held her tightly. He was overwhelmed by the depths of her grief.

After a few minutes, she took a long breath and looked up at him and said, "It can't be my father."

"I wish that were true," he said.

"Could Kiara see who was inside the Range Rover parked by the guesthouse?"

"No."

"She couldn't even tell if it was a man or a woman?"

"No."

"I'm sure it was Victoria. It *has* to be."

Cam suddenly wished he could make Victoria the guilty party because Raven wanted it so much. He looked down and saw the bandage on her wrist covering the wound from the bullet. He lightly stroked the injury with his thumb.

"Does it still hurt?"

"Not much. It's healing well." She shivered slightly and pressed her cheek into his shoulder. "I'll never forget what it felt like to be shot at."

"Nor will I."

"To think my father experienced that over and over during the Troubles."

"Did you know that he was lying about spending the night of February 13 at the Fairmont bar?"

"No." She shook her head slightly for emphasis. "That's what he told me, and it's entirely consistent with the way those two carry on. I'm a little surprised he told you the truth tonight instead of making up another lie."

"Really? Why?"

"Because he doesn't like to talk about his work during the Troubles, and he doesn't want anyone to know he's still involved."

"With the IRA?"

"I told you, and he told you, too, none of them ever admits to membership."

"Do you ever get tired of being lied to by your father?"

"Once in a while. I try not to because it does no good. He'll never change. He loves to tell stories, not necessarily true ones."

Cam tightened his arm around her, and she cuddled closer to him.

"I can't stay," he said.

"I know."

"But I wish that I could."

"I know."

* * *

He had expected that he would fall asleep as soon as he got into bed. But, instead, he lay awake in the dark, remembering every detail of the evening with her. She had felt so tiny and vulnerable in his arms. He knew he shouldn't admit it, even to himself. But he was more deeply in love than he'd ever been in his life. He couldn't act on it. But he could allow himself to feel it. And it seemed all the more exotic and exciting because it had to be kept a secret. Eventually, he fell into half-waking, half-sleeping dreams of being with Raven.

CHAPTER THIRTY-EIGHT

Tuesday, March 26, 2019, 4212 Ocean Way, Coronado, California

The next morning, Cam called Jess as soon as he woke up at eight thirty. He told himself that his call wasn't driven by his sense of guilt for being with Raven the previous night. But he knew that wasn't entirely true.

"Sorry my phone was off when you called," Jess said. "We went to bed early."

"How are things there?" Cam asked.

"Actually, I'm not sure."

"What do you mean?" Cam couldn't keep the note of alarm out of his voice.

"Mother and I took the girls to a movie last night. Steph had to use the restroom halfway through, and I went with her. There was a man standing outside our theater. He looked as if he was waiting for someone. The restrooms are off the main lobby, and he followed us. Fortunately, when we came out, he had disappeared. But it made me nervous."

"Did Steph notice?"

"I don't think so."

"Any sign of anyone around your mother's house?"

"Not that I've seen. How long is this going to last, Cam? I didn't sleep well last night because I was worried about something happening to you or to us."

"I hope not long. Meg and I and Lachlan have all agreed that we need to push this to trial as soon as possible."

"Well, hurry."

"I will."

"And be careful."

* * *

He went downstairs to the kitchen and made himself a cup of coffee while wondering how guilty he should feel for lying to Jess about why he'd been unavailable last night. Very guilty, he decided. He wouldn't let it happen again.

He was heading back upstairs to get dressed when he heard the sound of a car in the driveway and looked out to see Nash's fiery-red Ferrari parked behind his behemoth of a Mercedes.

"Wow, big brother," Nash said when Cam opened the front door, "still in your pj's at ten o'clock in the morning?"

"Late work night," he lied. "Want some coffee?"

"Of course."

Cam made another cup and led the way to the den where they settled on the sofa.

Nash took a sip and smiled. "You do make a great cup of coffee. Tell me about this late work night. You weren't at the office because I tried to find you there."

"I went to interview someone who'd like to work with you. Kiara Blake."

"Oh, Nora's personal assistant. Did it take the whole night

to find out if she killed Nora?"

"You know it didn't. She's been cleared by the DA's investigator. Nora was alive when she and Sonia left for the Fairmont."

"So Sonia was there, too?"

"Apparently the whole entertainment world went to Nora's that day and night, begging her not to interfere with Lachlan's movie. Surely you haven't come to talk about Nora."

"Of course not, although the question of who killed her intrigues me. Have you given any thought to the gorgeous Raven?"

"She was in Dublin." *Did I say that too quickly?*

"You're right. I haven't come about Nora. It's Dad. He's going to put the house on the market this week."

"No!" Cam felt as if he'd been punched in the gut. "Couldn't you and Addie talk him out of it?"

Nash shook his head.

"But Mom hasn't even been gone for a full week. Even if he hates the house, he should give the rest of us time to say goodbye. All of our family memories are there."

"Addie and I told him. He wouldn't budge. He said it was better to rip the Band-Aid off instead of pulling it off a fraction of an inch at a time."

"God, he's so unfeeling!" Cam felt helpless and exasperated.

"Well, we talked about that at the T-ball game, remember? He's the cold, rational one with hard edges. Mom was the soft, dreamy, fairy-tale memories person."

"What about McKenna? Did she talk to him before she went back to London?"

"She told him he could do whatever he liked with the house."

"That's horrible!"

"Maybe, but that's what she said."

"Did you offer to buy it again?"

"I did, and he refused. I've considered having an agent buy it and then transferring the title to me."

"That's the only way we're going to save it," Cam said. "Let's do it. I'll chip in some cash, too. We could hold title jointly."

But Nash shook his head. "We could do it, but what would be the point? It would sit there empty, slowly decaying. Even if we tried to host family events there, they'd never be the same without Mom. Everything would just be a pale shadow of what it used to be."

"What are you saying we should do, then?"

"As horrible as it sounds, maybe Dad's right. We should let it go and figure out new ways and new places to celebrate as a family."

Cam didn't reply because he felt as if he'd been gut punched yet again.

"You're not okay with that, are you?"

"No, I'm not."

"Keeping the house won't bring her back."

"But it would keep her alive."

"No, it won't. She's gone, Cam."

"Now you sound like Dad."

"He's not wrong about everything."

"What does Addison think?"

"The same thing you do—that I've lost my mind and become like Dad."

"And that doesn't sway you?"

"No. But here's what I'll do if you and Addie want me to.

I'll go ahead with my plan to find someone to buy it and then transfer title to me. You and Addie can figure out how to take care of it. Those roses alone will require a full-time gardener."

"And you'll pay for that?"

"You can afford a gardener, big brother."

"I'll think about it."

"Well, make up your mind fast. If I don't snap it up immediately in disguise, someone else will. It's a very desirable property."

"And I know that only too well." Suddenly, tears welled up in his eyes. Nash reached out and put his hand on his shoulder. His eyes were wet, too.

"Why?" Cam demanded. "Why did she do it when she knows how much we all needed her?"

"I don't think she did it," Nash said. "From the beginning, I didn't think she killed herself, but everyone else was so convinced, I hesitated to say anything."

"What do you mean?"

"I mean, I think it was an accident. She wouldn't have left us on purpose."

"But the box? And those stupid receipts?"

"She was standing at the top of the stairs, holding the box. She was upset because of the way Dad had treated her over the concert. She was wearing a long nightgown. That's a perfect recipe for a trip and fall."

Cam wiped his eyes. "You're right. Somehow, that makes it bearable. But only just."

* * *

Cam had intended to go straight to the office, but he decided to spend a few minutes at his parents' house first. At least there was no For Sale sign yet, he noted with satisfaction as he pulled into the driveway. He headed for his mother's garden first. He half expected to see her in one of her flowery smocks, pruning the roses.

But, of course, she wasn't there. Cam wandered around, studying the plants. Some of them were vintage varieties and fabulously expensive. He was hurt and a bit angry to find them with yellowing leaves and falling petals. He grabbed the hose and began to water, and as he revived them, he began to cry as he remembered that they would have been last watered by his mother.

It took some time to cover the entire garden. Nash had been right. If they kept the house, they'd need a full-time gardener who actually knew how to grow roses. It wouldn't be easy to find someone like that. Most people in California who called themselves gardeners only knew how to cut things down. A real pro would be difficult to find and expensive. But he'd do it no matter what it took because losing these plants would be losing Jackie all over again.

When he finished watering, he sat down on a bench under one of the arches covered in some of the antique climbers and breathed in their light, sweet, musky scent warmed by the midmorning sun. Their aroma made him think of Raven and her exotic perfume and aroused his seesawing emotions of desire and guilt. He was carrying more emotional weight than he ever had in his life. Nash's theory of Jackie's death comforted him. An accident made far more sense than suicide, and it made

Blaine's decision to sell the house understandable and even bearable. That's why Nash was willing to go along with it, Cam realized.

He decided that he could accept it, too. And he decided that this was his opportunity to say goodbye. He walked across the garden and the drive and went up the back steps to the kitchen door. He used his key to open it and stepped inside.

The house had already begun to smell stale and musty even though it had been closed up for only a week. Blaine would need to open all the windows and air it all out before showing it to prospective buyers.

Cam stood in the kitchen for a few minutes, considering how the dark-blue tile complimented the warm-yellow walls. So like his mother to make this room feel cozy and inviting. He opened the cupboard where Jackie kept her teapot and mugs. Should he make a cup, the last ever cup of tea he'd ever have in this house? But he decided against it. Tea without Jackie wouldn't be comforting.

He studied all the little pictures she had placed on the kitchen countertops. There was one of the girls with Jess and one of Addison with her girls. He had thought Callie and Steph would have more time with their grandmother. Time to learn the names of all the roses in her garden. Time to learn exactly how to make the perfect cup of tea. But then, when no one had expected it, it had all ended.

Cam walked through the dining room and the den and the living room and then went upstairs and walked through all nine bedrooms. Suddenly, it hit him. There'd be no more Christmases with all the rooms full of family and friends and everyone running around in pajamas on Christmas Eve, challenging the children to listen for Santa's sleigh on the roof. His eyes filled with tears as he thought of all the holiday magic that had been lost forever.

The last bedroom was the master suite. The door was closed. He assumed his father had closed it when he left the house for what apparently was the last time. He stood with his hand on the knob for several seconds, wondering if it would be wrong to go in. No, not wrong, he decided. He needed to say goodbye to this place, too, where he'd so often been summoned for praise or correction or both.

The bed was made with his mother's pristine blue and white down comforter that looked like an invitation to sink into its luxury and snooze the night away. Her brushes and combs and perfume bottles were just as she had left them on her dressing table. Chanel No. 5 had been her favorite.

Cam sat down and ran his fingers over the combs and brushes. He opened the Chanel bottle and let the lush, warm scent overwhelm him. His eyes teared as he closed the bottle. He turned to the tall jewelry chest that stood next to the dressing table. Jackie had had a large collection of very expensive jewelry, some from Blaine but a great deal of it from her father who had doted on his only daughter. Cam opened the drawers and studied Jackie's creamy pearl necklaces in different lengths, her drop pearl earrings the size of small bird's eggs, her dazzling array of diamond and sapphire and ruby earrings, broaches, and rings. She'd long ago made a list of which pieces went to Addison, McKenna, and Jess. Even divided three ways, each would receive a substantial collection of jewels.

The top drawer was the smallest in the chest, and he opened it last. Twenty or more pairs of earrings set with diamonds, rubies, pearls, sapphires, and emeralds sparkled against the drawer's black velvet lining. The sight reminded Cam of standing at the massive windows of the Adair condo with Raven, being enchanted by the lights of the city at night.

His eyes were drawn to a pair of earrings the color of Raven's light-blue eyes. They were large pear-shaped aquamarines surrounded by two rows of tiny diamonds. Cam remembered Jackie wearing them to a firm Christmas party as the sole ornament for a simple black dress. The effect had been stunning. He picked up one and then the other and studied them in the palm of his hand. After a long minute, he opened another drawer where Jackie kept small travel pouches and took out a small dark-blue velvet drawstring bag. He slipped the earrings into it and put it into the inner pocket of his suit jacket. There was so much here that no one would notice they were gone, and even if someone did, he or she would assume that Jackie had lost them or given them away.

He closed the jewelry chest and reminded himself to warn Blaine to lock up the contents while the house was being shown or go ahead with the distribution to Addison, McKenna, and Jess. He carefully closed the door to the bedroom as he left and headed down the hall to the stairs. He paused at the top of the staircase and looked down, mentally testing Nash's accident theory. After a long minute of observation, he decided that Nash undoubtedly was right. It would be easy to trip on the hem of a long nightgown while holding a small box and navigating the steps at the same time.

Relieved, he went downstairs. But when he reached the front hall, he paused and decided to sit on the last few steps to say his farewell to the house and all his memories of it. His eyes fixed on the spot where he'd found Jackie's body. She'd hit the back of her head as she'd tumbled down, and Cam could still see faint traces of blood where her body had come to rest. He wondered why whoever had done the cleanup had not been able to get all of the stain out of the oak floor. But it was barely noticeable. He doubted a prospective buyer would notice.

He glanced at his watch and realized it was nearing noon. He should have been at the office an hour ago. His heart hurt as he got up and retraced his steps to the kitchen where he paused for one final look before he switched off the lights and closed the back door.

CHAPTER THIRTY-NINE

Tuesday, March 26, 2019, Offices of Goldstein, Miller, and Mahoney, Emerald Shapery Center

Cam's emotions were still raw when he arrived at Meg's office to talk about setting a trial date. Meg was sitting at her desk in her suit skirt and floppy-bow blouse, reading some papers, and Finn and his babysitter, a dark-haired girl who looked like a college student, were building a Lego tower at his little table in the corner.

Suddenly, the tower collapsed and Finn, in a fit of pique, picked up the one remaining intact piece and hit it against the table, scattering Lego blocks in all directions. "I'm bored with Legos!" He yelled as he began to cry. "I'm bored with this office! I don't want to be here anymore. I want to go home and watch TV!"

Cam paused in the doorway, surprised by the child's anger. Finn had always seemed calm and composed beyond his years and willing to go along with whatever Meg wanted him to do.

"You can't go home," Meg said coolly. "You have to stay with me." She appeared to be entirely unmoved by his anger, but her voice had an edge to it as if she were about to lose control, too, and she had very dark circles under her eyes. She wasn't sleeping, Cam reflected. He remembered that she'd seemed upset last Tuesday even before he'd told her that they were all in danger because of their association with Lachlan. He'd guessed it was something to do with her ex. He wished he could ask her about it without upsetting her.

"I could stay with Brianna," Finn said, sniveling now instead of crying outright. "I used to stay at home with her all the time. I'm bored here."

"Well, things are a little different right now," Meg said.

"I don't care. I'm tired of being here every day. I want to go home and watch TV."

At that moment, Meg looked up and saw Cam in the doorway.

"Sorry," she said. "He had a slight fever this morning and couldn't go to school, and now he's just cross."

"Nothing I haven't seen many times before," Cam told her. "There's a TV in the conference room on this floor, and I know it's empty because I just passed it. Why don't you let Finn watch it with his babysitter while we talk?"

Cam could see that she liked the idea, but she hesitated. "I wouldn't be able to see him in there."

"But he'll be with the sitter, and firm security doesn't let just anyone wander the halls."

"Please!" Finn put his little hands together in prayer as a gesture of supplication.

"Well, okay. But you have to stay in there with Brianna."

"Of course! Of course!" Finn gave Cam a look of four-year-old gratitude as he danced a victory dance next to the table covered with ruined Legos.

"Come on, then," Brianna said, holding out her hand. She, too, looked happy to be released from the jail that Meg's office had apparently become. "Let's go see what's on that you want to watch."

"Thank you," Meg said as Finn and Brianna disappeared down the hall.

"I know you're worried, but maybe you should ease up just a little," Cam suggested as he sat down at the big table in the corner of her office.

"I can't," Meg said as she sat down across from him. "He's all I have. I can't lose him."

Her statement made him think of Raven's fear of losing her father. *And you. Don't forget that she is afraid of losing you.* But he forced himself back to business.

"I talked to Raven last night. She called after Lachlan went out." *Of course, I'm not going to say I was alone with her at the condo.*

"I assume Lachlan went to Seamus's to confirm the alibi story he told you."

"Probably. But we can't very well tell a jury that he was involved in an IRA retribution counsel on the night Nora died."

"Agreed. What did Raven have to say? Could she talk him out of an immediate trial?"

"If only. She said that once he's made up his mind, he never changes it. She insisted that she's absolutely certain that Victoria is the killer."

"Did she point to any more evidence of that?"

"Not really. Just what she knows about her mother and her father."

"So it's all based on Raven's testimony?"

"At this point. What she has to say makes sense. Victoria hated Nora passionately because she stole Lachlan from her and damaged her academic career. Victoria has a financial stake in the sequel, and a motive to frame Lachlan for murder because if he goes to prison, she will be in charge of his literary estate."

"What we need is some evidence to corroborate that testimony."

"Right. Raven insists that the Range Rover that went through the gates at eleven forty was the one Victoria borrowed from Seamus, but so far nothing's shown up on the surveillance footage."

"Do we have the license plate number of the vehicle Victoria was using?"

"It's on the roster from Seamus that Raven gave us."

"Have you finished reviewing your share of the surveillance footage from the mansion? Have you seen anything on it that might help us identify that car as Victoria's?"

"No. Sorry. I haven't finished. So much has happened—"

"Don't apologize," Meg interrupted. "I'll go through the rest of the tapes. Finn and I are in every night for the present, anyway. I think there's some footage from the cameras at the guesthouse."

"Kiara said the car was parked there, waiting for them to leave. Maybe we'll get lucky and be able to see the plate on the Range Rover."

"And maybe it will be the one Victoria was driving." *And Raven will be ecstatic. And so will I because I can do something to make her happy.* "We haven't tried to talk to Victoria," Cam pointed out. "We don't know what her story is for that night."

"She's refused to meet with anyone from either side. I already tried to get her to agree to an interview," Meg told him.

"Well, then that leaves us guessing."

* * *

That night, Cam lay awake into the wee hours, thinking of being with Raven the evening before. He got up several times and went into the guest room and looked out, hoping to see the little gray Fiat under the streetlight. But, of course, she wasn't there.

After the last time, he went back to his own room and took the earrings out of the top drawer of his chest. He opened the black velvet pouch and studied them in the low light. *Your mother never meant for her to have them. Put them back tomorrow and no one will ever know.* But I can't do that.

CHAPTER FORTY

Wednesday, March 27, 2019, 4212 Ocean Way, Coronado, California

It was a strange dream. Cam was alone in the hallway of his parents' house. Jackie was standing at the top of the stairs in her nightgown. She was looking down at him and pointing to a small jewelry box that she was holding. She was asking him over and over to bring the earrings back. He kept trying to tell her that he didn't have them, but no words would come out of his mouth. He kept struggling to speak without success.

Then a phone was ringing somewhere. Jackie didn't seem to hear it. She kept standing there, pointing to the empty box. He wanted to tell her that he needed to answer his phone, but he remained unable to speak. All at once, Jackie began to fall toward him, hurling through the air as limp as a rag doll. Cam woke with a start to find that the ringing was real. It was two a.m., and it was Raven.

"Thank God, you answered." She was whispering. "They've broken into the condo. They've shot up the living room and are headed this way."

Cam's heart was pounding. "Where are you?"

"I'm in the closet in my bedroom. I'm the only one home.

Please call the police and come as soon as you can."

"Okay. Stay on the line. I'm going to put you on hold and call 911."

"No, I can't stay on. They've got equipment to detect a call. They probably already know I'm here. Come as fast as you can. And, if I don't see you again, I love you." She added the last words in a rush, and the line went dead.

Cam's hands were shaking as he called the police and then grabbed his keys and ran downstairs. He stopped only long enough to throw his Burberry over his pajamas and then headed out to his car.

He gunned it as fast as he dared through the deserted streets of the island and then opened it up full throttle when he hit the Bay Bridge. His heart seemed to accelerate with the car. *I can't lose her,* he chanted to himself over and over to keep out the horrible possibility that his fear had already become a reality. *You took Jackie,* he told the Universe. *That's more than enough.*

The sight of police cars, SWAT vans, and an ambulance swarming around the Pacific Gate building ratcheted Cam's fears higher. The closest parking spot was a block away. He jumped out of the car and ran as fast as he could toward the entrance.

The lobby was teaming with police in uniform, in plain clothes, and in SWAT gear. The officer at the door allowed him in after he explained that he was Lachlan's attorney and showed him his bar card, but the officer immediately lost interest in Cam when he received a call on his two-way radio.

An elevator opened, and three officers got out. Cam ran for the empty car and managed to squeeze in before the door closed. All the way to the penthouse, he prayed that Raven was okay.

When the doors opened, he stepped into the hallway which was full of yet more police in uniform and SWAT gear. The double doors to the condo were wide open. He scanned the crowd for Raven, his heart beating faster and faster. And then he saw her. Someone had pulled the hall bench out of the condo and placed it along the wall opposite the elevator. She was sitting there, wrapped in a gray blanket, surrounded by two EMTs.

Her face was pale and drawn, and he could see that she'd been crying. As he hurried toward her, she looked up, clearly relieved and overjoyed to see him. When he reached her, he quickly took her in his arms and held her tight until one of the EMTs said, "We need to check her blood pressure again. It was a bit low. Are you her husband?"

"No, the family's attorney."

"I'm fine," Raven insisted, but she sat down again and let the EMT put the cuff on. Cam sat down beside her, still holding her as tightly as he could with one arm.

For the next few seconds, the EMT knelt by Raven, intent on the numbers on the blood pressure monitor. Then he sat back on his heels, took off the armband, and said, "Okay, it's better now." He looked at Cam and said, "We were initially afraid she was going into shock."

"I'm fine," Raven repeated.

"Were you hit?" Cam asked.

"No. They fired the first rounds in the living room, and then they headed for Dad's bedroom and his study and fired more rounds in there. They were coming for me when the first sirens went off. Someone in the building heard the initial shots and called 911."

"Thank God." Cam hugged her again. "Did the police arrest them?"

"No." She shook her head. "They used the service elevator to get in and out. They were gone by the time the first police cars arrived."

"Any identification at all?"

She shook her head again. "The police said the security cameras picked them up, but they were wearing all black and ski masks. There were three of them." She shivered, and Cam wrapped the blanket around her a little tighter.

"Are you sure you're okay?"

"I'm sure. Really."

"Does Lachlan know? Where is he?"

"He went to Los Angeles this morning. It was something about the sequel. He didn't say that he'd be staying overnight."

"Have you been able to reach him?"

"My phone's in there, and I don't want to go back inside. Will you try?"

Cam speed-dialed Lachlan, but the call rolled to voicemail. "I think his phone is turned off," he told Raven.

"I'm worried that he was followed, and something has happened to him."

"It's not likely. After all, they thought he was at the condo. They came here looking for him."

She leaned her head on his shoulder and closed her eyes. "I'm still worried."

Cam gave her another hug. "Try not to. I wish this hadn't happened to you."

She opened her eyes and gave him a tiny smile. "I'll be okay as long as you're here."

At that moment, a slightly heavyset man wearing a navy windbreaker, blue jeans, and Nikes approached them.

"I'm Detective Sanchez, Ms. Adair. I'm in charge of the investigation into what happened tonight."

Cam released Raven and stood up. "I'm Cameron Rhodes, the Adairs' attorney. Could we put off taking Ms. Adair's statement? She needs some rest. Here's my card. If you get in touch with me tomorrow, we can work out a time for her to be available." Cam took a business card out of his wallet and handed it to the detective.

"That will be fine." The detective handed him his own card. "The forensic team is going to be here for a while yet. As soon as the medics clear you, you can go, Ms. Adair. Do you know where Mr. Adair is?"

"He's in Los Angeles," Cam said. "He's not expected back tonight."

"Then we'll talk to him, too, whenever he becomes available."

* * *

After the hubbub and chaos at the condo, stepping into his house's dark, utter stillness was like stepping into another world. Raven stood in the hall which was lit by a single lamp on a small antique table in the corner and stared at the surroundings like someone in a trance. Cam watched her closely as he hung his coat in the closet and took out one of his sweaters for her.

"Are you all right?" he asked. "Here, give me that and put this on." He gently took the blanket from her and helped her slip his dark-blue sweater over her black silk pajamas. She hadn't wanted to go back into the condo for additional clothes before they left.

She accepted his help with the sweater but still said nothing. She seemed to be drinking in every detail of the house. Cam began to worry that the EMTs had been wrong to accept her refusal to be checked out at the hospital.

Just when he was about to suggest an ER visit after all, she shifted her gaze from the house to his face and said, "It's just as I pictured it when I sat outside at night, hoping for a glimpse of you."

He put his arm around her and asked, "Would you like to try to sleep now or would you like a drink first?"

"A drink. Whiskey if you have any."

Still keeping his arm around her, he walked her into the living room and wrapped her in a quilt as she settled on the couch. He opened the drinks cabinet and poured a larger whiskey for her than the one he poured for himself.

"Here."

"Thanks."

He sat down beside her, and she snuggled against him and laid her head on his shoulder. She sipped her drink but said nothing. Cam could see her eyes drooping, and he expected her to fall asleep immediately.

But just as he began to nod off himself, she said softly, "All I could think about in that closet when I heard the gunshots was what if I could never see you again."

He hugged her hard. "Don't think about it anymore. It didn't happen."

She was quiet again, and he thought she'd fallen asleep at last. But after a few minutes, she looked up at him, and he could see the tears on her lashes as she said, "But it will happen. One day, it will happen."

His heart hurt. He kissed the top of her head lightly and stroked her hair as he held her. Finally, he said, "You don't know that for sure, and right now, you need some sleep. Let's go upstairs."

He kept his arm around her as they navigated the steps, and he led the way to the guest room. He switched on a low light by the bed and turned it down for her and plumped the pillows as she watched, still wrapped in the quilt.

"Here," he said. "It's all ready for you. Are you cold? Do you want to keep the quilt?"

"No, just your sweater." She handed him the quilt and lay down. He pulled the covers over her tiny frame and reached over to turn out the light. But her hand on his stopped him.

"Do you want me to leave the light on?"

"No. I want you to stay. I'm terrified of being alone."

"Okay." He switched off the light and went around to the other side of the bed. *I'll stay until she falls asleep, and then I'll leave.* She turned away from him and snuggled her back against his chest, and he put his arms around her.

After a few minutes, her breathing became regular, and Cam thought that she was asleep. But as he began to let go of her, she grabbed his arm and held on frantically. "Don't leave. I'm afraid."

He kissed the hand that gripped his arm and put his own around her again. "I'm still here. Now go to sleep."

As he waited for her breathing to become regular again, he pictured her standing fearlessly in the path of his car that first night at the guesthouse. He'd believed that she was incapable of fear. But he'd been wrong.

CHAPTER FORTY-ONE

Wednesday, March 27, 2019, 4212 Ocean Way, Coronado, California

Cam woke at eight and lay quietly without moving for a few minutes, watching Raven as she slept. She looked like a child curled up with one hand tucked under the pillow, her legs drawn up in a protective pose. Her long dark lashes and her very dark hair highlighted her perfect pale complexion. Cam felt a tremendous wave of love and protectiveness wash over him. He reached over and straightened the blanket that covered her. Then he began to ease himself out of bed, trying not to wake her, but as soon as he moved, her lids fluttered. He went still again, hoping she'd stay asleep, but in a moment, her eyes opened fully and took in her surroundings. They went from the ceiling to the clock on the bedside table to the chair across the room and to the window beside it. Then she turned her head, and her eyes rested on Cam.

"I was trying not to wake you," he said.

"I know."

"Wouldn't you like to sleep a little longer?"

"Not now. Where were you going?"

"To call the office. I need to make sure Meg and Finn are

okay and warn them to be careful. I won't be long."

She nodded. "What about my father?"

Cam picked up his phone on the bedside table and scanned the calls and messages. "He hasn't called me back. I'll try now." He speed-dialed Lachlan, but the call rolled to voicemail. "His phone's still off," Cam reported.

She sighed and closed her eyes. He reached out and squeezed her hand. "Try not to worry."

She opened them again, two clear pools of sky blue. Cam thought of the aquamarines in the velvet pouch in his room.

"It's impossible not to," she said.

"Well, rest for now. When I talk to Meg, I'll see if she's heard anything."

On impulse, he leaned over and kissed her lightly on the forehead. Then he got up, pulled the cover around her snugly, and went down the hall to his own room to call Meg.

"Are you at the office?" he asked when she answered. "And is Finn with you?"

"I just got here. I dropped him at school. I'm picking him up at two as usual."

"I think you should go and get him and keep him with you today."

"Has something else happened?" The fear in her voice was palpable.

"Yes." And he proceeded to tell her about the incident at the Adair condo. "Raven's in the guest room. She was terrified, of course, and she didn't want to be alone, and she's worried about Lachlan. He went to Los Angeles yesterday and hasn't been heard from since. Has anyone there heard from him?"

"I haven't, but he wouldn't be likely to call me. Wouldn't he call Raven before you or me?"

"Yes, but she left her phone at the condo. The place is heavily damaged. She just wanted to get away from it. She came very close to being killed."

"Closer than the last time?"

Cam remembered that he'd lied about the first shooting. It was easier to go on lying. "Yes. I think one of us should let Hugh know what's going on. I can't leave Raven right now, so could you update him?"

"Of course. But first I'm going to pick up Finn."

When Cam hung up, he went back to the guest room to check on Raven. She was still curled up under the covers. Her eyes were closed, and she'd fallen asleep again. Relieved that she was resting, he went back to his own room and showered and put on his gray suit pants and a white shirt. He didn't feel like going to the office, and he didn't feel like wearing a suit, but it was likely that he'd be dealing with law enforcement today, so professional dress was best. At least he could wait to put on a tie.

He realized that Raven had no clean clothes, so he took one of Jess's many track suits to the guest bathroom for her to change into. Then he went down to the kitchen and made coffee. The same question had been spinning through his mind like a song on repeat ever since he woke up. Where would Raven be safe? *Not with Lachlan.*

As he was checking the refrigerator for eggs and breakfast potatoes, he looked up and saw Raven standing in the doorway. Her face was pale and drawn.

"I thought you had gone back to sleep."

"I tried, but I couldn't. I'm worried about Dad. Any word?"

"Not yet."

She burst into tears, and Cam hurried across the room and put his arms around her. She sobbed uncontrollably against his shoulder. He let her cry for a few minutes while he stroked her hair.

As she began to regain control of herself, he said softly, "It's going to be all right."

She looked up and wiped at her eyes with her hands. "I'm sorry."

"You don't have to be." *How can I keep her safe?*

"I haven't thought about life without my father. He's the one whose always been there when I needed someone."

"Are you sure that's true?" Cam asked gently.

"Of course." Her eyes said his suggestion troubled her.

"But you've been nearly killed twice because he's so absorbed in making a movie that he's been willing to leave you alone at a very dangerous time. He's not the one being shot at, Raven. You are."

She closed her eyes for a moment, and when she opened them, Cam could see new tears on her long, dark lashes. "We don't know that for sure. Yet."

"Where was he staying in Los Angeles? We could call his hotel."

"He didn't mention a hotel. He said he'd be back by suppertime, but Dad often changes his mind about when he comes home."

"Was he with Seamus?"

"I don't think so. He said this trip was about the movie."

"Why don't you take a shower? I've put some of Jess's clothes out for you. They won't fit, but at least you can change into something fresh. And I'll have coffee and eggs ready when you're finished."

"Okay. Thanks." She gave him a wan smile, and he released her.

She started to turn away, but she turned back and said, "You're dressed for the office. Do you have to go?"

"Are you afraid to be here alone?"

"Yes, terrified."

"I won't be gone very long. I still have to set up a time for the police to talk to you."

"Will that be today?"

"I'll try to keep it from being today."

"Okay. Thanks."

She turned away again, but stopped and looked back at him and said, "I can't go back to the condo."

"I know. You said that last night. Besides, it's too damaged from what I saw."

"I mean, I can't go back there at all, even to get my things."

"I understand. I'll find a way to get them for you."

He watched her turn and go down the hall toward the stairs. His too-large sweater overwhelmed her small frame and made him think of his daughters when they played dress-up in Jess's clothes. His heart ached with love and sympathy, and then he felt the familiar tug of guilt because he had daughters and a wife, and he wasn't supposed to feel this way. *But he did, and how could he keep her safe?*

He had just finished grinding coffee beans when his phone began to ring. Lachlan at last.

"Where's my girl?" he demanded when Cam answered. "I've called and called and she doesn't answer."

The question aroused his ire. "She's safe, no thanks to you."

"What do you mean?"

"Where are you? Don't you know what happened at your condo last night?"

"I'm still in LA. I, uh, decided to stay over."

"You're just some sort of tomcat with no thought for anyone else, aren't you?"

"I've never said that I could resist the invitation of a beautiful woman."

"What in the world were you thinking when you left Raven alone again knowing there are people everywhere it seems who want to kill all of us?"

"I thought I'd be back by supper. And I thought she'd be safe at home. Was there another gunman?"

"Three, in fact. They shot up the condo. Raven narrowly missed being killed. If the police hadn't shown up when they did, she'd be dead." Cam's voice broke at the thought of the double loss of Raven and his mother.

"Oh, God! Seamus and I thought they'd left town. But she's okay? Where is she? Why hasn't she answered her phone?"

"Because her phone is still at the condo. I brought her to my house. She called me while the gunmen were still there. I didn't know if she'd made it until I got there. She was terrified. I couldn't leave her alone."

"Oh, God!" Lachlan said again. "Can you put her on?"

"She's upstairs in the shower at the moment. She'll be relieved to hear from you. I'll have her call you as soon as she comes down."

"And I need to see her."

"And the police will want to talk to both of you. I'll text you my home address. Meet us here."

"Got it. Will be there in a couple of hours. And I'll do a better job of protecting her."

"No, you won't. I'm keeping her here with me."

And how are you going to keep that promise?

CHAPTER FORTY-TWO

Wednesday, March 27, 2019, 4212 Ocean Way, Coronado, California

"Lachlan's on his way," he told Raven when she came down after her shower. Once again, she seemed childlike and vulnerable in the clothes that didn't fit. "He called from Los Angeles. I told him what happened last night."

She looked relieved.

"Here, sit down." He pointed to the breakfast room off the kitchen. "The eggs and potatoes are ready. And I've made fresh coffee."

"Thanks." She took one of the two places that he'd laid at the table and dug into the food. He was glad to see that she was hungry.

"Are you leaving after breakfast?" she asked after a few bites.

"I'll stay until your father comes."

"Did he say why he didn't come back last night?"

Cam's anger flared. "Do I really have to tell you?"

She considered the matter thoughtfully between bites of scrambled eggs. Then she said, "No, of course not. He met a woman. The usual."

"I can't forgive him," Cam said. "He knew you were in danger."

She reached out and put her hand over his. "Don't, Cam. He can't change. If he could, he'd still be with Sinead."

"What do you mean?"

"I mean that's the great tragedy of his life. She was and still is his only love, yet he couldn't be faithful to her. He can't resist temptation, even when he wants to."

"Even when your life is at stake?"

"He didn't know my life was in danger."

"Yes, he did!" Cam's anger took hold again. "He knew the night you got shot. And nothing's changed since then."

Raven sighed and stroked his hand gently. "He'll do better now."

"I'm not giving him the chance," Cam said. "You're going to stay here with me."

She took back her hand and studied him for a few seconds with her clear blue eyes. Then she leaned over and kissed him softly on the cheek and said, "You know that's impossible."

"I don't care."

"Yes, you do. You have—"

"Don't tell me what I have. I know what I have, and what I don't have. And I know what I can't afford to lose." *Oh, God. What am I saying? What am I doing?*

* * *

Wednesday, March 27, 2019, Offices of Goldstein, Miller, and Mahoney, Emerald Shapery Center

Cam found a summons to Hugh's penthouse office on the thirtieth floor in Meg's handwriting in the middle of his desk when he arrived at noon. There were also messages from Detective Sanchez about interviewing the Adairs. Meeting with Hugh was the obvious priority.

"Come in, come in," Hugh said when Cam appeared in his doorway. He was sitting at his desk eating a salad from a plastic container.

"I can come back," Cam offered. "I didn't mean to interrupt your lunch."

"You're not interrupting. Horrible stuff unless you're a rabbit." He closed the lid and got up and motioned for Cam to join him on the sofa. He wasn't as heavy as he'd been in the old days when he'd been the most famous plaintiff's attorney in America bringing in multimillion-dollar verdicts month after month and destroying anyone and anything in his way, Cam reflected. The Andrews-Cooper Innocence Project that he had founded with Kathryn Andrews and his daughter Erin had changed his health habits as well as his work habits. He was much more approachable than formerly, although he was still capable of making unreasonable demands on everyone at Goldstein, Miller.

"Meg told me about what's been going on with the Adairs, and I told her to tell you to come and see me as soon as you got in. She's worried about Finn, and she says that you've sent Jess and the girls to Baltimore," Hugh began.

"That's right."

"And all this violence is coming from who or what?"

"Lachlan says he has enemies from his IRA days. Actually, this case has been dangerous since day one. Someone tried to break into the guesthouse at Rancho Santa Fe the night you sent me out there to talk to Raven. She shrugged it off as someone after her paintings and Lachlan's guns, but I think every one of these attacks has been an attempt to kill one or both of the Adairs."

"And not one suspect has been identified?"

"Not one."

"How close are you and Meg to trial?"

"Closer than we'd like to be. The Adairs are demanding that we go to trial immediately. But we still don't have a defense for Lachlan."

"Nothing?"

"Nothing we feel we can rely on. He's not a particularly truthful client. At first, he claimed he was sleeping with a student in Boston. But then the district attorney proved that he was in San Diego on the night Nora died. Then he claimed to be drinking at the bar in his hotel with his longtime sidekick at the time of her death. Recently, Meg and I have learned that he wasn't at the bar."

"Where was he?" Hugh raised his eyebrows.

"He claims he was at Seamus O'Malley's offices in the midst of a secret meeting authorizing the execution of an IRA snitch. Not exactly an alibi we can present to a jury."

"I thought the IRA wasn't active anymore."

"According to Raven, they're not bombing buildings or assassinating British sympathizers, but they are still a political organization. Lachlan is a legend because of his work during the Troubles in the early sixties and seventies."

"Meg said the Irish papers were full of angry editorials because he's going on trial for murder here. So you're gambling you'll have a defense by the time of his trial?"

"Exactly."

"It's a high-profile case that we don't want to lose, Cam."

"Meg and I are only too aware of that."

"I gather the Adairs can't go back to their condo?"

"Correct. The gunmen went through the place shooting at will with a ton of ammunition. Raven was there at the time, and she refuses to go back even to get her belongings."

"So are they going to stay in the house in Rancho Santa Fe?"

Cam shook his head. "Raven's still at my house. I had no other place to take her last night. Lachlan returned from LA just as I was leaving to come here. He says he was up there to talk about the movie. He's going to stay with Seamus who has a house in La Jolla."

"And Raven?"

"She can't be alone at the Rancho Sante Fe house, and I don't want her with Seamus and Lachlan."

Hugh raised his eyebrows. "But why?"

"Because Lachlan has been careless about protecting her. She's been wounded once and was nearly killed last night. He'll leave her alone unprotected again."

"So would a downtown hotel be better? The firm could order extra security."

"I'd rather have her where I could check on her. I was thinking a suite at the Hotel Del."

"I've got a better idea," Hugh said. "Erin's cottage is empty. She's on assignment for the Innocence Project in Virginia. Her place is very close to you, and it has state-of-the-art security. And I'll hire a some off-duty cops for extra protection."

"That would work." Cam was careful not to show any emotion about the arrangement.

"Good. Then I'll send some messengers to pack up her things and take them to Erin's. She can sleep there tonight."

CHAPTER FORTY-THREE

Wednesday, March 27, 2019, 910 Flora Avenue, Coronado, California

At midnight, he could hear the ocean as he lay awake next to Raven in the cottage's master bedroom. In the end, it all been much easier than he'd imagined. There had been no dramatic moment of decision or earnest discussion about whether what they were about to do was right or wrong. To the contrary, their evening had proceeded as if it had all happened a hundred times before.

They'd arrived at Erin's cottage at nine o'clock. Even in the dark, it looked as if it were straight out of a fairy tale. It was painted white and accented with green shutters. Roses spilled from the window boxes and climbed happily along the picket fence that surrounded the pocket handkerchief-sized yard.

Hugh's minions had assembled Raven's belongings in boxes in one of the two bedrooms. As they were enjoying a glass of wine in the cozy living room decked out in floral chintz slip-covered furniture, a delivery truck drove up and deposited dinner from the Hotel Del's kitchens at the front door. They'd eaten it by candlelight in the dining room on Erin's gleaming cherry table for two with more wine, and after that, it had been the most natural thing in the world to move on to the inviting queen-sized bed in the master bedroom.

Now, as he listened to the soft roar of the surf, he felt the first prick of conscience as he thought of Jess and his daughters, who, at that moment, seemed as remote as the stars. He knew that he loved them, but he knew that he loved Raven, too. How could he ever reconcile these feelings?

Suddenly, he thought of Blaine, and he wished that he had actually had an affair. The reality of a paternal affair would have helped Cam justify himself at this moment. And it would have made his mother's death meaningful instead of the act of a woman left alone too often to delude herself that her husband was being unfaithful.

Beside him, Raven stirred in her sleep. Cam turned and put both arms around her and pulled her closer. She responded with a sleepy kiss and a little sigh of contentment. He stroked her hair softly and thought of how he'd longed from the beginning to run his fingers through her long dark locks. This had been inevitable, he told himself, from the first moment she'd appeared like some magical being in front of his Mercedes on that cold February day. A force drew them together that he could not name or resist. So, for now, right and wrong did not matter. He only knew that he loved her, and that, for the present, that was everything.

* * *

Thursday, March 28, 2019, 910 Flora Avenue, Coronado, California

The hard light of midmorning and the sound of his phone ringing in another room woke Cam on Thursday. Panic seized him because Raven's side of the bed was empty. He pulled on the pants he'd discarded the night before and his T-shirt and hurried to find her.

He didn't have to go far. Wrapped in a dark-blue silk robe, she was curled up amid the flowery pillows on the sofa, sipping coffee and studying the view from the window.

"There you are at last," she said when he appeared. "Your phone kept ringing, and I wondered if I should wake you. But I decided you needed your sleep."

Cam glanced at the gold carriage clock on the mantel. Ten o'clock. He had been tired. He walked over to the dining room table where he'd left his phone the night before and looked to see who'd been calling. Nash.

"It's my brother. I'd better see what he wants."

"I'll make some breakfast. The messengers from your firm left us the basics."

She got up and walked toward him and lifted her face for him to kiss before turning toward the tiny kitchen. He went back to the bedroom and sat down on the bed and called Nash.

"Finally. You're answering your phone," he said when he answered.

"I'm sorry. I slept in."

"Are you at your house? I went by this morning at six thirty, but your car wasn't in the driveway."

Oh, God! I didn't expect anyone to come looking for me.

"It was in the garage. I've noticed that the sun is beginning to damage the paint." *A plausible lie, at least.* "Why were you looking for me so early? Are you still in San Diego?"

"I'm on the road to LA as we speak. That's why I came looking for you early. I had promised Dad that I'd meet the realtor at the house this morning to let her go over what needs to be fixed before putting it on the market. But my agent set up a big audition for me this afternoon for a part I really want, and it's my only chance to try for it. So I was hoping you'd deal with the realtor. Her name is Marjorie Wilson. Nice, middle-aged lady. She was a member of Mom's book club. I know you're opposed to selling it but—"

"I'm not anymore. I spent some time there on Tuesday and made peace with everything. I'm okay with letting it go."

"That's a relief because Addison and McKenna still want to keep it."

"I thought McKenna said Dad could do whatever he wanted."

"She changed her mind and joined Addie in opposing the sale."

"Well, Dad has the final say. What time was I supposed to meet her?"

"Right now. But I called and told her that I couldn't get in touch with you. Could you be there in an hour?"

Cam realized he'd have to go home to get fresh clothes, but his parents' house was only minutes away.

"Sure."

"Okay, eleven thirty it is then."

* * *

Raven had breakfast ready when he went back into the living room. She put two plates of eggs and toast on the table in the dining room and said, "Sit and eat while it's hot. I'll fetch the coffee."

She was back in a few seconds with two steaming mugs and handed him one.

He took a sip of the rich, dark brew, sighed contentedly, and smiled as he watched her sit down opposite him and begin on her own breakfast.

Her clear eyes met his. "What are you smiling about?"

"About how wonderful it is to be here with you at this exact minute."

"I gather you have to go to the office at some point."

"I do. But first I have to go home and get clean clothes and meet the realtor at my parents' house. My father's in a hurry to sell it."

"Isn't it too soon?"

"I thought so at first, but now I think it will help all of us move on. Will you be all right here today alone?"

"Yes, but this isn't a proper Irish breakfast. No sausages or potatoes. I need to go to the market."

"One of the bodyguards Hugh hired can take you."

"I was going to have Dad and Seamus arrange for someone to bring my car here."

"Well, of course you can do that. But you shouldn't be out alone, so the bodyguard will go with you."

She smiled and leaned across the table and stroked his cheek. "It's so amazing to be taken care of this way."

He picked up her hand and kissed it lightly. "You should have always been protected. I can't forgive Lachlan for being so careless."

"When do Da and I have to talk to the police?"

"This afternoon at three. Detective Sanchez agreed to come to my office. It won't last long. I don't think either of you have much to say. The bodyguard will drive you there, too."

"There's nothing I can tell the detective. I heard them, but I never saw them."

"Do you think these are the same people who tried to break into the guesthouse that first night when Hugh sent me to Rancho Santa Fe to see you?"

"I couldn't say. It's possible, of course. But Lachlan has a lot of enemies, as he's told you."

"So separate attacks from separate sources?"

"He's so exposed right now because he's going to go on trial. I wouldn't be surprised if more than one old enemy has seen his chance and tried to take it."

Cam nodded. "The detective is going to be disappointed. He will want you or Lachlan to point a finger at a suspect."

"I know, but neither of us can."

Cam finished breakfast and gathered up his clothes from the previous day. When he came back into the living room, Raven was clearing the breakfast dishes.

She stopped when she saw him in the doorway. "Are you leaving now?"

"Yes, I have to be at my parents' place by eleven thirty. I've just got time to go home and put on clean clothes."

He saw disappointment in her eyes as she followed him to the front door. Before he opened it, he turned to her and pulled her to him and held her tightly.

"Be safe while I'm gone."

"I will."

"See you this afternoon." He gave her a long kiss and turned to open the door.

"Cam, wait!"

He turned back to her, and she gently pulled his face closer and kissed him again. "I want to make the most of the time we have," she said when she let him go. He saw tears in her eyes.

"We will," he said. "I promise we will."

CHAPTER FORTY-FOUR

Thursday, March 28, 2019, Caminito Bella Luna, Coronado, California

Marjorie Wilson was already waiting for Cam when he arrived. She was standing by the back door with a tall man in jeans and a red windbreaker who was also carrying a camera. She was toying with a large ring full of keys, so Cam wondered if she intended to go into the house without him.

"Sorry I'm late," he said as he hurried up the steps to join them by the door.

"You're not," Marjorie said. "We're a tiny bit early. This is Roger Milton of Milton Inspections. He's here to make a list of what needs to be repaired before the house goes on the market."

Roger offered his hand, and Cam shook it. Then he asked Marjorie, "Do you have a key?"

"Yes, your father gave me a set. But we were waiting for you regardless. Are you ready to go in?"

Cam thought he was ready because he'd said his personal goodbyes on Tuesday, but he felt overwhelmed by sadness as soon as the three of them stepped into the kitchen. The air inside felt even more heavy and stale than it had felt on Tuesday, and the thin layer of dust that had settled over everything was more noticeable than before. His heart hurt because these were just more signs that Jackie was gone and never coming back.

Marjorie and Roger walked toward the front of the house. Cam remained in the kitchen, picturing Jackie taking out the tea things to make tea for everyone. He could hear the realtor and the inspector's voices rising and falling as they discussed some problem that they found in the entry hall. Then they were silent while a camera's shutter clicked, and then the sound of their footsteps indicated they had moved on to the living room.

Cam walked around the kitchen, studying the little pictures of Jess and the girls and listening to the low hum of voices as Marjorie and the inspector progressed through the first floor of the house. The sight of Steph and Callie's bright smiles that Jackie had treasured enough to keep in this place where she herself had spent so many hours plunged the guilt knife into Cam's gut and twisted it over and over as he thought of the joy he'd felt at being with Raven last night. Yet, even as he berated himself for betraying his daughters and his wife, he also saw in his mind's eye Raven's white-faced terror as he'd held her and comforted her over the past couple of days. How could something as wrong as being unfaithful to his marriage and his family seem not wrong at all because a woman he loved was in danger? But this was a question he knew that he'd never be able to answer.

He heard footsteps behind him, and he turned away from the pictures on the counter to find Marjorie standing in the doorway. There were tears in her eyes.

"Are you okay?" he asked.

She walked into the kitchen and came to stand beside him. "No, not really. Sorry. I've been in this house so many times for book club and your mother's parties, and it hurts so much to see it like this without her."

Cam nodded, only too aware of the tears in his own eyes. "There's nothing to be sorry for. We all miss her."

"She was so bright and vivacious. So *alive*. It just doesn't seem possible that she would have chosen to end her life."

"She didn't," Cam said. "It wasn't suicide."

"What? But your father said—"

"I know what he said. But he's wrong. Mother's fall was an accident. She never meant to leave us. My brother Nash and I figured it all out. She was upset that night, and she was wearing a long nightgown. She was coming downstairs for something, and she tripped and fell. We all blame ourselves because we left her alone knowing that she was very emotional about a family issue, but she would never have chosen to leave us voluntarily. Her family was everything to her."

"That makes a lot more sense," Marjorie agreed. "In all the years that I knew Jackie, nothing was more important to her than the four of you and Blaine. And I'm glad to hear this news for another reason."

"What's that?"

"We will have to disclose to prospective buyers that a death took place in the house. An accidental fall isn't going to hurt the value as much as suicide would have."

"That sounds so crass."

"It does. But it's true. Your father says that your sisters are opposed to putting it on the market."

"They are. But McKenna lives in London, and Addison has been settled in Mission Hills for a long time. I don't think either of them really wants to buy the house and live in it."

"I understand," Marjorie said. "I realize how hard this must be for all of you."

"How long before we can list it?"

"A couple of weeks, I think. Roger hasn't found much that the family should repair. You'll have to remove all of the furnishings, of course."

"But why? My mother decorated this house beautifully. It won't be the same without her things."

"That's just the point," Marjorie said. "It will sell faster with rental furniture staged to make the house seem impersonal."

"That's a truly horrible idea."

"It's in the contract your father signed. You and your siblings will have to come and get what you want to keep right away."

"Mother made a list of who gets what." *A list that didn't include her aquamarine earrings going to Raven Adair.*

"Then it will be even easier to empty the house in preparation for the sale."

* * *

Thursday, March 28, 2019, Offices of Goldstein, Miller, and Mahoney, Emerald Shapery Center

"Thank God, Cam. I've been trying to reach you."

He had wondered how he would feel the first time he talked to Jess after sleeping with Raven. The answer was simple: overwhelmingly guilty.

"Sorry. A couple of gunmen shot up the Adair condo on Wednesday night. There's been a lot to do because of that."

"That's horrible. Is everyone safe?"

"The Adairs are fine. Lachlan wasn't home when the gunman broke in, but Raven was."

"Was she hurt?"

"No, but very shaken up."

"What's going on there? Have you or the girls been followed by any strangers again?"

"No. Mother and I have decided that was a coincidence, but it's hard not to be overly concerned."

"I'm not sure you are overly concerned," Cam said. "Don't let your guard down."

"I won't."

"Dad's hired a realtor to sell the house. I had to go over there this morning for a house inspection. It's Marjorie Wilson. I think you know her from book club."

"Yes. I like her. Jackie would be happy with that choice. Are you okay with letting it go?"

"I wasn't at first, but now I agree with Dad and Nash. We all need to move on. Addie and McKenna don't agree."

"But they're outvoted."

"I wouldn't put it that way. Dad's vote is the only one that counts."

"When is it going to be listed for sale?"

"In a couple of weeks. Marjorie says we have to get all of Mom's things out right away."

"Oh, God! That seems so harsh."

"She insists. I know Mom had a list of who gets what. Do you know where it is?"

"Addison has it. Will I be back before you start dividing it all up?"

"Probably not."

"Well, don't give anything away."

"I won't."

"I'll make room for all of it. The girls will want their grandmother's belongings someday. If you don't know what to do with anything, put it in the garage until I get back."

"Of course. I've got to go to work now."

"Love you."

"I love you, too."

Cam ended the call and studied his phone for a few minutes. Jess's comments about his inheritance had reminded him that his life was one seamless, family piece without room for his feelings for anyone other than his wife and his children. And yet he was deeply, impossibly in love with Raven Adair.

CHAPTER FORTY-FIVE

Thursday, March 28, 2019, Offices of Goldstein, Miller, and Mahoney, Emerald Shapery Center

"Any luck on identifying the Range Rover on the surveillance tapes?" Cam asked at five o'clock that afternoon. He and Meg were seated at the conference table in her office. Lachlan and Raven had just finished their interview with Detective Sanchez, and Cam had returned to Meg's office after escorting them to their waiting cars driven by bodyguards hired by the firm. Lachlan was returning to Seamus's house in La Jolla, and Raven was going back to Erin's cottage where she would be waiting for Cam when he finished his meeting with Meg. Finn and his babysitter had been dispatched to the TV in the conference room to keep him entertained.

"Not yet. And I'm almost at the end of what we have."

"Should I take some back and help out?"

"No, I'll probably finish them over the weekend. There aren't many left."

"So if we can't identify the car, where does that leave us?"

"With speculation about who was in it."

"What about the slip and fall expert? Did you find someone?"

"Dr. Marvin Talbot. He's a Ph.D. forensic kinesiologist. He teaches at UCSD. I sent him your file of photos because it was more complete than mine."

"Do you have a report from him?"

"Not yet. I called yesterday and left a message to let him know we are closer to trial than we originally thought we'd be."

Suddenly, Cam heard someone running down the hall toward them. A moment later, the door to Meg's office burst open, and Finn appeared with Brianna chasing him.

To Cam's surprise, Finn ran to him and, in one swift movement, threw his arms around him and buried his head in his shoulder. Instinctively, Cam put his arms around the little boy.

Meg looked shocked. She half rose from her seat to disentangle her son, but Cam held up one hand as he continued to comfort the child.

"It's okay," he told her. "Just give him a minute."

"I'm so sorry," Brianna said. "He was watching TV, and all of a sudden, he jumped up and ran."

Cam looked down and saw that Finn's face was streaked with tears. "It's okay," he soothed the child, patting him gently on the back. "It's okay."

But Finn pulled away from Cam's shoulder and said in one angry burst, "No, it's not okay! It can never be okay! My father doesn't want to see me anymore!"

When he finished, he hid his face again, this time against Cam's chest, and cried as if his heart was breaking.

"Here, let me take him." Meg stood up and came around to Cam and put out her arms to hold her son.

But Finn raised his face long enough to push her away and say, "No! I don't want you. It's all your fault!"

As Cam held the sobbing little boy, he felt as if every ounce of the child's grief was being poured into him as well. He sat still, rubbing Finn's back softly as he felt Finn's pain flood his own body.

Meg stood in front of him, her eyes full of tears, paralyzed by the magnitude of her child's suffering. Brianna sat down at Finn's miniature table in the corner and began to draw doodles on a piece of paper with a blue crayon.

After a bit, Finn's sobs began to ease. Cam lifted him up so that he was sitting in his lap. Meg handed him a wad of tissues, and Cam dabbed at the child's eyes.

"I know your mother loves you, Finn, more than anyone ever could," he began gently.

Finn regarded Meg blankly for a few seconds but said nothing.

Cam tried again. "And whatever has happened with your father, your mother is the one who has always kept you safe and who always will."

Finn sniffed and Cam wiped his eyes again. Then he said, "But I want to see my dad."

Meg looked uncomfortable, and Cam's heart went out to her. No matter how hard she tried, she couldn't leave the uncooperative ex behind.

"Finn, this isn't the time and place to decide all that," Cam said. "Grown-ups say a lot of things, and they change their minds. It's the end of the day, and your mother and all of us are very tired. I bet your mother has a special treat tonight to cheer you up."

Finn wiped his eyes again and looked at Meg expectantly.

"Let's go home and order burgers and fries and ice cream and watch *Sam and Tucker*."

Finn gave this a few seconds of thought. Then he said, "Okay." He extended his arms toward Meg and let her pick him up from Cam's lap. She held him close with her eyes closed for several seconds. Then she opened them and whispered over Finn's shoulder, "Thank you."

CHAPTER FORTY-SIX

Thursday, March 28, 2019, 910 Flora Avenue, Coronado, California

Cam was bone-weary, but he could not sleep. He lay awake in the dark next to Raven and concentrated on the soothing sound of the sea as he tried to block the disturbing thoughts that flew thick and fast through his mind.

First, and foremost, was the memory of Finn's grief. Cam still felt as if all of the child's sadness had poured into him and settled around his heart permanently.

Second was his joy at coming home to Raven that night which had been almost immediately dulled by the memory of his call with Jess that morning and her direction to keep everything that Jackie had left to them. It wasn't fair, Cam thought, that as much as he loved Raven, there were parts of his life that only Jess could share.

Third, although he would never abandon Callie and Steph the way that Finn's father had abandoned him, there was still the great grief that he would thrust on them if he left their family in favor of a life with Raven. Just as he had felt Finn's despair this afternoon, he could feel the terrible sadness that would break Callie and Steph's hearts if he followed his own. It wasn't fair, he told himself again, that the price of having the one love that he desperately wanted seemed to be too high.

"Why are you crying?" Raven had awakened and rolled over on her side to cuddle close to him. She gently wiped away a stray tear that had trickled down his cheek as she asked her question.

"I didn't realize that I was," he said. "I thought you were asleep."

"I'm not now. Can you tell me about it?"

"I don't know if I can."

"Try."

"This morning, the realtor my father hired walked through my mother's house with me, telling me about the preparations to sell it. She said we have to empty it of all of my mother's belongings. We have to make it bare and impersonal and remove all traces of the person who created our family in that house."

Raven leaned over and kissed him softly on the lips. "I never had a place like that to miss," she said. "But I can understand how much that hurts you."

He looked down at her in the dark and saw a tear on her cheek, too. He wiped it away gently and said, "And that makes me sad, too."

"What?"

"That you never had a home like the one Jackie made for us."

"It's okay."

"No, it isn't."

"So what will become of your mother's things?"

"The four of us will divide them. And Jess will decide where they fit into our house when she comes home. In the meantime, she told me to store them in the garage if I can't find a spot in the house myself."

"I'll help you do that," Raven said. "I'll help you find places for every single one."

The thought of sharing that bit of Jackie with her cheered him. "I'd like that."

She kissed him again on the lips and stroked his cheek softly. "I wish I'd met your mother. She sounds so special and amazing and loving."

He smiled. "She was all of those things. And I wish you'd met her, too."

"What else made you sad, today?"

"How do you know there's something else?"

"Because I love you."

It always sounded so easy and natural when she said it, as if there were no obstacles in the way of loving each other.

"Meg's little boy crawled in my lap this afternoon and cried his eyes out because his father, who's in New York, has said he isn't going to see him anymore. He's only four, and he's heartbroken."

"Everyone comes to you for comfort, don't they?"

Her comment made him smile. "I hadn't thought of it that way."

"But it's true."

"Maybe. I'm not sure."

"I am. But the little boy has his mother, doesn't he?"

"Absolutely. Meg adores him."

"Then that's all he needs. I had my father, and that was enough. He'll be okay."

"It didn't feel as if he'd be okay when I was holding him in my lap today. It felt as if he'd feel the loss of his dad for the rest of his life."

"Maybe. I don't know. I'm pretty sure losing Victoria by being sent away to boarding school in Ireland was better for me than being with her day and night."

She was quiet for a few minutes, and Cam thought she had nodded off to sleep again. But after a bit, she said, "And Finn made you think of your girls."

He felt himself tense up at the thought of trying to explain the conflict in his heart. He couldn't find any words to describe it, so he stayed silent.

She raised herself up on one elbow and looked deeply into his eyes. All the love in hers delighted him and yet broke his heart. She said, "You don't have to tell me. I know."

She lay down and laid her head on his chest. Once again, he thought that she'd drifted off to sleep, but once again her soft lilting voice wove its spell in the dark. "I envy them."

"Who?"

"Your wife and your girls." Her voice broke, and he realized that she was crying.

He took her fully in his arms and held her tight. Her grief seemed to pour into him, the way that Finn's had earlier, but this time he could find no comforting words for her or for himself.

CHAPTER FORTY-SEVEN

Friday, March 29, 2019, 910 Flora Avenue, Coronado, California

"Mr. Rhodes!"

As Cam headed toward his car at ten o'clock the next morning on his way to the office, one of the bodyguards came running toward him. The security people had set up their station just outside the picket fence that bordered the front yard. The bodyguard, a beefy guy wearing a black track suit, had opened the gate and was running up the driveway toward him.

"Wait, Mr. Rhodes! I have to talk to you!"

The urgency in his voice made Cam's stomach tighten. He gripped the driver's side door handle and braced himself for bad news.

The bodyguard was winded when he reached him, so Cam had to wait for him to speak. "Sorry."

"That's all right."

"My partner and I caught one of them sneaking around back at three a.m.," he said after he caught his breath.

Cam's blood ran cold. "We didn't hear anything inside."

"That's because he didn't get close enough to the house for you to hear him."

"So did you catch him? Is he in police custody?"

"Afraid not. He heard us coming and managed to disappear."

"Not even a glimpse of his face?"

"Nothing. He was dressed like the shooters who came to the condo: black clothes, black ski mask. The thing is, the guys at Mr. O'Malley's place also saw two guys over there at roughly the same time."

"And I'm guessing they got away, too."

He nodded.

"So no chance anyone at Seamus's place got any information on identification?"

"Correct."

Cam wished he didn't have to go to the office and leave Raven alone, but he didn't have a choice.

"I've got to go to work," he said, "but I'm worried about Ms. Adair."

"We're on it. After all, we didn't let anything happen last night."

"That's true. But whoever they are, they'll certainly be back."

"And we're prepared." He smiled, turned away, and jogged back down the drive to the improvised station where the other security guard waited.

Cam suddenly realized that he was still hanging on tightly to the door handle of his car. He started to open it and get in, but the image of the man in black creeping toward the back of the cottage last night wouldn't stop playing over and over in his head. What if something happened to Raven today while he was away? What if last night had been their last time together? He turned abruptly and hurried up the front steps.

He found her in the kitchen, putting the last of the breakfast dishes into the dishwasher. She looked up, surprised to see him. He hurried across the room, took her in his arms, and held her tightly to him.

"What's wrong?" she asked, freeing herself just enough to look up at him while he still held her close.

"The guys out front stopped another gunman around three this morning. He was headed for our back door. He was fully covered, like the ones who broke into the condo, so they couldn't get an ID. There were two more at Seamus's at about the same time."

He felt her shiver as he held her. "Are Dad and Seamus okay?"

"Yes. The guys over there were on their toes, too."

"I've got to call Dad to make sure he's all right."

He kissed her lightly on the top of her head. "I know. And I've got to get to the office. But they'll be back, Raven. And next time they might not give up and run away when they see the security people."

"I'm aware that's a risk."

"It's not a risk. It's a certainty."

She closed her eyes for a moment. When she opened them, she said, "I keep thinking of what it was like that night when we were crouching under that bench and bullets were flying all around us."

"I know. But try not to think about it."

"I wish you didn't have to leave."

"Me, too. But Meg and I have a lot of work to do if we are going to get your father's case to trial quickly. Promise me you'll stay in today. Don't go out."

"I have to go to the market, so I can make dinner for us."

"No. We should order in."

"I'd rather cook for you. I promise I'll take someone with me."

"Just to the store and back then. Promise me."

"I promise."

CHAPTER FORTY-EIGHT

Friday, March 29, 2019, Offices of Goldstein, Miller, and Mahoney, Emerald Shapery Center

When he reached his office, Meg was waiting for him.

"Where's Finn?" he asked as he put his briefcase and coffee down and turned on his computer. "Should we go back to your office to talk?"

"No, we can talk here. I let him go to school. I haven't seen anyone watching our house, and he's so bored here with Brianna. Why? Did something happen?"

"The security people spotted a gunman at Erin's place last night, and they saw a couple at Seamus's also. They escaped when they were discovered."

"What about at your house?"

"Nothing there." *It's a true statement even if a misleading one.*

"I don't think you and I are in the front line of fire," Meg said.

"Maybe not. But I'm keeping Jess and the girls in Baltimore until the trial is over. Are you sure you don't want Finn with them? The offer is still open."

"Thanks, but no. I'll pick him up after school today, and

Brianna will be here to keep an eye on him until it's time to go home. Thank you for talking him off the ledge yesterday. His father didn't say he wouldn't see him again. I made that decision."

"You don't have to explain to me."

"I know. But I wanted you to understand. I have to protect Finn. The situation with his father was just too confusing for him."

"I could see that. He's only four. His father's far away and only appears occasionally. Does this change your intention to move back to New York? If you don't want him to be hurt by his father's indifference, wouldn't it be worse for Finn if he knew that his father lived close by? Wouldn't it be better for both of you to stay here?"

"No, it wouldn't. We're going back just as soon as this case is over."

The tone of her voice said she wasn't prepared to share any more, and she quickly changed the subject back to business. "I've finished the surveillance tapes from the mansion, and I've got bad news."

Cam sat down and sipped his coffee. "I'm listening."

"There's nothing that identified a license plate for the Range Rover that arrived at eleven forty. I found the footage of it waiting by the guesthouse. The camera also picked up Sonia's car leaving just after midnight."

"Do you know if Axel has seen this?"

"Unfortunately, he has. He sent over a discovery update this morning with the changed time of death and a copy of the video that I found over the weekend."

"What is the new time of death?"

"Between twelve fifteen and one a.m."

"So Axel is going to say that it was Lachlan waiting by the guesthouse."

"Yes. He's noticed a hearing next Wednesday to amend the charges to include murder by lying in wait."

"Special circumstances murder is bad news. Is he seeking the death penalty?"

"No. Life without parole."

"Has he added Kiara as a potential prosecution witness?"

"No. He did send us a summary of their investigator's interview with her. There's nothing in it that's different from what she told you. But I doubt he would call her as a witness since she can't identify the occupant of the Range Rover. She's no help to his circumstantial evidence claim that it was Lachlan in the car."

"That's true," Cam agreed.

"Axel intends to ask for a trial date on Wednesday when he moves to add the special circumstance."

"Well, everyone wants this to be over," Cam observed. "But we don't have a defense for Lachlan other than to argue their circumstantial evidence doesn't prove he's the killer in the Range Rover."

"And I assume Lachlan is still opposed to asking for a continuance?"

"He is."

"Then relying on the weakness of the prosecution's circumstantial evidence might be the best we can do," Meg said. "After all, Seamus has a large fleet of black Range Rovers, and

Lachlan's not the only one with a motive to get rid of Nora, and the video doesn't show the parked car heading for the house after Sonia left."

"Victoria's motive is as strong as Lachlan's."

"But she won't talk to us, and even if she was willing, she's not going to admit she was in the car waiting by the guesthouse."

"I'm afraid you're right. But we haven't talked to Seamus, yet. Maybe he'll have something that will help us prove that it wasn't Lachlan's Range Rover on the guesthouse video."

"If he won't come to us, would you mind going to see him alone? After what you told me about last night, I don't feel comfortable leaving Finn and Brianna here without me."

"I agree. You should stay with them. I'll see if he's available this afternoon."

* * *

As soon as Meg left, Cam called Seamus's office and set up an interview through his assistant for one o'clock.

Just as he ended that call, his cell phone rang, and Nash said, "The meeting with Marjorie Wilson must have gone well. She's decreed that the house has to be emptied by Monday for staging."

"Oh, God! I was hoping she'd back down on that."

"Nope! And Dad's ecstatic."

"When's the official listing date?"

"I think a week from Monday if the four of us cooperate by taking everything out of the house this weekend."

"Do we have a choice?"

"Not really."

"Look, little brother, I was willing to sub for you with the realtor, but I cannot empty that house by myself in two days."

"Don't worry. That's not the plan."

"I'm relieved to hear that." *But I don't like it because this is going to interfere with my time with Raven. And I've got to be careful not to let anyone know what's really going on.*

"I've hired four trucks and ten movers who are going to show up at nine a.m. tomorrow morning. The only one of us who can't be there is McKenna, and Addison has agreed to put her share in a storage unit and keep an eye on it until she comes back to the States. I've made copies of Mom's list of who gets what. All you have to do is make sure your things wind up on the truck assigned to you and show the guys the way to your place when everything's loaded up."

"I'm impressed by your organization. What happens to anything that's left behind?"

"Dad's arranged for an auction house to pick up the remainder on Monday and auction it off at one of their sales."

The thought of strangers pawing over Jackie's treasures and bidding on them lodged like an arrow in Cam's heart. But the process was already underway, and there was nothing he could do to stop it. It was painful, but it was necessary, he told himself.

"All right. Nine in the morning. See you then, little brother."

CHAPTER FORTY-NINE

Friday, March 29, 2019, Celtic Analytics Campus in Rancho Bernardo, San Diego, California

Celtic Analytics occupied a huge campus in the upscale suburb of Rancho Bernardo. Seamus's office covered the entire top floor of the four-story building that housed the company's administrative staff. From this vantage point, he could see his empire spread out below. There were four separate buildings joined by a web of twisting paths that wound through palm trees and lush greenery and ended at a huge fountain in the center of the courtyard in front of Seamus's building. This was only one of five tech campuses under his rule. He had one in Dublin, one in London, one in Zurich, and one in Dubai.

He welcomed Cam warmly into his office and led him to the corner with the best view of the fountain and surrounding buildings and gestured for him to take one of the comfortable chairs grouped around a small glass table. Without asking if he wanted any, Seamus poured a cup of tea for each of them from a green and white china pot.

"How do you take yours? Milk, sugar, or both?" he asked.

"Black is fine."

Seamus handed him a cup and saucer that matched the pot and then picked up his own cup and sat down across from Cam. He took a long sip of tea. "Earl Gray, my favorite. Although, a pint of Guinness would be better. But it's working hours." He gave Cam a conspiratorial smile.

Seamus O'Malley was short and heavyset. He had a sparse thatch of gray hair, a round, heavily lined face, alert brown eyes, and elf ears that protruded on each side of his head. He was wearing dark slacks, a white shirt without a tie, and an Irish tweed sport coat. He and Lachlan were the same age, but Seamus looked ten years older. Cam could see why, in the ladies' man department, he was only a wannabe.

"I hear there was a gunman at your place last night as well as at mine," Seamus said.

"Yes. And two at yours. Did you or Lachlan see them?"

"No. The security people got rid of them before they came close to the house."

"Which means they'll be back."

"My security people will be ready for them. Have you come to ask me to be an alibi witness for Lachlan? He was with me that night."

"But the two of you were not drinking at the bar at Fairmont until closing time."

"So he told you the truth."

"He didn't until we talked to Kiara Blake, who actually was at the bar with Nora's agent until closing."

"Okay, you caught us. Where did Lachlan say that we were?"

"Maybe it's better if you tell me your version of where you were."

"At my office. Some old business left over from the Troubles."

"Signing someone's execution warrant."

"So Lachlan told you about that, too."

"I'm afraid that's not an alibi that Meg and I can use. The story that he did not kill Nora because he was busy arranging to kill someone else wouldn't play well to a jury."

"Agreed."

"So what were the two of you really up to that night?"

"Dinner and the meeting afterward."

"So you actually had dinner at the Fairmont?"

"Yes."

"And then?"

"And then Lachlan drove us here in the fleet Range Rover that he was using to set up for the meeting."

"What time did you finish dinner?"

"Around eleven thirty."

"Did you know that Lachlan received a text from Michael Bernstein about that time telling him that Nora had rejected their offer?"

"No. We had our phones silenced during dinner. I have no idea if any calls or messages came in to Lachlan's phone while we ate."

"What about during the meeting?"

"All phones were off."

"How long did your meeting last?"

"Until dawn. We had a difficult decision to make."

"What about after?"

"I drove Lachlan to the airport. He had an early flight to Boston. We were both exhausted. I'm sure he slept on the plane."

"So there's no possibility that Lachlan was driving the Range Rover that went through the security gates at Nora's at eleven forty?"

"None. We were just heading out for our meeting then."

"Any idea who it was?"

"My money's on Victoria."

It sounds rehearsed. I want to believe him, but it sounds rehearsed.

Cam placed his cup on the little glass table and stood up. Seamus responded by standing also.

"I'm glad we had a chance to chat," Cam said. "It looks like you'll be an important witness for the defense. We don't have to talk about your overnight activities. You can testify that you and Lachlan had dinner at the hotel, and he was with you at eleven forty, so he couldn't have been at Nora's. But there's just one more thing."

"And that would be?"

"Any receipts to prove that dinner was actually at the Fairmont?"

"You're suspicious because we weren't in the bar later."

"I don't want to be blindsided by a prosecutor who did his research so that he could impeach you with the truth."

Seamus was quiet for a few moments as if thinking something over.

"You're hesitating," Cam observed. "Does that mean you weren't at the hotel?"

"I was going to say we charged dinner to Lachlan's room, but you'd be able to find out that was a lie. I'm afraid you've caught us again."

"Where were you?"

"At Mille Fleurs."

"Less than ten minutes from Nora's."

"And you did know that Lachlan got that text from Bernstein at eleven thirty?"

"Yes."

"So Lachlan was in the Range Rover that arrived at Nora's at eleven forty."

"I'm afraid that's true."

* * *

Thursday, March 28, 2019, 910 Flora Avenue, Coronado, California

Cam lay awake that night while Raven slept soundly beside him. He kept thinking about the gunman who'd been intercepted last night. Outside, the winds were high, and the sound of every branch falling or the creak of the roof of Erin's vintage cottage made his heart race. The gunmen would be back. But when? And where? It likely wouldn't be here where they were surrounded by bodyguards.

To take his thoughts off the danger they were in, he replayed his conversation with Seamus. He almost wished that Seamus hadn't told him the truth. Meg was right. Both of them had represented guilty clients before, but that didn't make the thought of doing it again any easier. He'd called Meg from the car and had given her the bad news.

"Well, it's not unexpected," she said. "We still have our circumstantial evidence defense as long as Axel doesn't find out the two of them were at Mille Fleurs. Kiara didn't tell him that

Lachlan and Seamus weren't at the hotel that night, did she?"

"No. The DA's investigator was only interested in the texts that showed Nora was alive when they left her."

"Unfortunately, that information hurts Lachlan since Axel is going to argue that Lachlan was the one in the car."

"Yes," Cam agreed. "But as you said, Axel still can only guess about who it was out there waiting for everyone to leave."

"Let's hope he never finds out that it was Lachlan."

"Agreed. Be careful this weekend, Meg. Keep Finn close. Those gunmen are still out there, looking for a target."

Raven sighed and smiled in her sleep. Cam turned toward her and put his arm around her protectively. He was still angry when he thought of Lachlan's leaving her in the condo all alone, knowing assassins were looking for her as well as for him.

"You look upset," Raven had said after dinner as they sat on the couch finishing off their last glasses of wine.

"Do I? I guess I'm just tired."

"I think something's bothering you. Is it moving everything out of your mother's house in the morning?"

"Yes."

"Don't worry. We'll get it all taken care of."

He smiled. "I know. Thanks."

They sat in silence for a few minutes. Cam felt Raven studying him again thoughtfully. Finally, she said, "That's not the only thing on your mind."

He sighed. "I met with Seamus today."

Her eyes held his full of concern and without any trace of apprehension as if she already knew what was coming. "Can he help Dad?"

"No." The word seemed to hang in the air between them like something palpable.

"So bad news?"

"The worst."

"I want to know." There were tears in her eyes.

"Are you sure? Maybe it's best if you leave this to me and Meg."

"No, I want to know. I *need* to know."

"Seamus first lied and said they had dinner at the Fairmont the night Nora died. But then when I pressed him for proof, he admitted they ate at Mille Fleurs. They finished around eleven thirty."

"So that means that Dad was close enough to be at Nora's at eleven forty."

"Worse than that. He told Seamus that's where he was going after he got Bernstein's message."

Raven stared at a spot on the floor between them for a long time. Finally, her eyes met Cam's, full of pain and grief, and she said, "I didn't know."

He put down his wineglass and put his arms around her. He held her in silence for a few minutes.

Then she drew away and looked up at him. "Do you believe me? I didn't know."

"I believe you." He kissed the top of her head lightly.

She laid her head against his shoulder and said, "Even if it's true, please don't let him get convicted, Cam. Please do everything you can to keep him out of prison."

"I will. I promise."

CHAPTER FIFTY

Wednesday, April 3, 2019, Offices of Goldstein, Miller, and Mahoney, Emerald Shapery Center

The atmosphere in the conference room on the twenty-ninth floor at ten a.m. was tense as Meg and Cam waited for Lachlan and Raven. Cam was tight as a wire, not only for professional reasons, but for personal ones as well.

On Saturday, moving Jackie's belongings out of the house had gone off without a hitch. Four moving trucks and a small army of movers had swarmed like locusts through the rooms until, by one thirty, all of them were empty except for the items that no one wanted. Addison had had the task of dividing Jackie's jewelry, and Cam had been relieved when she failed to mention the aquamarine earrings.

He had been the one who closed up the house after the four trucks rolled out of the drive. He had wandered through the nearly empty rooms upstairs and then had gone downstairs to stand for one last, long moment in the front hall, truly at peace with Blaine's decision to let it go. Without Jackie and her things, it was no longer home for him. It was just a building where there were still faint traces of blood on the oak flooring at the foot of the stairs. Someone had tried to clean them because they were fainter than the last time Cam had been there. But he could tell that the stains were still visible, and they brought back the awful moment when he'd seen Jackie lying there, her head turned toward the front door, eyes fixed, as if she was forever expecting someone to arrive.

True to her promise, Raven had met him at his house after the truck arrived, ready for work in jeans and a head scarf. She had an artist's eye, and she did an excellent job of incorporating his mother's items into Jess's cozy, welcoming decor. Cam hoped that his wife would be so delighted that the garage was not filled with moving boxes that she would just assume that Addison had helped him put it all away.

There was too much to finish that afternoon, so they began again on Sunday morning. By five o'clock, they were done. After Cam had taken the last of the cardboard and packing paper to the trash, he had decided to celebrate by opening a bottle of champagne. He had carried the bottle and two glasses into the den, expecting to find Raven, but she hadn't been there. He had looked through the entire first floor without success, so he had gone upstairs where he found her in the playroom. She had been sitting on the floor in front of the three-story dollhouse that Jackie had left to the girls, and she had been meticulously unpacking the tiny furniture and placing the delicate pieces, one by one, in each little room.

He had paused in the doorway to study her as she freed a miniature bed from bubble wrap, studied it for a moment, and then found a place for it in the house's attic. Next, she opened the matching chest and dresser and spent several seconds arranging them. He could tell that she was enjoying herself in an almost childlike way, and he thought of the contrast between the sophisticated Raven who helped to run her father's empire and the Raven who was deeply absorbed in the dollhouse.

As she reached into the large box for another piece, she felt Cam watching her and turned toward him.

He held up the bottle and the glasses. "I thought we should celebrate."

She smiled. "I'm almost finished."

He watched for a few more minutes as she put the last of the carefully wrapped pieces away. Then she turned toward him again and said, "What do you think?"

"Callie and Steph will be surprised and thrilled. Addie's girls already have a dollhouse so Mom left this one to them."

"I always wanted one," she said as she stood up. "I asked every Christmas, but since I was at boarding school and rarely home, Lachlan and Victoria said I didn't need one."

The note of disappointment in her voice touched Cam as he thought of the lonely little girl shuffled from house to house. He put the bottle and the glasses down and took her in his arms and kissed her, long and deeply.

And it was at that minute that he heard footsteps in the hallway and turned with Raven still in his arms to see Nash standing there.

He'd turned back to Raven immediately, and a few seconds later he heard his brother's footsteps on the stairs, and then the front door closed. Raven, who was turned away toward the dollhouse hadn't seen Nash, but she sensed something was wrong.

"What is it?"

"Nothing."

"But I thought I heard the front door."

"One of the bodyguards came to take us back to Erin's place."

* * *

Now, as they waited for Lachlan and Raven in the conference room, Cam reassured himself that Nash would never tell Jess. But his text later that night had stung.

She's playing you, big brother.

Cam had told himself a thousand times since reading it that it wasn't true. But was it?

The conference room door opened, and Raven entered, followed by Lachlan. Cam rose with Meg to exchange professional greetings. Raven kept her face neutral as did he. She and her father sat down at the table facing Meg and Cam.

"We apologize for being late," Lachlan began. "Raven was ready, but I had to take a call from Michael about the movie."

"Is the sequel still going forward?" Cam asked.

"Yes."

"It's not the best timing," Meg observed.

Lachlan frowned. "What do you mean?"

"It adds fuel to the prosecution's case that you killed Nora, Da," Raven said softly.

"Well, I didn't, and the opportunity to make a sequel is too important to turn down."

"We really need more time before we go to trial," Cam said.

"But didn't you set a date this morning?" Lachlan asked.

"Isn't that why you wanted to talk to us today?"

"Trial setting is this afternoon at two o'clock," Meg told him. "We were hoping to talk you into more time and to tell you about Cam's interview with Seamus on Friday."

"I know all about that," Lachlan said. "He told you I went to Nora's after dinner."

"You were the one entering the security gate at eleven forty," Cam said.

"Okay. I admit it was me."

"And you parked by the guesthouse until Sonia and Kiara left."

"True. But I didn't know who was in Sonia's car. I only knew I wanted to talk to Nora alone."

"So what happened?" Cam asked.

"I went in through the back entrance to avoid the security cameras, and I went up the back stairs to Nora's bedroom. It was empty. I walked down the hall toward the front stairs, and I found Nora there, drunk and trying to balance on one foot. She was mumbling about being a great dancer and the goddess of love."

"Did you push her?" Meg asked.

"No. I put my arms around her and led her back to her room. It wasn't hard to do. She had labored under the delusion that I was in love with her for a long time and that eventually I'd resume our marriage, so she thought I was there to make love to her."

"What happened next?" Cam asked.

"I laid her on the bed, and she started to try to undress herself. But when I told her it was over for good and all and that

I'd never give her another penny if she tried to stop the movie, she started to cry."

"What then?"

"I left. She was drunk, but she understood me. It was sad to see how hurt she was when the truth finally got through to her. Maybe she really loved me. I don't know. But I never loved her, and life with her was miserable."

"What time did you leave?"

"The clock in the car said twelve thirty when I got in. I went into the house about five minutes after Sonia and Kiara left. So I guess I was there with her for about fifteen minutes. Twenty at the most. I tried to get her to stop crying because she sounded like such a lost soul and I could tell that her heart was broken. But I could see that being there made it worse, so I left."

"Where did you go after that?" Cam asked.

"To the meeting at Seamus's."

"So that was a real thing?"

"Absolutely. Seamus told you it lasted until dawn, and then I headed back to Boston. I didn't learn about Nora's death until I got off the plane."

"And did you see anyone else around when you left Nora?"

"No."

* * *

Wednesday, April 3, 2019, San Diego County Central Courthouse, Downtown San Diego

"Are you sure you want to go to trial this soon?" Judge Parker Anderson frowned at Axel Saldana who was standing at the podium and who had just requested a trial date. "You've added a special circumstance today," Judge Anderson reminded him. "Are you certain you are up to proving that two weeks from now?"

"Yes, Your Honor. The prosecution is ready for trial."

"How about the defense?" Judge Anderson turned to Cam, who was standing at the defense table.

He glanced quickly at Meg who shook her head imperceptibly and then over at Lachlan sitting beside her who nodded affirmatively. Cam sighed inwardly and then said,

"The defense is prepared."

"That's not the same as 'ready,'" Judge Anderson said.

"We're ready." *And that's the biggest lie I've ever told in my career.*

* * *

"What are we going to do?" Cam asked Meg at four that afternoon as they sat at the table in her office while Brianna built Legos with Finn in the other corner.

"Lose. Unless there's a miracle in the next two weeks, and we find some evidence that someone other than Lachlan was in the house after Sonia and Kiara, but we've been through all of the surveillance footage and found nothing. There's no other place to look for another suspect. Lachlan's it."

"Do you believe his story that she was alive when he left?" Cam's stomach tightened as he asked the question. He desperately wanted to believe Lachlan for Raven's sake, but his rational attorney side knew better.

"Not one bit."

* * *

Raven was anxiously waiting for him when Cam reached Erin's cottage at eight o'clock that night. He entered feeling tense and out of sorts. After his conference with Meg, he'd had a long conversation with Jess about the upcoming trial and when she and the girls might be able to come home. And now he felt torn between his duty to his family and his desire to be with Raven. Jess and the girls seemed distant and faintly unreal after weeks of separation. Raven, on the other hand, shared his bed, and he couldn't imagine life without her.

But overlaid with that conflict was his brother's words, *"She's playing you."* And, indeed, maybe she was. He'd sat for a while in his office, sipping some good Scotch that he kept for these moments of intense emotional turmoil as he stared at the city, watching the lights come on in the early spring dusk. He was torn between his gut feeling that Lachlan was a liar and Raven's intense wish for him to believe her father. Finally, after the last drop of Scotch was gone, he decided it was time to go back to the cottage.

"I waited dinner for you. It might be a little overdone." Her expression said that she knew something was wrong and she was braced for bad news.

They were standing in the living room just inside the front door. She was wearing her black silk pajamas and a white silk robe and the aquamarine earrings which intensified the effect of her clear blue eyes. He was still in his court suit with his tie loosened. Even though he was in emotional turmoil, he felt that hard jolt of desire that being near her always aroused in him.

"I worked late." But they both knew that he had never worked late since the day he'd come to share the cottage with her.

"You don't believe Da, do you?"

Damn, she could always read his thoughts. "It doesn't matter what I believe. It matters what the jury believes."

"But doesn't that affect your ability to persuade them?"

"What affects my ability to persuade them most is that Meg and I haven't had enough time to prepare a solid defense."

"I know."

The two words startled him. He hadn't expected agreement.

Once again, she read him perfectly. "Don't look so surprised. I know you need more time."

"Then why wouldn't you try to talk Lachlan into giving us more?"

"Because there's a target on the back of everyone involved in this case. Someone is going to die if this doesn't end soon. I don't want it to be you."

His heart melted when he saw the tears in her eyes. He dropped his briefcase and hurried to take her in his arms. As he held her, he felt sobs shake her tiny body as if the case was already lost, and Lachlan was already in prison. He remembered how alone she's had always been since childhood and how since he'd been with her, he'd felt deep happiness in a way that he never had before.

"Don't cry," he whispered into her hair. "Nothing is going to happen to me."

WITCH TRIALS

CHAPTER FIFTY-ONE

Wednesday, April 24, 2019, San Diego County Central Courthouse, Downtown San Diego

"This is a simple case, ladies and gentlemen of the jury," Axel Saldana said as he began his opening argument at three o'clock on Wednesday afternoon.

Cam's heart sank as he sat at the defense table with Meg on his left and Lachlan on his right. Raven was on the end by her father. The courthouse had been swamped with media since Monday morning when jury selection began. He and Meg had shepherded Lachlan and Raven quickly past the throng of microphones and cameras each morning while Axel held forth on the courthouse steps, confidently briefing the press on the stunning victory he was expecting. Cam could see how much he was enjoying the prospect of convicting an Irish celebrity with a Hollywood connection.

The two weeks between the trial setting and the start of the trial had netted the defense team nothing. There was not one shred of evidence that anyone had entered Nora's house after twelve thirty when Lachlan claimed he left.

"Not really a surprise," Meg observed at their last trial prep conference. "Neither of us believes him, and a jury won't either."

"Right. He stays off the stand," Cam agreed.

On top of the frustration that Cam felt over going to trial with a wholly inadequate defense was the unexpected lack of interest in his parents' house. It had been on the market a full two weeks and not a single offer. His father was upset. The realtor said the death disclosure was chilling interest. Although Jackie's fall had been an accident, buyers still shied away. Blaine was so anxious to unload the place that he'd already cut the price twice.

"He's in too big a hurry," Nash had observed last night when he phoned Cam to wish him well at trial. Thankfully, his brother omitted any reference to Raven.

I shouldn't let my mind wander. Focus, focus.

"The evidence will show," Axel continued, "that Nora Carson was alone and helpless on the night of February 13—"

"Objection." Meg was on her feet. They had agreed that she would be the lead at trial. "Improper argument."

"Agreed," Judge Lisa Watson intoned from the bench. "The jury will disregard the description 'alone and helpless.' Stick to a recitation of what you believe the evidence will show," she advised Axel.

And that might be the only victory we get in this trial.

"Thank you, Your Honor." Axel accepted the admonition without expression. He went on. "The evidence will show that the defendant had opportunity and motive to carry out the threat he made to kill his wife earlier that morning. Alicia Cortez, Ms. Carson's housekeeper, will testify–"

Cam tuned out. He knew what was coming all too well. *We*

used to call these suicide missions in the public defender's office.

His mind wandered to Sunday and the night before trial began. It had seemed surreal. Lachlan had wanted the defense team plus Raven and Seamus to spend the evening drinking and listening to him read his poetry in the Irish pub in the Gaslamp that he favored. But for security reasons, Seamus had created a mock pub around his pool, ringed by the bodyguards.

Meg had, of course, flatly refused to be involved. Cam, too, had told Raven it wasn't the best use of his time on the night before jury selection. But eventually, she had persuaded him to go for an hour or so as a show of support for her father. He'd wound up staying until midnight, marveling at how much whiskey Seamus and Lachlan could hold and how carefree Lachlan seemed as the music grew louder and louder between bouts of reading poetry about his longing for Sinead. *Doesn't he know he's on his way to prison for life?*

"Ms. Courtney, is the defense going to make an opening statement?" Judge Watson's question brought Cam abruptly back to the harsh reality of starting a trial there was no hope of winning.

"Just briefly, Your Honor."

Cam watched Meg take the podium and smile at the jury.

"Good afternoon, ladies and gentlemen. You've heard Mr. Saldana's claims about the evidence that he thinks will prove my client guilty of murder. But what you haven't heard is how flimsy the prosecution's case really is. Mr. Saldana's entire case rests on identifying the person in the black Range Rover who was parked by the guesthouse that night at eleven forty p.m. Mr. Saldana claims it was Professor Adair, but he has not pointed to one single piece of evidence that establishes that it was my client. Mr. Saldana does not have a witness who will testify that it was Professor Adair. Mr. Saldana does not have a license plate that will identify the vehicle as the one Professor Adair was driving that night. Mr. Saldana doesn't have any DNA or fingerprints that establish my client was in that car. All the prosecution has is speculation based upon some angry words that were uttered during a husband-wife quarrel hours earlier. And who, ladies and gentlemen, hasn't quarreled with a spouse and made empty threats? Mr. Rhodes and I are confident that after you've heard the full story of February 13, 2019, you will acquit Professor Adair of all charges. Thank you."

"Thank you, Ms. Courtney. Mr. Saldana, you may call your first witness."

"The prosecution calls Deputy Harold Riddle."

Cam watched a middle-aged, balding man in a tan deputy sheriff's uniform take the stand. After the preliminary identification and occupation questions were out of the way, Axel asked, "Did you answer a 911 call on the morning of February 14, 2019, at 2530 Via Del Charro?"

"Yes. I was the first officer on the scene. I arrived about eight that morning. The housekeeper had called for help."

"Would the housekeeper be Alicia Cortez?"

"That sounds right. May I review my report?"

"You may," Judge Watson said.

"And was it Ms. Cortez?"

"Yes. She found her employer, Nora Carson, at the bottom of the stairs when she arrived for work that morning. Ms. Carson appeared to be deceased."

"And what did you observe?"

"Ms. Carson, dressed in a nightgown, was lying at the foot of the stairs, within a foot of the last step. Her eyes were closed. She wasn't breathing."

Cam drew a deep breath. For a moment, he was back in his parents' house looking down at Jackie, eyes wide open, head turned toward the front door.

"And did you summon the paramedics?" Axel asked.

"911 had already put in the call. They arrived just a few minutes after I did, but she had been deceased for some time."

"Thank you. No more questions."

"Any questions from the defense?" Judge Watson looked at Meg, but it was Cam's turn.

"A few, Your Honor."

He took the podium and breathed deeply as he studied his notes. He felt all the eyes in the packed courtroom on him. *Now I remember why I haven't done this for sixteen years.*

"Good morning, Deputy Riddle. Just a few brief questions. Was Ms. Carson lying face down?"

"Yes."

"Could you see bruising on her body?"

"Nothing stood out as obvious, but she was fully clothed. That sort of thing was for the coroner and the autopsy."

"Of course. But you did take scrapings from under her fingernails, did you not?"

"I did."

"And what was the purpose of that?"

"To see if she'd fought off an attacker and to try to identify that person."

"And what were the results of the fingernail scrapings?"

"I never received that report. You'd have to ask the coroner."

"Thank you, Deputy. No more questions."

Strike one. And it's only going to be downhill from here.

CHAPTER FIFTY-TWO

Thursday, April 25, 2019, San Diego County Central Courthouse, Downtown San Diego, Morning Session

"Good morning, Mr. Saldana, you may call your first witness." Judge Watson beamed benignly at the courtroom packed with media and spectators.

"Thank you, Your Honor. The People call Deputy Coroner Maria Sanchez."

Cam watched the coroner take the stand and be sworn.

"Dr. Sanchez," Axel began, "did you perform an autopsy on the body of Nora Carson on February 15, 2019?"

"Yes."

"Could you summarize your findings for the jury?"

"Ms. Carson was five feet six and weighed one hundred and sixty pounds. Internal organs were normal. She had a broken neck and a fractured right arm which I concluded were sustained in her fall. She had significant bruising on her torso, particularly on her back."

"And what was her cause of death?"

"Her death was a homicide caused by the fall. Someone applied strong force from behind."

"So she was pushed down the stairs?"

"Yes."

"What about drugs in her system?"

"Her blood alcohol level was .02. That would cause altered mood, relaxation, slight loss of judgment."

"Would her sense of balance have been affected?"

"Not at all."

"What about narcotics?"

"No evidence of narcotics."

"Thank you, Dr. Sanchez."

He and Meg had agreed that he would cross-examine the coroner, so he took Axel's place at the podium.

"Good morning, Dr. Sanchez. Were the fingernail scrapings from Ms. Carson's body tested for DNA?"

"Yes."

"And what was the result?"

"Only her DNA was present."

"So she wasn't fighting off an attacker, was she?"

"I can't say because I wasn't there."

Got me.

"Now, turning to your conclusions about Ms. Carson's blood alcohol level in your report. What is the difference in a BAC of 0.2 and 0.8?"

"At 0.8, someone is too intoxicated to drive in California. The impairment of speech and coordination is much less at .02," Dr. Sanchez said.

"But Ms. Carson could still have been somewhat off-balance at .02, couldn't she?"

"No. That wouldn't have been enough to affect her footing.

She was pushed. The bruising on her back proves the force came from behind."

Damn!

Cam sat down at the defense table and watched as Axel replaced Dr. Sanchez with Alicia Cortez. Just as she had done at the preliminary hearing, she kept her eyes fixed on Axel as she occasionally tossed her long dark hair over her shoulder. She was obviously nervous.

"Ms. Cortez, how did you know the victim?"

"I was her housekeeper for the five years before her death."

"And did you know the defendant?"

"Somewhat. He was Ms. Carson's husband, but they did not live together."

"Where did he live?"

"In Boston."

"Did you observe the defendant with Ms. Carson on the morning of February 13?"

"Yes. He came to visit her around eleven o'clock."

"Did Ms. Carson discuss the purpose of that meeting with you?"

"Yes. She said–"

"Objection, Your Honor," Cam was on his feet because this was his witness. "What Ms. Carson said is hearsay."

"Sustained. Next question."

"What happened when the defendant came to visit his wife that morning?

"I heard them fighting. I heard the sound of china breaking and Professor Adair came out of Ms. Carson's study with blood on his forehead."

"Did he say anything when he came out?"

Cam stood. "Same objection, Your Honor."

"This is admissible as an excited utterance," Axel asserted. "He was under the stress of the fight with his wife when he uttered the statement. It's also a declaration against interest."

"Overruled. You may answer."

"He said, "I'll kill you before I'll give you a part in this movie."

"And did you happen to observe the vehicle that Professor Adair was driving that day?"

"Yes. A black Range Rover."

"Thank you, Ms. Cortez. No more questions."

Cam took the podium with a heavy heart.

"Good morning, Ms. Cortez. Now you said that you worked for Ms. Carson for five years?"

"Yes."

"Had you observed Ms. Carson with Professor Adair on other occasions?"

"Yes."

"Many occasions?"

"Yes. She was always trying to get him to visit her."

"So she liked to be with him?"

"Oh, yes. She wanted him to live with her, but he wouldn't."

"Had you observed them quarrel before?"

"Yes. Frequently."

"And had Professor Adair ever said anything similar to Ms. Carson during one of their previous heated exchanges?"

"Oh, yes."

"And how did Ms. Carson view those statements?"

"Objection." Axel stood up.

"It's her state of mind," Cam said.

"Overruled."

"Ms. Carson knew he was Irish and had a temper."

"So she didn't take them seriously?"

"Not at all."

"What about on February 13? Did she think Professor Adair had made a genuine threat?"

"No. She cried after he left because they had quarreled. She wanted him to come back. I heard her trying to call him almost as soon as he left. She was upset because she'd hurt him, and she wanted to apologize."

"To your knowledge, has Professor Adair ever harmed Ms. Carson?"

"No, he has not."

"Thank you, Ms. Cortez. No further questions."

But Axel was back at the podium immediately.

"Was the quarrel on February 13 more intense than the quarrels you had witnessed in the past?"

"Not really. Ms. Carson had a temper, too. She often threw things, but she usually missed."

"Thank you. No more questions."

* * *

"We scored a few points with the housekeeper," Meg observed over lunch in the conference room on the twenty-ninth floor at Goldstein, Miller. Lachlan, Raven, and Cam were sitting around the large conference table which held a plate of sandwiches and fruit along with bottles of water.

"There's a juror who keeps staring at Cam," Lachlan said.

"The woman on the end of the first row," Cam said. "I noticed. I don't know her."

"She said she's an elementary school teacher," Meg said. "Did we ask her if she lived in Coronado? She could know you from there."

Cam's stomach tightened. They hadn't asked her. He didn't remember her address from the juror questionnaire. He never went out with Raven in public, but what if she had somehow found out?

"Well, they were all asked on voir dire if they knew any of us," Cam reminded them. "If she knows me and didn't disclose, Judge Watson has to remove her."

"We can bring it up after lunch," Meg said. "Be prepared this afternoon. It's probably not going to go our way. Bernstein is Axel's next witness."

Cam looked over at Raven, wondering why she was so silent. Her eyes met his, and he realized that she knew the truth: her father was on the path to conviction.

* * *

Thursday, April 25, 2019, San Diego County Central Courthouse, Downtown San Diego, Afternoon Session

"Before the People call their next witness, Your Honor, the defense is requesting an in-chambers conference about a jury matter," Meg said when they returned to the courtroom at one thirty.

"Very well. We'll adjourn for fifteen minutes," Judge Watson agreed.

After they had settled in the judge's office, she turned to Meg and asked, "What is the matter the defense wants to raise?"

"We've noticed that Juror No. 6 in the front row seems to be preoccupied with my co-counsel," Meg explained. We were wondering if she failed to disclose during voir dire that she knows him."

"Mr. Rhodes?"

"Yes, Your Honor. She seems to be very focused on me. I don't know her."

"Let's call her back and talk to her."

A few minutes later, the bailiff brought Juror No. 6 into Judge Watson's chambers. She appeared to be in her early forties. She had dark-brown hair and hazel eyes. She was conservatively dressed in a black dress and matching jacket. Cam was sure that he had never met her before.

"Juror No. 6, counsel for the defense has noticed that you seem to know a member of the defense team, Mr. Cameron Rhodes. You seem to be observing him more closely than the other attorneys."

"I don't know him," Juror No. 6 said. "It's just that he reminds me of my brother who passed away a year ago."

"Condolences," Judge Watson said. "In that case, perhaps this isn't the trial for you. I'm going to thank and excuse you."

"I'm glad, Your Honor. I didn't know how to tell anyone about the resemblance."

When Juror No. 6 was gone, the bailiff put slips of paper with the numbers of all the alternates in a bowl and drew one. The new juror was male, and Cam was relieved. They'd started out seven/five, and he'd been concerned that the female jurors would dislike Lachlan's womanizing ways and hold out for conviction. Six/six was at least a chance at a hung jury. So they'd had two small victories so far today: Alicia Cortez's testimony and a shift in the balance of the jury.

* * *

Thursday, April 25, 2019, San Diego County Central Courthouse, Downtown San Diego, Afternoon Session

Michael Bernstein was the first witness when they returned to the courtroom. He looked calm and confident in his gray slacks and navy blazer with an open-necked light-blue check shirt.

"Please state your name and occupation for the record," Axel directed.

"Michael Bernstein. I'm a film producer."

"And how did you know Nora Carson?"

"I met Nora not long after she came to Los Angeles looking for movie roles. She had parts in a number of my films, the most notable being *Unforgettable*."

"And are you acquainted with the defendant, Lachlan Adair?"

"Yes. *Unforgettable* was based upon his best-selling novel."

"At the time of her death, was Ms. Carson being considered for a role in another of your films?"

"Not really. Lachlan and I were in talks to make a sequel to *Unforgettable.* Nora wanted a role in the movie, but neither Lachlan nor I thought she was suitable for a part."

"And why was that?"

"At forty-six, she was too old for the movie we were

discussing. Professor Adair had a younger actress in mind for the part."

"And who was that?"

"Kiara Blake. She was Ms. Carson's personal assistant."

"Were you with Ms. Carson on the night of her death?"

"Yes. I had dinner with her at her house. I arrived around seven thirty."

"Did you talk about the sequel to the prior movie?"

"Yes. Ms. Carson had a contract right to appear in the new movie, and she was threatening to prevent the production if her contract was not honored. I was there that night to offer her a share of the profits of the new movie if she would let us make it without her."

"And what was her response?"

"She refused my offer."

"I'm going to show you some surveillance video from Ms. Carson's home that night." Axel played the tape that showed Bernstein's car exiting through the security gate. "Is that your red Tesla leaving Ms. Carson's at eleven thirty-three p.m.?"

"Yes."

"Did the defendant know on the night of February 13 that Ms. Carson had turned down your offer for a share of the profits in the new movie?"

"Yes. I had texted him to that effect as I was leaving her house."

"I'm showing you a printout of your text messages that evening. Could you tell the jury what time you sent that text to the defendant?"

"At eleven thirty-one."

"And do you know if the defendant was driving a black Range Rover that night?"

"Yes, he was. He was at my house earlier that day in a black Range Rover."

"No further questions."

Bernstein was Meg's witness, so she took Axel's place at the podium.

"Just a few questions, Mr. Bernstein. Did you see a black Range Rover approaching Ms. Carson's house as you left that night?"

"No. I didn't see any cars coming toward the house as I went through the security gates."

"So you have no idea who was driving the car that went through the gate at eleven forty?"

"Correct."

"Are you acquainted with Victoria Adair?"

"Yes. She is Professor Adair's ex-wife and his literary executor."

"Did she have a substantial financial interest in the proposed sequel that Ms. Carson was going to block?"

"Yes. She stood to lose millions if the movie didn't get–"

Before Michael Bernstein could finish his answer, the doors in the back of the courtroom opened to reveal a small army of deputy sheriffs standing there. Cam's heart skipped a beat. Were they there for Lachlan? But they couldn't be. He was already under arrest.

The deputy approached Judge Watson and handed her a note. Her face went white as she read it. Then she addressed the courtroom.

"Ladies and gentlemen, our building must be evacuated at once. These deputies are here to assist in helping us exit the courtroom in an orderly fashion. The jurors, the parties, my staff, and I will all exit through the door to my chambers while everyone else will be assisted through the doors of the courtroom."

Cam's heart was hammering as he stuffed papers into his briefcase. Meg was doing the same as was the entire prosecution team.

"Just leave it," one of the deputies said who had appeared at the defense table. Cam glanced over and saw another deputy delivering the same message to Axel. The last of the jurors had just vanished through the door to the jury box.

"Follow me, now!" the deputy said.

Cam motioned for Meg to follow the deputy, then directed Lachlan and Raven to go next. Finally, he brought up the rear. They went through the doors usually used only by the judicial staff, down a short corridor, and then through a door into the main hall. The deputy sheriff glanced back several times to make sure his charges were following him. Cam caught sight of Axel and the prosecution team also in line behind another deputy headed down the same hall just ahead of them.

"Hurry!" The deputy threw the word over his shoulder, urging them to go faster as they approached the door to the stairs at the end of the hall. The deputy opened the door and held it open while the four of them passed into the stairwell. Meg, in the lead, started down the stairs with Lachlan and Raven following her. They were on the fourth floor, so they had a number of flights of stairs to go before they could leave the building. Cam was the last to pass through the door. As he did, he asked the deputy who was still holding it open, “What’s happened?”

“There’s a bomb in the basement. The FBI is down there trying to disarm it.”

CHAPTER FIFTY-THREE

Thursday, April 25, 2019, Offices of Goldstein, Miller, and Mahoney, Emerald Shapery Center

Cam, Raven, and Lachlan joined by Hugh Mahoney assembled in the conference room on the twenty-ninth floor around two thirty. The lunch fare had been replaced with coffee and an assortment of pastries. Cam poured coffee for himself and Hugh. Everyone else declined food and drink. Meg was in her office down the hall with Finn and Brianna. Cam had promised to summon her when she was needed.

The phone rang, and Hugh answered it and exchanged a few words with the caller. When he hung up, he said, "That was my secretary. Two FBI agents are downstairs. She's bringing them up to talk to us."

"I'll get Meg," Cam said.

He hurried down the hall to her office where he found her sitting with Finn at his little table. Brianna was at the big table, working on her computer. Meg had her arm around Finn and was hugging him close as they colored a picture together.

She looked up immediately when Cam entered.

"We need you down the hall."

She nodded, but she held Finn a minute longer before she got up and put her suit jacket back on and followed Cam out into the hallway.

"I don't want to leave him."

"I know. But at least he doesn't know what's happened. The FBI is here to talk to us."

The two agents in gray suits were already seated at the conference table when Cam entered with Meg and sat down.

"I'm Special Agent Todd Martin, and this is Special Agent Robert Wallace. We've already interviewed Judge Watson, and two of our agents are meeting with the district attorney right now."

"One of the sheriff's deputies said that there was a bomb in the basement of the courthouse," Cam said.

"That's right," Robert Wallace agreed. "It was found by sheer luck. A couple of the maintenance people went down there to work on a problem with the electrical system and saw it."

"But you disarmed it?" Meg asked.

"Yes, but it was a very sophisticated device."

"Do you know who is responsible?" Hugh asked.

"A group called the 'New Irish Volunteer Brigade' has claimed credit. They aren't on any list of recognized terrorist organizations, so we are skeptical of their claim."

"Have you heard of them, Professor Adair?" Special Agent Martin asked.

"No. I have not been involved in Irish politics for many years, and I was never a member of any of the paramilitary organizations. Just a peaceful supporter of a united Ireland."

Cam kept his face neutral and avoided looking at Raven. Meg, too, kept her face expressionless.

"We've withheld any mention of the New Irish Volunteer Brigade from the press because it could taint the jury in Professor Adair's trial," Special Agent Wallace said.

"Judge Watson indicated she'd be in touch with the parties later this afternoon about further proceedings. This is all that we know for now, but we were all very lucky today as I'm sure you realize. Do you have any questions?"

Hugh looked around the conference table before he said, "No. Thank you for coming."

As the agents rose to leave, Cam felt his phone vibrate. Jess.

"It's my wife," he said to the room in general. "I've got to go to my office and take this."

* * *

"Cam, what's happened?" The fear in her voice was palpable.

Cam sat down at his desk and drew a long breath before answering. It was as if he'd been numb to the danger they'd all been in until this moment. He realized that his hands were shaking as he held the phone. "Sorry I couldn't call before. We've been in meetings ever since we were evacuated from the courthouse. We just finished talking to the FBI."

"I heard it on the news."

"We're fine. Everyone got out safely, and the FBI shut it down. Do the girls know?"

"Fortunately, they don't. Mother and I decided not to say anything until I talked to you. But I should tell them."

"It would just worry them. I don't think it's necessary."

"But it is. They'll hear it from someone else if we don't. And that would be worse."

"Well, please don't make it sound scary."

"But it was."

"Yes, but they don't need to know that."

"I don't see how they can not know that their father might have been killed today. Cam, for our sakes, you've got to get out of this thing now."

"I can't, Jess. My co-counsel is a single mother with a four-year-old. I can't leave her alone in danger." *Not to mention Raven.*

"Do they know who did it?"

"Not really. A group claimed credit, but the FBI thinks it's bogus. They aren't releasing any information to the press."

"Because it would prejudice your client? Was it some Irish paramilitary organization?"

"No." *Close enough to the truth.*

"Cam, have you and Meg thought about the fact that things don't add up with Lachlan Adair?"

He felt his stomach tighten. She was a superb attorney, even if she hadn't practiced for six years. "We haven't seen it that way, Jess."

"Well, think about this: he's a Harvard professor who owns three expensive pieces of real estate, one in Boston and two in San Diego. You've said that he was the sole support of the deceased wife who couldn't have been cheap to keep. And you've said that he had enough money to get her started making her own movies if he'd chosen to. And, on top of that, he can afford you and Meg to defend him."

"That income is from the residuals from the movie version of *Unforgettable.*"

"Really, Cam? That movie came out in 2007. What movie pays those kinds of residuals for twelve years? Has Nash ever had that much financial success from any of his projects?"

"Stop, Jess!"

"Stop what?"

"Stop trying to analyze the Adair case! You're not counsel of record."

Cam regretted the verbal slap the moment he'd let it fly.

Jess's silence stretched on endlessly.

"I'm sorry," he said.

"I'm not. I told you in the beginning not to get too wound into this case. I told you that the girls and I needed you. And Jackie."

Cam's conscience stabbed him hard. "My father wasn't having an affair. And it wasn't a suicide. She tripped and fell."

"I don't believe any of that for one minute."

"Well, I do. Besides, Hugh–"

"Don't blame your unUncle Hugh. You wanted this case."

Not in the beginning. But now—

"Jess, this is pointless. Please go to bed and rest. We can talk more tomorrow."

"We're growing apart, Cam. You're putting your career ahead of me and our girls."

"No, I'm not." *I'm putting Raven ahead of you all. God, help me, but I am.*

* * *

Thursday, April 25, 2019, Offices of Goldstein, Miller, and Mahoney, Emerald Shapery Center

The meeting in the twenty-ninth floor conference room had ended when Cam finished his call with Jess. Hugh and Meg had gone back to their offices. Raven and Lachlan had departed, Raven to Erin's cottage, Lachlan to Seamus's La Jolla mansion.

Cam walked down to Meg's office to find her packing up to leave, too. He glanced at the clock on her desk; it was short of four o'clock.

"Did I miss anything after I left?" he asked.

Meg looked up from tucking papers in her briefcase. "Judge Watson's clerk called. We're going to be on a conference call with her and the prosecution team in the morning at nine. Finn's had enough of my office for one day. We're headed home."

"Of course. I'll see you in the morning. But call me if you need anything tonight."

"We'll be fine. They're not after Finn and me. They're after Lachlan."

"I would have agreed with you this morning, but after what happened this afternoon, I think you and Finn are in danger, too."

"Hugh agrees with you. He's sending extra security with us tonight. We'll be fine. Come on, Finn. Time to go."

"Finally," Finn said as he jumped up from his little table. "Here, put my picture in your briefcase. I want to hang it up in my room tonight."

Meg opened the briefcase that she had closed and obeyed him. "Okay, now let's go."

"First, I want to give Cam a hug," Finn announced.

"Mr. Rhodes," Meg corrected.

"Cam is fine," he said as Finn embraced him mostly around his legs and seemed to hold on just a touch too long.

"That's enough, Finn." Meg walked over and gently disentangled him.

Cam walked with them to the elevator and waited until the door closed before returning to his own office. He sat down at his desk and stared at the bay in the thinning afternoon light. He kept thinking of the almost desperate quality of Finn's embrace.

He's missing his father. I know Meg had her reasons, but his little heart doesn't know that. It would be like that for Callie and Steph if you– But it was a thought he could not finish.

* * *

Raven met him at the door when he reached the cottage at five thirty. She put her arms around him and held him close as soon as he shut the door. He felt the same urgency that he had felt in Finn's embrace earlier.

"I've made dinner." She let go of him and stepped back slightly. "I thought food might help."

"I don't think I can eat," Cam said. "At least not yet." In the low light of late afternoon, he could see that her face was pale and drawn. "How are you? How's Lachlan?"

"Lachlan's been through these things before. Although he's shaken up enough to stay in tonight."

"He was thinking of going out carousing?"

"It's his answer to almost everything. Life is short. Enjoy."

"And you?"

"Exhausted and shaken. Let's have a glass of wine and talk."

Cam changed into his sweatpants and a sweatshirt and joined her on the couch in the living room, where she'd poured two glasses of wine and set out some fruit and cheese.

"So what happens now?" Raven asked.

"The judge will tell us tomorrow. Meg and I haven't talked about it. She just wanted to be with Finn this afternoon. But I'm sure we'll move for a mistrial in the morning."

"A mistrial? You mean stop the proceedings and start all over?"

"Lachlan can't possibly get a fair trial after something like this. I'm sure the jurors are as upset and frightened as we are."

But she shook her head. "No. If the trial doesn't go on, we'll have to do it all again. It won't end. It has to end. Now."

"But your father will go to prison."

"No, he won't. He didn't kill Nora."

Cam put his wineglass on the table and studied her face. They had drawn the curtains and the low light accented the worry lines in her expression. He put his arms around her and said, "Even if he didn't, it looks very much like he did."

He had expected her to contradict him, but instead, she leaned her head against his shoulder and said, "I know."

"He lied to the FBI today."

"I know."

They sat quietly for a few minutes. Cam let himself sink into the enchantment of her perfume and her warmth.

Then Raven said, "He won't agree to a mistrial."

"I know," Cam said.

At that moment, his phone began to ring. The caller ID said Axel Saldana.

"Axel's calling," he told Raven as he released her. "I'd better answer this."

He went into their bedroom and closed the door.

"Axel?"

"Hi, Cam. We need to talk ahead of the meeting in the morning."

"Sure. What do you want to talk about?"

"We have to find a way to end this before one or all of us get killed."

"Agreed. But ending it is up to you at this point."

"My boss has authorized me to make an offer."

"Of what?"

"A plea to voluntary manslaughter with a sentence of three years providing Lachlan will cooperate with the Feds."

"What kind of cooperation?"

"Naming members of the IRA."

"But they're no longer active."

"But there's no statute of limitations on murder, and the Brits are leaning on the Feds to pressure your client to name names. Three years would be a gift since the midterm for voluntary manslaughter is six and tops is eleven. He won't die in prison if he takes this, and it'll all be over."

"You know it's not my call. I'll convey your offer."

* * *

Friday, April 26, 2019, Offices of Goldstein, Miller, and Mahoney, Emerald Shapery Center

"This case should be settled," Judge Watson said at ten o'clock the next morning as soon as all the parties were on the conference call. "I don't see that a mistrial motion would cure the harm to any of the parties caused by yesterday. Mr. Saldana, has your office made a settlement offer?"

"We have, Your Honor. A very generous offer. A plea to voluntary manslaughter and three years plus cooperation with the FBI."

"That is generous," the judge agreed. "Mr. Rhodes? Ms. Courtney?"

Meg gave Cam a look across the conference table that said she didn't want to deliver the bad news. Fortunately, before Cam had to speak, Hugh intervened.

"Professor Adair has declined as is his right to do." Somehow it sounded more acceptable coming from the most influential partner at Goldstein, Miller.

"I see," Judge Watson spoke slowly, a sure indication of her disapproval. "You know, Professor Adair, I was a prosecutor before I took the bench. I don't think you should be too hasty to reject the district attorney's offer. So far, in my view, the evidence has weighed heavily against you. If convicted, you'll die in prison."

"I have faith in Mr. Rhodes and Ms. Courtney," Lachlan said.

"Your Honor, the district attorney's office will leave our offer open over the weekend. Perhaps things will look different to Professor Adair on Monday."

"I hope that's the case," Judge Watson said. "So we'll plan to reconvene on Monday at the courthouse and see how things stand then. I'll order the jurors back, but let's hope we do not need them."

CHAPTER FIFTY-FOUR

Monday, April 29, 2019, San Diego County Central Courthouse, Downtown San Diego, Morning Session

Although Cam had not tried a case for sixteen years, he was well aware that it's always a bad idea to piss off the judge. He had agreed to take the heat that morning by sparing Meg the task of telling Judge Watson that Lachlan still would not agree to take the district attorney's offer. Her Honor's morning smile had immediately dissolved into a frown, and she had been so visibly angry that she had addressed Lachlan directly instead of through counsel.

"You do realize, Professor Adair, that if you are convicted, you will not be able to raise prejudice from the interruption on Thursday because you haven't asked for a mistrial, and you are insisting on continuing these proceedings?" Frosty did not even begin to describe her tone.

"I am aware," Lachlan said, although Cam doubted he actually understood this technicality of appellate practice. He had made it clear that he wanted to continue the trial, he would not plead, and damn the consequences.

"Very well, then. Bailiff, bring in the jurors. Where are you going to resume, Mr. Saldana?"

"I'm recalling Michael Bernstein."

Meg stood up. "The defense objects to a repetition of his testimony."

"But these are unusual circumstances," Axel replied.

"I'll allow it," Judge Watson said.

Of course you will. You're so pissed off at Lachlan that you're going to let Axel do anything he wants from here on out.

Cam only half listened to Bernstein's repetition of the damning eleven thirty-one text message. He'd spent the entire weekend going back over all the surveillance video to try to find even a tiny hint that someone had entered Nora's house after Lachlan left at twelve thirty. He had even pressed Raven into service in his desperate mission to save her father from prison. But neither of them found anything.

"Cross-examination?"

Cam jolted himself back to the present.

"Thank you, Your Honor." Cam took the podium. "Now, Mr. Bernstein, when we left off last week, I believe you testified that you did not see any cars approaching Ms. Carson's residence as you were leaving."

"That's correct."

"So you have no idea who was driving the black Range Rover that entered the security gate at eleven forty, correct?"

"Correct."

"And was there a reason that Professor Adair did not accompany you to Ms. Carson's that night?"

"He had dinner plans of his own at his hotel."

"And which hotel was that?"

"The Fairmont."

"And how long does it take to drive from the hotel to Ms. Carson's house?"

"About thirty minutes."

"So if Professor Adair received your message at eleven thirty-one at the Fairmont, could he have been at Ms. Carson's nine minutes later?"

"No."

Finally, a home run!

"Now, last week we were also discussing your acquaintanceship with Professor Adair's ex-wife, Victoria."

"Correct."

"And I believe you testified that she had a financial interest in the sequel that Ms. Carson was threatening to block?"

"That's correct."

"Do you have personal knowledge of the extent of her interest?"

"I do. Victoria's divorce settlement entitled her to ten percent of Lachlan's share of the profits."

"And how much do you think that might be worth?"

"I would say upward of ten million. Maybe more."

"No further questions."

Meg gave him an imperceptible smile as he sat down between Lachlan and Raven at the defense table. But his victory did not last long.

"Your Honor, the People call Jacob Bertrand."

"Objection." Meg stood to object. "Mr. Bertrand was not on the pre-trial witness list."

"His testimony will be very brief and is related to the defense's cross-examination of Mr. Bernstein," Axel explained.

"I'll allow it."

Because Your Honor wants to teach Lachlan Adair a lesson in just how reckless he's been to continue this trial.

Jacob Bertrand was a heavyset man with very dark hair who appeared to be in his mid-forties. He was wearing the standard West-Coast executive uniform: jeans and a suit coat over an open red-checked shirt.

"And what is your profession, Mr. Bertrand?" Axel asked after the witness had identified himself and been sworn.

"I am the manager of Mille Fleurs restaurant in Rancho Santa Fe."

"And do you recall the evening of February 13, 2019?"

"Yes. We were very busy that night, so I helped the waitstaff at the tables."

"And do you recall personally serving any special guests?"

"Yes. Seamus O'Malley was there that night with Lachlan Adair, and I took care of them."

"I'd like for you to examine this receipt and identify it for the jury."

Cam looked at Meg. They should object to the authenticity of the document, but they already knew how Judge Watson would rule. Meg shook her head faintly. It wasn't worth trying.

"This is the bill from Mr. O'Malley's dinner that night."

"Is there a time stamped on the bill?"

"Yes. Eleven twenty-eight p.m. That's the time that Mr. O'Malley's credit card went through the register."

"So that would be the approximate time when their dinner ended?"

"Correct."

"And are you familiar with Nora Carson, Mr. Bertrand?"

"Oh, yes. She was a regular guest."

"So do you happen to know how long it takes to drive to her house from the restaurant?"

"Objection." Meg stood up. "No foundation. Lack of personal knowledge."

"I was just getting to that," Axel said.

"Overruled."

There's going to be plenty of evidence of bias against the defense for the appellate attorney to find.

"I do know the travel time," Jacob Bertrand said. "I have driven Ms. Carson home on numerous occasions when she was too intoxicated to drive."

"So what is the travel time?"

"Under ten minutes."

"Thank you. No further questions."

"Cross-examination?"

"No, thank you," Meg said.

"Any more questions, Mr. Saldana?"

"Not for this witness. The prosecution would like to call Detective Sanchez."

With a sinking feeling, Cam watched Axel cue up the surveillance footage of the Range Rover waiting by the guesthouse.

"Detective Sanchez, did you obtain surveillance footage of Nora Carson's house from the night of February 13-14, 2019?"

"I did."

"And did you find anything of interest on those videos?"

"Yes. I found an image of a black Range Rover parked by the guesthouse on the estate with someone inside close to eleven forty-five p.m."

"With the court's permission, I will now play the video that the detective has just described."

Axel's paralegal lowered the lights in the courtroom, and the image of the Range Rover waiting by the guesthouse filled the gigantic overhead screen. He enlarged the image of the sole occupant, and Cam was thankful that it was even more blurry when enlarged.

"And is this person in the driver's seat Nora Carson's killer?"

"Yes."

"And why is that true?"

"Because we know that Nora was still alive shortly after midnight when her last visitor left. No one entered the security gates after eleven forty."

"No more questions."

"Cross-examination?" Judge Watson looked at the defense table.

"Thank you, Your Honor," Cam said as he stood up and replaced Axel at the podium. "Just a couple of questions for the detective. First, Detective Sanchez, does this video show the Range Rover doing anything other than parking by the guesthouse?"

"That's all that it shows."

"So you agree that it does not show the car moving toward the house after Sonia Siebert's car drove away."

"It doesn't show that, but—"

"Objection, Your Honor," Cam said. "The witness is trying to go beyond the scope of the question."

"Sustained," Judge Watson agreed. "Just answer the question that has been asked, Detective."

"Yes, Your Honor."

"Now, Detective, can you identify the person in the parked Range Rover?"

"No."

"Can you tell if it's a man or a woman?"

"No."

"So the person in the Range Rover could be anyone?"

"Well—"

"Stop, Detective, and listen to my question. Could the person in the vehicle be someone other than my client?"

"Yes."

"Could it be a female, based on this image?"

"Yes."

"So it could be Victoria Adair, assuming she was driving a black Range Rover that night?"

"Yes."

"Thank you, Your Honor. No further questions."

Axel was on his feet as soon as Cam sat down.

"Detective Sanchez, is there any evidence that any vehicle other than this black Range Rover was on Ms. Carson's premises after Sonia Siebert left?"

"None."

"So even if the video did not capture the Range Rover in the act of moving toward Ms. Carson's home, is there any evidence that anyone else could have driven from the guesthouse to her residence when she was alone?"

"No evidence of anyone else."

"And finally, Detective Sanchez, do you have any evidence that Victoria Adair was driving a black Range Rover that day?"

"No, I do not."

"Thank you, Your Honor. No further questions."

* * *

The sandwiches sat untouched on the platter in the middle of the table in the conference room during lunch break. Cam sipped water from a plastic bottle. Lachlan sat at the end of the conference table, looking worried. Raven was next to him, her face pale and drawn. Hugh sat next to Meg who was restless because she wanted to go down to her office to check on Finn and Brianna.

"I take it things didn't go well this morning." Hugh was the first to speak.

"They did not," Meg agreed. "It looked like Cam had hit a home run when he cross-examined Michael Bernstein. He established that Victoria had a strong motive to kill Nora, and Lachlan could not have reached Nora's house from the Fairmont within nine minutes after Bernstein texted him at eleven thirty-one that she had rejected their offer."

"I was going to put on Seamus O'Malley for the defense to establish that Victoria was driving one of his black Range Rovers that night, but Axel made that fact irrelevant."

"How?"

"Axel called the manager of Mille Fleurs who served Seamus and Lachlan that night which meant Lachlan was only nine minutes from Nora's when he received Bernstein's message."

"I see." Hugh frowned. After a few seconds of thought, he asked, "But isn't it still true that no one knows for sure who was driving the car that entered the gates at eleven forty?"

"In theory, I suppose," Cam said.

"Was that all of their evidence this morning?"

"Axel played the video that shows a black Range Rover sitting by the guesthouse, waiting for Nora to be alone."

"Were you in that car?" Hugh looked at Lachlan.

"Yes, but I didn't kill Nora. She was alive when I left her."

"Do you have any evidence of that?"

"Nothing but my word."

"Can the prosecution identify you as the person in the car?" Hugh asked.

"No," Cam answered.

"We're left with only one argument," Meg said. "And that is Axel can't establish beyond a reasonable doubt who was in that vehicle."

"Would you buy that if you were a juror?" Hugh asked.

"Probably not," Cam said. "And that's our problem."

At that moment the conference room door burst open and Cam's secretary hurried into the room.

"Sorry to interrupt. There's someone here to see you, Mr. Rhodes. I put her in your office. And your babysitter needs to see you, Ms. Courtney. She isn't feeling well."

Meg got up and shot out of the room like a rocket. Cam, on the other hand, hesitated.

"Who wants to see me?" he asked.

"Her name is Kiara Blake."

* * *

Kiara was pacing back and forth in Cam's office when he entered. She stopped pacing and said as soon as she saw him, "I have to testify for Lachlan." She looked frightened and desperate.

"Why?"

"Because Lachlan is going to be convicted if I don't."

"But you don't have any testimony that will help him," Cam objected. "You can only say what you told me in our interview: you saw a black Range Rover waiting by the guesthouse. You weren't able to identify who was inside."

"But I can now."

"How come?"

"Because it's the only way to keep Lachlan from being convicted. It was Victoria. I can testify that it was Victoria."

"But you don't know that to be true."

"But no one knows that except you and me."

"You're offering to perjure yourself for Lachlan?"

"It's not perjury if I believe it's true."

"But you don't believe it's true. You want Lachlan to give you the leading role in the sequel."

"Yes, but it's more than that."

"How?"

"He's asked me to marry him."

"Lachlan Adair has asked you to marry him?"

"Yes."

"When?"

"Actually, before Nora died. He said that if she wouldn't agree to a divorce, he'd file himself."

"And the marriage would be good publicity for the new movie. Just like his marriage to Nora when the original movie came out."

"No. He's in love with me."

"I can't put you on the stand."

"Why?"

"Because I could lose my license if I put on testimony that I know is false."

"But no one knows what I saw except you and me. No one can prove it's false."

"Victoria could."

"How?"

"By being called by the prosecution in rebuttal to say where she really was that night. Lachlan has already admitted to us that he was the one waiting by the guesthouse. We know you're lying, and the ethics rules say we can't put you on the stand."

She looked more and more desperate as Cam spoke. "Please, you have to let me do this. My life will be ruined if Lachlan goes to prison."

"That's a bit of an exaggeration, isn't it?"

"No. The movie won't be made because there's no one else to write the screenplay. This is my big break. You have to let me testify."

The door stirred, and Raven slipped into the room.

"I came to see what's going on." Her eyes told him that she knew she shouldn't be there.

Kiara ran to her and hugged her. "Thank God, you're here! Tell Mr. Rhodes I have to testify for Lachlan. I can say it was Victoria in the car."

Raven looked quizzically at Cam. "That's good news, isn't it? We need her testimony."

"But we know it wasn't your mother. I can't knowingly present false evidence."

"Even if it could be true?" Raven pleaded.

"But it can't be. Your father admitted he is the person in the car on the video."

"But he didn't kill Nora. He said that, too. We don't have a video of my mother's arrival at the house, but logically, since Dad didn't kill Nora, it has to be my mother. Somehow, she came after Dad left. The prosecutor thinks the killer is on his video. Since my mother is the killer, it isn't really lying to let Kiara identify the driver as my mother."

"And what happens when Axel puts on your mother in rebuttal to say she wasn't anywhere near Nora's that night?"

"He won't be able to do that because my mother killed Nora. I'm certain of it."

Cam remained silent.

"Please." Raven had tears in her eyes. "If you don't let Kiara testify, you know my father will go to prison. You, yourself, just told Hugh that the jury won't buy the argument that the prosecution has failed to prove who was in the car. Please."

Cam was amazed that he was actually considering using Kiara as a witness when all of his professional training said he'd be in ethics trouble if he did.

"The decision isn't mine," he finally said. "Meg is the lead trial attorney. We'll discuss it, and she will decide. I'll go down to her office now. The two of you should go back to the conference room and wait."

Raven ushered Kiara out, while Cam headed down the hall to Meg's office. Brianna, the babysitter, passed him looking pale and ill.

"I'm glad you've come," Meg said as soon as he entered.

"Brianna is vomiting and running a fever. I've had to send her home. I'm going to have to take Finn back to court with us. I'll sit in the back with him."

"That's not a good idea," Cam responded. "My secretary can watch him here until the afternoon session is over."

Finn looked from his mother's face to Cam's. Then he said stubbornly, "I don't want to be with a stranger. I want to be with my mother." He put his arm around her neck as if to prevent any possible separation.

Cam felt his patience thinning, but he made a mighty effort at self-control. "Finn, your mother is the head lawyer in a very big trial. You won't like sitting through court. It's long and boring."

"I don't care," Finn said. "I'm not staying here with a strange person."

"What did Kiara Blake want?" Meg asked.

"She wants to testify for Lachlan. She wants to say the person she saw in the Range Rover by the guesthouse was Victoria."

"But that's not true. She couldn't identify the person in the car."

"She wants to lie for Lachlan so she can star in the sequel."

"I hope you told her we can't present perjured testimony."

Cam suddenly felt guilty that he had shifted the decision to Meg. "I did." *That part, at least, is true.*

"Look, we don't have any evidence to put on," Meg said. "The afternoon will be spent deciding on jury instructions. You can do that without me. I'll sit in the back in case we need to confer."

"You know that Judge Watson is not going to let a four-year-old in her courtroom. She's furious with Lachlan for not taking the deal. This is going to solidify her prejudice against us."

"I don't care," Meg said. "Finn is my first priority, and I want him with me this afternoon."

CHAPTER FIFTY-FIVE

Monday, April 29, 2019, San Diego County Central Courthouse, Downtown San Diego, Afternoon Session

At twelve forty-five, Cam set out with the rest of the defense team on the three-minute walk to the courthouse. Proceedings would resume at one o'clock. Meg walked on his right with Finn's hand firmly in hers. Raven, Kiara, and Lachlan followed behind. Cam worked as hard as he could to convince himself that Judge Watson would somehow agree to let Meg sit in the back with Finn while he put his entire career in jeopardy by calling Kiara as a witness. Lachlan had insisted that she be called, and Raven's tears had made it impossible for Cam to refuse. All he could do was pray that Victoria would not be able to establish her whereabouts on the night of Nora's death.

They were just starting up the steps to the front door of the courthouse when Cam heard a loud pop. First one and then another and then another. Suddenly, Cam realized that they were being fired on from the roof; and at the same minute that he realized he was under fire, he saw Finn go down on the steps followed by Meg. Cam dropped his briefcase and threw himself over Meg and Finn. He was aware of bullets flying around him, like the night in Coronado near the ocean. Return fire was coming from somewhere, but he did not know where. Then he heard a woman scream somewhere behind him, and he hoped it wasn't Raven.

The gunfire stopped as suddenly as it had begun, but Cam lay still covering Meg and Finn, too afraid to move. Then he felt a tap on his shoulder and a voice said, "It's all over. We got the sniper. You're safe now." A San Diego police officer in SWAT gear helped him to his feet. "Were you hit?" he asked.

But before he could answer, he heard Meg screaming as she held Finn's little body close.

Oh, God! No! Who shoots a child?

Suddenly sirens were screaming and ambulances seemed to be converging on them from every direction. Cam turned for a moment to look behind him and saw Raven and Lachlan slowly getting up. He prayed they hadn't been hit. But when he looked back one more time, he saw Kiara's lifeless body lying on the courthouse steps. Within a few seconds, he was surrounded by EMTs holding a stretcher.

"I don't need that," he insisted, but they put him on it anyway. He heard one of them say, "You've been shot, buddy," and then the world went dark.

* * *

Monday, April 29, 2019, USCD Hospital, Hillcrest

When he woke up, Raven was standing by his bed. His right shoulder was throbbing, and her left arm was in a sling. He tried to push back the sheets so that he could get up, but she stopped him.

"Stay still. You've just had surgery."

"Surgery?"

"There was a bullet in your shoulder. You threw yourself on Meg and saved her life. They had to operate to take it out."

"What about Finn?"

"He's stable, but his condition is critical. He's in a room down the hall. Meg's with him, and one of the nurses said that his father is on the way."

"What about you?" He reached out and touched her sling.

"I'm fine. Just a scratch on my forearm from a bullet that missed me. It's sore and bruised, so they gave me a sling."

"And your father?"

"He was very lucky. A bullet grazed his temple, but nothing worse. He's got a laceration and a bruise. They've admitted him for overnight observation because of his heart, but he's fine. Your wife called while you were in surgery. I talked to her and told her that you were going to be all right. I hope you don't mind."

"Not at all. I'm glad you did."

"She's very nice." There were tears in her eyes, and she looked away.

Cam reached out and pulled her close enough to hold her to him. "I'm just so glad you're safe," he whispered against her hair. "Lie down with me," he invited. "I need you close to me right now."

She managed to crawl onto the bed beside him, and in a few moments, he heard her breathing become regular, and he realized that she was asleep. Cam felt his own eyes droop and within minutes, he, too, was sleeping.

CHAPTER FIFTY-SIX

Tuesday, April 30,2019, USCD Hospital, Hillcrest

When he woke, Raven was gone and bright sunlight was streaming through the blinds. The clock on the nightstand said eight a.m. A moment later, the door opened, and a man in a white coat entered.

"I'm Dr. King, the surgeon who took the bullet out of your shoulder. How are you feeling?"

"A bit sore. But ready to get out of here. Can you tell me how everyone else is doing?"

"The little boy is still critical. The Adairs have been discharged. Ms. Adair is waiting for you in the hall. I told her that she could take you home, if you were ready to go."

"I am. But I need to see Finn's mother first."

"He's in 219, several doors down on the left. You can walk over after you've dressed and signed your discharge papers. Ms. Adair brought you some fresh clothes so you don't have to put your suit back on. It's covered in blood."

* * *

A half hour later, dressed in sweats, Cam entered Finn's room while Raven waited for him outside. The blinds were only half-open, and what light was allowed in fell in bars on the white tile floor. Meg was sitting in a chair next to Finn's bed, leaning toward him, and gripping his hand tightly. The sight of the tiny body in the big bed, surrounded by machines and tubes, made Cam's heart ache.

Meg turned when she head the door opening. She'd been crying so much that her entire face was swollen. Cam hurried over to her and gave her a hug as she stood up.

"How is he?"

"About the same. The bullet lodged in his right lung. He got through the surgery to take it out, and he opened his eyes once when they brought him in here, but that's all. He hasn't really been awake. How are you?"

"Just a little sore."

"You saved my life." Her eyes met and held his for a long moment.

"I–"

"Don't deny it or try to say it wasn't what it was," she said. "I'm here because that bullet went into your shoulder instead of my heart."

"I'm being sent home to rest for a bit. I'll come back later and sit with him to give you some time off if you want."

"I can't leave him. I'm sleeping in that chair over there." She pointed to a recliner at the foot of the bed.

"What about fresh clothes? Raven is with me. We could bring you some from your place later if you have a spare key."

"No need. I'll be fine just as I am until Finn wakes up."

"But your suit is covered in blood," Cam objected. "I'll come back later with a few of Jess's things. You're close to her size."

But Meg's face suddenly wore that guarded look that took over whenever Cam offered her assistance or any form of companionship. As much as she needed his help, she was determined not to take it.

* * *

Tuesday, April 30, 2019, 910 Flora Avenue, Coronado, California

Hugh called almost as soon as Cam and Raven reached Erin's cottage.

"How are you?"

"I'm fine. Finn's in serious trouble."

"I know. Meg isn't coming back to this case."

"I realize that."

"You'll have to take it from here alone."

"I realize that, too."

"Axel called me this morning. Judge Watson is itching for the defense to move for a mistrial. The DA doesn't want to do this all over again."

"Neither do I."

"Axel is renewing the plea offer. Voluntary manslaughter, three years, and cooperation with the Feds and the Brits."

"But he already turned that down. Emphatically."

"But he hadn't been nearly killed on the courthouse steps back then. Surely now he'll be sensible and take the offer."

* * *

As soon as Cam hung up with Hugh, he called Jess.

"Are you home from the hospital?" she asked.

"Yes, but right now, I'm at Erin's cottage." *It's a lie, but not a very big one.* "Axel has renewed the plea offer. I have to present it to Lachlan." *That much was entirely true.*

"Thank God!"

"Jess, there's a very good chance that he won't take it."

"So you'll move for a mistrial?"

"So far, he's been dead set against a mistrial."

"Have you come up with a better defense than questioning who was in the car that night?"

"No."

"Then it's practically malpractice not to ask for a mistrial to give yourself some more time to come up with something better."

"I know that and you know that, but Lachlan refuses to acknowledge it."

"Then he's going to be convicted."

"And that's what Meg and I have told him."

"You have the right to ask for a mistrial over his objections. That's a tactical decision of counsel," Jess pointed out.

"I know. I'm considering it."

"The girls and I are ready to come home, Cam. We're growing apart."

"You said that the last time we talked."

"Don't you agree?"

"I can't go into that at the moment, Jess. I'm now lead counsel on this case. I haven't tried a criminal case alone in sixteen years. Right now, I've got to stay focused on finding a miraculous way to get a not guilty verdict for a guilty client."

* * *

"Did you talk to Jess?" Raven asked when Cam came out of their bedroom. She was sitting on Erin's couch with a mug of coffee. She looked apprehensive. "Want some?"

"No, thanks. Yes, I talked to her." He sat down beside her and put his good arm around her.

"She's in a hurry to come home."

"She told you that?"

"Yes, when I answered her call while you were in surgery."

"It's too dangerous now."

"Agreed." She looked relieved. He gave her a reassuring hug.

"Hugh called, too. Axel doesn't want a mistrial. He wants this case to be over. He's renewed the offer to your father."

"Three years and turn snitch?"

"They call it being a 'cooperating informant.'"

Raven sighed. "He'll be dead set against it."

"I know. But we've got a child's life hanging by a thread. You're wounded, and if the bullet had come any closer to Lachlan's temple, he'd be dead. And Judge Watson is furious because he didn't agree to a mistrial after the bomb scare. Isn't cooperation better than going on with a trial before a hostile judge, in front of a pissed-off jury, with a rusty defense attorney who hasn't tried a case alone in sixteen years and who doesn't have much of a defense to offer?"

Raven gave him a rueful smile. "Yes, if you put it that way."

"Then will you work on your father and try to make him see reason?"

"Yes. I was going to Seamus's to talk to him this afternoon. I'm worried about Da's heart."

"I'm going to stop by my house and pick up a few of Jess's

clothes for Meg. Yours won't fit. You're too small. But she can't sit there for days and days in that bloody suit. And I want to see how Finn's doing."

His good arm was still around her, and she leaned into his shoulder for a moment before she drew away. But he wasn't ready to release her. He pulled her to him again and held her tightly for a long moment. Then he said, "I'm not going to lose you. I've never felt this way for anyone. I don't know how I'll work it out with Jess, but I'm not going back into the straitjacket that my life was before you came into it."

* * *

Tuesday, April 30, 2019, UCSD Hospital, Hillcrest

The blinds were closed in Finn's room when Cam entered around one thirty that afternoon. He was holding a small bag of items that he'd pulled from Jess's closet, mostly sweatpants and t-shirts. Meg was sitting by the bed in almost the same position as the previous day, but she was wearing gray yoga pants and a hoodie. Cam was relieved that she wasn't in the same bloodstained suit, but he wondered who had brought her fresh clothes.

She turned toward the door when it opened. She regarded Cam apprehensively as he stepped into the room.

"I brought you a few things in case you needed a change of clothes," he said. "How is Finn?"

"Thanks." She let him cross the room to put the bag of clothes near her chair. "They had to take him back to surgery this morning. They had to drain his chest. They're keeping him heavily sedated."

Cam couldn't bear the anguish in her voice and on her face. He leaned down to give her a hug. "Why didn't you call me?"

But she drew away from his embrace. "I'm fine, Cam, really. I–I don't need your help."

"One of the nurses told Raven that Finn's father was coming? Has he arrived from New York?"

"He's here. He went to get coffee for us. Please, Cam. It would be better if you weren't here when he comes back."

Apparently, the tension between her and the ex hadn't improved.

"Okay. I don't want to make anything worse for you. Hugh's taken you off the case."

"Yes, he told me. Did he give you anyone else to help out?"

"No. I'll be fine because Axel's renewed the plea offer. No one wants to resume the trial."

"Except Lachlan?"

"I haven't talked to him yet. He was grazed on the temple. If the sniper had improved his aim by a quarter of an inch, he'd be dead. It's my job to sell him on taking the deal. I'm hoping he'll see reason."

Meg glanced nervously at the door again.

Cam took the hint. "I'd better get going. Will you keep me updated on Finn?"

"Of course."

But it was too late. The door opened, and his father entered carrying two cups of coffee.

Cam stared at him. Suddenly, the room seemed to be spinning. "Dad? What are *you* doing here?"

"I'm Finn's father," Blaine said.

CHAPTER FIFTY-SEVEN

Wednesday, May 1, 2019, Offices of Goldstein, Miller, and Mahoney, Emerald Shapery Center

Hugh had decided that he and Cam should meet with Lachlan and Raven in the twenty-ninth floor conference room on Wednesday afternoon. Cam had already told him that he wasn't optimistic about his own ability to sell Lachlan on the plea deal. When Raven had returned to the cottage last night from Seamus's, she'd told Cam that Lachlan had refused to budge from his demand that the trial resume. She promised to do what she could today at the meeting to persuade her father to change his mind, but she wasn't optimistic about the outcome.

Cam had decided not to tell anyone about Meg and his father. He was still in shock. He kept thinking about the Sunday when he'd seen Meg and Finn at the firm in the early afternoon and then later when he'd found Blaine in his office reading depositions. Finn had told him that he'd had breakfast with his father that morning, but Cam had never connected that breakfast with Blaine, nor had he connected it with the fact that all of them had turned up at the firm at nearly the same time that afternoon, apparently to create a work-related cover story. As a result, he'd told Jackie that now monstrous lie: Blaine wasn't having an affair. But, of course, he was. And it seemed likely that he'd run out on Jackie's symphony party and broken her heart to be with Finn and Meg. But the worst part of his discovery was that it wiped out Nash's theory that Jackie's death had been an accident. She'd been holding the box of receipts when she'd thrown herself down the stairs. At least, she hadn't known about Finn. His father's decision to stand her up that Sunday afternoon had been the reason that she'd taken her life. Cam hoped that if he kept his father's secret, he would be the only one besides Blaine who knew the truth about their mother's death.

But this wasn't the time to think about his family's problems, Cam reminded himself as he studied Lachlan, who was sitting on the opposite side of the conference table. The abrasion on his temple stood out, ugly and red, a reminder that he'd had a close brush with death on Monday. Hugh lost no time in reminding him of his extraordinary luck.

"You're aware that the FBI thinks there will be further attempts on your life if this trial resumes?"

"I am, but that's nothing new for me."

Hugh frowned, and Cam, sitting beside him and across from Raven and her father, reflected that Hugh was used to winning verbal sparring matches. Cam saw him frown because he hadn't expected to be checkmated on his first move.

"Well, it may not be new for you," Hugh resumed, "but it's new for the attorneys of this firm. Ms. Courtney's child is now in critical condition, and Cam only has one good arm at the moment. We agreed to represent you in a courtroom, not to be casualties in your political war."

"But as I've said before, I have no control over these people. I don't even know who they are."

"Da," Raven, who was sitting at his side spoke softly but firmly, "your heart isn't going to take much more of this. The American attorneys are right: you shouldn't demand a resumption of the trial. The judge hates you at this point for going on after the bomb was planted. Putting many lives in danger is not a good idea."

Lachlan seemed to soften at his daughter's words, and Cam saw Hugh shoot her a look of gratitude.

"It's not pleading guilty that bothers me," Lachlan said. "It's having to snitch."

"So you'd plead if being a cooperating informant wasn't part of the bargain?" Hugh asked.

Lachlan sighed. "I suppose I would."

"Suppose isn't good enough," Hugh said. "I have to have a definite answer before I go back to the DA with a counteroffer."

Lachlan was silent for several moments. Cam noticed that Raven was watching him anxiously. "All right. I'll plead and take the three years if I don't have to turn snitch."

Cam could see the relief in his eyes when Hugh got up to pull the phone on the conference table within reach. Within a few minutes he had the prosecutor on the line.

"Good afternoon, Axel," Hugh began. "I'm putting you on speakerphone. I have Lachlan and Raven Adair here with Cam Rhodes. Meg Courtney isn't coming back to this case as you know."

"Good afternoon," he responded. "How is Ms. Courtney's son?"

"Still critical, I'm afraid."

"Please tell her our whole office is thinking of her and her little boy."

"I will," Hugh agreed.

"Do you have an answer from Professor Adair to our offer?" Axel went on.

"I have a counteroffer," Hugh said. "Professor Adair is willing to plead to three years providing he does not have to be an informant."

Axel was silent on the other end. Finally, he said, "But his cooperation is the only reason why my boss is willing to offer him a low term. Without an agreement for cooperation, we couldn't offer less than ten years."

"But that's likely a life sentence for a sixty-nine-year-old man," Hugh objected.

"Three years and cooperating informant or nothing," Axel said.

"Then nothing," Lachlan spoke loudly. "I've spent my entire life fighting the British. I'd rather cut my own throat than turn snitch on any of my lads at this late point in my life."

"Well, then, the trial has to resume." The disappointment in Axel's voice was palpable. "We should set a conference call with Judge Watson in the morning to tell her the news. I'll call her clerk and set it up and let you know what time she's given us."

"Thanks, Axel," Hugh said and ended the call. He looked over at Lachlan and said, "As good as our attorneys are, they aren't miracle workers. You've just signed up for a long stint in prison."

* * *

Thursday, May 2, 2019, Offices of Goldstein, Miller, and Mahoney, Emerald Shapery Center

"Your client wants to resume this trial?" Judge Watson did not even make a pretense of sounding neutral and judicial on the call with all the parties the next morning.

Cam winced and looked over at Lachlan, but he remained impassive in his seat at the conference table.

"Professor Adair has rejected our renewed plea offer," Axel said. He, at least, managed to sound unbiased.

"He's giving up three years in order to be convicted and be sentenced to life?" There was a note of hysteria underlying the judge's incredulity.

"Your Honor, the terms of the plea deal are not acceptable to my client. He does not wish to be a British informant, and I will remind you that Professor Adair is an honored Irish patriot for his service against the British in his own country," Cam said.

The reference to Lachlan's status in Ireland knocked Judge Watson off her high horse, as it was meant to do.

"Very well. It's your client's choice. We will convene at nine a.m on Monday morning. I assume that we'll start with the jury instructional conference or does the defense have any evidence it wishes to put on?"

"No, Your Honor," Cam said. "We aren't putting on any evidence. We are prepared to discuss the jury instructions first thing on Monday morning."

* * *

That afternoon, Cam was alone in his office, going back over the Adair file meticulously, hoping against hope to find any fact that he could use to cast doubt on Lachlan's undoubted guilt. Despite his best efforts, he kept coming up dry. Lachlan was guilty. Nothing could shake that conclusion. Then, just after two o'clock, his phone rang. It was Dr. Marvin Talbot, the professor of forensic kinesiology at UCSD, whom Meg had hired to be an expert witness. There was no report from him in the file, so Cam had assumed that he hadn't come up with anything that would help the defense. A defense expert would not put unfavorable results in writing because of the risk that the court would order it turned over to the prosecution in discovery.

"Hi, Cam. Meg Courtney said you'd taken over the Adair case."

"That's right," Cam said.

"I've found something that I think you should know about."

CHAPTER FIFTY-EIGHT

Monday, May 6, 2019, San Diego County Central Courthouse, Downtown San Diego, Morning Session

"You've changed your mind?" Judge Watson was no happier with Lachlan's decision to continue the trial than she'd been the previous week. "Now you do have a defense case to put on, Mr. Rhodes?"

"Yes, Your Honor." *Smile. Don't let her see that she's intimidating you. At least my arm is out of the sling even if my shoulder is still stiff and sore.*

The courtroom was packed with media and spectators who had been lined up since five a.m. to get a seat. Cam felt very alone without Meg. The doctors were still keeping Finn heavily sedated. Cam had wanted to go and see him, but Meg had not been encouraging, and Cam was sure it was because Blaine did not want him there. When the trial was over, Cam would confront his father. Or would he? Didn't he have the same desire to leave his marriage in order to be with Raven?

"So we aren't going to talk about jury instructions this morning?"

"No, Your Honor."

"Very well." Judge Watson made no effort to hide her exasperation. "Call your first witness."

"The defense calls Dr. Marvin Talbot."

Cam watched Dr. Talbot state his name, take the oath, and be seated. He was a pleasant, round-faced man. He was wearing a navy suit and a maroon tie, and the combination added to his air of authority. He had salt-and-pepper hair, and he wore black-framed glasses that also added to his scholarly appearance. He was quite fit, and he took the witness stand with an air of confidence that Cam thought would play well with the jury. Dr. Talbot's bio stated that he was fifty-two and a Distinguished Professor of Biology at the University of California, San Diego. And in addition to these credentials, he had three pages of publications in major scholarly journals.

Cam quickly elicited all of this evidence from Dr. Talbot, and Axel a bit reluctantly, agreed to accept him as an expert in his field.

"Dr. Talbot, what is kinesiology?"

"It is the scientific study of human body movement. Kinesiology addresses physiological, anatomical, biomechanical, pathological, and neuropsychological principles and mechanisms of movement."

"And do you apply your knowledge of human movement to a particular area of interest?"

"Well, actually, I have several areas of interest that I research. But I have researched and written extensively about how to distinguish an accidental fall from a fall caused by external force being applied to a human body."

"So the difference between an accident and a homicide?"

"Or the difference between someone who intentionally falls downstairs intending to take his or her own life and someone who is pushed by another person."

"And did the defense ask you to study the details of the death of Nora Carson?"

"Yes. I considered the coroner's autopsy report, the police report, and the witness statements compiled by the defense and the prosecution."

"And did you reach any conclusions about how Ms. Carson died?"

"I did. I concluded that Ms. Carson's fall was an accident and likely caused by heavy intoxication."

"Now, Dr. Talbot, the coroner has testified that Ms. Carson's blood alcohol was only 0.2. Would a BAC of 0.2 cause her to be drunk enough to fall down the stairs?"

"No, but that wasn't her actual BAC. The 0.2 was a typo in the coroner's autopsy report. The original lab data shows a BAC of 0.12." *Thank God, he called me and told me about this finding last Wednesday. We finally have a defense even if it's not airtight.*

"Your Honor, the defense would like marked as Defense Exhibit A the original lab report that Dr. Talbot just testified to as a basis for his accidental death conclusion."

"No objection." But Cam could see that Axel was not happy about this discovery.

"Now, Dr. Talbot," Cam resumed, "what are the symptoms of a BAC of 0.12?"

"Obvious physical impairment, loss of judgment, and blurred vision, loss of coordination and balance."

"So if Ms. Carson were standing at the top of the stairs, she was drunk enough to lose her balance and fall?"

"Objection. Counsel is testifying."

"Sustained." Judge Watson gave Cam a look of pure irritation.

Okay, rookie mistake after sixteen years as a corporate lawyer.

"Now, Dr. Talbot," Cam continued, "is there anything other than Ms. Carson's BAC level that caused you to conclude that her death was caused by an accidental fall?"

"Yes. Her body was found within five inches of the bottom stair."

"And why is that significant?"

"Because when a body is pushed, its weight plus the force of the push causes it to land at some distance from the stairs. When body weight is the only force causing the fall, it lands much closer to the stairs. I am certain that Ms. Carson was not pushed because of her position near the bottom stair."

"So, to sum up, what conclusion did you reach in your report?"

"That Nora Carson died as the result of an accidental fall with intoxication as the contributing factor."

"No further questions." And Cam sat down.

"Good morning, Dr. Talbot," Axel began as he took over the podium. "How many falls have you studied in your academic career?"

"At this point, thousands."

"And in every accidental fall, is the body always found within inches of the staircase?"

"No. The laws of basic physics apply here. Body weight isn't always the only factor we have to consider. In some falls, we also to take into account whether someone runs or jumps into the fall, as well as the specifics of the location where the fall took place."

"So you cannot say, as a hard and fast rule, that in every accidental fall down a staircase, the body of the victim is always found close to the stairs?"

"Not in every one, but in the majority."

"What about a man coming up behind a very drunk Nora Carson and giving her a slight nudge? Would that cause her body to land far from the staircase?"

"Well, probably not. But I'd have to know more about how much force was applied to answer that question accurately."

"But you do agree, don't you, Dr. Talbot, that Ms. Carson's balance was significantly impaired with a BAC of 0.12?"

"Yes."

"And with that much impairment, it would not take much force of any kind to cause her to fall?"

"Yes."

"No more questions, Your Honor."

"Mr. Rhodes? Redirect?"

"Yes, Your Honor." And Cam took the podium again. "Dr. Talbot, did you find any evidence that force had been applied to Ms. Carson?"

"I did not. The coroner attributed the bruising on her back to being pushed, but there were no hand patterns or fingerprint patterns to support that conclusion."

"So what caused that bruising?"

"She hit the stairs on her back as she fell. If she'd been pushed, she wouldn't have hit each stair on the way down. The spacing of the bruises on her back is consistent with the distance between the steps."

"Thank you, Dr. Talbot."

"Mr. Saldana? Recross?"

"No, Your Honor."

Cam felt a huge wave of relief as Dr. Talbot exited the courtroom. Axel had made inroads into his testimony, but he hadn't destroyed it entirely.

"Does the defense have another witness?" Judge Watson's expression said that she hoped the answer was no.

"Yes, Your Honor. The defense calls Sonia Siebert."

Sonia made a dramatic entrance in a black suit, relieved by a red silk scarf tied around her shoulders. To appease Judge Watson's impatience, Cam made quick work of establishing that Sonia was Nora's agent and longtime friend who had lunched with her on the day of her death.

"Now, Ms. Siebert, after you left Nora Carson's house on the afternoon of February 13, did you see her again that evening?"

"Yes."

"About what time did you see her?"

"It was just before midnight. Kiara Blake and I went to talk to her after Michael Bernstein left. We wanted her to agree to let Michael make the sequel to *Unforgettable*."

"And did you talk to her about the project?"

"Somewhat. Kiara and I found her in her den. She was pretty drunk and still drinking wine. We tried to persuade her to take the financial package that Michael was offering, but she wouldn't see reason. She believed that making the movie would boost her career but more importantly, she thought that making the movie with Lachlan would rekindle his feelings for her."

"Did you do anything to disabuse her of that notion?"

"Yes. As her agent, I knew that the movie wouldn't help what little was left of her career. And as her friend, I knew that her husband, if he had ever been in love with her at all, no longer had feelings for her."

"So you were able to change her mind about blocking the sequel?"

"I don't know about that. Nora was far more fixated on having Lachlan back. I could see that after I talked to her about her marriage, she seemed to understand for the first time that he had never loved her and he would never come back to her. She began to cry, and it looked as if something inside of her just fell apart."

"What happened after that?"

"She agreed to let Kiara and I help her upstairs to bed because she was too drunk to get there by herself. We left her sitting on her bed. I tried one more time to make her see that taking Michael's offer was best for everyone, but that upset her. She asked us to leave, so we did."

"What time was it?"

"It was right at midnight. I heard the clock chime as we went downstairs."

"No further questions."

"Mr. Saldana?"

"Yes, Your Honor."

Cam watched Axel take the podium. "Now, Ms. Siebert, you just testified that you found Ms. Carson in her den that night.

Is that room on the first or second floor of her residence?"

"The first floor."

"And you testified that you and Ms. Blake helped her to her bedroom. Was that on the second floor?"

"Yes."

"Could Ms. Carson have navigated those stairs to the second floor without your assistance?"

"I don't know."

"But she didn't go up on her own steam that night, did she?"

"We did help her up the stairs."

"And you said that you left her sitting on her bed?"

"Yes."

"Did she have any reason to go back downstairs alone after you left?"

"I don't know."

"But did it appear to you that she was going to bed when you left her?"

"Yes."

"Did you ever see her alone on the stairs that night?"

"No."

"Now, you also just testified that you and Ms. Blake left Nora around midnight. Is that correct?"

"Yes."

"And what vehicle were you driving?"

"I have a black BMW."

"You say you were with Nora that night, but there's no BMW shown entering the security gate, isn't that true?"

"I used the back entrance. It's a turnoff from Del Charro, the main road."

"Does that back driveway go past the guesthouse?"

"Yes."

"And did you see a vehicle by the guesthouse that night as you were leaving Ms. Carson's?"

"Yes."

"What kind of vehicle was it?"

"A black Range Rover."

"And could you see who was in the car?"

"I could see that someone was in the driver's seat, but I could not see who it was."

"Could you tell if it was a man or a woman?"

"No."

"Thank you, Ms. Siebert. No more questions."

"Mr. Rhodes?" Judge Watson seemed slightly less hostile for a moment.

"Yes, Your Honor, just one question. Ms. Siebert, did you see the Range Rover drive toward the house?"

"No. It wasn't moving when I saw it."

"No more questions."

"Mr. Saldana?"

"No, thank you, Your Honor."

"Any more witnesses, Mr. Rhodes?"

"One, Your Honor. The defense calls Seamus O'Malley."

Seamus took the stand and quickly established his ownership of Celtic Analytics and his friendship with Lachlan.

"Now, Mr. O'Malley," Cam continued, "do you own a fleet of black Range Rovers in connection with your business?"

"I do."

"And do you also make these available to Professor Adair and his family and friends, including his ex-wife, Victoria?"

"Yes."

"And did Victoria Adair have one of your vehicles on February 13, 2019?"

"She did."

"And when did she return that car?"

"The next morning around ten."

"So Professor Adair was not the only member of his circle of family and friends driving one of your cars on February 13, isn't that correct?"

"Yes."

"And were you personally acquainted with Victoria Adair's feelings toward Professor Adair's current wife, Nora Carson?"

"I was aware that she hated Nora."

"And do you know if Victoria had any financial interest in the sequel that Professor Adair wanted to make?"

"Yes, she did. Lachlan had given her an interest as part of their divorce settlement."

"No further questions."

Axel was on his feet quickly. "Mr. O'Malley, do you have any knowledge of where Victoria Adair went in your vehicle on February 13?"

"No."

"So you have no idea if she drove to Nora Carson's house that night do you?"

"I do not."

"No further questions."

"Redirect, Mr. Rhodes?"

"Yes, Your Honor. Briefly." Cam took over the podium again.

"Mr. O'Malley, does the fact that you do not know where Victoria drove your vehicle on February 13 conclusively prove that the Range Rover parked by the guesthouse was not the one Victoria was using?"

"It does not."

"So it's entirely possible that Victoria was the one parked by the guesthouse that night?"

"To my knowledge, yes."

"No further questions." And Cam sat down.

* * *

Monday, May 6, 2019, Offices of Goldstein, Miller, and Mahoney, Emerald Shapery Center

"It went well," Hugh said as they assembled in the twenty-ninth-floor conference room around the familiar platter of sandwiches and bottles of water. "I don't think Axel did much damage to Seamus's testimony that Victoria had a Range Rover that night that matched the one parked by the guesthouse."

Cam was relieved to hear that. Hugh had insisted on being in the audience that morning to monitor his solo flight without Meg. Even if he was Tyler Miller's grandson, he still had to turn in a performance that Hugh would approve of.

"Now I have to testify when we resume after lunch," Lachlan said.

"What for?" Hugh demanded. "Don't you know how risky it is for the defendant to testify?"

"But I'm innocent," Lachlan insisted. "I have to explain to the jury how I found Nora that night at the head of the staircase, impossibly drunk and trying to balance on one foot."

Hugh looked from Lachlan to Cam, and he knew he was expected to have the answer. "If you testify to that, you'll have to admit that you were in the Range Rover."

"Well, I was."

"But a key point of our defense," Cam reminded him, "is that the prosecution can't prove who was in the car."

"But I can testify that Nora died because she was drunk and she fell."

"Did you actually see her fall?" Cam asked. "The last time you told this story, you said you took her from the staircase to her bed and left her there."

"That's true. I did. She was in bed when I left."

"So if she fell, she got up after you left and went back to the stairs?"

"Yes, of course."

"Except you don't know that," Hugh broke in, "because you never saw it."

Lachlan stared at Hugh. "But I know that has to be true."

"Why?"

"Because I didn't kill Nora."

The conference room became silent as Lachlan looked from Hugh to Cam several times. Finally, he said slowly, "You don't believe me, do you?"

"It doesn't matter what we believe," Hugh said. "Our job is to defend you."

"But Dr. Talbot said–"

"Dr. Talbot is an expert," Cam explained, "who's been paid for his opinion. In litigation, you can find an expert who will testify to almost anything—for a price."

"So you're saying that you bought an expert opinion that Nora's death was an accidental fall?"

"No, we're not saying that," Hugh answered.

"I very much disagree," Lachlan responded.

"Da," Raven broke in. "It's up to your attorneys to decide how to defend you and that includes relying on the testimony of an expert witness if they feel they need one."

Lachlan smiled fondly at her. "You're telling me this is when I should keep my trap shut."

"If you want to put it that way." Raven gave him a gentle smile.

"Very well, then," Lachlan conceded. "If you think I shouldn't testify, I won't insist."

"To be clear," Cam said, "this is one place where you do have the right to override my judgment. You have an absolute right to testify if you want to."

But Lachlan shook his head. "If my daughter thinks I should listen to you, then I should listen to you."

"Do you want to sit through the conference on jury instructions?" Cam asked. "That's what we'll do when we go back."

"No."

"Then you can waive your presence when court resumes and leave for the day. Closing arguments will be first thing in the morning."

* * *

Monday, May 6, 2019, 910 Flora Avenue, Coronado, California

Cam couldn't sleep that night. He got up, went into the living room of the cottage, and poured himself a small scotch, then sat down on the sofa to drink it. Too much alcohol would impair his performance tomorrow.

As he sipped, he reflected on the fact that the defense case rested entirely upon the testimony of Dr. Talbot, and juries were often quick to reject an expert as a hired gun whose opinion could be bought by a wealthy defendant. Doubts about the strength of his case began to gnaw at him. Maybe he should have let Lachlan testify. Maybe hearing him explain how he tried to rescue a very drunk Nora from doing ballet exercises at the head of the stairs would have had more appeal than Dr. Talbot's somewhat dry testimony about the laws of physics.

But Lachlan's story didn't sound true, and Cam was sure that it wasn't. After all, Lachlan had proven himself to be a chronic liar. He had even admitted that he could no longer distinguish the truth from a lie. And there had been so many lies in this case, beginning with Leslie Ryan and continuing right up to the lie about dinner at the Fairmont. A sinking feeling in the pit of his stomach told him that the jury was not going to be impressed with Dr. Talbot. Lachlan was guilty, and there was nothing Cam could do about it.

"Why are you awake?" Raven was standing in the doorway in her black silk pajamas. She crossed the room to sit beside him on the sofa.

"I couldn't sleep. I'm worried about tomorrow."

She put her arms around him and nestled against his

shoulder. "You'll do a wonderful job for Dad."

"But I don't think it's enough."

"It will be enough."

He shifted so that he could put his good arm around her, and they sat in silence for a few moments. Finally, Cam said, "No matter what happens, I want you to stay with me."

She reached up and cupped his cheek with her hand before she leaned over and gave him a long kiss. Then she said, "Finish your drink and come back to bed."

CHAPTER FIFTY-NINE

Tuesday, May 7, 2019, San Diego County Central Courthouse, Downtown San Diego, Morning Session

"As I said to you, ladies and gentlemen, at the beginning of this case, this is a simple story." Axel Saldana began his closing argument at nine the next morning. "The defendant wanted to make a movie, but not just any movie. A movie that was worth so much that the defendant offered to pay his wife millions to keep her from blocking it. But Nora Carson wasn't willing to be bought. She had a right to the lead role, and she wasn't going to back down.

"On February 13, many people tried to talk Nora out of her right to be in that movie. Michael Bernstein, the producer, tried to talk her out of it. Her agent, Sonia Siebert, tried to talk her out of it. And, above all, the defendant tried to talk her out of it. But Alicia Cortez heard Nora's answer: 'Over my dead body.' And that's exactly what happened. That night, as soon as the defendant found out that Mr. Bernstein had not been able to persuade Nora to take the financial deal, he went straight to her house and he took care of it. Now he could make that movie, over her dead body."

Axel paused to play the video clip of the Range Rover parked by the guesthouse. Then he continued. "Now the defense wants you to believe that it makes a difference whether Nora's BAC was.02 or .12, but it doesn't make any difference at all. Why? Because there's no evidence that Nora, whether at 0.2 or 0.12, was ever standing on those stairs alone."

Lachlan shot Cam a look. *I still think putting him on the stand would have been a bad idea. But if he gets convicted, he'll say his testimony would have made the difference. And maybe it would have.*

"The defense's own witness has told us that the only time Nora was on the stairs that night was when Ms. Siebert and Ms. Blake helped her to her bedroom. The next time Nora was near those steps was when her husband pushed her. Ladies and gentlemen, the prosecution has proven its case beyond a reasonable doubt. There is no doubt that the defendant was the person Ms. Siebert saw in the Range Rover that night. He was waiting for Nora to be alone. As soon as he saw Ms. Siebert's car drive away through the back entrance, he immediately went into the house and made sure that he could make his movie over his wife's dead body. Ladies and gentlemen, I am sure that you will return a just verdict in this case: a verdict of guilty."

Axel ended with a dramatic pause and then sat down.

"Mr. Rhodes?" Judge Watson invited Cam to the podium.

"Thank you, Your Honor." Cam took a long breath to steady himself before he began. He couldn't lose this case, and yet, he already had.

"Ladies and gentlemen, this case is not as simple as Mr. Saldana says it is. What Professor Adair and his wife said in a moment of anger is not the real story. The real story is the scientific evidence that the prosecution has done nothing to refute. You heard Dr. Talbot. The prosecution got Nora's BAC wrong. It wasn't .02. It was 0.12. Why is that error significant? Because the prosecution did not want you to know that Nora was so drunk that she couldn't navigate those steps alone. You heard Sonia Siebert. Nora needed help to go upstairs. What that means is after Sonia left Nora, she went back to the stairs and tried to go back down. But because she was so drunk, she slipped and fell to her death.

"And how do we know that Nora returned to the stairs alone and that her death was accidental? Three reasons. First, Nora was only sitting on her bed when Sonia left her. Sonia didn't say she got in and prepared to go to sleep. So we know she went back to the stairs at some point, drunk and alone.

"Second, and more importantly, there wasn't much force behind her fall. Dr. Talbot told you that she fell within inches of the stairs. If she'd been pushed, the force would have made her land much farther away.

"Third, the prosecution has never proven that anyone went into Nora's house after Sonia left. The prosecution wants you to believe that Professor Adair was sitting in that Range Rover on the surveillance footage. But as Seamus O'Malley established, the occupant of that car could also have been Victoria Adair. And, in fact, no matter who it was, the prosecution is only speculating that the car drove to the main house after everyone left. And the prosecution is only speculating that whoever was in that car went into the house. The surveillance video is worthless in this case because it doesn't prove that Nora's death was a homicide, and even if it was, it doesn't prove the identity of the killer.

"The prosecution has not proved its case, ladies and gentlemen. The defense is certain that when you've considered all the evidence, you will find Professor Adair not guilty."

Cam realized that his legs were shaking as he left the podium and resumed his seat at the defense table. *Thank God, that's over.*

"Rebuttal, Mr. Saldana?"

"Briefly." And Axel replaced Cam at the podium.

"Three things, ladies and gentlemen. Remember that Dr. Talbot was highly paid for his opinion about the amount of force applied to Ms. Carson. Professor Adair, as we know, is worth millions thanks to *Unforgettable.* Second, if her BAC was really 0.12, it wouldn't have taken much force from the defendant to push her down the stairs, so that means ending up five inches from the bottom of the stairs does not prove an accidental fall. Third, the evidence proves that the defendant was the only person who knew at eleven thirty-one p.m. on February 13 that Nora had rejected Michael Bernstein's offer. And the defendant was the only person driving a black Range Rover who could have passed through the security gate at eleven forty. I'm confident that you will find the defendant guilty of his wife's murder. Thank you."

CHAPTER SIXTY

Wednesday, May 8, 2019, UCSD Hospital, Hillcrest

Meg didn't look happy to see Cam the next morning when he opened the door to Finn's room while she and Blaine were sitting on either side of his bed.

She immediately got up and motioned for him to follow her into the hall. "Why are you here?"

"We finished closing arguments yesterday. The jury is currently out. I wanted to check on you and Finn and bring him these." Cam handed her a package of Legos.

"How did closing go?"

"Well enough, I guess. Hugh was pleased. But I think we're looking at a guilty verdict. I hadn't heard from you, and I was worried about you and Finn."

"Thank you," she said a bit abruptly. "But there's been nothing new to tell you. The doctors haven't been willing to lift the sedation until today."

"Isn't that good news?"

"They aren't sure that he'll come out of it."

Cam's heart sank. "I—"

"Look, I know that I owe you an explanation, but now isn't the time."

"You don't owe me anything," Cam said. "I didn't come for an explanation. I came because I'm worried about both of you."

The door to Finn's room opened, and Blaine came out. He walked over to Meg and put his arm around her possessively. "You don't need to worry about Meg and Finn," he said. "They are my responsibility."

"I'm not questioning that, Dad," Cam said. "But I care about them, too."

"Then you'll leave us alone to deal with this."

"I haven't told Nash or Addie or McKenna if that's worrying you," Cam replied. "I'm leaving that for you."

"I appreciate that." Blaine seemed to soften slightly. "But you aren't needed here."

Cam looked directly at Meg. Her eyes were pleading with him to leave.

"I'll call you with any news," she said. "I promise. And you have to let me know what happens when the jury comes back."

"Okay." Cam turned and began to walk down the hall toward the exit. When he was halfway there, he heard the door to Finn's room close behind them.

* * *

He went back to the office, hoping to lose himself in work for other clients.

His phone rang: Jess.

"The news said that the Adair case has gone to the jury."

"It has. Yesterday morning."

"It sounds like they're taking their time. Good news for the defense."

"Yes."

"How's Meg's little boy?"

"We'll know more later today."

"I'm going to book a flight home for tomorrow."

"Not yet, Jess." He did not try to keep the urgency out of his voice.

"We've been gone too long, Cam."

"Please be patient a little longer. The situation is still volatile. We don't know what's going to happen when the verdict comes back."

"But it looks like you've got a chance at a defense verdict."

"Jess, there's no doubt that Lachlan's guilty. He's an important figure in Ireland, and we are all still under heightened security. There's going to be some kind of trouble when they reach a verdict. I want you and Steph and Callie to stay where you're safe."

* * *

As soon as he hung up, his phone buzzed again. The jury had sent a note to the court. The jurors wanted a readback of the coroner's testimony. Judge Watson wanted to know if anyone had any objections. There were none. *If they're focused on the coroner, a guilty verdict is on the way, and it won't be long now.*

* * *

Wednesday, May 8, 2019, 910 Flora Avenue, Coronado, California

That night, Cam and Raven had just sat down on Erin's couch after supper when Cam's phone rang.

"I'm at the guard station," Nash said. "They won't let me come up to the house unless you say it's okay. I need to talk to you."

Cam verified his brother's identity. When he finished, he said to Raven, "Nash is on his way."

"Does he know about us?"

"Yes."

"But how?"

"He came by my house the day we were putting away Mother's things. When he saw us together, he left without saying anything. Don't worry. He hasn't told anyone."

A few seconds later, the doorbell rang, and Cam opened it to let Nash in.

"Sorry to intrude," he said, "but something important has come up."

"You're not intruding. Come into the living room and sit down. Drink?"

"No, thanks."

Raven, who was sitting on the couch, stood up when they entered. Nash hesitated for a split second and then decided to kiss her on both cheeks. "Hi, Raven," he said when he finished.

"It's good to see you again," she said. "I'm going to leave you two alone to talk."

She went into the kitchen. As soon as she closed the door behind her, Nash said,

"Dad called me today."

"And I'm guessing he told you about his affair."

"Yes."

"And I'm guessing you realized that Mom's death wasn't an accident."

"She didn't trip and fall," Nash said. "She did it deliberately."

"Yes," Cam agreed.

"When did you find out about Dad?"

"A little over a week ago when I went to the hospital to see Meg and Finn. He wanted to tell everyone himself. Has he told Addie and McKenna?"

"Not yet. He said he would when he's ready."

"Then he will. After all, he told you. All of his attention right now is focused on Finn. You're his hero by the way."

"Whose?"

"Finn's. The *Sam and Tucker* movie. Jess suggested inviting Meg and Finn to Mother's party after the symphony concert. She was going to show the movie to the kids and have you surprise Finn that night. But Meg wouldn't agree to come. I see why now."

"Jess called me today," Nash said.

"She called me, too." Cam knew he sounded defensive.

"She's anxious to come home."

"I know. But it's still too dangerous."

"Is that the real reason, big brother?"

"It's at least one of them. Did you come here to talk about Dad or me?"

"Both," Nash said. "Dad can't take back anything he's done, but there's still time for you."

"Are you telling me what to do?" Now he sounded angry and defensive.

"No."

They sat in silence for a few minutes. Finally, Cam said, "I can't go back to the way things were."

"What do you mean?"

"I mean I've marched in lockstep my whole life."

"Doing what was expected of you," Nash added.

"Right."

"And now you can't go on doing that anymore?" Nash's eyes were sympathetic.

"Right. I can't. I love Jess, but what I feel for Raven is a different kind of love. I can't go back to being without that feeling or being without her."

Nash was quiet for a few moments.

"Do you hate me?" Cam asked.

"Of course not." His smile seemed a little forced but still reassuring.

"Then what?" Cam probed.

"Jess is strong. She'll handle it and probably even get over it. But you'll be turning your girls' lives upside down."

"You mean they'll hate me."

"That might be too strong a word. They won't accept Raven as a stepmother, and they'll probably never trust you again."

"Then it will just have to be that way," Cam insisted. "I can't go back to my old life."

"No one thought much about what you needed in that life," Nash observed. "Everyone expected you to take care of them."

"And with Raven it's different."

"Is it different, or is she playing you?"

"It hurts for you to suggest that the one person who has put me first isn't sincere," Cam said.

"Then I'm sorry, and I apologize." Cam could tell Nash meant it. "If you're really serious about making this thing with Raven permanent, then you owe it to Jess to tell her before she comes back."

"You're right. I've thought about that."

"Then do it," Nash said.

"Okay, I will. Tomorrow."

* * *

Raven came out of the kitchen when Nash left.

"How was it?" she asked.

"Difficult and frank. He wanted to talk about my father's affair with Meg."

"Did he talk about us, too?"

"Yes. He told me to tell Jess before she comes back that I'm staying with you."

She studied him in silence for a few minutes. Then she asked, "What about Callie and Stephanie?"

"They'll love you."

"I doubt that."

"You'll see."

"You look tired," she said. "We should go to bed."

"Yes," he agreed.

They turned out all the lights and made their way to the bedroom. When Cam reached for the light on the bedside table, Raven put out her hand to stop him.

"No light. Let's undress in the dark."

CHAPTER SIXTY-ONE

Thursday, May 9, 2019, 910 Flora Avenue, Coronado, California

When Cam woke the next morning, Raven's side of the bed was empty and the bars of light coming through the blinds were etched on the floor with hard distinct lines. He immediately knew that he had grossly overslept. He grabbed his phone in a panic, imagining the worst: the court had called because the jury had reached a verdict. But he was safe because it was eleven thirty, and there were no incoming calls.

He lay still for a moment, savoring the freedom of lying naked under the sheets in the late morning. He could not remember a time when he had had the luxury of rising slowly instead of rushing to get up and dressed and off to deal with some family or professional crisis. Nor could he recall a time when he'd made love all night long.

The thought made him want to resume. He would find Raven and lead her back to bed. He got up and pulled on his pajama pants and went into the living room, expecting to find her. But she was not there. Instead, a man in dark slacks and a tweed jacket was standing with his back to Cam. He seemed to be studying the view through the front window intently until he turned and said, "Oh, hello there."

He spoke with the same lilt that made Raven's voice so mesmerizing, and like Raven, he was very attractive. His six feet lent him an air of authority and importance that was somewhat softened by his large dark, sympathetic eyes, the most striking feature of his oval face. He had a full head of thick, dark hair, and seemed vaguely familiar, although Cam was certain they had never met.

"I'm Raven's half brother, James," the man said pleasantly.

Of course he seems familiar. He looks like Raven's portrait of Sinead. Cam's half-nakedness suddenly made him feel hot with embarrassment. His shirtless, shoeless, disheveled appearance spoke volumes about how he'd spent last night.

"I— She didn't say— I didn't know you were coming." Stammering was even more embarrassing.

"Well, we weren't sure. I've been on assignment in Riyadh, and I couldn't leave until I'd finished. Raven asked me to come if I could, so she wouldn't be alone. She said Dad's likely to be convicted."

But she's not alone! Last night was meant to tell her that once and for all. Cam felt as if he'd been punched in the gut. He wanted to turn and flee to hide the disappointment that he was certain was visible on his face.

The door to the kitchen opened, and Raven entered the living room. She walked over to Cam and gave him a kiss on the lips. The intimacy of the gesture in front of her brother reassured him. "I see you've met James," she said. "I asked him a few weeks ago to turn up if he could. You were saying then that things weren't looking good for Dad, and I thought he should be here. James and I have eaten, but you need some breakfast."

"No," Cam said. "I'll grab something on my way to the office. I've overslept. I need to be downtown if the court calls."

He went back into the bedroom and quickly dressed for work all the while wondering if today would be the day of Lachlan's conviction and if last night had meant to Raven what it had meant to him.

* * *

The minute Cam entered his office, Hugh appeared. He didn't look happy.

"Where have you been?"

"I—I—"

"Judge Watson's clerk has been trying to call you. She finally got through to me instead."

Oh, God! He pulled out his phone and realized that he'd turned it off last night. When he turned it on, he could see all the missed calls from the court.

"Did the jury reach a verdict?" *I knew this would happen. I've screwed up big-time.*

"No. They sent a note asking for a readback of Dr. Talbot's testimony. Judge Watson was so angry, she was going to go ahead without hearing from you."

Cam's knees were weak with relief. "Well, I'd have hardly said no to that."

"True. But you know better than to be out of touch during jury deliberations."

"Sorry. I must have accidentally turned my phone off last night. Nash came by with some family business that's a bit stressful. I was preoccupied with that."

Mentioning Cam's family reminded Hugh that he was chastising Tyler Miller's grandson who had, not very long ago, lost his mother, Tyler Miller's only daughter. "It's fine," Hugh backtracked. "Don't worry about it. I'm sure there's a lot on your mind. How is your father doing?"

Oh, God. Not Dad. Not now. How is my father planning to explain to Hugh and the rest of the firm that he was unfaithful to Tyler Miller's daughter and had a child with a senior associate?

"Blaine's under a lot of stress." *At least that much was true.*

"We're all a bit lost without Jackie," Hugh said.

* * *

Cam made himself sit at his desk until five o'clock as penance for missing Judge Watson's call that morning. But there were no further communications from the court, and by five o'clock it became clear that the jury had gone home without reaching a verdict. Tomorrow. It would be all over. He knew he'd broken his promise to Nash to call Jess today, but it just hadn't been the day to tell his wife he couldn't go on with their old life. Tomorrow would be soon enough.

He was relieved to find Raven alone when he got home. She rushed to the door to kiss him and tell him that supper was almost ready.

"Where's James?"

"He's with Dad and Seamus. Nothing from the jury today?"

He told her about the request for Dr. Talbot's testimony.

"That's good news, isn't it?"

"Let's hope it is." But in his heart, he knew better.

CHAPTER SIXTY-TWO

Friday, May 10, 2019, Offices of Goldstein, Miller, and Mahoney, Emerald Shapery Center

Anxious not to make the same mistake of being late two days in a row, Cam made it to his desk by nine the next morning. His punctuality paid off. At nine thirty, Judge Watson's clerk called. Another jury request for a readback. This time they wanted the testimony of Michael Bernstein and Jacob Bertrand.

"Are they asking for the complete testimony, the defense cross as well as the direct?"

"Judge Watson said to tell you they asked for all of it."

"Okay, then. The defense has no objection."

If they wanted to hear cross as well as direct that meant they hadn't completely caved into the prosecution's case. But still, it didn't look good for Lachlan even though they were taking their time. Bernstein established an ironclad motive, and Bertrand made it impossible to deny Lachlan hadn't been at Nora's that night. The only evidence left was Sonia's observation of the black Range Rover. *At least they didn't ask for Sonia's testimony,* he told himself when he hung up on the call. But two hours later, just before eleven o'clock, they did.

* * *

Friday, May 10, 2019, UCSD Hospital, Hillcrest

The readback of Sonia's testimony was the nail in the coffin for the defense. Clearly, they hadn't believed Dr. Talbot's opinion that Nora's death was an accident because they'd moved on to Bernstein, Bertrand, and Sonia, the evidence that proved that Lachlan was the shadowy figure in the black Range Rover. *Maybe I should have let him testify about why he was there and what he did. No, that's ridiculous. Who would believe he just led her back to bed when a multimillion-dollar movie deal was at stake?*

Cam knew that they'd have a guilty verdict by early afternoon. He hadn't heard any news from Meg since Wednesday when she'd told him the doctors weren't certain whether Finn would come out of the sedation. He told himself that if things had gone wrong, he'd have heard by now. But the silence worried him. He decided that he would go to the hospital in the interval between the damning readback and the time to assemble in the courtroom to hear the inevitable bad news.

The hall outside Finn's room was empty. Cam took a deep breath, steeling himself to face Blaine, and then he pushed open the door. Meg, who was sitting by the bed, turned toward him, surprised. To his great relief, Cam could see that Finn was propped up on pillows, absorbed in something on an iPad, and Blaine was nowhere to be seen.

"I didn't mean to startle you," Cam said. "I hadn't heard any news, and I was worried."

Finn looked up and said, "I got shot, and I had to sleep a

long time to get well. But I'm going to be okay now. Want to watch *Sam and Tucker* with me?"

"I'd like to do that a little later. I want to talk to your mother now. Can I give you a hug first?"

Cam's heart turned over when Finn held out his little arms as best he could attached as he was to IVs and medical monitors. *Thank you, God,* Cam thought as he hugged him gently.

The door stirred again as Cam let Finn go, and he braced himself to see Blaine. But it was a doctor and a nurse instead.

"We've come to change his dressings," the doctor said. "Would you mind stepping outside for a few minutes?"

Meg gestured for Cam to follow her out into the corridor. The light in Finn's room had been dim, but in the brighter hall light he could see just how pale she was.

"Changing his dressings takes a little while. I've been needing to talk to you alone, but this is the first time that Blaine has been willing to leave the hospital," she said.

"Where is my father?"

"He went back to his suite at the Grant to shower and change and return some calls to a couple of clients who've been trying to reach him. Come in here where we can talk." She gestured toward an empty waiting room. She entered and took a seat on one of the red plastic sofas. She motioned for Cam to sit beside her.

"This thing with your father was never meant to go this far," she began. "We met in 2010. He had a corporate client who was in some trouble for wire fraud. I was the Assistant U.S. Attorney assigned to the case. I knew he was married, but our attraction was instant. At first, we tried not to act on it, but the feelings were too strong."

Oh, God. If only I didn't know exactly how that feels.

"In the beginning, we always met in New York when Blaine was in town on his client's case. When it settled, he had fewer reasons to be in the city, so we saw each other less often.

"But Blaine went to DC quite a bit, so he persuaded me to start meeting him there. We got tired of weekends in hotels, so we began taking trips to little B & Bs, usually in Virginia, but sometimes he'd fly up to New York, and we'd find romantic little places in Connecticut."

Mother's box of receipts.

"Eventually, Blaine talked about making it permanent, but for me that was never a possibility. I liked my job in the U.S. Attorney's Office. I liked living in New York. I didn't want children. I liked the thrill of having an affair with an attractive, older man, but that was all that I wanted."

"Did you tell him that?"

"He never asked me what I wanted, but I thought it could never go any further than it had because he always talked about the complications from his position at the firm as the son-in-law of Tyler Miller. From what he said, it seemed as if he could never divorce your mother without losing his spot as the number two partner in the litigation section."

"That was true as long as my grandfather was alive. But things changed after he died."

"That must have been when he started leaving receipts from the B & B weekends for your mother to find."

"How did you know about that?"

"He told me. He wanted her to file for divorce, but he didn't want to confront her with our affair. Blaine thought she would end the marriage for sure when she saw the evidence, but she didn't, and I was relieved."

"Why?"

"Because I didn't want anything with your father other than our romantic weekends. By this time, I knew about your big family and your mother's devotion to it, and I didn't want to turn that upside down. I liked my single life and my job and my tiny New York apartment. I didn't want your father to run my life."

"Was he trying to do that?"

"He did after he found out about Finn. Obviously, the pregnancy was an accident. I was surprised to find that I did want a baby. I tried to end the affair to avoid telling him I was pregnant. But it didn't take long for Blaine to figure it all out. I stuck to my decision to end things between us. I wanted to raise Finn on my own. I wanted to keep my job at the U.S. Attorney's Office and stay in New York. I told Blaine all of that, but he wouldn't listen."

"So he was responsible for your going to Goldstein, Miller's New York office?"

"Yes. He arranged for me to join the firm, so he could pull strings to give me more time off when Finn was born and to increase my salary. And the arrangement allowed him to claim that he was working with me in New York when, in reality, the two of us were in my apartment taking care of Finn as a newborn. Blaine was determined to be hands on, and I didn't have anyone else to help me. I thought having his father in his life would be better for Finn, and Blaine really loved him from day one. And as you've seen, Finn adores him. So I began to believe that maybe we could make it work without hurting your mother."

"And then things changed when he retired?"

Meg nodded. "Yes. He lost his excuse to travel as much as he wanted to New York, so he arranged for us to come here. I tried to talk him out of that. I still wanted to live in the city, and I thought I could go back to the U.S. Attorney's Office when Finn was old enough for preschool. Everything in my personal life and my career had become too entwined with your father, and I wasn't in control of anything anymore. And Finn, at three, was growing more and more confused about the father who came and went. Blaine insisted that he could see more of him if we were all in San Diego."

"So you accepted the transfer?"

"I didn't have a choice."

"And did things improve?"

"No, everything got worse. Finn now saw Blaine more often, but he began to realize that fathers live with their families. And he couldn't understand why Blaine didn't live with us."

"So that's what you meant when you said that Finn was confused enough about the male figure in his life?"

Meg nodded. "And then Hugh assigned me to work with you. I begged Blaine to change that, but he wouldn't. He told me that it was my chance to get to know his children so that all of you would accept his eventual divorce."

"So that's why you didn't want to come to Mother's party and let Finn meet Nash and that's why you didn't want Finn to go to Baltimore with Jess and the girls."

"Yes. I could see that I was losing my identity and control of my life. Blaine kept telling me that a big win in the Adair case would make me a sure thing for partner next year, and then he'd divorce your mother and marry me. He was pushing Finn and me to be part of your family, and I didn't want that for us. I didn't want to marry him, and I didn't want him to destroy your mother's life.

"And the situation was growing more and more destructive for Finn. He was increasingly upset because Blaine didn't live with us. He kept asking when he'd get a father who didn't have to leave after every visit.

"So I decided to go back to Rochester and raise Finn on my own, the way I'd planned to from the beginning. But when I told Blaine that the situation wasn't good for Finn and that it all had to end, he threatened to take him away from me."

"So that was when Finn said his father didn't want to see him again?"

"Yes. It broke his heart, but Blaine was going to break it even more if he stayed in our son's life. I was terrified that Blaine would get custody because he has so much money and influence in this town. But I knew that I'd just have to take a chance that he'd let us go because he wouldn't want all of you to know about Finn. But now it's too late. You know."

Her eyes filled with tears, and Cam could see that she was exhausted. He put both arms around her and held her as best he could with his injured shoulder. And for a few moments, she let herself lean into his embrace. He said softly, "I could never do anything except love and accept Finn. And I'm sure my siblings would agree with me. And my mother would have loved him, too, if she'd known."

But Meg pulled away and shook her head. "No, you don't understand. Your mother couldn't accept Finn."

"But she didn't know about him," Cam said.

But Meg was crying harder now, and she had pulled away entirely from his embrace. "No," she said again. "She did know. Your father told her that night."

"What night?"

"The night she died. He didn't want to go to the symphony concert with the rest of you because he wanted to see Finn. He left Jackie at the concert and came to my house. When he told me how he'd stood Jackie up, I asked him to leave and that upset him. He called me in the wee hours and said that he'd gone home after Jackie's party was over and told her about Finn. Then the next day, when I heard about her death, I knew that she'd killed herself rather than face the loss of her marriage. And I knew I had to get Finn away from Blaine because it would destroy him to know why Jackie died."

"He doesn't have to know," Cam said.

"But if he grows up here, around all of you, eventually he'll figure it out. He's incredibly bright. But now it's too late to get him away from Blaine."

"No, it isn't. You can go as soon as Finn's out of the hospital."

But she said with a resignation that broke his heart, "No, I can't go. Don't you see? If I'd left Finn at the firm on Monday instead of insisting that he come with me to court where he really didn't belong in the first place, he wouldn't have been hurt. He couldn't bear the thought of being left with a stranger, and I gave in, and it was a stupid decision."

"That's a bit harsh, don't you think? It's been difficult to know what to do under the circumstances we've faced in the Adair case."

"But because of my bad decision, I nearly lost him. And now Blaine says I can't be trusted to raise Finn alone. He says I have to marry him so he can make sure Finn is always safe. Otherwise, if I try to take him to Rochester, he will see that I lose custody."

"That's ridiculous," Cam said. "You're Finn's mother, and I know he loves you best."

"I know that, too. But your father doesn't care."

"I won't let him hurt you and Finn," Cam insisted.

Meg stood up and gave him a gentle, sad smile. "You're the one who takes on everyone's burdens. Your father said that about you."

And that's what Raven said when she asked me who takes on mine.

"But you can't take on this one. I've made my mistakes, and I have to live with them. I can't leave Finn any longer. Call me when the jury comes back with the verdict."

CHAPTER SIXTY-THREE

Friday, May 10, 2019, Offices of Goldstein, Miller, and Mahoney, Emerald Shapery Center

Cam found his way to his car in the parking lot, almost unaware of where he was. All his attention was focused on Jackie at the head of the stairs, already broken and hurting from Blaine's public humiliation earlier in the day. He imagined her standing there in tears, clutching the evidence of Blaine's unfaithfulness, no longer able to ignore it because his betrayal had produced a child. Had his mother felt free as she stepped off into the void? Had she felt as if falling through time and space was the only cure for her heartbreak?

He shivered at the thought. His homing instincts drove him back to the office. That's where he went to handle any tragedy or trauma because that was where he could lose himself and ignore his feelings.

But even though he was sitting at his massive desk, surrounded by important work for million-dollar clients that demanded his undivided attention, grief overwhelmed him.

I can't give in. I've got to keep this at bay. It's one thirty, and the judge's clerk is likely to call at any minute to say the jury has reached a verdict. He decided to call the only other person who knew the truth about his father.

"Has your jury come back, big brother?" Nash asked.

"Not yet, but it can't be long now. They've been out for nearly three whole days."

"So what else is up?"

"I went to see Meg and Finn today. He's going to be okay."

"Well, that's good news."

"Nash, Mom knew about Finn."

"But how?"

"Dad told her. He went back to the house that night after we all left. That's what made her do it."

"How do you know?"

"While I was at the hospital, Meg explained her side of the story. She never wanted Dad involved in Finn's life because of what it would do to Mom and to us. She tried to end things when she found out that she was pregnant."

"Dad said they were going to get married."

"She doesn't want that. She wants to take Finn back to Rochester where she grew up and start over."

"Does she have family there?"

"No. She's alone, but she doesn't want Finn to know about Mom."

"I see her point," Nash said, "but Dad isn't going to let go of them. And shouldn't Finn have cousins and aunts and uncles? Mom made her decision that night. No one else is responsible for that."

Cam's phone blinked, and he saw an incoming call from Judge Watson's chambers. "I don't know the answer," he told

Nash, "but the judge is calling. I'm pretty sure we've got a verdict."

* * *

Friday, May 10, 2019, San Diego County Central Courthouse, Downtown San Diego

It was three thirty before all the parties could assemble in Judge Watson's courtroom to hear the verdict. Axel and his two assistants stood at something that nearly looked like attention at the prosecution's table. Cam was first on the defense side with Lachlan next, Hugh next, and Raven on the end. James Adair was in the first row of the public gallery behind them.

The courtroom was packed with media. Judge Watson had ordered the cameras turned off to protect the jurors' identities. Cam could see relief on her face when the foreperson announced that the jury, indeed, had reached its verdict.

"If you will please hand the verdict form to the clerk," Judge Watson said with a pleasant smile.

The foreperson was a woman in her early thirties, the only attorney on the panel. She looked crisp and professional in her black suit and white blouse as she handed the verdicts to the clerk, who, in turned, carried them over to the judge.

The butterflies in Cam's stomach were almost unbearable as he watched Her Honor scrutinize the papers in front of her. He tried to calm himself by thinking about life with Raven after the ordeal of this trial was over. Lachlan would be in a California prison. They would visit often. He'd be able to make Jess understand that he couldn't go back to his old life. Callie and Steph—

"The jury's verdict is in order," Judge Watson said as she handed the papers back to the clerk, who returned them to the foreperson.

Cam's butterflies were unbearable again.

"Madam Foreperson," Judge Watson began, "as to count one, the premeditated murder of Nora Carson, what is the jury's verdict?"

"Not guilty, Your Honor."

* * *

Hugh called ahead and ordered champagne to be waiting for them in the twenty-ninth-floor conference room when they got back to the firm. To be cautious, and ever mindful of the drive-by murder of Charlotte Estes on the courthouse steps after the Andy Owens trial, the defense team had exited through the back doors. Nevertheless, the savvy media had been waiting with cameras rolling.

"Now you officially walk on water at the firm," Hugh said to Cam as they followed Raven, Lachlan, and James through the hail of camera flashes.

"No one is more surprised that I am," he replied. "Meg deserves the credit. Dr. Talbot won this for us. She hired him."

"But you put him on the stand," Hugh insisted.

The conference room was full of staff and the sound of champagne corks popping when they entered. Cam was happy to let Hugh, Raven, and Lachlan take center stage while he went down to his office to call Meg.

"You aren't going to believe this, but we got a not guilty verdict," he told her.

"*You* got a not guilty verdict."

"No, Meg. I couldn't have done this without you. I'm sure my father was right when he said you're a sure thing for partner now."

"Except that's not what I want."

"I know."

"I've got good news on my end," she said. "Finn can go home tomorrow."

"Thank God! Nash was saying that you might want to reconsider Rochester. Finn might like to have aunts and uncles and cousins."

"I'm not in a position to make those decisions right now." The strain had returned to her voice.

"Sorry. Dad's there, isn't he? We'll talk later."

"For now, Cam, congratulations."

"Give Finn a hug from me."

"I will."

* * *

Thanks to more champagne, the celebration had kicked into higher gear when Cam returned to the conference room. Lachlan saw him enter and immediately sought him out.

"There you are! I'm going to dedicate my next book to you."

The genuine warmth in his light-blue eyes touched Cam, but he still thought of Nora, drunk and vulnerable, at the top of those stairs. *This was another thing I hated about the PD's office. Even when I won, I couldn't feel good about it.*

"Thank you, but that really isn't necessary."

"Still, I want to. And I wanted you to know that Raven and I are heading back to Dublin tomorrow. Seamus is giving us a ride."

Cam's world seemed to spin and collapse all at once. "Not tomorrow!" he blurted out before he could stop himself.

Lachlan looked mildly surprised. "Yes, tomorrow," he repeated. "I'm sure you're anxious to have your family back, and you personally have been in danger too long. We should go. Then you'll be safe."

No! No! No! He wanted to shout it at the top of his voice. But he remained silent, sipping his champagne as he scanned the room for Raven. She was talking to Hugh, but when she saw his face, she disengaged and walked swiftly over to him.

"Dad's told you the news," she said only for him to hear.

"Yes, but–"

"We'll talk about it tonight." She gave him a reassuring smile.

So it isn't going to happen. Cam took a deep breath as James Adair approached.

"Our entire family can't thank you enough," he said.

* * *

The party went on for another hour before breaking up into groups headed for dinner in the Gaslamp. Hugh pressured Cam to accompany him, but he managed to get a rain check, pleading fatigue after the long day. As he headed for his car in the parking garage, his entire attention was focused on getting back to Raven and the cottage and ending her plan to leave. His phone buzzed as he backed out of his parking space, and he glanced at the message. Jess.

> *"Congratulations. You pulled it off. The girls and I will be home on Sunday."*

CHAPTER SIXTY-FOUR

Saturday, May 11, 2019, Lindbergh Field, Private Jet Terminal

At ten o'clock the next morning, Cam was numb as he watched Seamus's private jet being readied for takeoff at Lindbergh Field's Private Jet Terminal. The plane was bound for Boston where Lachlan wanted to pick up some important papers from his academic office and then on to Dublin. Raven and Lachlan were on the tarmac, waiting to board. Lachlan was joking with Seamus, but Raven had turned and was looking toward the window in the private lounge where Cam was standing. Seamus had arranged for them to say their goodbyes there.

* * *

She had already been packing by the time he'd returned to the cottage from the party the night before.

"Aren't we going to talk about this?" Cam asked as he closed the front door, his heart sinking at the sight of the open suitcases in their bedroom.

"Yes, of course, but first let's eat. I've made some supper."

It was a comforting meal of roast lamb and potatoes, but Cam found it hard to do it justice. He was too upset. Afterward, she disposed of the dishes quickly and poured them a glass of Jameson.

"Come sit in the living room," she said.

Cam settled next to her on the couch. The whiskey soothed his jangled nerves but did nothing for the emptiness he felt inside. "I don't want you to leave," he said.

"And I don't want to go." Her eyes were sad.

"Then you don't have to."

"But I do. Your wife–"

"Will be here on Sunday. But I'm not going back to that life."

"Have you told her?"

"No, I haven't had the chance."

"Then that's for the best, Cam. Because I can't stay here."

"I don't understand. Of course you can, or don't you want to be with me?"

"I do want to be with you." She leaned over and gave him a long kiss. "But it's too dangerous. Dad and I have to go back to Ireland."

"But why are you safer there? Isn't that just playing into the hands of the old enemies who've been after you here?"

"No, because Dad's friends far outnumber his enemies in Ireland. He's a patriot and a national treasure."

"You mean more of his old IRA comrades are there to protect him."

"You could put it that way, if you want to. But he has friends beyond his fellow soldiers."

"So why can't he go alone?"

"Because I'm a target, too."

"You?"

"Why?"

"Because killing me punishes him."

"There has to be some way for us to be together," Cam insisted. "Or was Nash right when he said you were just playing me?"

He could see that the accusation startled her. She drew a long breath and suddenly there were tears in her eyes. Cam put his arms around her and pulled her to him.

"I'm sorry I said that."

She drew away slightly and wiped the tears off her cheeks. "It's all right. I understand why. But no, I haven't been anything but sincere about the way I feel about you. I've waited to meet someone like you all my life. And now you're here, but there are too many things between us."

"Jess is strong. She'll get over it. Nash said that."

"Even if that's true, your children won't."

"I love them, but I also deserve some happiness in my own life."

"It's not just your family between us."

"I don't understand."

"All I can tell you is that you'll be in danger if I stay. And I can't let that happen to you."

* * *

They were boarding now. Cam's heart sank as he watched Raven go up the steps. She paused at the top and turned toward his window and waved. Then she went inside. Lachlan and Seamus followed.

Cam held his breath, praying that somehow Raven would change her mind and decide not to go. He focused on the closed door, hoping to see it open and the steps being pushed back up to the side of the airplane. It was a futile hope, he knew. But it gave him comfort in the long pause before the plane began to move away from the gate and taxi slowly toward the runway.

Suddenly, he heard the sound of urgent footsteps behind him. He turned and saw James Adair running toward him.

"Where are they?" he shouted. "Are they on the plane? We've got to stop them."

He had reached Cam's side by the time he finished. He was out of breath and his chest was heaving. He looked out the window. The plane began to increase its speed as it headed down the runway.

"Oh, God! No!" James rushed over to a uniformed airport security guard standing by the door to the jetway. "There's a bomb on that plane!" he shouted. "And my father and sister are on it. You've got to stop them. I'm a Reuters journalist. This is a tip from a reliable source. Please, for the love of God, stop them!"

James waved his press credentials in the guard's face as he begged for help. The guard, still regarding him skeptically, picked up his phone and spoke into it.

"There's a journalist here who says there's a bomb on the private jet that just got underway."

Cam's heart was pounding as he watched the plane's speed continue to increase.

The guard ended the call and looked back at Cam and James. "I'm sorry. The tower says it's too late to bring them back."

And then, at the moment when he should have seen the plane lifting off into the sky, Cam saw, instead, an orange ball of flame at the end of the runway, and then he heard the thundering explosion.

CHAPTER SIXTY-FIVE

Monday, May 13, 2019, Offices of Goldstein, Miller, and Mahoney, Emerald Shapery Center

Cam sat at his desk at nine a.m. on Monday morning, feeling as if half of himself had been blown away. Saturday had turned into a long, confused blur as he stayed with James, who talked to the authorities all afternoon, explaining his journalistic credentials over and over and refusing to name the confidential source who had tried to help him save Lachlan and Raven.

Around midnight, Cam had found himself back at his own house at Ocean Way, getting as drunk as possible on Irish whiskey supplied by James.

"You still don't know the truth, do you?" James had asked as they sat in the den with their drinks and the bottle.

"About Nora's death? Sure, I do. Lachlan killed her."

"No, not about that," James said. "Raven never told you who was trying to kill them, did she?"

"Yes, she did. She said it was Lachlan's old enemies from his IRA days."

"Ha!" James tossed back his drink and poured another from the bottle on the table. "And you believed that?"

"What's not to believe?"

"That the IRA is still active enough to be shooting at people in the States. They never told you the truth."

"What is the truth, then?"

"Lachlan is—that is, was—one of the biggest arms dealers in Europe."

"*What?*" Cam could feel the whiskey now. *I'm drunk. I didn't get that right.*

"Just what I said. Lachlan was one of the biggest arms dealers in Europe. Surely you didn't think all that money came from his academic career and that one movie."

"Meg Courtney, the other attorney on his file, did mention that something seemed wrong with the financial picture, and so did my wife, who's also an attorney. But being an arms dealer? That never occurred to me."

"And that was the beauty of my father's position. He was a romantic and a poet and the last person anyone would suspect. But gunrunning has long been an Irish occupation."

"What do you mean?"

"I mean the Irish learned the value of acquiring and selling arms in World War I. There's never been any reason to give it up, especially because the money and the guns came in handy to fight the British in Ireland."

"Who did Lachlan sell to?"

"Anyone with enough money. The Chinese, the Russians, the Saudis. Probably some unnamed terrorists, too. It would be dangerous to actually know."

"Seamus?"

"He was part of it. He was into it with Dad in their IRA days before Celtic Analytics made him rich."

"And Raven?" Cam was afraid to ask.

"She ran all of Dad's business affairs."

"Including the guns?"

"As I said, all of his business affairs."

"I loved her," Cam said, too drunk to care about the consequences of his admission.

"I know," James said. "And she loved you, too. She tried to think of a way to stay with you, but she was too deeply into Dad's business to pull out. Here..." He reached into his pocket and took out the aquamarine earrings. "She wanted you to have these."

Cam stared at them. "How did you get them?"

"She wanted you to have them back."

"Did she know what was going to happen?"

"I suspect she did."

"She said she had second sight?"

He nodded.

"Who did it?"

"My money is on the Chinese. Dad and Seamus were loading weapons to send to them the night Nora died. They didn't want anyone to find out."

"But Lachlan said they were in some meeting at Seamus's office to sign a death warrant for an old IRA operative."

"Ha!" James tossed back the rest of his drink and poured another. "That was so he didn't have to tell you the truth."

"But he said he was at Nora's that night before the meeting."

"That was BS, too. He didn't want you to know he sent Victoria to deal with Nora."

"Oh, God, of course. She had a black Range Rover, too. And she refused to talk to Meg or me. But why would Lachlan lie to protect her?"

"Because he was the one who sent her, so he thought he should take the heat. He had a soft spot for Victoria because she gave him Raven. And you know he adored Raven. And he felt guilty for leaving Victoria and Raven when she was a little girl."

"So Victoria killed Nora?"

"No. I know Raven wished that she had and wished she'd gotten caught, but she didn't kill her."

"How do you know?"

"I've talked to Victoria. That night, Lachlan sent her to persuade Nora to take Bernstein's deal, but she was so drunk that Victoria couldn't get anywhere with her. She found her doing ballet poses at the top of the stairs and managed to get her back to bed."

"That was Lachlan's story."

"Right. He was covering for Victoria, who was covering for him because he was gunrunning that night with Seamus."

"So who killed Nora?"

"Nora."

"What?"

"I knew Nora well. The only things that mattered to her were her career and Lachlan. That night, Victoria told her that Lachlan was never coming back to their marriage, and she told her that her career was over."

"And Sonia had already told her the same thing earlier."

"So Nora got the message and decided she didn't want to go on without the hope of having Lachlan back. Nora killed Nora."

Cam, even though he was drunk, was stunned. He said nothing for a few minutes. Then he said, "That makes sense. Sonia said that something seemed to collapse inside of her when she realized Lachlan didn't love her."

"You didn't think your expert got it right, did you?" James smiled.

"I didn't."

"So who was trying to kill us during trial?"

"Probably the Chinese. They didn't want anyone to know what Lachlan had really been up to that night. But it could have been any of Lachlan's clients."

"My family is coming back tomorrow. Are we still in danger?"

"Not now. You don't actually know anything that could damage them."

"What about you?"

"I'm a journalist. I'm always in danger. Tomorrow I'll go undercover for a while."

But now it was Monday, and Cam wasn't drinking Irish whiskey with a daring journalist. He was back in his own stodgy world, sitting at his own stodgy desk, trying to find a way to shore up the hole in his heart. He took comfort in the fact that James had left Sinead's address so that Cam could write him. And he took comfort in the fact that James had said, as the last thing before he left in the wee hours of Sunday morning, "My sister truly loved you. Never doubt that."

He had carried that assurance like a talisman with him through the last twenty-four hours when he'd had to go back to the airport to get Jess and Callie and Steph. At least the terminal location had been different. But he hadn't been able to hide the tears, and Jess had taken them as happiness at their return. *If you only knew what it felt like to be back in the harness, trying not to feel anything and knowing there's no chance of escape.*

Now, as he sat at his desk, he reflected on the fact that Dr. Talbot had been right after all, and Cam didn't have to feel guilty about the outcome of the trial. Lachlan hadn't killed Nora.

Suddenly his phone rang. Dr. Talbot himself.

"Hello," Cam said.

"Marvin Talbot," he said. "I wanted to congratulate you on your not guilty verdict."

"Thank you, but it was your work that did it."

"I just wanted to ask you one question. When is the other one going to trial?"

"The other one?"

"There were two slip-and-falls in your file. Nora Carson was definitely an accident. That was clear. But the other one, the victim named Jackie, that was a homicide."

Oh, God. Meg said she was sending over my file to the expert. And the police photos of Mom were in that file. Oh, God. Oh. God. Please, no. Please, no.

EPILOGUE

Friday, September 27, 2019, Offices of Goldstein, Miller, and Mahoney, Emerald Shapery Center

Cam sat at his desk at four thirty, thinking about the coming weekend. He had just completed a large corporate merger that had taken two weeks to pull off. In spite of his victory in the Adair case, Cam had refused to let Hugh put him into the white-collar crime section.

Cam was tired, and he wished that he could rest all weekend. A good book and a tall glass of chardonnay sounded perfect. But Jess had already told him that he was responsible for taking Callie and Steph to their soccer games. That meant he'd spend most of Saturday sitting on uncomfortable bleachers watching his daughters and their friends chase a soccer ball up and down a field. Sunday, Jess told him, was going to be the four of them for lunch at the Yellow Door followed by supervised homework with the girls in preparation for school on Monday. He was trapped, and he felt it. But there was nothing he could do.

His father had adjusted to prison life well enough. When Cam told Nash about Dr. Talbot's report, the two of them had gone to Axel and worked out a deal. Blaine pled to voluntary manslaughter for a six-year sentence. It didn't seem like enough to Cam, but it was better than putting the family and Meg and Finn through the agonizing ordeal of a trial. If Blaine lived long enough, he might get out of prison before he died, but he would never be part of the Rhodes family again. Cam and all of his siblings had severed all ties with him.

Eventually, a San Francisco investment banker bought Jackie's old house and tore it down to build a faux chateaux as a vacation home. The only part about that transaction that hurt Cam was the destruction of Jackie's rose garden. But even that, in the end, seemed better than preserving a monument to the past.

For a while, driving past Erin's cottage, which she had now returned to, brought tears that he had to hide before he drove into the drive at Ocean Way. But eventually he'd persuaded Jess to sell their house in the spirit of new beginnings and buy a place overlooking the Pacific in La Jolla. Cam could afford a seaside mansion with his share of Jackie's estate, and he found tranquility in watching the tides come and go.

Meg did not set up shop in Rochester. Instead, she returned to work as an Assistant U.S. Attorney in New York. She found a two-bedroom apartment, so Finn could have his own room and that softened the blow of having to leave his friends in California. Cam and Nash arranged for generous child support from a trust that they forced their father to set up before he reported to prison. At Meg's request, Cam and Nash did not tell the rest of the family about their little half brother. Finn's future in the Rhodes family would be decided when he was older. Meg had suspected that Blaine was responsible for Jackie's death, and that's why she had conceived her original plan to leave San Diego. If she hadn't been assigned to the Adair case, she and Finn would have been clear of Blaine much earlier.

When the sequel to *Unforgettable* came out, Cam left work early one afternoon and went to see it alone. Maybe it was just a coincidence, or maybe James had written the screenplay from his undisclosed location. But for two hours, Cam watched a tall blond actor who resembled himself find love with a tiny, dark-haired woman whose eyes were the color of the sky.

AFTERWORD

Please write to me at dhawkins8350@gmail.com, and tell me about your experience with *Unforgettable*! I always love to hear from my readers, and I am so happy that you decided to give my story this chance to entertain you. You can find me at deborahhawkinsfiction.com or on Facebook at DeborahHawkins,Author.

This turned out to be a challenging story to tell because the theme of infidelity is woven throughout the plot. Betrayal is not an easy subject to tackle, and it is difficult to craft sympathetic, attractive characters who are unfaithful to the intimate partners who trust them. Yet Cameron Rhodes finds himself at midlife shouldering more than his share of responsibility for the troubles of others, and he cannot help being drawn to Raven Adair, the only person who senses that his own needs are being ignored by the loved ones who lean on him to solve their problems and to shore up their grief.

I hope that you'll leave reviews for *Unforgettable* on Amazon, and please do sign up for my newsletter at deborahhawkinsfiction.com so you won't miss any updates on new books. Again, thank you so much for this opportunity to entertain you for a few hours with a story and characters that I hope you enjoyed getting to know as much as I did.

NOVELS BY DEBORAH HAWKINS

THE WARRICK-THOMPSON FILES (5 BOOKS):
DARK MOON, A Legal Thriller
MIRROR, MIRROR, A Legal Thriller
KEEPING SECRETS, a Legal Thriller
THE DEATH OF DISTANT STARS, a Legal Thriller
VENGEANCE, A Legal Thriller
AND AWARD-WINNING FICTION:
RIDE YOUR HEART 'TIL IT BREAKS
Winner Beverly Hills Book Award 2015

DANCE FOR A DEAD PRINCESS
Finalist Foreword Reviews, 2013
Honorable Mention, Beverly Hills Book Award 2014

Made in the USA
Middletown, DE
18 January 2025

69762590R00274